For Robert

Una apis, nulla apis
One bee is no bee

(proverb)

AUTUMN TERM

THE FIRST DAY OF TERM

8.45 A.M. DROP-OFF

There was Bea, standing over the other side, in the shade of the big beech tree. Rachel, clearly waiting in the wrong place as usual, moved to go and join her and then stopped short. Uh-oh. She could read the signs even from that distance: taut, watchful, smiling . . . Bea was building up to one of her Big Announcements. The playground was so noisy and frenzied—it always was the busiest morning of the school year—that a normal person might have to shout, bellow even, to attract everyone's attention. But not Bea. She would never raise her voice around school, especially after the bell had rung. Anyway, there was no need. She just picked her moment, cleared her long hair from each side of her face as if parting the curtains on a stage, gave a little cough and began: 'Welcome back, welcome back. Hope your summer was amazing.' And at once the chaotic back-to-school clatter dropped to a placid, steady hum.

The groups that were scattered about, catching up after the long break, all stopped and turned around. Those who were standing alone, anxious about the first day in a new class, forgot their nerves and stared. 'Now then, everyone. Listen up. Please.' Bea held up her enormous bunch of keys, gave them a sharp rattle and smiled some more. 'I have been asked . . .' she paused, 'by the *new head* . . .' the words ruffled through the gathering crowd, 'to pick a team.' She was on tiptoes, but there really

3

was no need. Beatrice Stuart was the tallest of them all by far.

Rachel, sinking back against the sun-trap wall of the pre-fab classroom, looked on and smiled. Here we go again, she thought. New year, new project. What was Bea going to rope her in for now? She watched as the keenos swarmed to the tree and clustered round. Their display of communal enthusiasm left her with little choice but to stay put, right there, keep her distance. She could sit this one out, surely. She was bound to hear all about it from Bea later. She would wait here. They would be walking out together in a minute. They always did.

The tarmac in the playground needed restoration and was already tacky from the unusual morning heat. Rachel had to keep peeling up the sole of her shoe to stop it sticking. While August had been dank and dark, the summer had bounced back buzzing and full of beans for the start of the new school year. It was funny, she thought, how the seasons seemed to take the holidays off, too. The last few Christmases had been warm and wet. Only in the Easter term had winter eventually shown up, buried them all and shut the school completely. And now here they all were, after a month of fleeces and cagoules and more *Simpsons* than was good for them, back for the autumn and sweltering. Perhaps it wasn't just schools that came alive according to the academic calendar: it was a pattern to suit the whole of the natural world.

Rachel tried to tune in to Bea's little rally without actually moving, but she could only hear snippets. There was something about the *fabulous* new headmaster. And the latest *savage* cuts. And, guess what, some fund-raising. Of course. Yet more

4

fund-raising. She shifted her weight on to the other hip and tuned out again.

She watched idly as a tractor measured out lines on a field beyond the games pitch, gazed up at an aeroplane drawing a perfect curve in a sky the colour of Quink. Christ, it was hot. What was she doing wearing jeans? This weather was doing nothing to help her general feeling of listlessness. Unlike, apparently, the rest of nature, Rachel had no back-to-school bounce. She was buzzless. Bean-free. She'd had to drag herself up the hill to get here this morning—Sisyphus and his wretched rock rolled into one. But still, after a holiday like that one, even Rachel was, if not quite glad, definitely relieved to be back.

She always did like this school, and even from the murky puddle at the bottom of her own little well of misery she could see that today it looked pretty much like paradise. St Ambrose Church Primary teetered on a hill, clinging to the edge of its market town, enjoying the view of the luscious green belt while it could, before the inevitable retail park came along to ruin it. Rachel loved its mock-ecclesiastical architecture, its arched front door and sloping roof—so resonant of the splendid nineteenth-century social values that had brought it into existence. She could lose herself for hours in the different shapes thrown above the playground by the puzzled branches of the old beech tree, under which the children played in the day and their parents were assembling now.

And of course she liked the people. OK: most of the people. St Ambrose, after all, was famous for its people. It was known throughout the county for its one-big-happy-family schtick. They all looked out

5

for one another at St Ambrose; prided themselves on it. Well, some of them did. And Rachel had always, instinctively, made a point of having as little to do with that lot, thank you very much, as was politely possible. Still keeping her distance, she watched them all over there, one-big-happy-family-ing round Bea, raising their hands to volunteer for something or other, jittery with excitement. Rachel shook her head: frankly, she despaired sometimes, she really did. But, at the same time, she did think Bea was amazing; it was impressive, really, to give people some thankless task of joy-quenching tedium and make them feel truly thankful. To see her surrounded by women—outlining plans, issuing commands, thinking big, rearranging a few mountains—was to see a creature in its element. It was just who she was. Rachel could only look on, with love and enormous admiration. Really, she and Bea might as well belong to different species. But it didn't matter: they had been great friends— best friends, really—since the day they met, when the girls first joined Reception five years ago.

The soundtrack of the first day of term—the chanted good-mornings, the little chairs being scraped in to low tables, plastic trays thumping back against classroom walls—drifted out of the open windows. And suddenly the corner of Rachel's eye was caught by someone she had never seen before—tall, dark, a study in elegance from her clean, swinging bob to her pretty ballerina pumps. And, Well, well, well, she thought to herself as she turned to get a better look. Well, well, well. That was a rare and wonderful sight: an actual exciting-looking newbie. In her long and wearying experience of that playground, the September

6

intake was so strikingly similar to the previous term's leavers as to be virtually indistinguishable— as if she had sat in the dark through to the end of the credits and the same boring old movie just started playing all over again. Could it be that this year might turn out to be different? The same story but remade, with a fresh new cast?

The newbie approached the crowd around Bea and hovered on its edge, circling. She seemed to debate whether to join in, weigh up the pros and cons, before drifting off through the gate and towards the car park. While Rachel wished she would hang around, just for a minute so they could meet, she also had to applaud the wisdom of getting the hell out without being nobbled. But even as she did so, some grudging admission that she really should be doing her bit was born within her and grew until, like a nagging small child, it was pulling and pushing her somewhere she didn't want to be. There was nothing for it but to give in. Rachel sighed and dragged herself over to the tree to be given a minor, lowly, inconsequential task—some small token of belonging.

'Aw, that's *amazing*. Thanks, lovely,' Bea was saying to the unlovely Clover, who was always hanging around on the edge of things, like a black cloud at a picnic. 'And I've got Colette, Jasmine and Sharon on board. All old hands.'

How did Bea do that—know who everyone was? Rachel had seen them every day since for ever, but she still found it hard to tell that lot apart. Well, that wasn't quite true: since Colette's marriage broke up last year and she released her inner teenager, Rachel did now know Colette. It was hard to shut out the gossip, however much you

7

wanted to, and the gossip seemed to suggest that every single bloke within quite a significant radius also now knew Colette. But Jasmine and Sharon— she defied anyone to know who was who there. They could swap lives and no man or child would necessarily notice. And even if they did, would they bother to mention it? Those two exercised together, shopped together, thought—even spoke—as one. Rachel didn't know if they had holidayed together too, but she did know they'd had too much sun— they looked like a little helping of snack-box raisins.

That was always the striking thing about the first day of term—the children had all gone trotting into class trimmed and polished and shiny, but the mothers looked about as groomed as Robinson Crusoe. Rachel couldn't quite recognise half of them. Give them all a few weeks, and their turn at the hairdresser or the spa, and the situation would be reversed: the kids would be a mess and the adults reborn. Apart from Heather, of course. Heather didn't really do polish, or trimming, or grooming. She had been the same reliable recognisable figure, in the same reliable clothes, for the past five years. Right then she was on tiptoe— she did need to be—and using her left hand to push her right up yet higher, waving it frenetically. And as she did so her specs were slipping dangerously far down her nose.

'All right, er . . . Heather, isn't it? Perhaps you can . . .' Bea looked stumped, then inspired. 'I know! You can be secretary to the committee! We'll give it a go anyway. No promises, mind. But let's see how you get on.'

Heather flushed with triumph. It was a shame, thought Rachel with genuine sympathy, that

8

Heather did not meet triumph more often. All pink like that, she didn't look quite so tragic and mousey.

'Ah.' A note of something like mischief came into Bea's voice. 'Georgina. Joanna.'

Georgie—who, to be fair, was as kempt as the average castaway whatever the season—was trying to sneak past. Her hair was even wilder than usual after the long weeks of holiday, but Rachel still thought she looked quite lovely. However much she tried, Georgie could never quite hide her natural, classy, skinny good looks. Jo, stocky and strong, stood beside her like a minder.

'What'—Georgie sighed as she stopped and turned towards Bea—'now?'

'The new headmaster is determined to somehow overcome the absolutely *appalling* attacks on the St Ambrose budget this year—it's a *scandal* what's happening, we are *so* lucky to have someone with his *wealth* of financial expertise—and he has asked, um, *me* to form a fund-raising committee. I just think it would be nice if you two joined in. For once.'

'Me? No. Sorry. Really. Love to. But couldn't possibly.' She picked up the toddler padding along beside her and held him up as her passport out. 'I've got Hamish . . .'

'Georgie, he's hardly a baby any more! And you do have more children in this school than any other family.' Bea smiled at the crowd as she spoke.

'But you don't want me. Really. I'd be useless.' She moved closer to Jo. 'We'd both be useless.'

'Yeah,' nodded Jo. 'Rubbish.'

'Well, thank you. It's great to have you on board.' Bea wrote down Georgie's name. 'And you,

Jo.' Another little tick. 'Excellent.' They retreated, muttering, indignant.

Rachel was hardly going to raise her hand like everyone else. She was not a total loser. But she was preparing to attract Bea's attention and make a small, subtle yet ironic sign that she might help in some way vague and tangential, when someone else she had never seen before stepped to the front and addressed the whole crowd. Hello, what was this? Not another stand-out newbie? They were reaching levels of excitement here that were really quite unprecedented. Rachel chortled away to herself. She did hope St Ambrose was up to it . . .

'Oh, OK,' said the exotic stranger, who was as tall as Bea, as blonde as Bea and actually—golly— as good-looking as Bea. 'Surrender! No excuse. Career break. *Extraordinary* feeling! Nothing for it. Do one's bit. Yikes! Here goes. *I* will come and help you all.'

Bea raised an eyebrow. Oh dear, thought Rachel. Bea didn't raise an eyebrow very often—risk of skin damage to the forehead—but when she did . . . blimey. It was on a par with an ordinary mortal, say, throwing a chair out of a window or driving a car into a lamppost. Christ. The eyebrow. Rachel gave a low whistle.

'Sorry.' Bea's voice was as warm as her smile, but that eyebrow was still way up there. 'I don't think we've met . . .'

'I'm new. First day. Just *loving* it.' She swept her enormous sunglasses off her face and up into her long hair. 'You know that feeling: *done the right thing*. We're so pleased we chose St Ambrose. *Perfect*. Gad. The private sector! Escapees. *Never* again. I'm Deborah.' She stopped to dazzle the

10

assembly with her teeth. 'Deborah Green. But everyone calls me Bubba.'

Woo and hoo, thought Rachel. We've got a right one here. That's it. I'm in after all. This is going to be a laugh. She raised her hand, just as Bea flicked back her hair and declared that her work there was done.

'Thanks, all.' Bea laced the strap of her enormous handbag into the crook of her elbow, shook her gigantic bunch of keys. 'I really do think this is going to be a very interesting year.' And she swept out of the school gates and off to her car.

Rachel stared after her. She had hardly had a clear thought in weeks, what with the murk, the well, the puddle, the depths etc., but at that moment, as she stared at the blonde-on-dark stripes on the crown of Bea's retreating hair, she had several. One after the other. Clear as day.

The first was: Huh. Weird. She didn't speak to me. And I haven't spoken to her for ages.

The second: Hey. Have I actually clapped eyes on her since Chris walked out?

And the third, very, very sharp this one: Hang on. Bloody hell. She didn't pick me.

ST AMBROSE CHURCH SCHOOL EXTRAORDINARY FUND-RAISING COMMITTEE

Minutes of the First Meeting
Held at: The Headmaster's house
In attendance: Tom Orchard (Headmaster), Beatrice Stuart, Georgie, Jo, Deborah Green, Sharon, Jasmine, Colette, Clover

Secretary: Heather Carpenter

THE MEETING began at 8 p.m.

MR ORCHARD thanked everybody for giving up their evenings and wished to—

BEA seconded that and also informed the committee that HEATHER was to act as SECRETARY for the very first time and informed HEATHER that all she had to do was take down exactly what everybody said and make it sound a little bit, she knew, more official-sounding if she could. She also would like to add that she really loved those new shoes.

MR ORCHARD continued that he was touched by the dedication of so many parents in the community. He explained that this was his first post as headmaster after several years in the City, that the financial situation was as grim as the rumours suggested, but he was in possession of a number of proposals which in his view would lead the school out and up to a brighter—

BEA thanked THE HEADMASTER on the committee's behalf and stressed the excitement at its hearing of all his plans, which she already knew to be awesome and which she totally promised would happen so soon.

COLETTE informed the meeting that she had made some nibbles, nothing much, just a few cheesy bits into which the committee should simply dive.

MR ORCHARD requested that the meeting just took the time to hear—

BEA thanked THE HEADMASTER again and proposed the coming of first things first. This committee needed a chair.

MR ORCHARD informed the meeting that he presumed he was the—

CLOVER wished to add that she had bought some Wotsits.

SHARON requested to inform all present that BEA was the obvious choice for Chair—

JASMINE explained that this was because BEA was always Chair.

BEA proposed that she really did not want to be appointed Chair for the reason that she was always Chair. And perhaps it was time for someone else and the doing of their bit.

DEBORAH requested that the committee call her BUBBA as everybody did, announced that she would be delighted to be Chair and would like now to take this moment to outline in depth her professional experience in the world of HR, the career from which she was having a break.

BEA let it be known that goodness gracious of course she could not compete with BUBBA. She also had to say how thrilled everybody felt to have someone of such status among them and that one day she would just love to hear lots and lots more about BUBBA's amazing career, simultaneous to putting the world to rights, over a bottle of something completely delicious. Meanwhile all she could add was that she had five years of tireless work for the community of St Ambrose, a deep knowledge of every member of the happy school family and her own record of fund-raising success behind her. That was all. She had nothing more.

MR ORCHARD proposed that he would also like to be considered for the—

COLETTE said all in favour of BEA say aye. And all in favour of BUBBA say aye.

JO informed the meeting that there was a surprise.

BEA thanked her many supporters for their kind vote of confidence and her astonishment that she should be chosen in the face of such frankly terrifying competition.

SHARON requested that her absence be recorded for just a minute and enquired of THE HEADMASTER if it, you know, was upstairs?

MR ORCHARD agreed, and added that it was the second on the right.

JASMINE informed SHARON that she would come with.

BEA commenced the outlining of her plans. Her number-one fund-raising priority was the introduction of a LUNCH LADDER, the having of which was already happening over at St Francis. In brief: one person has a lunch, charges £15 a head, and those who attend have a lunch in turn and so on. And even more money could be made for this venture if we took down all the recipes that are used and published them as THE ST AMBROSE COOK BOOK. She happened to know that that was something of which St Francis had not thought and that therefore we were already up on the game. Also she announced the happening of THE QUIZ in the summer term and proposed the holding of a CAR BOOT SALE as soon as possible before it got too wet.

CLOVER apologised but wanted to ask if GEORGIE was quite all right?

JO informed the meeting that she was just

having a snooze and enquired if anyone had a problem with that.

COLETTE proposed the introduction of a termly GOURMET GAMBLE in which everyone made a dish for supper, put it in a room and bought a raffle ticket. Then they won a completely new and different thing for their supper. As well as raising money, this encouraged within the community the trying of new things and also guaranteed the making of a change.

JO woke GEORGIE and instructed that the Minutes record their absence from the meeting for the smoking of a fag.

SHARON requested permission to ask THE HEADMASTER a little detail about which there was wondering. And that was, she could not but help the noticing of just the one toothbrush in the bathroom and enquired of THE HEADMASTER whether Mrs Orchard would be relocating soon?

JASMINE seconded that question, and added that the committee was very excited about meeting her.

MR ORCHARD suggested not to get too excited as there was no MRS ORCHARD for the meeting to meet and added that while he had the floor, now might be the time to raise the subject of—

BEA proposed the pressing on of the agenda and requested the declaration of volunteers so that the fund-raising might begin. Of course, BEA herself would be in charge of THE QUIZ as usual. And enquired who would like to start THE LUNCH LADDER?

15

THE MEETING was silent.

HEATHER proposed that if nobody else wanted to she was happy to do it but she was keen to avoid getting in the way of others or indeed the treading on of their toes.

BEA said that hmm, well, in her view GEORGIE should be the first and that the meeting must inform her of this in due course when she chose to return. She then requested volunteers for the GOURMET GAMBLE.

THE MEETING was silent but the Minutes record that HEATHER raised her hand.

BEA informed CLOVER that here at last was her chance to shine. That just left THE CAR BOOT SALE which in her view was not in any way difficult.

THE MEETING was silent. HEATHER raised her hand again.

BEA informed HEATHER that she could organise THE CAR BOOT SALE but also informed COLETTE that she would oversee that.

COLETTE said that was fine, she did only have her living to earn and it would sometimes be nice if people

BEA enquired of THE MEETING if it had any suggestions on how she might exist without COLETTE and her amazing support? And also if it had noticed her jacket which was so gorgeous? Furthermore, she wished to praise the committee for its making of an excellent start.

MR ORCHARD seconded that, but expressed some regret that no other male members of the community had been able to turn up this evening.

16

BEA stated that that was because she hadn't invited any of them and asked if there was any other business.

JASMINE said she would like to enquire of THE HEADMASTER if he had considered the possibility of knocking this room through to the kitchen.

SHARON personally guaranteed both the creation of a more spacious living area and the bringing in of more light.

The Minutes show that here GEORGIE and JO returned to the meeting.

GEORGIE enquired whether they had missed anything important.

HEATHER said yes, that she was starting THE LUNCH LADDER.

GEORGIE stated that the committee did have to be joking.

JO informed GEORGIE that she had predicted something along those lines and that they had done her up like the proverbial kipper.

COLETTE then enquired of THE COMMITTEE, Hello? Like, excuse her? But what was THE COMMITTEE to be called and was it going T-shirts or wristbands?

SHARON sought clarification that THE COMMITTEE was surely an off-shoot of PASTA?

BEA suggested to the meeting that a little definition was needed between PASTA and this committee. The thing about the Parents' Association, which was so excellent and so motivated, was that it was open to simply everybody and that was so lovely and so friendly that up she sometimes welled. But as this committee was invitation-only, it was useful to

17

erect a few boundaries to prevent the creation of confusion and the giving of offence. Perhaps something along the lines of COMMITTEE OF ST AMBROSE, to be known as COSTA?

COLETTE seconded that, and proposed wristbands, as those T-shirts did nothing for anybody and those with light should not be hiding it beneath bushels.

GEORGIE announced that that was it, that was enough of that and that furthermore she was off.

THE MEETING closed at 8.32 p.m.

3.15 P.M. PICK-UP

Rachel had cut it a bit fine and arrived at the school gates with just a few minutes to spare. Georgie and Jo were both in their usual place by the green metal fence, under a grey-blue micro-cloud, with a fag on. They were on their own there, of course—they tended to be on their own. Rachel had never worked out if it was fear of the smoke that kept everyone else away, or fear of Jo, whose zero tolerance of any extraneous social nicety was prone to being misunderstood.

'Hello, my love,' Georgie greeted her warmly. Jo didn't bother. 'Good day?'

'Uh. Um. You know. All right. S'pose.'

'O-K. I'll take that as a no.'

The school bell rang. Georgie and Jo turned to stubbing out cigarettes and containing dog-ends with sober ritualism, like clergy at the end of the Eucharist. Suddenly Jo broke off what she was doing and looked at Rachel for the first time.

18

'Yeah. Chris. Heard about that,' she said gruffly, abruptly.

'Oh. Mmm.' Rachel loathed these conversations. Really loathed them. The first time she had to acknowledge the separation with every single person she knew was excruciating. They all wanted to talk it over, was the worst thing. Pick at it. Examine all sides of the problem. She was losing count of the number of deep-and-meaningfuls she'd been put through lately, and every single one was wretched and humiliating.

'Yeah. Well,' Jo began.

Rachel braced herself for what was coming.

'He always was an arse.'

She waited for more.

But that was it. Jo was already stomping off towards school. Her powers of oratory were seemingly exhausted. The subject was, apparently, dismissed. And as she followed through the gate, Rachel found that she was almost—not quite, mind, but almost—smiling. Jo had hit just the right level of depth and meaning there. She genuinely felt a tiny bit better.

'Bit chillier today. Brrr . . .' Heather was waddling beside them.

'Is it?' Rachel hadn't noticed. She had been working all day, completely up against it, and this was the first time she had been outside. 'How was the other night, by the way? The meeting?'

'Bloody awful,' harrumphed Georgie.

'Worst night of my life,' added Jo.

'Actually, I really enjoyed it,' said Heather dreamily. 'Everyone was so nice, and guess what? I got the Car Boot Sale!'

Rachel did not quite know how to respond.

19

'Er . . . congratulations?'

'Thank you.' Judging from Heather's expression, there was even more good news where that came from.

'And,' she was pink again, 'Bea's asked me to join them all exercising in the mornings.'

It had worked once. Rachel might as well try it again. 'Congratulations.' It seemed to do the trick. Then the school door opened and a tide of children washed into the playground and swirled around the legs of those who stood there.

Poppy flung her arms around Rachel's waist. She too was pink. 'The headmaster wants to see you, Mummy. But I haven't done anything, I promise.'

*   *   *

Rachel rounded the corridor towards the head's office just as another woman emerged. She flew past Rachel, mouthing the word 'gorgeous', rolling her eyes, fanning her face vigorously with both hands to convey some sort of transporting sexual joy. Blimey, thought Rachel. One man on the staff and suddenly we're *Fifty Shades of St Ambrose*. The grumpy school secretary gave a withering look and cocked her head in the general direction of the office.

Rachel knocked, and entered.

'Ah,' said the head, looking up from a spreadsheet. 'Mrs Mason?'

'Er, I'm not really sure,' Rachel wanted to say. What with the swift and nasty buggering-off of Mr Mason, I don't know if I am, any more, Mrs Mason. Especially as there is, apparently, a second Mrs Mason waiting in the wings . . .

20

But what she said was: 'Yes,' and 'Hello.'

Well. She didn't know what that other woman was on. He was fine, this Mr Orchard, but he was nobody's definition of 'gorgeous'. There at the head's desk sat a perfectly normal bloke of early middle age. He was wearing a normal bloke's suit, and his hair was, well, the colour of any white bloke's hair—that sort of browny-greeny, sort of bleuch colour.

'Thank you for your time.'

It was a puzzle, Rachel always thought: blokes and hair. By the time they hit thirty-five, they either didn't have any or they just had the same as the next bloke. Imagine us lot out there all with the same hair colour: Bea without her butter-blonde highlights, all Bea's mates without their pale—actually brassy—imitations, Georgie without the occasional when-she-got-round-to-it chestnut rinse, Rachel with her signature auburn *née* ginger. We wouldn't know anything about each other. So how do these men, in their regulation grey suits and their brown/green hair, how do they do it? What are their markings? How do they even know who they are, themselves?

'Everything's fine with Poppy,' Mr Orchard assured her. 'Nothing to worry about on that score.'

Well, that was how much he knew. 'Oh, that's a relief,' she said. 'I was wondering why . . .'

'Yes, of course. Actually I had been hoping to see you at the fund-raising committee meeting earlier in the week—'

'Oops. Sorry. Babysitter.' Rachel was pleased with that. Babysitter: very smooth. Much better than 'I didn't get picked.'

'It's fine. No worries.' He laughed nervously. 'I'm

21

not going to put you in detention.'

She smiled politely and thought, God, he's lame.

'Only I heard you're an artist.'

'Well, yes—children's illustrator these days . . .'

'Great. Even better, actually. The committee got off to—er—a flying start the other night, but I'm not sure I quite managed to get across exactly what the fund-raising is for. These new cuts mean that, unfortunately, we are not going to get the planned extension after all. Which I'm afraid also means—'

'Oh no! No new library?' She hadn't realised.

'Exactly.' He looked genuinely downcast.

'But that's terrible.'

'I know. And I'm so glad to hear we're of the same mind on this one. But I think we can still do something.' He shifted in his chair and looked at her straight on. 'Not as smart, maybe, but not as costly either. And we can do it ourselves.' His eyes, Rachel noticed, started to shine. Just at that moment, for a brief flash, she thought he might not be quite as lame as all that. 'Look. You know all the outbuildings off to the side over there?' He pointed across the playground to a small collection of sheds and storerooms with high windows and a brick-and-flint cladding. 'We could raise the funds to knock those together and turn them into the library.'

'Oh, yes . . .' He was right, as well. Rachel could see it at once.

'It's just not good enough to have the books crammed about all over the school. They deserve their own space, where the pupils can retreat for some quiet time. Where readers can be nurtured and books can be respected.'

'Couldn't agree more.' This was encouraging. She had heard this new headmaster was just a money man. It was more than a bonus to hear he was actually a books man, too.

'And I would love it to be more inspirational than the rest of the school. No bare walls. Above the shelving, it can be a gallery. For the children's work, and perhaps the adults'. And artists within the wider school community. Don't you think?'

'Absolutely.' She might go so far as to describe him as a breath of fresh air . . .

'And I would love you, Mrs Mason, to design a timeline depicting the history of the school, to go around the cornicing. Would you like to do that?'

Eh? What? Woah there. Where did that one suddenly come from? Extra work? By her? For nothing? Noooooo, she wanted to scream. She would not. She had neither the time nor the financial security any more to be pissing around doing voluntary work to provide fripperies for the children that would make not a jot of difference to their educational experience. They came here to learn to read and write and do their bloody tables— and just to get out of everybody's hair, frankly—and that was why they paid their taxes. And now she was broke. She was knackered. Drawing bloody pictures in a quite nice way was the only way she had, in the foreseeable future, of making things comfortable for her own kids at home. So why the hell should she waste one precious minute of her precious free time on meaningless nonsense to be ignored or unvalued by other people's children?

But what she said was 'Yes, of course.' And then added, in a casual don't-mind-if-I-do-don't-mind-if-I-don't kind of way: 'Does that, um, mean . . .' she paused, hooked her hair behind her ears, looked out of the window at the children throwing a ball

23

into a net, 'you want me on the committee?'

At the word 'committee', his body seemed to sink slightly. 'You are more than welcome, Mrs Mason. More than welcome. But, in a way, what I am asking you to do here is a little different from being just a member of a committee.'

'Oh?'

'I see yours as a more advisory role. Sort of artistic adviser, type of thing. The committee will raise the funds so that you can do the important stuff.'

'Ooh. So, you mean, it's sort of, more important than being on the committee?' she squeaked. Damn—that was not just lame. That was super-lame.

'Well.' He looked down, shuffled a few papers on his desk. 'I can't guarantee that the committee will see it that way, but that would be my view. Yes. Mrs Mason.' He spluttered a bit and seemed to be struggling to control himself in some way. 'You are more important than the committee.'

Was he laughing at her? Who knew, who cared? They thanked each other, and she left the office. This time, the grumpy secretary's look of contempt couldn't touch her.

She swung back down the corridor, her nostrils closed against the stale air of afternoon school, and out into the day. There was Georgie, hands in the sleeves of her oversized sweatshirt, skinny little legs crossed in baggy jeans, watching all her own children and Poppy playing on the bars. Rachel rushed towards them, punching the air in ironic triumph, was actually on the brink of shouting a satirical 'Yesssss!', when she became aware of Georgie's expression and the atmosphere around

24

her.

Bea was back under the tree again, and today the crowd around her was bigger: mothers, fathers, a lot of the older children too. And they were all silent.

'It's Laura. You know, mum of the twins in Year Three, breast cancer,' Georgie whispered into Rachel's ear. 'Died last night. Bea just heard. And Dave took all his leave when she was sick, poor love, so he's going to be all over the shop. Bea is just setting up a rota for the next few months—school runs, hot meals, lifts to Brownies. All that stuff.'

Rachel's arm was still out, mid-punch. She wrenched it back and looked around quickly to see if anyone had noticed. No. She hugged herself. Nobody was looking at her. They were all locked into their mutual misery, looking up at Bea. Georgie put an arm around Rachel and said softly, 'Come on.' Leaning in on each other, head propped against head, they walked together over to the tree and took up their places on the edge of the sombre crowd.

THE DAY OF GEORGIE'S LUNCH

8.50 A.M. DROP-OFF

It was a brittle, bright October morning. Their tins for harvest festival were clinking in the carrier bag and the cold air snapped in their faces as they walked up the hill. Rachel's head was thick with tiredness, but she had to muster from somewhere the energy to say something. The silence was driving her nuts.

'What's the story, morning glory? You're very quiet.' She knocked on the top of her daughter's head. 'Anyone in?'

'I was just thinking about Scarlett,' said Poppy.

Bet you weren't, thought Rachel. 'Scarlett? What's she up to? Still your best friend this term?'

'She's being a bit funny. There are these two new boys and she thinks she's just like the boss of them. And one of them she likes a lot and says we can't play with him. And the other one she doesn't like at all and she says we can't play with him either. She says he's a weirdo.'

'Excuse me. Do we use that charming word about our classmates? I think we do not.'

'I didn't!' Poppy's ponytail swung round with the force of her denial. 'I said Scarlett did!'

'Well. Who is this boy? What's he like?'

'He's called Milo. And, OK, right . . .' Poppy stuck her ponytail in her mouth and chomped on it. 'He's not a weirdo, but . . . He is a bit weird, Mummy.'

Rachel sighed. Was the real problem here

Scarlett and the weirdo? Was that really what was bothering Poppy? Or was it actually Chris, and what happened last night, and all sorts of other stuff that was a lot harder to talk about . . .

Three o'clock the previous afternoon: Chris, out of the blue, announced that he'd blagged two tickets to the football for that very night, and whisked Josh off, just like that, with half an hour's notice. The whole evening had been chaotic, unsatisfactory and badly handled. Josh was clearly unsettled by suddenly finding himself going out with his dad again, Poppy was clearly struggling with the way she was just left out of it. And the stifling, ghastly silence had been there from the beginning of breakfast. That ghastly silence was becoming increasingly familiar to Rachel. She seemed to hear it on average twice a day, lately, and it was getting quite deafening. She knew what it was: the involuntary silence of the frustrated inarticulate; the silence of the disgruntled young who cannot begin to discuss the source of their own disgruntlement. So cheers, Christopher, she thought bitterly. Here's to yet another parenting triumph.

'Morning all!'

Phew. Heather appeared, with a basket of harvest goodies wrapped in cellophane and tied with a bow. It was always at this point, when they came to the corner of Beechfield Close, that Heather and Maisie joined them. Did Heather sit behind her curtains every morning, twitching, watching, stalking the Masons on their walk up the hill? Or was it mere coincidence? Rachel preferred not to think about that. And anyway, she didn't really mind. She rather liked the way they came

27

together, changed partners and proceeded in pairs. It felt like a line dance. Or a porridge advert. And Poppy needed a change of subject.

'Hey, look at you, Sporty Spice. What's with the trackies?'

Heather blushed. 'Oh, I'm working out with Bea and the gang again. It's a run this morning. Wednesday. We always run on a Wednesday.'

Poppy had been walking ahead with Maisie, but at that moment came back. 'So should we say something?'

'Say what?' Heather froze, alert, strangled on the edge of panic. 'What's happened?'

Oh Lord, thought Rachel. We don't want Heather getting wind of this silly nonsense—she'll turn it into something requiring a resolution from the UN. 'Nothing. At all. Is that right? Do we indeed always run on a Wednesday?'

'Yes, generally. But just to confirm, Bea sends out a group text every evening telling us what we'll be doing next morning. Where to meet, what to wear and so on . . .'

'Gosh. There's a thing.' Rachel turned to Poppy. 'Go on. Quick. Catch up with Maisie.'

'And then,' Heather was so pleased with herself today, 'time for a quick change and round to Bea's to wash some stuff for the Car Boot Sale, and then it's the lunch! Not even a minute for the internet!'

A Range Rover thundered past. Through the tinted windows, they could just make out the murky shape of its driver waving maniacally.

'Who's that?'

'Not a clue.'

They reached the car park. Rachel got a glimpse of the promising newbie in the ballerinas heading

28

off to her car. Drat. Missed her again. Around Bea's people carrier, four or five women in running gear were already warming up. One had her right foot in her left hand, another was tipping her left elbow over her right shoulder. The rest were gently jogging on the spot.

'There in a sec,' Heather called to them. No one looked up. 'Don't go without me!' No one replied.

'Hey. Baby.' The walk was over; the girls were waiting by the gate. Rachel stopped, squatted and got her head down to Poppy's level. 'Don't worry about it. Least said . . . It's bound to blow over. OK? Now.' She got up again. 'In you go. And please. For once in your life. Can you Just. Try. And. Somehow. Be. Good?'

Rachel stood and watched her trotting off. She was officially the Goodest Girl in the world, her daughter. The champion of the Good Girls' League Table, gold medallist at the Good Girl Olympics, and she knew it. But she hadn't laughed at that, or even smiled.

The school door swallowed Poppy in, and spat out Georgie, who emerged towing a toddler and wearing a hunted look. 'OK. This is weird. Total strangers keep coming up to me and saying, "See you later." It's giving me the creeps.'

A woman in something resembling her pyjamas bumped into them and swung round. 'Oh! Hi! See you later.'

'What the—?'

'It's your lunch, Georgie!' giggled Heather. 'Today! You can't have forgotten a thing like that?'

'I bloody have. And I don't blame me, either. God.' She pulled down her mouth, put on the voice of a sitcom grumpy teen: 'What time is it, then, my

29

lunch?'

'Twelve-thirty drinks, sit down at one. Everyone's looking forward to it . . .'

'Are they just? And where do you think you're going?' Rachel was tiptoeing away as subtly as she could. Georgie grabbed her by the collar and pulled her back. 'Don't even think it. You're coming. If I've got to put up with it, you bloody well can.'

'Oh Georgie, I can't face it. I'm not ready to—'

'Do you good,' butted in Georgie crisply. 'Here . . .'

Amazing: she had clearly forgotten the lunch again already. It was one of the things Rachel loved about Georgie. You could actually see what she was thinking. You could look into those clear blue eyes and watch the lunch just fly out of her mind, like a trapped bluebottle out of a newly opened jam jar. And there was obviously something else—bigger, more important—worrying away in there now.

'Heth', Georgie began. 'No offence, but . . . You do know you're dressed like a complete and utter total arse?'

11 A.M. MORNING BREAK

It was, Georgie reflected, like grief. She was reminded of those first few strange and cloudy months after her mum had died. She'd go pottering along, as if everything was normal, then, just as she was doing something routinely simple—plonking the baby in its cot, or forking the spuds out of the soggy ground—the truth would come and thump her right there, in the gut.

She'd been just like that this morning. Come

home from dropping the children off, dumped the current baby in the playpen, put the kettle on, scraped the scraps into bowls—one for the pigs, one for the chicks—and then it hit: a different truth, but still hard, still right there, nearly winding her: she had all these bloody women coming round. And she was supposed to be bloody feeding them.

She stood, bottom against kitchen sink, and surveyed this morning's damage. She was perfectly well aware that her standards of domestic hygiene did not meet those that were generally upheld as the norm and, broadly speaking, she gave not a tinker's toss. She knew how much she did. She knew that she never stopped working from the minute she opened her eyes in the morning. She felt perfectly confident that the important things, the things that counted, always got done. The children were fed, the children were clothed, the animals lived their expected span. OK, so you could tell the difference between Martin's Farm and the Martha Stewart residence. But then Martha Stewart didn't have too many kids and a big, messy husband in the agricultural sector, did she? It's a darn sight easier being a perfect home-maker, Martha, if there's nobody actually at home.

Still, even she had to admit that today wasn't quite up to snuff. There was—she had noticed this for some time now—always something. Her household was like one of those biblical lands that never knew peace and order; that was always battling against some pestilence or elemental catastrophe sent by the Almighty to try it.

Today, He had sent shoes. There were so many shoes—and boots, and pumps, and trainers and wellies encrusted with hard, dried mud—scattered around that you could not actually see the dirt on the flagstone floor. 'Proof,' she said to Hamish, 'that there's always an up side.' Hamish reclined against the bars of his pen and sucked on his rusk.

'Of course, what we need, Hammy my boy, is a system.'

Hamish gurgled.

'We need a place for the footwear. That's what that Bea would do, you know: bet she's got a special Designated Footwear Place. And we could have that. What's to stop us? And, see, this would have an added advantage'—Hamish was riveted. His rusk had stopped, mid-air on the way to his mouth—'because then, when we go out again, we would know where to find our footwear. And then nobody would ever have to ask me the whereabouts of their footwear, as we would all know that their footwear would be in the footwear place.'

Georgie and Hamish both had a faraway look— their eyes focused on a distant parallel universe with a parallel home that ran smoothly on routine and order. Then Georgie took a sip of her coffee, shook herself and came round.

'Of course, it'll never happen.'

And Hamish went back to his rusk.

She did, though, need to come up with something now, if only to get her through lunch. And though she might be a stranger to the long-term strategy, Georgie was the unassailable mistress of the short-term domestic fix. Where could she stuff it all? A solution was lurking in the fluff beneath the skirting-board of her mind, she just needed a brush-around to get it out . . . And there it was. Ha! The dishwasher! The dishwasher that had been broken for weeks, but about which she had done nothing. The baskets had disappeared off to Henry's bedroom days ago, commandeered by Action Man for the war effort. That left a nice spacious cupboard. Of sorts. It would do. For the mean time . . .

'Come on, babe. Work to do.'

Hamish got the hang of it immediately, bombing round the kitchen on all fours, hurling things into the dishwasher till it was packed full. Georgie had to force it, hard, shut. And then she noticed that the floor was filthy even by her spectacularly low standards.

*   *   *

Bubba headed back towards the house, two clinking mugs in one hand and a bunch of drying lavender in the other, smiling happily to herself. There's nothing wrong with it, she thought. She wasn't going to apologise. She just did love domesticity. It was as simple as that. She'd had Mark in absolute stitches over dinner last night, when she said the highlight of her day was the morning coffee break, but it was all true. The routine—the ritual—of it was just so reassuring . . . Every day, eleven sharp—you have, she told Mark, to run a tight ship, or the whole thing goes *completely* pear-shaped—she made three coffees. She left two on the Aga to keep warm, and took one into the laundry to Kazia. Hand on heart, she said to Mark, some of the cosiest chats she'd had since they'd moved here had been in that laundry, with Kazia, while Kazia did the ironing. 'You would not believe,' she'd said, 'how many hours I spend in there, talking about the children's clothes and what we need next time they go to Waitrose.' Mark

33

said he wouldn't believe it. And, she had added, she simply never got bored . . .

Anyway, then it was back to the Aga, collect the other two mugs and out into the garden. Tomasz was doing amazingly out there. The beds were going to be glorious and he'd got her plans for a veg patch well under way. He leaned on his fork while they chatted away—pruning, ground elder, ya-da-ya-da-da-da, it was actually *hysterical* to listen to—and then she took a little turn around, drinking in the air, and the beauty, of her little corner of England. It was, she'd told Mark more than once, very heaven.

This morning's chat was all about the lake—or, to be more precise, what Tomasz called 'the lake' but which she preferred to call 'the pond'. True, the estate agent called it the lake, when he'd first showed them round at the beginning of the summer. And the previous owners—they were lake this, lake that, lake the other. But Bubba knew a lake when she saw one—like when she honeymooned on Como, or stayed with her granny in Windermere. She was no geographer—hands up, first to admit it—but, as she understood it, a lake was a big thing. And this, this body of water in her own back garden, was not a big thing. Not at all. This was something over which she and all geographers could unite and call, as one, a pond.

'Mrs Green,' Tomasz had said. 'About the lake.'

'The pond, Tomasz. We don't want to sound pretentious, do we?'

'Mrs Green. About the pond . . .' Such a quick learner, Tomasz, thought Bubba. Which was no great surprise. He'd got about ten PhDs or something. She wasn't quite listening to the rest of

34

it. Something about banks or borders or some such. What-*ever*!

'Good point, Tomasz.' She'd taken the mug from his gloved hands. 'Thank you for your input.' Always a useful phrase in meetings when her mind had wandered. 'I'll talk to Mark this evening.' And she'd headed back to the house. As a general rule of thumb, Bubba was beginning to realise, while there was no such thing as too much Kazia—God, that girl was a gem—there was such a thing as quite enough Tomasz; and she'd had it, yet again.

*   *   *

'Right.' Georgie was talking things through with Hamish. 'We can now, at least, traverse the floor. We are, my little love, up on the game.' She put her bottom back against the sink, picked up her coffee again, started to think that actually it was about time she started to think about what anyone was going to actually eat at this wretched lunch . . . and then noticed the kitchen table. It was almost, in its way, in her view, an art form. Still-life: 'Family Breakfast'. Only a true artist could stick the *Beano* to *Girl Talk* to *The Enchanted Wood* to Biff and Chip—bugger it. That should have gone into school—with egg yolk and Frosties and apple juice; all these inanimate objects combined together to create an animated discourse on Nourishment of the Young. It was a masterpiece, really . . .

But she could also see that it was, in another way, to other eyes, a screaming mess. And the problem, Georgie knew, went deeper than the naked eye was able. A true art historian could take this morning's still-life, scrape away at it and find another, older

35

one: 'Last Night's Supper'. And beneath that, there were scores of other masterpieces, 'The Sunday Lunch' and 'The Party Tea', going all the way back—Georgie happened to know—to a surface of ingrained glitter entitled 'Christmas Six Years Back'.

The thing was that, when the floor was in such a state, nobody would even notice the kitchen table. Now the floor was, well, clear at least, the kitchen table was sort of leaping out at her. Mocking. It had its thumbs in its ears. It was waggling its fingers. It was standing there looking at her, poking out its metaphorical tongue. 'Oh dear,' she said to Hamish, who was back in the playpen, filling his nappy with quiet intent, 'what on earth have we started?'

Of course, she could just throw the whole lot in the bin, but there was stuff there that was needed. She could only sort it by sitting there like a pathologist and pronouncing life or death on every colouring book and felt pen and all the rest of it, and there just wasn't the time for all that. She still hadn't worked out what she was giving anyone for lunch. She glanced up at the clock. Fine. Not quite twelve o'clock. No panic. Got a while yet. Just time for another creative solution . . .

*   *   *

Bubba brushed her feet on the mat, coiled her lower leg round the back door, flicked it back into its frame. And suddenly, just like that, she had what she liked to call one of her lightbulb moments. Ding! she thought. Then doubted herself. Did light bulbs actually go ding? What did she mean? Flash!

Or just tah-dah! Anyway, the point was, she had a stonkingly bright idea. Her garden was, indeed, very heaven. She didn't want to sound too boasty or anything but she thought it was probably a lot more very heaven than the gardens of any of the other families at St Ambrose—what Mr Orchard, bless him, kept calling 'our community'. Yikes! Anyway . . . Why not share it with them in some small but special way? They could throw something magnificent here, which would knock everybody's socks off and raise an enormous amount of money for those poor kids. She had felt so sorry for Bea the other night, at that meeting. All those pathetic little ideas of how to make a few bob here and a few bob there. They'll still be at it with one foot in the grave at this rate—selling raffle tickets at their own funerals, holding a cake stall at the back of the crematorium . . .

The Greens should make a substantial contribution, and this could be it. A summer ball. For St Ambrose. The St Ambrose Summer Ball. She could see it now: a marquee down by the pond . . . No, by the lake. For one night only, she would allow the pond to be the lake. A Lakeside Summer Ball. A-*mazing*!

'Kazia!' Kazia jumped, dropping the iron with a clatter. All Bubba's fault—she didn't normally appear in the laundry *twice* in one morning.

'Sorry—did you burn yourself?—but listen: I've had an incredible idea.' Kazia listened intently as Bubba outlined her grand scheme. It was growing as she spoke: it was already a sit-down dinner for up to two hundred people, with fireworks and dancing and a jazz band by the lake. She was so excited that it was quite a shock when Kazia chucked a bucket

37

of Eastern European cold water all over her.

'Mrs Green, I'm not so sure . . .'

God, what was it with these people? Kazia was as bad as Tomasz. Honestly. Meet our live-in couple, Mr and Mrs Strindberg—Gloom and Grump. If Strindberg *was* actually Eastern European. Which she might have to check . . .

'Won't it mean a lot of work?' Kazia studied a rising blister on her finger.

'Oh, Kazia,' Bubba said, putting her hand on the ironing board in a gesture of affection. 'You know I'm not afraid of hard work.'

Friendship restored. She trotted into the kitchen and dumped the dirty mugs on the draining board, happy once more. *Now* she had something to get her teeth into. Heavens, was that the time? Twelve o'clock. Where did the mornings go? She was due at this grim-o lunch over at Cold Comfort Whatever any second. She could announce the ball idea right there—that would cheer them all up, bless 'em. *Christ!* She only had twenty-five minutes to tart herself up. Better crack on.

12.30 P.M. LUNCH BREAK

Georgie was bent over the table, gathering up piles of stuff with her arms and shovelling them all into a bin marked COMPOST—it was empty for once, and amazingly non-smelly; well, just the odd whiff of cauliflower leaf and potato peel—when Will burst in from the yard.

'HELLLLOOOOOOO!' He did make her laugh, her husband. Spent all day every day right here on the farm, but whenever he came back into the

38

kitchen—which was only about ten times a day—he was as a Spartan back from Thermopylae, a hero home from the war.

'Two of the most gorgeous beings on the planet, both in my kitchen at once. How lucky am I?' He pulled off his boots, spun them across the floor and picked up Hamish out of the playpen—'Phwoar. Pongeroo, my darling'—and dropped him again.

'Sorry, babe. Just having a bit of a tidy up . . .'

Will took in the scene of devastation around him and guffawed. 'Going well then, I see.' For Georgie, it was one of the beauteous miracles of their marriage that her husband took such delight in domestic chaos. It just cracked him up every time.

He walked up behind her, slapped her quickly on the bottom and pulled her up and into his arms. 'Why bother? I came in search of lunch, but now it occurs to me, perhaps we could use our time more wisely . . .' He nuzzled into her neck, and she leaned back into him.

'Mmmmmmm . . .' And then that kick of grief again. 'I can't!' she wailed. 'It's "The Wreck of the Deutschland" in here, Hamish's nappy is a health hazard, and I've got all these sodding women turning up in half an hour for a lunch that I haven't even begun to think about and for which I appear to be charging fifteen quid apiece . . .'

'Doh. Is that all? Then surely a quick shag shouldn't be out of the quest—'

What was that? They swung round together in alarm. It sounded—could it be?—something like a sharp little kitten heel on the flagstones in the yard . . .

'Golly. Gosh. Um. Hi. Are you OK?'

Bubba's first thought on entering the Martins' home was that she was actually walking into an as-it-happened crime scene. All the signs were there. She recognised them immediately. She did watch a *lot* of detective programmes on the telly—anything from *Midsomer Murders* to *CSI*. Loved them; couldn't get enough. As she said to Mark the other night, she was, to all intents and purposes, practically a *policeman*, she knew all the procedures so well.

So there she was, on the threshold of a kitchen that had clearly been ransacked in the most unbelievably *brutal* manner—God, she would hate to have her home violated like that; they'd never been burgled, *so* lucky, touch wood. And there was poor Georgie, gripped in a stranglehold by some *huge brute*, literally *the Gruffalo*, all unshaven and wild and woolly, bushy eyebrows, *exploding* nasal hair, with—she was trying to take in as much as possible for the police report later—filthy, almost *crusty* hands. And there was the baby, being forced to watch—oh God!—from a *cage* . . .

She was about to go in there, all guns blazing, but something stopped her. Something in the atmosphere . . . It was sort of . . . what was it? She wasn't quite sure. Happy. Cheerful. Or something. So she coughed politely—she could still, she reckoned, attack if attack were needed—and made her presence felt.

'Ah,' said Georgie. 'Good. You're early'—though without sounding all that pleased. 'This is . . .' she began, to her husband, but her voice trailed away.

'Call me Bubba.' Bubba held her hand out in peace to the huge woolly mammoth person, which guffawed an enormous guffaw.

'Nothing could delight me more.' He roared again. 'I'm Will. I gather you're actually paying to come here for lunch. That's a family first. I hope you're not the litigious sort.'

You know what? thought Bubba. He's oddly attractive, this Will—in a noble-savage kind of way. But, golly. Poor, poor guy. Do they really have to live like this? Should we be fund-raising for *them*?

Georgie had moved away to the table, where she seemed to be putting the strangest things in the compost bin. Felt-tip pens? Bubba was only just getting to grips with the whole compost *scene*—she and Tomasz had had more conversations about it than she would like to remember—but she was pretty sure you *couldn't* compost a felt-tip pen. Still, they were all farmers round here. They must be greener-than-one, she *supposed*. But you'd think: Felt pen? *Toxins?*

'Oh, sorry,' she said to Georgie's back. 'Am I the first? What can I do? Chop something! Let me chop!' She looked around. It was funny, but it seemed, oddly, *foodless* . . . 'Isn't this lovely?' She and Kazia always had everything *out* by this stage in the proceedings.

'Chop?' Georgie turned round. She was pink from the exertion of composting all those toys and so on, her hair was on end—she looked, in Bubba's opinion, seeing her in her home environment for the very first time, really quite bonkers. 'We're not quite at the chopping stage, thanks anyway. More at the—um—picking stage. Will, can you entertain . . .' her mouth opened, flapped like a codfish, but

41

nothing came out, 'for me, while I just nip out to the greenhouse?'

*　　　*　　　*

There were two things in this life that gave Georgina Martin a profound sense of existential contentment. One was walking around with a child—one of her own, obviously—tucked into her hip. The other was the growing and picking of her own fruit and veg, on her own patch of land, for immediate cooking by her and consumption by her loved ones, in her very own farmhouse kitchen. She wasn't quite sure why. She didn't really these days have the time required to think this kind of stuff through. She guessed it was to do with anchoring herself—vertically to the landscape beneath her feet, laterally to the generations that flanked her; establishing her position in the cosmos, her connections to the past and the future.

Humming quietly, she walked back through the yard with a basket full of future lunch. She was completely engrossed in totting up the elements she had—pitch-perfect cherry tomatoes, purple basil, figs, plus tiny beetroot, thyme, shallots and garlic—and how they might be combined together to form a coherent whole. Those that can, cook; those that are completely hopeless need a recipe book—that was her philosophy. She remembered the blackberries that the kids had picked and the mascarpone in the fridge. Simple, stylish, delicious. Hamish could have the leftovers. Perfect.

So she was actually, consciously, smiling when she looked up to see the cloven hooves of a flock of mutton dressed as lamb clip-clopping across towards her. Sharon, Jasmine, Heather—well, Heather was, to be fair, more mutton dressed as mutton . . . But who the hell was that with her? Colette? Colette, in her yard, done up like she was off to some sodding cocktail party . . .

OK. That was it. She was the victim of some hilarious bloody practical joke by Bea, and she wasn't putting up with it for another second. If they thought she was giving houseroom to every loser and loony with a kid at St Ambrose they had another think coming. 'Oi!' she was about to say. 'Hop it! Bugger off out of here!' But Will, unfortunately, got there first.

'Hey, Heather.' Kiss, kiss. 'Great skirt.' He was having a high old time. And: 'I don't believe we've met. I'm Will Martin,' he swung round with a gesture of openness towards the back door, 'and you are very, very welcome.'

Georgie thought she might actually hit him.

Drinks

Jo's bottom—not an insignificant thing, everyone agreed, but as that didn't seem to bother Jo it didn't seem right for anyone else to add it to their burden of worry—was protruding from the cupboard under the sink. Hamish's little neat one was beside it. They were both in search of something. 'Come on, Hamish.' Jo's voice was muffled by the U-bend, but her irritation with the baby could clearly be heard. 'There must be an ashtray somewhere. Else where does your mother stub her fags out?'

Bubba leaned against the fridge, wondering if she was ever going to be offered a drink. Heather

43

was laying the table—someone had to—while chatting happily to Georgie over one shoulder.

'How many are we?' She opened the drawer of the enormous kitchen table in search of paper napkins, shut it swiftly and gulped.

'How would I know?' Georgie was chopping shallots in a frenzy. She flung open the fridge—Bubba dived out of the way just in the nick—grabbed the butter, slopped olive oil into a wide-bottomed pan and lit the gas beneath. She picked up a mortar and pulverised three garlic cloves—smash, smash, bash—and tossed them in. 'Why would anyone bother to tell me?'

Bubba took up a fresh position against the dishwasher and, to no one in particular, smiled a hopeful, friendly smile.

'Is that Melissa coming?' Heather turned her attention to glasses, drummed her fingers against her lips. Where to start? 'Bea thought she might turn up.' She headed towards the dishwasher—Bubba moved off towards the dresser—and opened it. 'She looks lovely.' She shut the door sharply, pulled a face. 'Know the one I mean? Tall, dark, bob . . . Wears ballet pumps.'

Jo reversed out of the cupboard, headed for the dresser and grabbed a bone-china dish. She bashed the side of Bubba's head as she did so. 'Sorry,' said Bubba, as it seemed that someone ought to.

Colette and Clover were already seated tightly together around one end of the grubby table; they seemed to be at a separate social occasion all of their own. 'The tricky one,' Colette was saying, 'is Saturday . . .'

'Oh God,' Clover moaned. 'Nightmare.' Her head shook, her eyes closed. 'I don't know how

44

anyone could expect you . . .'

'. . . what with the football in the morning and pick-up from the sleepover and the dance recital in the afternoon . . .'

A curious sound started to come out of Clover from deep within. Words now beyond her, she had moved on to some sort of funereal ululation: 'Tut, owwwww,' it went, 'tut, owwwww.'

'. . . then I said to him, "Touch rugby? Sunday morning? You have to be kidding me . . ."'

Clover's moans and Colette's detailed itinerary rose up to the blackened gables of the kitchen ceiling. And there they met the manic chatter of Bubba making friends with Heather—

'. . . all we ever wanted was a quiet life, and average bright, and we end up with this *extraordinary* boy. Little Martha's perfectly straightforward, thank *goodness*, but Milo . . . Oh, I don't know. It just feels like such a responsibility to, you know, do the right thing . . . So. Anyway. How about you?'

'Oh, um, yes, well. Just the one. Sadly. I would say she is, yes, sort of average bright, perhaps. On,' Heather tried a cheerful laugh, 'ha, a good day . . .'

—and the sizzling and chopping of a large lunch being hurriedly cooked. And all these noises came together to make a huge umbrella of sound, beneath which Georgie and Jo were free to talk.

'How's it going? Things any better with Steve?' It wasn't yet common knowledge that Jo was having trouble at home. Only Georgie was aware of it. And knowing Jo, she would like it to stay that way: if anyone else dared ask, they would probably get their heads stoved in. Georgie stole a sideways look as she reached for the wooden spoon. Jo never went

45

in for make-up and all that at the best of times—it was one of the many admirable things about her—but today she was looking particularly ragged: pale face, shadowed eye, a furrow cut through her brow that wasn't there last year. Something deep in Georgie gave a sudden lurch of sympathy.

She was so fond of Jo. Anyone who knew her well had to be fond of Jo; to the mere acquaintance, though, she could be proper scary. She was just like a girl Georgie had really liked at school: only ever referred to by her parents as her 'bad friend' and in that tone of voice reserved for a dose of measles.

'Bloody awful.' Jo took over stirring the shallots in the butter, so giving her back to the rest of the room. 'He didn't get the job he went for the other week, and there's nothing else in the offing. You know'—she was talking directly to the wall tiles now. Georgie had to come next to her to hear—'I got back from night shift at half-six this morning and the tea things were still sat on the kitchen table from half-six the night before. Spaghetti hoops sort of fossilised on to the plates. And he's stretched out on the sofa asleep in front of the telly. Hadn't even got himself up to bloody bed.'

Georgie slid the chopped herbs into the foaming butter. Of course, this was what people round here didn't quite get: not only was Jo perfectly harmless, she was also as vulnerable, deep down, as all the rest of them. She just didn't bang on about it to anyone and everyone, and very refreshing it was too. 'He needs a doctor, Jo. He needs proper help.'

'Yeah. Well. He doesn't want it. I couldn't help myself this morning. I was so knackered. I just flew at him.'

'And?'

46

'Huge scene. Nice for the boys to wake up to. . . '

'Oh, love. But they're all right.'

'Oh, they're all right. I'm all right, really.' Jo shook herself. 'But I'm starting to think we'd all be a bit more all right without him around . . .'

She gave a dry laugh and turned back to the kitchen. 'What's all this about then?' Jo cocked her head in the direction of the table while popping a cherry tomato in her mouth. 'Colette and Clover? That's new, isn't it? An unholy alliance if ever I saw one . . .'

'Poor Colette.' Georgie glanced over there. She was now painting olive oil on to bread slices. 'All she needs. The minute she got the decree nisi, she somehow got Clover as her new BFF.' She tossed over some rock salt. 'It's like those bugs the kids pick up at school. If you're on good form, they can't touch you.' Then crunched over some black pepper. 'But if you're already a bit on the low side, that's it. They're in. Worming their way round, sickening your system . . .'

'She gives me the right creeps.' Jo gave an involuntary shudder. 'And I bet she's pleased with herself. She's never managed to get in with the Sporties before, has she? What with that wart on her face and legs like a Shetland Pony . . .'

'Shhhh.' Georgie nudged her friend in the ribs. They were both sniggering when they looked up, saw two women standing there proffering their fifteen quid, and stopped immediately.

'Hi,' said the braver of the new arrivals. 'Bea suggested that we . . .'

Georgie wiped her fringe away with the back of her arm. 'Oh, of course. I'm quite sure she did.' Jo looked them up and down, and took up position

47

on Georgie's side of the chopping board. 'Come in, come in. Oh yes. Just make yourself at home. Everybody else has.' She gestured at a roomful of women, none of whom had been offered so much as a glass of water.

The women looked baffled. One was halfway to putting her money back in her purse when Rachel put her head round the door.

'Well done.' Georgie stepped forward and kissed her warmly. 'I was beginning to wonder if you were going to flake on me.'

Rachel stepped gingerly over the threshold. 'Sorry. Tons of work to do and had to wait for the new washing machine. Whose is the Range Rover? Parked like a total nutter. Give us a nice big glass of something, will you? I could do with a little fortification.'

Starter
Bruschetta of cherry tomato on the vine, wild garlic and purple basil. Served with roasted figs and British goat's cheese

Preparation time: 15 minutes

Cooking time: 10 minutes

'Mmmm, shish ish shcrummy,' said Rachel through a full mouth. 'Schtarving . . .'

'So are we!' said Heather, glancing at Colette. 'We did an hour's run this morning.' Clover scowled at her, but Heather was just too cheerful to notice. 'And then a good old session on the Car Boot Sale.'

Clover put a hand on Colette. 'You must be

48

shattered . . .'

Jo shot them a bitter look. 'Chrissake . . .'

'Oh,' said one of the late arrivals, saving Heather from the scrutiny of her friends. 'The Car Boot Sale.' She was desperate to join in somehow. 'Sunday after next, is that right?'

Rachel put down her ciabatta. Her appetite was suddenly gone again. 'Chris has finally announced that that will be his first weekend with the kids.'

'Then that's great for you!' said Heather, delighted. 'Just what you need, a car boot sale. That'll take your mind off it all!'

'I doubt that's possible. It is, after all, my first Sunday on my own in—what?—fourteen years . . .'

'But it's so important, a bit of *me*-time,' chipped in Clover.

'Heather, dear,' called Georgie from the stove in her Mary Poppins voice. 'You are developing, if I may say so, a rather car-boot-centric view of the universe . . .'

'Well, I just hope you're all coming,' said Heather with a frown. 'This is a major fund-raiser for the school.'

Jo snorted.

'And they're always such fun.'

Jo snorted again, and louder.

'And'—time for the big rallying cry, a quote from Bea, as it so happened—'it's a great chance to just get rid of all your old bits.'

The table fell momentarily silent.

'Oh,' said Bubba. 'I'm not sure I've actually *got* any "old bits".'

'I have,' said Jo in a mournful tone. She wasn't snorting now. 'I've only got old bits.' She was looking quite wretched.

49

'Ooh, actually,' brought in Bubba. 'Lightbulb! Now I think of it, there's a *cupboard* full of old Alexander McQueens and stuff . . .'

'Oh, Bubba, really? That would be amazing.' Heather spoke to the table, aglow. 'You know, it really could be quite something, this car boot sale. With a bit of positive energy and good will, we could really do something remarkable here.'

'On the subject of fund-raising,' cut in Bubba, picking her moment. 'I've had an idea. What say you all to . . . a summer ball!'

'A what?' said Jo.

'A summer ball! By our lake!'

'Hangon hangon hangon. Woah there. Your *lake*?'

'Friend of mine once, she had a lake,' Clover chipped in. 'It was absolute hell . . .'

'Well. Pond. Ish.' She flicked her hand airily. 'We're very lucky. Anyway. Dinner. Dancing. About a hundred quid a head.'

'One hundred quid???'

'All right then,' obliged Bubba happily. 'A hundred and fifty!'

'But that's more than a night shift!' spluttered Jo. 'Do you have any idea how many incontinence pads I have to change for a hundred and fifty quid?'

Bubba did not have any idea and nor did she look like she would care to.

'Oh dear,' said Clover. 'It does sound a huge amount of bother. Is it going to be one of those things that is so much more work than it's worth?'

'Bubba.' Heather was practically swooning. 'I think it's the most brilliant idea I've ever heard.'

'Does Bea know about this? Have you told her you're thinking of this?' demanded Colette. Her voice was edgy. 'I mean, I really think Bea should be told . . .'

'Well, this does sound interesting.' They turned, as one, to the open door. They sat up, reflexively, straight. All faces, save those of Georgie and Jo, were instantly lit from within. Suddenly, lunch was looking up.

'Do tell. What exactly should I be told?'

Main Course
Risotto of fresh herbs with truffle shavings, served with roasted baby beetroot

Preparation time: 10 minutes

Cooking time: 25 minutes

Rachel shuffled up to make room next to herself on the long pine bench, but Bea went and half perched—like she didn't really want to catch something—beside Colette instead.

'A ball. Wow. Awesome. And heroic of you, Bubba, I must say. Heroic.'

Bubba was modest. 'Oh, you know: From each according to their abilities . . .'

Bea cocked her head. 'Really? No. I don't think I do know. Anyway. One thing to get straight: it can't be a *summer* ball, I'm afraid.'

'Oh?'

'No. I always do The Quiz in the summer.' She checked her phone quickly. 'The Quiz is the summer . . .'

'But . . .'

'. . . The summer is The Quiz.' She picked a cherry tomato from Colette's bruschetta.

51

'Let me get you a plate,' said Heather.

'No thank you.' Bea took some goat's cheese from Clover's. 'I'm not staying.'

Bubba was defiant. 'But what about the weather? It doesn't matter what the weather is like for a quiz, but for a ball it's crucial. The whole point is to be in the garden, drinks around the lake . . .'

Rachel and Jo cleared away the plates from the starter. Bea lifted an entire bruschetta from one as it passed, and continued as if Bubba had not spoken.

'I think the best thing would be a Christmas Ball. Sounds marvellous. The English summer so loves to disappoint, anyway. Let's not even give it the option. A Christmas Ball. It's decided. Bubba, you're completely brilliant.' And she checked her phone again.

Georgie thumped her over-sized, heavy-bottomed pan in the middle of the table with a brisk 'Help yourselves.'

'My favourite,' said Colette.

'Poor you,' chipped in Clover. 'Risotto's a nightmare.'

'Yeah.' Georgie stuck a ladle in the rice. She passed the Parmesan and grater. 'Poor, poor me.'

'Isn't this fabulous?' Bubba swept her arms to take it all in: the humble meal served straight from the pan at the rough-hewn country table. 'Straight out of—I don't know—*Wuthering Heights* or *Jude the Obscure* or something.'

'Christ,' muttered Jo, striking her familiar pose of bored crossness—she was in a one-woman war against the pretentious.

Heather was racking her brains. 'Have I read those, Georgie? What happens?'

'Oh. You know. Usual. Everyone's miserable-slash-bonkers and then they snuff it,' said Georgie briskly. Jo snorted. 'Cheers, *Blubber*. Hey, it's not my idea of a good time either, but one is trying one's best . . .'

'Sorry. And it's actually, um, *Bubba*?' She laughed nervously. 'That came out wrong. I meant, you know, the sort of rustic *charm* of it all.'

Bea was using Colette's dessert spoon to scoop risotto off Clover's plate and periodically checking her phone, which remained disobligingly mute.

Clover spoke through a mouthful of rice. 'Why on earth would you ask Georgie what books you've read, Heather? We all know you're scatty,' she raised her eyebrows to the rest of the table 'but . . .'

'Well actually . . .' Heather drew herself up and smiled a small, smug smile, 'we were at school together.'

'Yup.' Georgie settled Hamish in his high-chair beside her. 'And she was a pain in the arse then like she's a pain in the arse now.'

Will wandered through in his socks. 'Look at this. The Long and Leisurely Ladies' Lunch.' He tousled his son's hair. 'It's another world for you lot, in here. Another world . . .'

'That's right. It is. So you can sod off out of it,' said Georgie cheerfully.

'I will when I've found my mucking-out boots.' He leaned over and swiped a baby beetroot. 'Have you seen them?'

'Umph.' She had a fork to her lips and a spoon to Hamish's. She cocked her head. 'Dishwasher . . .'

Munching loudly, Will padded over there, opened the door and rooted about for a bit. 'It's quite full in here, babe . . . Ah, here we go. My

53

wife—right as ever.' He pulled his head out again and beamed proudly over to the table. 'You can't fault her.'

Bubba looked at Will, at Georgie, at the dishwasher and back again. Bea smiled a particular smile—the same smile that a pope would smile on first looking upon a miracle, say, or Stephen Hawking an alien. A smile that said: There. See? I *knew* it!

Then Will tapped the boots sharply against the dishwasher, stood patiently while the mud fell off all around him and with a cheery 'Smell ya later, ladies!' headed out the door.

Dessert
Blackberries served with lavender sugar and mascarpone cream

Preparation time: 5 minutes

Cooking time: none

'Get stuck in, everybody. In a charming, rustic sort of way.'

Bea leaned over the huge bowl of blackberries and took a handful. 'I won't, thanks anyway, Georgina. I'd better be getting on. Gosh. We can't all sit around all day. See you at school later.' She gathered up her silent phone and left.

'You sit down, Georgie,' said Rachel. 'I'll put the kettle on. Who's for tea? Coffee? Lesbian?'

'Thanks, Rach.' Georgie scooped Hamish out of his high-chair. 'I'd better just take this one off for his nap.' She knew even before she said it that Heather would leap from her seat and all but rip

54

the child from her arms. Sure enough:

'Ooh, let me.' Heather leapt from her seat and ripped the child from her arms. 'He'll come with me, won't you, my gorgeous?' They headed for the thick oak door that separated the warm sunny kitchen from the dark fridge-freezer that was the main house. 'We're the best of friends.'

Hamish was the best of friends with all mankind, was the truth. If Myra Hindley walked in now he'd nuzzle her neck and share his rusk. But let Heather think she was special; she needed the boost.

And Georgie needed the rest. She sat down, closed her eyes and started to drift away. She could hear the others exclaiming over the blackberries— they were damned good, their blackberries—and wondering what she had put in the mascarpone. But it was like the sound of seagulls when you're lying against a harbour wall, or a tractor in the fields at harvest: it was distant, coming from somewhere else, beyond.

This was what happened to her, these days, whenever she stopped and the kids weren't around and Will wasn't there to make her laugh. It happened the other night in that ghastly meeting. It wasn't that she nodded off exactly; it was that she went into some sort of suspension, like a computer going on standby, Georgie imagined: she'd gone to screensaver. Her body just wouldn't waste its energy on this lot; it was storing it up for the only stuff that mattered.

'Wanna ciggie, love?' Jo was nudging her, but she was too far away. She couldn't come back yet.

'Owp! We seem to have lost our hostess.'

'Look at her, she's knackered. Leave her to it.'

'God, it's *awful.* Look at the *state* of it all.'

Georgie knew that voice: that was the ridiculous Blubber person, sounding like she was on some fact-finding mission in a Third World country. 'Can they just not *afford* any help?'

'Oh, they're loaded.' Heather was back downstairs then. So Hamish must have gone off all right. That was good. Georgie could sink a bit further down now. Down, down . . . 'She just won't do it. And we just can't understand why.'

Can't we just? thought Georgie. And that'll be because I'm not mug enough to tell you. She might not know everything about the female condition, she would admit that. But this much she did know: she knew what not to talk about with her fellow woman. And number one on that list was any suggestion, not even the merest hint, of marital or domestic contentment. She knew not to say that her husband still liked to have regular sex with her. She knew never to suggest that she might also rather like having regular sex with him. She wouldn't let on to a living soul that Kate was on grade-five piano. Or that Sophie had started Dickens. Or that Lucy was great at gym. And she would never, ever in a gazillion years admit to anyone that she had her whole little set-up exactly as she liked it.

'Hey. Why don't we have a good clear-up while she's asleep? There's only half an hour till pick-up. If it doesn't get done now it'll still be here at Christmas . . .'

She did have an au pair once, and she was brilliant. Absolutely brilliant. The whole house was a new pin and there was no need for them to do anything. So they didn't. The children were either out in the garden or in their rooms and she, Georgie, well . . . she had all day to do whatever she

56

wanted. And it was as if her whole family had been blown apart—this great, pulsing, vital organism just split into lots of simple, pointless little cells, capable of only the lowest form of existence, never connecting with each other at all.

'Blimey. The dishwasher's a no-go, that's for sure . . .'

'OK. Sleeves-up time. Come on, girls. Clover? Cloth. Catch!'

So she sacked Whatsername. And, yes, she had been up to her ears ever since. And some people found her housekeeping wanting. She would admit that there are one or two things that she never quite got round to, though ought. But the kids got their chores back. And every evening, they were not just together during supper but before—when one was peeling the potatoes and another laying the table. And after, when Will docked an iPod and they danced around the washing-up. That nightly ninety minutes was the coping-stone of their family life. But she wouldn't let on about that to this lot.

She heard Clover lumbering to her feet, saying, 'It's my day to pick up the twins and keep them at home until Dave gets back. I'd better slip away.'

Then the sound of the back door closing, and retreating, stomping steps across the yard. It was Jo who broke the silence: 'God, life, eh? First they lose their lovely mum to cancer, then they've got to have tea with that miserable old cow.'

'Jo. That's a *terrible* thing to say.'

'Mebbe. But it's what you're all thinking . . .'

Georgie found the energy to prise open one eyelid. There was Bubba at her sink, having a Petit Trianon moment, holding up that green scourer as Marie Antoinette might a fan. 'I haven't done this

57

for ages! Do you know, it's rather good *fun*?'

Then someone hit the iPod, and the song they'd had last night—'Dancing in the Moonlight'—started up where it had left off. Immediately, Rachel was flicking her hips and jiving with the risotto pan. She was a cool little groover, that Rachel. Jo started head-banging away. Heather was—what was Heather doing? It looked like, sort of, early ballet . . . Bubba's neat little buttocks were twitching along while she washed. Colette—well, there was a surprise—slipped quietly out the door.

And Georgie reckoned she'd got just about ten minutes. Ten minutes left to give in to a nice, quiet snooze . . .

3.15 P.M. PICK-UP

Bea was standing in the playground with Colette, being fully debriefed on the day's events. They each had an eye on a cluster of Year 5 girls nearby. At the centre of it was Bea's eldest, Scarlett. She was going to lend her Sylvanian squirrels out just for that evening, and she was trying to decide to whom. The potential candidates gathered around, each desperate to be the chosen one.

'Georgina! What a success. You really got things off to a flying start.'

'As usual, all the hard work comes down to the likes of *moi*. Here you go.' She handed Bea a fistful of notes. 'I'm pretty sure there were twelve of them, but there was only a hundred and fifty quid in the pot at the end of it. Someone's on the fiddle. Perhaps we should call the fraud squad in.'

Colette had the grace to look shifty. Bea was

merely puzzled, and said to no one in particular, 'Well I was only popping in. I didn't eat anything, obviously . . .' Then her phone rang. She gave a little jump, snapped it open and vanished.

Poppy Mason pulled away from the cluster and approached Georgie.

'Hi, Pops. How're you doing? Where's my rabble?'

'Josh went out with Daddy last night. Just the two of them. To the football.'

'Oh. O-K . . .'

Then children flooded out of school, parents in from the car park. And they were swamped.

'Georgie! Back with us! Wasn't that fun?'

'No. It was a bloody nightmare.'

'And—ahem—did you notice anything—ahem—different about your kitchen when you woke up?'

'Yeah. It looked a lot better. Cos you lot had all buggered off out of it. Thank the Lord.'

THE WEEKEND OF THE CAR BOOT SALE

8.50 A.M. DROP-OFF, FRIDAY

'Have you heard?' Heather and Maisie were standing on the corner, already waiting. There was no longer any pretence of bumping into Rachel and Poppy every morning. They were now clearly visible—waiting, fidgeting—from Rachel's cottage door. With narrowed eyes, she had just been able to make out Maisie throwing sticks into the conker tree, the sheaves of papers in Heather's hands and the toes of her trainers, tapping.

'You'll never guess!' The girls assumed forward formation; the four began their progress. 'Bea. Has. Got a job!'

At once Rachel felt a sharp flash of pain, located somewhere in the region of her own pride. Or, at least, where once she used to keep her pride back when she had some . . . For years, Bea had not only told her everything, she had told her first, before anyone else. And it had always been a source of simple amusement—nothing more—that, once Bea had dispensed some snippet of something, people would then hover around Rachel in the hope that she might pass it on to them. Sometimes, she could almost look down on herself in the playground and snigger at the way she would have to dole out the news to a hungry multitude, second-in-command of the Information Food Chain: 'Spain, I gather, they've just booked it'; 'Yes, late last night. So tanned!' And now where was she? Hearing about Bea from Heather, of all people. That was quite

60

some declassification: she wasn't even the creature at the bottom of the food chain these days. She was now just some lowly parasite feeding thereon . . .

Rachel still had no idea what she had done to deserve any of this, but one thing was for sure: she would refuse to show much interest. 'Um. Oh.' Anyway, in her world, jobs were not quite the exotic objects of dazzled wonder that they were in Heather's. She even happened to have one herself, which just about summed up their utter banality. And though she had never asked, she did have a sneaking suspicion that Heather didn't stop people in the street to tell them about it. But, clearly, this job was different.

'It's hot news. I saw it on Facebook last night.'

'Bea announced it on Facebook?' Did anyone round here—except, of course, the children—plan to grow up any time soon?

'No, Bea didn't. I'm still waiting to be accepted by Bea on Facebook. I'm "Pending".' Heather shrugged. Pending didn't seem to bother her. She was fine with 'pending'. Better, obviously, than being dropped from a great height. 'But Colette—I'm friends with her—'

'Hey. Congrats.' Funny, she always seemed to be congratulating Heather at the moment. Just one stupendous triumph after another. It was like walking into school with Alexander the Great. 'To think, I knew you when you were nothing.'

'Aw. You are sweet. I was pleased. Anyway, Colette changed her status to "Colette is very proud xxx".'

'And what's all this then?' Rachel indicated the papers that Heather was clutching.

'Posters. Bea wants people to make as many

cakes as they can, for us to sell at the Car Boot Sale. She says if we run a tea and coffee stand there, well, that could be another really, really good, positive source of income for the school.'

Enough. Rachel was suddenly overwhelmed by a deep yearning for the sophisticated company of the two ten-year-olds ahead.

'Hey, girls.' She skipped lightly to catch up with them. 'What's up?'

'Look at my conkers,' said Maisie proudly.

'You know that big box the washing machine came in?' Poppy's eyes were gleaming. 'I'm going to make a Dalek suit!'

'And you know Mr Orchard?' chipped in Maisie. 'Destiny in Year 3 told us why he's come here.'

'He fell in love with a pop star.'

'And the pop star was going out with a footballer.'

'Our Mr Orchard? Well, who'd have thought it?' said Rachel.

'I know! And the pop star loved Mr Orchard.'

'Who can blame her?'

'So the footballer thumped him. Bash.' Poppy pressed her little fist into her cheek. 'He said, "Mr Orchard you must never be seen in Chelsea again."'

'And so Mr Orchard came to St Ambrose.'

'Ah yes,' Rachel sighed. 'The old pop star/footballer/primary-school educator triangle. Is there nothing new under the sun?'

'Is that quite common then?' Heather was alongside them now, and genuinely interested. 'I've never seen it in the paper . . .'

'That reminds me! Guess what, guess what? You'll never guess this one,' gabbled Maisie.

'Scarlett's mummy's got a job!'

To the bulk of the community of St Ambrose, rushing into the playground and then rushing out, it was a morning just like any other. But to a little section of it—a section that was now gathered, agitating, in the corner under the big beech tree— it felt like the dawn of a new, and very different, world: Bea was wearing clothes.

Bea had turned up in some sort of sportswear every morning since Scarlett was in Reception. And yet here she stood, today, transformed; in her professional finery of sharp jacket, knee-length skirt and nude tights, elevated slightly—just her heels or, perhaps, some sort of podium, or possibly just the moral high ground—and swinging her bunch of keys, smiling down upon the merely gym-bound.

'PA-slash-manager with the promise of some PR. Thank you *so* much.'

And 'That's right. For a TV chef. You've had your hair cut! Satellite at the moment, but we're hoping . . .'

Scarlett stood to one side, swinging her book bag and adding the footnotes. 'I know, she does so much! But she'll manage. She always does.' She turned to Rachel: 'I *love* your boots.'

'Thank you, Scarlett. What's your mum up to over there? She looks like a bride about to throw her bouquet.'

'Oh, she's just choosing who's going to take us home for her tonight. It's so sweet. Mummy's going to be so busy now, but she says *everyone* will want to

63

do their bit.'

That was it for Heather. She was off, flying over to the beech tree as fast as her Nikes would carry her, waving her hand in the air, scattering posters across the tarmac and calling, 'Bea? Bea? Is there anything I can do, Bea?'

'Well,' said Rachel to the girls. 'It looks like I'd better do my bit and deliver you both in to school.'

*   *   *

Rachel could hear the phone ringing inside, but she just could not find her door key. Which pocket? Brrring brrrring. Flat little Yale thing. Where's it gone? Brrring brrrring. Trouble is, she'd lost weight and her jeans were nearly hanging off and all bunched up and she couldn't get to the bottom of the pockets. It wasn't that she was grief-stricken. Well. Perhaps not only because of the grief. It was more that when Chris left, although she pretty much held most aspects of home life together, the whole diurnal meal routine system thing instantly fell apart. Brrring brrrring. She would not, in other areas, put her estimation of self at 'low'—Aha! Found it!—but the facts spoke for themselves: an evening with her and Chris and they always went in for two courses, set places and a modicum of culinary excitement. Now she was on her own, it was a bowl of Alpen and a Kit-Kat.

She burst through the door, tripped on a cardboard box and lunged for the phone. Just in time.

Oh.

'Yeah. Hi, Mum.'

It should not be this bad when her mother rang.

She should just tuck the handset into her neck, go about her business and say yes from time to time. That was all that was required. Simple. And yet . . . Though Rachel knew and accepted herself to be a forty-year-old woman, when the phone began to trill, just the sound of her mother's voice—the very words 'It's only me'—and she was magically transported back to her own difficult, challenging, recalcitrant adolescence.

'I had coffee with Mary yesterday.' Rachel went upstairs to gather the latest thrilling instalment of dirty clothes. 'Her nephew—you know the one that went to Canada—it's all going *brilliantly* for them.' Neh neh neh, mimed Rachel, pulling an unattractive face. She trotted back down the uneven cottage stairs—

'The schools are wonderful, apparently.'

—and tripped over another cardboard box at the bottom.

'And they say his *daughter* is a *marvel* on the ice rink . . .'

Big deal. Rachel filled the washing machine. 'Well I'm sorry if Josh fractured his wrist the first and only time he went ice-skating. And I'm sorry he wouldn't go back again so that you could boast away to Mary. Or Torvill. Or Dean.'

'Oh really, Rachel. You know I wasn't saying . . .'

Yeah. She was going round the sink now with a scourer. She did know her mum wasn't saying that. But the trouble was, Rachel wasn't quite sure what she *was* saying yet. Where exactly were they going with this? Their 'little chats' always followed this familiar path: her mum led her down these twisting, turning conversational alleyways that seemed to be leading nowhere, until Rachel was completely lost, partially blind, limping and then bam! The real stuff, the subtext, the subject that her mum really wanted to get on to leapt out of some shadowy doorway and hit her in the face. Rachel's only method of self-defence was to fight her all the way.

She had no idea as yet where the riveting topic of Mary's Canadian nephew was leading her. She was pretty sure that her mum didn't want them all to emigrate. And it didn't seem to be about ice-skating in their lives, the lack thereof . . .

'But poor girl, she has to be at the rink at five every morning, to practise before school. I think it's monstrous . . .'

OK, so it wasn't a campaign for her children to do more extra-curricular stuff.

'As I said to Mary, "She's lucky she's got two parents," I said. "Rachel couldn't manage anything like that. *Now she's on her own . . .*"'

There: ambush. It was a *divorce* conversation.

'Josh and Poppy have two parents, Mum. As it happens. In fact, I do believe you've even met the other one. Remember? That guy? At my wedding?'

'Well in the past I have, yes. But a long time ago . . .'

'He only left—we only decided to separate—last month.' She started to mumble, 'Or month before last . . .' Christ, it was actually coming on for three.

'And he's certainly not been as *around* as I'm sure he made out he would be.'

'He's always around!' Brilliant. How had this happened? Rachel was suddenly the chief cheerleader of the Chris Mason Fan Club. Always around? Hilarious. 'He took Josh to the football only the other night.' The week before last, actually.

'How nice. And Poppy? Hmm? When did he last

66

see his daughter?'

Good question.

'He's got them both for the entire weekend!' She could barely believe the triumph in her own voice. Listen to it! Her children's father was finally getting it together to have them for the first time since the summer, and suddenly he was Brad bloody Pitt.

'Well I don't see how he's going to manage it, if he hasn't got them any beds . . .'

'He's getting beds this week!' Hurrah hurrah for him. Let us all worship the Great One who provideth beds even unto his own children.

'Yes, well, he won't, will he? Anyway. I was wondering if you could pop over and help me some time.'

'Sure. Hey. I'm only a struggling single mother.' She hated herself as she said it. 'All the time in the world. What can I do for you?'

Her mum ignored that one.

'It's my bees. I need to open them up and I don't really like being out there with them on my own . . .'

So here was something else that Chris had dumped her with: her mother's permanent quest for self-sufficiency that seemed to suck in the energies of everyone around her. Rachel turned her back to the sink and slumped against it in defeat. It was a mystery of physics, as yet unexplained, that the longer she had to get used to her husband's absence the larger became the hole he had left behind. While it had registered the departure of her co-parent and her lover—and how—her brain had, until that very moment, failed to compute what was going on at the peripheries. Like the fact that her mum had lost a son-in-law in the process. A son-in-law who, she had to admit, was remarkably good-humoured about popping round there whenever summoned by Her Imperial Highness.

So she must miss him too, then. Rachel hadn't thought of that.

'Yeah. OK. But I'm working all this week.'

'Oh yes. Of course. Your *"job"*.' Her mum always somehow contrived to convey vocally those inverted commas: it was still a struggle for her to equate drawing pictures with earning a living.

'Yes. My "job". It's very "busy". I'll come at the weekend.'

She hung up, and her head started to clear. Her arsey, difficult fourteen-year-old self shimmered, faded away and was replaced with an entirely reasonable adult once again. Poppy the *Dr Who* expert would be fascinated: it was a transmutation worthy of a pretty convincing alien.

Rachel would go round on Sunday and, she vowed, be as nice as pie. But now she must get down to some work. She sat down at the table, put a pencil in her mouth with one hand and smoothed the other over the blank paper in front of her, and then her mobile chirruped. Oh God, she thought. A text. Her stomach clenched. A bloody text. It ripped her apart that all communication with the man to whom she was technically still married was reduced to a sequence of electronic messages. Presumably before the invention of the mobile phone, separating couples actually had to talk to one another to make arrangements about the kids. And presumably, occasionally, a conversation might erupt about something other than arrangements about the kids. And presumably, more than once, that might have led to something else: peace, harmony. Dinner. Bed. Perhaps that's why the

68

divorce rate was lower back then.

Please let this one not be from . . . She opened the message. And of course: it was from the all-round great bloke, the merciful provider, the Pitt-alike himself. Now what?

'Got to work Sat. Soz. Will get kids Sun a.m. OK? Cheers.'

10 A.M. MORNING BREAK

Heather, thrusting her trolley before her, strode up the aisle towards Baking Accompaniments. She was fresh out of the gym, due shortly at Colette's and, while her pulse might not be exactly racing, it was certainly going at a brisk little jog. She stood in front of the self-raising flour. The trouble was, it was so hard to know how many cakes she should make herself. She took two kilos. Would anyone respond to her posters and make any more? She plucked down another two. And how many cars would come? Or what Bea called 'punters', doing that inverted-comma thing with her fingers? Six in total, that should cover it. She threw into the trolley the same amount of caster and icing sugars, grabbed three dozen eggs and marched off to Dairy.

She had never had cause before to buy those ginormous cartons of milk. They belonged in those vast fridges, in different kitchens, in another world. Her little family would have to bathe in it to use all that up. Guy didn't really like too much dairy anyway—not an allergy as such, just an intolerance, really. Sensitive gut. And, with them just having the one child . . .

A trolley came and parked next to hers. A food

69

mountain was piled up behind the two benign small children perched within. Heather stared at it all in wonder. Jumbo this, family-sized that, one hundred fish fingers? How could any family possibly ever eat one hundred fish fingers? The woman reached over for a gallon of milk and glanced into Heather's trolley. She took a second gallon, turned and tossed her eyes skywards in a look of sisterhood—'Weekly nightmare, eh?'—and on she pressed.

Heather looked down at what she was buying, the sheer bulkiness of it. Of course. That perfect stranger had not seen it as the trolley of a mother-of-one who was organising a car boot sale. Perhaps she didn't even know about the car boot sale. (Though that was a worrying thought. Surely this was a huge thing locally? Had she not advertised enough? Perhaps she should run after the woman and just mention it . . .) No. She had looked at Heather's trolley and she had just assumed stuff. She had assumed a big busy household full of open, hungry mouths like a nest in spring. She had assumed a host of small skeletons that needed calcium to grow; that Heather was, like herself, as busy as could be. She had, in fact, assumed that Heather was actually living the life that Heather herself had always expected to live.

She started to walk a little taller. A different woman was trying to manage a furious toddler, and the new Heather peered over her vast trolley and smiled at her. We've all been there, said her look. Though she, personally, never had. Maisie had never gone in for tantrums, on the whole. Always a quiet little thing, from the get-go. Too easy, Heather thought, and instantly that sad empty feeling came over her. She took four loaves of

70

bread, though she wasn't sure why. Do you need bread at a car boot sale? Well, the sheer quantity of it somehow made her feel better, filled a sort of gap.

The Detergents aisle now. She didn't need any at home, and couldn't see that she had to get any for Sunday. But Oh! she thought. Just look at them: the multi-packs of Flash that she would be buying if she had ended up with the large gang that was her due. She saw her other self—dragging out the mop and bucket twice a day, moaning about the mud on the kitchen floor and the football boots slung in the hall and all the other million and one things she had to do and did nobody appreciate her round here or might she just as well be talking to herself—and smiled wistfully. Hey, why not? What was to stop her?

Heather hadn't felt this wickedly naughty in a shop since she nicked an eye pencil from the Rimmel counter when she was thirteen. And that was all Georgie's fault. After a quick scout around to see if anyone was watching, she grabbed the reassuringly solid multi-pack—Oomph, that's heavy—and balanced it on the bumper tub of Stork margarine in the trolley. Where was the harm? She wasn't sure if anyone was looking, but if they were then so what? Woman, forty-two, buys floor cleaner—it's hardly the first sign of madness, is it? They weren't going to lock her up. And anyway, she might get that look again. Someone else might look at her, and assume those boys and that mud and the way that nobody appreciated her round there. Someone who didn't already know that the muckiest thing that ever happened in her kitchen was when Maisie went over the lines in her colouring-in, and that didn't happen very often because she took a lot of pride in her colouring-in, did Maisie.

Sometimes, just sometimes, in her darker moments—and they did get very dark, her moments; increasingly so—she just wondered if, well, if she wouldn't have been better off having no children at all, rather than just the one. There. There it was, the awful thought, and there was nothing that she could do about it. It just kept popping up—ping!—of its own accord. Wow. Look at that—a container of Ribena so huge that it needed its own built-in handle. She'd have two of those. Of course, Maisie was everything, everything, to both of them. Guy worshipped the very ground . . .

She grabbed a Cadbury's Party Selection. And then another one. In for a penny . . . She and Guy had always agreed that when they had children she, Heather, their mother, would be there for them. She would get them up every morning, be there at the school gates and read their stories, know their friends and boil their pasta, kiss their little heads good-night. That was what made a child sane and secure in their opinion. And Maisie had come along, and Heather had left her job and then . . . Despite their very best efforts and those of the medical profession, nobody else had come along afterwards. And Maisie had turned out sane and secure, thus proving all their theories correct. But she was so wretchedly sane and secure that it didn't leave Heather with very much at all to do. And she could find a job of some kind; but then if she did, well, she wouldn't be being at home with the one child she had managed to produce and she wouldn't know its friends or boil its pasta. And she might have to work late sometimes so then she wouldn't kiss its little head good-night. And so it—she, Maisie—wouldn't be sane and secure any more. She was, to use one of Guy's favourite expressions, 'in a bit of a pickle'. She thought enviously of Bubba and her Milo. 'An *exceptional* child', that's what Bubba had called him, and he did sound so original. Bubba'd certainly got her hands full there. Lucky thing.

As her mood sank, Heather's progress started to slow. She dragged herself towards the till, only to be cut up by that woman with the food mountain, who was practically breaking the speed limit. 'Rush hour', that's exactly how Bea described these years the other morning, over coffee after pilates. She had said that when our children are small, that's the 'rush hour' of our lives. She started to unload her mega-shop on the conveyor belt. Well if this is my rush hour, thought Heather, it's an odd one. Like a rush hour after some hideous atrocity, or a member of the royal family has snuffed it or there's a really big football match which England could win and then doesn't: it's all quiet and under-populated and eerie.

It was her turn at the checkout and the cashier prepared herself for the onslaught. 'Well you're a big shopper and no mistake.'

'Oh no, not really.' Heather rubbed her fingers against the opening of the carrier bag. 'It's not all for me.'

*　　　*　　　*

Rachel had been slumped over her drawing table

73

since she'd read the text. Her clean sheet of paper was now soaked to the point of uselessness. The sound of her thick, choking, snotty sobs bounced off the walls and echoed around the empty rooms of the rest of the cottage. The cat was studying her with an air of amused superiority. Actually, now she thought about it, it was technically Chris's cat—and something else he'd deserted. She lifted her head up—'So you needn't look so bloody smug'—and sank right down again.

She used to love the daytime quiet of her own house. When it had been the noisy teeming hub of a happy family life, to get it to herself every day seemed such a luxury. The last few precious moments before everyone came clattering back home were always her favourite—like a party venue before the revellers arrived. And first thing in the morning, after Chris had done his swearing at 'Thought for the Day' on the radio—'Bishop, you are a *tosser*'—and gone off for the train, and Josh had thundered up and down stairs for the final time and rushed to get the bus by its usual regulation-length whisker. She would stand at the door, after dropping Poppy off, and listen, just listen for the quiet like a doctor might listen for a heartbeat. Then she would sigh with pleasure and feel free to get on with her day.

It wasn't like that any more. There was still a party every night, clearly. But it was going on elsewhere and Rachel wasn't invited. There might still be a heartbeat, but the patient was in a coma. They were all so quiet now, especially in the evenings. And especially Josh. Her once loving, laughing, darling boy now was always in his own room, on another planet, and communicated only in a series of grunts. But was that because his father had moved on or adolescence had moved in? Rachel was finding it hard to tell. And the only other person who might know chose not to be around.

The worst thing—no, not the worst thing. Let's face it, this separation business was one big worst thing. It was a whole wide world of pain, you couldn't pick out one particular landmark and declare that the most horrible. One was genuinely, miserably, spoiled for choice. But she could say that the aspect of the separation that was occupying the bulk of her available mental space at that moment was this: the much-loved father of her beloved children was a total and utter scumbag. How could that be true?

Eight o'clock in the evening, thirteen years and nine months ago: their first night out together after the birth of Josh. Rachel was—miraculously—ready to go, her mother was on the sofa, studying the TV listings, ready to babysit, but Chris? Where was Chris? Where had he got to? She found him upstairs, studying his baby's face by the soft nursery night-light, utterly lost and absorbed. Rachel had tiptoed in—they were so new to it all then, didn't know you needed gelignite to actually wake a sleeping baby that wanted to sleep—and touched his arm. 'This is the point of it all, isn't it?' he had said to her. His eyes were damp. 'The point of us: it was him, all along.'

One Sunday morning, nine years and—what?—six months ago. Chris and Rachel were sitting, squashed together, on the sofa. Josh was outside on the swing. They had the garden door open, they could see him, he was fine. Chris's feet were

75

up on the coffee table, and laid out on his long, lean thighs was their new daughter. They felt like a single organism then; like when you take lots of little Play-Doh figures and mash them together to make one big blob. Chris had his left arm around Rachel, and with the forefinger of his right hand he was stroking Poppy's face in rhythm, from the top of her forehead to the tip of her nose, and they were trying to decide: when should she be weaned? The health visitors had changed their guidelines, inconveniently, somewhere between Josh's infancy and Poppy's, and they were desperate, completely desperate, not to do the wrong thing. They had laid aside that time so that they could discuss it properly: to stewed-carrot or not to stewed-carrot? It had seemed, at the time, quite overwhelming.

They had embarked on the journey of family life together. So what happened? Chris saw someone else through the windscreen, threw Rachel out of his still-moving vehicle and swerved off course, on to another journey of his own. Was that really all it took? Not an unusual story, of course. Nor was it unusual for one departing parent to find that there was no room, as it were, in the back seat for the children after all. Not unusual, but depressing. Definitely depressing. That the man she chose could go from worrying about baby rice to 'Got to work Sat. Soz' in less than a decade. That he should have been so concerned about the development of the lining of that little tummy, when all along he was just going to take that little heart and a great big club and just mash it to a pulp, week after week after week . . . Well. It was just depressing. That was all there was to it.

Stop. No more crying. She had cried so much

76

that she was actually bored of it. But she couldn't see that she was going to get any work done now either. Yet again. Funnily enough, it just wasn't easy drawing pleasant little pictures when one was in the grip of a murderous fury. Rachel's current project was a story book—*Ellie's Wellies*—in which a pair of little red Wellingtons went off on their own adventures when the size 1 feet of their little moppet owner were otherwise occupied. Yet the only image that kept coming to her tortured mind, demanding to be realised, was that of a hobnail boot having its own adventure on Chris's stubbly gob.

She breathed deeply, pinched her eyes together to halt the tears, pushed her chair back and collided with another cardboard box. That was enough. Although Chris himself had moved out at the end of the summer, these wretched little boxes of his treasured possessions had remained, strategically placed around the cottage like chips on a roulette table: he hadn't completely gone, he was still hedging his bets. Well, she was going to make up his mind for him. Something she could do right now was sort out her 'old bits'—Christ, Heather—to dispense from her car boot on Sunday, and amass all Chris's stuff for him to take at the same time.

She made a pile of the boxes he had already filled, and then grabbed a couple more. As well as Chris's clothes, his 'effects' as they say when someone has snuffed it—which he sort of had, or might as well have done—he could also take his books. Not that he ever read any more—nothing beyond the iPad and his BlackBerry—but Rachel did and she could do with more book space.

When they'd first got together, she couldn't

believe how well-read this man was. How knowledgeable, how bloody clever he was on not just novels, but pretty much every other subject under the sun as well. Rachel had given up reading once she'd had to give up Enid Blyton—the rest of world literature had, frankly, failed to come up to snuff. After that, she'd done nothing but draw and paint and model and just float around really, somewhere inside her own head. So she'd spent the first two years of their relationship just sort of sitting at his feet, drinking it all in. Then she had got up, promoted herself to her own chair, and had had her nose in a book ever since. And sometime after that, she noticed, Chris stopped reading altogether.

She took down all the paperbacks he had once known and loved. The ones he—they—used to talk about, with such passion, once upon a time. *The Secret History*, *Persuasion*, the Anne Tylers and their mutual top favourite: all the Graham Greenes. It was strangely comforting to think of him taking them all into his new life: like a dirty river dragging debris from its pure, clean source. Trace elements of the better man he used to be.

And now she'd got Saturday free to spend with Poppy. They could make that Dalek suit. What did they need? Eggboxes. Silver paint. Kitchen utensils. It would take everyone's mind off things. And on Monday morning the cottage would be cleansed. Ordered. And Rachel would be able to commence the rest of her life.

12.30 P.M. LUNCH BREAK

Heather stood at Colette's kitchen sink, her hands in the soapy water, looking out at the bare square garden. 'So is that where you work, then, in that little wooden hut out there?' It looked a bit like Maisie's Wendy house. In fact, wasn't it exactly Maisie's Wendy house?

'That's the Serenity Spa Sanctuary Beauty Therapy Suite, yes.' Colette was squatting in front of the tumble dryer, reeling in the latest load.

It had been Bea's idea, at their special meeting about the car boot sale, that they have a stall of jumble there as well—except she preferred to call it the 'donated nearly new'. It had been Bea's idea, too, that they gave all the jum—sorry, donated clothes—a good old wash beforehand, because they always sold better that way. And it had been Bea's idea that everyone went round to her place to do the washing together. They had all been really looking forward to that. But, sadly, when the great day dawned, it turned out that Bea had carpet fitters or some such. Wasn't it always the way? So in the end, Heather and Colette told her not to worry, and to just leave it to them. But to be honest, Heather wasn't really enjoying it all as much as she thought she would.

'This stain's not coming out, whatever I do, but I don't think we can be bothered with a second wash, can we?' Heather kept rubbing at a stubborn patch on a tatty little jumper. She hoped it was ketchup, although the phrase 'organic matter' kept springing, unbidden, to mind.

79

'Well Bea did say, the cleaner the stuff the higher the price . . .'

'Yeah . . . but . . .' They'd been slaving away for ages, and though Heather's enthusiasm and energy had noticeably diminished, the bin-bag mountain full of grubby donated clothing had not. She smuggled the yucky top out in a clutch of other dripping things and took them to the dryer.

'Hang on! We can't tumble-dry the woollens! Bea warned us about shrinking anything . . .' Colette filled up the basket and headed out to the clothes line and Heather ambled out after her. She made a tunnel with her hands and peered in through the window of the Serenity Spa Sanctuary Beauty Therapy Suite. Always been an Immac girl herself. Immac or just the Ladyshave. Goodness, look at all that clobber in there. What on earth do they get up to?

'Do you get a lot of your customers from school then?'

'The bulk of my client base, yes. I know everyone's little secrets.' Colette was talking through a mouthful of clothes pegs. 'Every Brazilian in St Ambrose'—Brazilians? Heather hadn't met any Brazilians. Weren't they normally Catholic?—'was rrrrrrrrrrr-ripped into place on that table.'

Brazilian! Heather had read about Brazilians, of course, but she did not till that moment really believe in them. She had them down as one of those things of which the human race was obviously capable, but that nobody in their right minds could possibly want. Like total nuclear warfare, say, or child slavery . . . Her legs had at some point, involuntarily, crossed. She uncrossed them, but

80

kept her thighs firmly plastered together as she waddled uneasily back to the haven of the kitchen.

The bin-bag mountain was still there, uneroded. 'Colette, we couldn't have a little break, could we? I mean, I know there's still loads to do, but . . .'

'Go on then. Sit down.' She put the kettle on and got out the biscuit tin. 'To tell you the truth, I'm beginning to wonder if we're going to get all this done.'

'Or even,' Heather said without thinking, 'if we need to.'

Colette froze. 'But Bea said . . .'

'Yes, of course.' She took a Hobnob—'Silly me'—and dunked it. 'So, any gossip?'

'Only about me . . .' Colette raised her left shoulder and peered over it, adopted the voice of Dolly Parton. 'Only that I am pretty sure that I have found myself a very nice new man.'

'Oh wow, Colette! I thought you were looking particularly gorgeous. That glow. Anyone we know?'

'Well, promise not to tell a living soul . . .'

They were both leaning in over the table, heads close together. Heather thought she might actually burst, it was all so thrilling. 'Promise . . .'

'. . . IT'S TOM!'

Er.

Tom.

Who's Tom? Did she know a Tom? Was she supposed to know a Tom? She could tell, from Colette's excitement, that she ought to know this Tom. Tom. Tom . . . No good. Nothing doing.

'Um . . . Tom?'

'Orchard! Tom Orchard!'

There was the faintest ringing of a distant bell . . .

81

'THE HEADMASTER!'

'Oh! *Mister* Orchard!' Tom? She's calling him Tom? 'Hey. You're a quick worker.' This wasn't quite the thing, was it? Headmaster and single mother? She didn't have him down as the type. Bea might have a few words to say about this . . .

'Oh, nothing's happened yet.' Colette twisted the top of the Hobnob packet and put it back in the tin. 'But you know when you just know?'

Heather wasn't entirely sure if or how you did know when you just knew. Not much experience in the just-knowing department. Her own romance, if that was the word, with Guy had moved at what you might call a careful pace. They'd met at a disco in the lower sixth and married the year they both hit thirty. Georgie had made the best-woman speech. She had said something about how exciting it had been, seeing the relationship blossom—like watching pandas mating. Then she'd done her David-Attenborough-in-a-bamboo-tree impersonation that she was so proud of, and everyone had laughed. It was a bit annoying, now she remembered it . . .

'He used to go out with a pop star, apparently.' Heather was keen to share all she knew on the subject of Mr—er, Tom.

'Did he?' Colette was pleased with this. 'I'm not surprised.'

'And the pop star used to go out with a footballer . . .' Even as she repeated it, Heather became less confident of her information.

'Well he is very attractive.' Colette was studying

82

her cuticles.

'Have you told Bea yet?' Heather wanted to know for a few reasons. Had Colette confided in her first? Before Bea? That was a rather delicious thought, and Heather was enjoying it. But at the same time, she needed to know where Bea would stand on one of their own entering into a relationship with the new headmaster.

'Bea.' For the first time, Heather heard something other than adoration in Colette's voice. 'Not yet, no. I haven't. It's sort of early days. I mean I haven't actually spoken to him yet, but we do have a meeting in the diary next week. To discuss my "concerns about Johnny's progress". Though I haven't actually got any!' She giggled, and then her face darkened again. 'If you want my opinion, it wouldn't actually have hurt Bea to have thought up this very obvious match and made it herself. But she didn't.'

Colette stood up, took the mugs, turned around and saw anew the laundry mountain.

'And I'll tell you what: you're right. We don't need to do any more of this horrible smelly revolting washing.' She kicked the nearest bin bag.

Heather was shocked: 'But Bea says we'll make more money . . . !'

'Yeah, right. Ten p? Twenty? So bloody what?'

'But she . . .'

'Heather! She isn't even here. She will never even know!'

'Ooo-er,' said Heather. And 'Gosh!' And 'But . . .' And 'She's got a job . . .'

'No buts.' This was a new, commanding Colette, and one that Heather had not previously seen. 'And I'll tell you something else. *Lewis* is on ITV3 in a

minute. Find yourself an armchair. I'll give you a
free mani-pedi while we watch.'

THE DAY OF THE CAR BOOT SALE

7.30 A.M.

Heather marched up and down the playing field feeling quite sick. For two days she had eaten nothing more than raw cake mixture off the back of a palette knife, and she wasn't sure if it quite agreed with her. She was overstuffed, undernourished and sleepless, so nervous was she about today. She had tossed and turned, tossed and turned as the words 'major fund-raiser for the school' pounded repeatedly upon her brain like a mallet on a gong.

Her jacket said that she was a STEWARD, in large black letters on its yellow neon front and its yellow neon back—so that someone could find her instantly if trouble broke out. And trouble could break out at car boot sales. She had done her research. She knew that the real professionals, the ones that came early with sharp elbows and wads of cash, could be really difficult. If two of the pros wanted the same thing, it could get very ugly. It was all such a worry . . .

These poor normal mums and dads who were just coming along to do their bit, they probably had no idea what to expect. Heather knew—from the internet—that the second you got there, these 'punters' started to surround you like those monkeys in the safari park. They hung upside-down off the roof and prised open the windows with long dirty fingers and nicked all your good stuff before you turned off the ignition.

Guy had suggested that they write a list of dos

and don'ts—like their Thomas Cook rep had done for them when they went to the souk in Tunisia last year, forewarned being forearmed. He and Maisie were handing out the printed sheets at the entrance now. And he had gone out and bought her a whistle, although she wasn't convinced that if a burly 'punter' was really angry a whistle would actually calm him. Did the local police station have a TASER? She really should have checked.

7.45 A.M.

'What a hoot, eh?' Bubba trilled, to no one in particular. Her Range Rover was parked at right-angles to the rest of the row. She was carefully arranging outfits, plastic-wrapped from the dry-cleaner, on a portable clothes rail, which was divided into categories: £20; £40; £60; £80 and so on, upwards. She was delighted to be getting rid of it all, to be completely honest. And wondering what she might do with the money she made today. It could be really quite a bit . . .

*   *   *

Georgie was three cars down, in the front of her Land Rover, with her feet up on the dashboard, a nice cup of coffee in her hands and the papers spread out on her knees. She hadn't actually bothered to check, but it sounded like the kids were doing a brisk-ish sort of business with their used toys at the back there. Very nice way to spend a Sunday morning, all told. A change being as good as a rest. In fact, she thought, putting down her

86

coffee and wriggling deeper into her seat, this might be the perfect opportunity for a proper, actual rest. Everything seemed to be ticking over. She might just close her . . .

8.00 A.M.

Heather, gripping her whistle and her walkie-talkie, her knuckles white, her eyes on stalks, surveyed the scene. The playing fields were filling up nicely.

Bea had been right about the cake stall— that was a very nice touch. Raised the tone. And when she had seen the great spread of cakes that Heather had made, Bea had volunteered to run it herself! She had been down to sell the jumble— sorry, donated nearly new—with Colette. But then she said, 'No! *I* shall sell those gorgeous cakes!' She was kind, Bea. Really lovely. There she was, over by the fence, wearing her apron that said THE BOSS on it, all ready for business. She also had on—and Heather was a bit surprised by this—one of those headsets, with a thingy stuck in her ear and a mouthpiece. If she needed one of those, surely Heather should have one too? Who else, after all, was Bea planning to communicate with if not the actual organiser? . . . Strange. Heather gave her a little wave. But if she had had her own headset, she could have said something. Like 'Hi!' Or something like that.

Although she wasn't letting go just yet, Heather was beginning to wonder if the whistle was entirely necessary.

8.10 A.M.

A Volvo estate came bumping over the grass towards Heather and stopped. Rachel emerged, leaving her door wide open. The list of dos and don'ts was clearly visible on the dashboard. '1,' it said. 'DON'T leave your car door wide open.'

'Morning. Nice turn-out. Well done.'

Rachel went round to the passenger side and opened the front door for Poppy and the back door for a Dalek. 'I wouldn't put it on now, love. Why not wait till Daddy gets here, and then . . .'

But Poppy was clambering into the large box even as Rachel was urging caution. 'Look, Heather! Look what I made. Daddy's picking me up from the entrance, and he said wouldn't it be really funny if people saw him just drive up all normal and then a Dalek gets in! They'll be like hey wow that's really weird and random . . .' She peered out of the eye holes and waggled the protruding sink plunger in farewell. 'See. You. Lat-er,' she said in a Daleky monotone, and stomped back across the field.

The two women watched her go. 'If he is even one fucking minute late,' said Rachel, 'I promise you I will fucking murder him right there in front of the fucking coffee and the fucking tea and the fucking fancy fucking cakes.'

Heather groped for her whistle. And then voices started to rise around the cake stall. It sounded like some sort of commotion was breaking out over there. She hurried off.

88

8.15 A.M.

'How's it going?' Heather asked nervously as she passed Colette at the Donated Nearly New table. She was looking really very groomed for early on a Sunday morning, but not quite so cheerful.

'Oh, great. Couldn't be better. Stuck here on my own behind a mountain of stinking jumble. Never been so sodding happy in my entire sodding life.'

'Oh dear. Sorry. Only Bea felt she was needed on Cakes.'

'Humph. And why couldn't she have felt I was needed on Cakes. Eh?'

'Well, it doesn't really matter, does it? Long as we're all doing our bit?'

'Well, yes. Actually. It does matter.' Colette was so cross it was really quite scary. 'Some of us aren't just here to do our bit. Some of us are here because today was a good, you know'—she pulled a face and flicked her eyes a bit. Were those eyelashes false?—'opportunity.'

'Sorry, I'm not quite following you . . .' She really needed to get over to Cakes . . .

'You know. To get to know him a bit better.' She dropped her voice to a hiss. 'Tom. Tom Orchard. And very tasty he's looking this morning too, in his civvies.'

'Well . . .' Heather started to pull away.

'I mean, he's bound to go over and buy a slice of something, isn't he? He's a bloke. OK, I do not have the world's best track record'—she lifted up her manicured hands—'first to admit it. But facts are facts and here is a fact: you're a darned sight

89

more likely to nab a single bloke with a slab of Victoria sponge than you are with a load of jumble.'

Here, Heather felt she could usefully chip in. 'Um. Donated nearly new?'

Colette stopped to deal with a customer. 'All of that? Thirty-five p altogether.'

'So thanks a lot, everybody,' she spat as she tinkled the coins into her float. 'Thanks a bloody bunch.'

*   *   *

Rachel went round to open the boot of her car. There was a bit of sorting out to do before she started flogging stuff—she had the boxes of Chris's things here to give him. And she wanted to keep her eye on Poppy just until he arrived. He wasn't late quite yet, but he would be very soon . . .

A black Chrysler that Rachel did not recognise came purring along the track and glided gracefully into position beside her. The door opened. Ooh, thought Rachel. How exciting. The promising newbie from the first day of term. First came her legs—long, lean, nicely denimed and culminating in yet another, very nice, pair of ballerinas. Then came the top of her glossy dark head, and the swinging, clean bob. With a neat little gesture, she tucked a thread of it behind one ear as she lifted her face to give Rachel a warm, thoroughly straightforward smile. And Rachel was just about to respond, would have loved to respond—she hadn't clapped eyes on anyone this promising for ages—but just at that very moment she found herself under a sudden, unprovoked and most vicious attack.

Heather had warned her, but Rachel hadn't

really listened. She was fine, Heather, perfectly sweet, but she did talk utter tripe. So how odd, Rachel thought, that on this one occasion Heather should be right: that she really was being overwhelmed by large, burly, pot-bellied boot sale enthusiasts, coming right into her face and saying, 'How much for this, love?'; that some were even now climbing into her boot and others were crawling over the front seat; that her car should actually be rocking at the force of their intrusion.

And how absolutely awful—so awful that now she couldn't breathe, her chest hurt so, she was gulping hard and sharp—that Poppy was still standing there, in the drizzle which was dampening them all, still on her own, still clutching her sink plunger. Waiting, waiting, waiting . . .

8.25 A.M.

'Cakes! That all you got? We've been up since the crack. Where's the bacon sarnies?' The situation at the cake stall was starting to get tricky. There were quite a lot of punters around the table now. Bea's hands were hidden in the wide pocket of her THE BOSS apron. She had removed her headset. Her jaw was clenched. 'They're all home-made.'

'Yeah, but haven't you got anything a bit more substantial than all this stuff?'

'How about this Angel Cake?' Bea tilted the plate towards the punters. 'I made this one myself. It's fat-free.' She looked really quite tense as she scanned the faces around her. And then she spotted Heather. 'Ah. Good. There you are. This,' Bea shot out a warm and generous smile, 'is The Organiser.'

91

She untied the strings and lifted her THE BOSS apron over her neck. 'These nice people have been up since, er, the crack. They feel they would prefer bacon sandwiches rather than cake. Or at least something a bit more substantial.' She draped the apron over Heather's shoulder. 'I see my mother's just arrived. I really must go and help her.'

*   *   *

No one was going near Bubba, Rachel could see that. She was sitting in the boot of her car, dangling her long legs over the back as if it were the side of a yacht. The sky was slate grey, yet her sunglasses were in her hair. Her eyes were smudged, her lips shimmered. 'Armani!' Rachel could hear her call politely. 'Lacroix!'

And the nice newbie, well, she was attracting a very nice class of customer. They seemed to be forming an orderly queue. So why was it only Rachel's boot that was buried beneath this teeming mass of voracity? It must be something about those cast-offs from her previous life, she thought, that was drawing them all in. People were now crawling over and through her car like maggots on a rotting corpse: the rotting corpse of her rotten marriage. She could have sold all of Chris's bits and pieces three times over: the market for crap wedding presents from the groom's side fifteen years back was, apparently, bullish.

'Sorry,' she called out for the tenth time, 'not for sale,' while keeping one eye trained on the entrance.

Do you have to be a mother, she thought, to be able to look at a box fifty yards away with a child in

92

it, and just know that the child in that box is crying? Scarlett Stuart and a group of Year 6 girls— swinging their shoulder bags, dressed for a disco— were walking up and down and round. Every time they passed the entrance, Rachel saw them fold in on each other, helpless with giggles. She wondered whether Poppy could hear them through the cardboard. Why had she let the child set off looking like that in the first place? But there was just no way she could get over there to stage a rescue. She couldn't even reach her phone. She was completely penned in by these crazed punters.

'Have it for fifty p.'

She was trapped in a nightmare.

'Fine. Twenty-five. Whatever.'

She might be having a panic attack. She . . .

The nice newbie next door was giving a large tray of something chocolate to one of her boys. 'Run this over to the cake stall, will you, Felix?' She then came over to the Volvo, put her hand on Rachel's arm and looked into her eyes.

'Excuse me.'

Ah. She had a lovely voice.

'Are you OK?'

8.35 A.M.

Heather stood, whistle in one hand, apron strings in the other, dejected. She could hardly believe it. She'd gone sweet and she should have gone savoury, she'd gone sophisticated and all the time she should've gone substantial. She thought she might actually puke. She'd had this feeling before, of course. Standing on a school field, feeling

93

rubbish—it was hardly anything new. 'Heather! You should have passed! You couldn't score!' Or 'Heather! You could've scored! You shouldn't pass!' Indeed, it was the pain's dull familiarity that hurt, more even than the pain itself.

Here, she thought, we are again. Heather, she said to herself, you've let the team down, you've let yourself down. She looked across the infinity of lemon drizzle. It was all so neatly and nicely made. (Delia. Foolproof.) And yet it was all so woefully, hideously and embarrassingly wrong.

Bea's apron seemed a little too tight in places; you'd think they'd make them one-size-only, be more sensible really. Even the neck was a bit tight. The whole morning was a total humiliation and the sooner it— There. Apron on, head free. Now for the mean and hungry punters.

But what had suddenly happened? Somehow, in the past few seconds, a huge tray had appeared on the stall in front of her, bearing neat slices of possibly the most delicious-looking thing she had ever seen in her entire life. It was chocolate, and it was—What's in there?—biscuit and Maltesers and it smelled amazing and there was tons of it.

Where had it come from?

*   *   *

'You cannot go over there.' In the past five minutes, the nice woman in the ballerina pumps had taken over Rachel's life—like a five-star general arriving in a war zone—and Rachel was close to tears of relief. First off, she had taken control of the Volvo. It was simple, really. She had just shut—slammed— the boot. The teeming maggots had all just melted away.

And now she was taking control of the wider Mason family. 'You can't go over to her. She's humiliated enough as it is. If you acknowledge it, she'll feel even worse.' Her tone was calm and kind, her eyes on Poppy in the box.

'But I can't leave her there, on her own. Who knows when the scumbag is finally going to show?'

'Leave it to me.

'Sweetheart?' The newbie called over to another good-looking boy. 'Look after the car for me, will you? I'll just be at the entrance.'

8.45 A.M.

Heather could not believe it. The cake stall—and, who knew?, possibly even the whole wide beautiful world in which she lived—was suddenly a new and happy place. The terrible mood had lifted.

'Now you're talking,' said one burly punter, eyeing up the Malteser cake. 'Slice of that, please, and a cup of tea.'

'Just what the doctor ordered,' said another. 'I'll have two, please, love.'

It seemed like a miracle to Heather—a bit like the one at Cana. It was funny, but it had always got to her, that particular Bible scene. Those poor people, on their actual wedding day, not having enough for their guests. Imagine! Heather honestly could not think of anything worse. She did suffer so with catering anxiety. And then along comes Jesus and just sorts it. Lovely story, that one . . .

Well, she had no idea who had performed the Miracle of the Car Boot Sale, but she did know there was no more catering anxiety at the St Ambrose Cake Stall on this Sunday morning, thank you very much. Just a polite and orderly collection of happy, satisfied customers.

'Two more slices, coming up!'

It did look scrummy. She would love to know who made it . . .

* * *

Rachel had reopened her boot and resumed business. She could see that Poppy was still waiting, but no longer alone. The visitor from the planet Skaro and the wearer of the ballerinas were chatting away merrily, the oldest of friends. Together they gave a personalised welcome to each new arrival—one with a wave, the other with a waggle of a sink plunger. And each new arrival smiled back, gratefully, in return. Ah, you could see them thinking, a Welcome-Dalek! At a car boot sale! How nice.

9.10 A.M.

Bubba was baffled. Although these clothes were, technically speaking, cast-offs they were damn good quality. And much better quality than any of the other tat on sale around her. Hanging here, under protective plastic, were all the outfits from her previous professional life. She, personally, wasn't going to need them any more. But that did not make all this 'jumble'. Not at all. This was an exceptional pre-loved wardrobe up for grabs here. The pre-loved wardrobe of an *extremely* successful

96

woman. This was a wardrobe that could smash you through any glass ceiling. Christ alive, you could win *The Apprentice* decked out in this lot. And yet none of these funny people wanted to buy a thing. She despaired sometimes, she honestly did. But there are some people who just don't want to *get on*.

* * *

Not only, thought Rachel, does a Dalek at a car boot sale suddenly not look quite so incongruous; it was starting to look perfectly normal.

'That's seventy-five p altogether then.'

Indeed, she thought rather grandly, one might almost feel sorry for all future car boot sales that did not have a Welcome-Dalek.

'How much for that stuff on the back seat?'

'That's not for sale,' said Rachel automatically, and then pulled herself up. Why on earth was she doing this? Why, when that bastard could not be bothered to turn up on time to see his own daughter, was she gathering up and cherishing and protecting his paltry possessions?

'Actually, excuse me?' she called to the back of a donkey jacket. 'My mistake. How much are you offering?'

'These three boxes for a tenner, love?'

'Make it a fiver—love—and they're yours.'

9.20 A.M.

Heather tapped on the car window, interrupting Georgie's snooze.

'Hello. You've been released from the tyranny of

97

the cake stall, have you?'

'Rachel's mum came and took it over. Bless her. She's a brick, that one.'

'Indeed she is,' agreed Georgie. 'The best. Unlike some I could mention.' She flicked her eyes over to the left. There, perched on the empty boot of a Passat, were Scarlett, Bea—with her headset back on, Heather noted—and Bea's mother.

'Know what they remind me of?' asked Georgie. 'Those posters we used to have in the science lab at school. With a small insect, and then a medium insect and then a big insect. And there were big red washed-out arrows going from one to the other. And it said "Life Cycle of Some Insect" over the top. Those three are exactly the same: small, medium and old versions of the same horrible thing.'

'Oh really, Georgie.' Heather was quite shocked. 'You are mean. Bea's been fantastic today. So supportive. Pamela's a brilliant chair of the governors, whatever you might think of her. And Scarlett is adorable. Maisie worships her. Are they doing good business over there? They seem to have sold out . . .'

'That's the blissful thing,' sighed Georgie, who really had been having a lovely morning. When she wasn't snoozing she was people-watching, and every prospect was pleasing. 'She came with a completely empty car, and has been sitting there patiently in the boot all morning. She just seems to be waiting for nice little worker people to come up and sell her things. I may be wrong, but I rather fear that Bea's mum might have failed to grasp the fundamental tenets of the car boot sale altogether.'

'Coo-ee! Heather!' called out Bea's mum from

98

her boot. 'I was so hoping you'd drop by. I hear you're doing teas? *Could* you be so kind as to bring me a nice cup?'

*   *   *

'Morning. How's business?' Mr Orchard was out of his off-the-peg suit. He was into his denims and his crew-neck and his leather bomber jacket. And Rachel could not help but notice that he didn't look quite such a—well—such a plonker as he normally looked in school.

She'd always been a sucker for that. Not now, of course. Not any more. But back in the day, she had never really gone for the man-in-uniform thing. No. It was when the man in uniform turned up without his uniform, revealing his own self. That, in Rachel's experience, was when something started to stir. In the gallery she used to work in, in another life in a different universe, there was a brilliant chef in the restaurant over whom everyone except Rachel used to swoon. She didn't get it at all. Until the day she met him out in the street, being scruffy old him and not the brilliant chef. And she was suddenly—rather fittingly, under the circumstances, looking back on it—toast.

'Roaring, thank you very much. I've earned more this morning than I have all week.'

Mr Orchard laughed. Which he probably wouldn't, thought Rachel, if he knew it was actually true.

'Are you buying, then, not selling?' she asked casually.

'Very much so, I'm afraid. I need to gather possessions, not shed them. I've been doing a bit

99

too much of that lately . . .'

Rachel thought, Oh yes?

'Where have you come from, Mr Orchard?' Her tone was teasing, she hoped, rather than flirty. 'Outer space?'

'It sometimes feels like it, I must admit.' The headmaster looked around him as he spoke.

Rachel saw it through his eyes: the rows of parked cars, the guffawing dads, the groups of kids charging around—they were all normal enough. Perhaps he was focusing more on the little oddities. Bubba could certainly pass as an alien, alone and shouting strange words in her own mysterious little language: 'Moschino! Miu Miu! Acne! Roll up!'

And that Dalek at the entrance, climbing clumsily, unsteadily—finally—into a neat little blue saloon, catching its sink plunger on the window. She supposed you didn't see that sort of thing every day.

'But no. Even further, really. Actually, I've come from Chelsea.'

No actual way, she thought. Wait till I pass that on. But before she could step neatly on to the topic of footballers, pop stars and that damned eternal triangle of lurve, he had moved his attentions to the back seat of her Volvo. 'Are these books for sale too? Mind if I have a look?'

9.30 A.M.

Heather's whistle was idle around her neck. Cars, their boots now empty, were queuing up to leave. The cakes—well, most of them—were sold. Guy was counting the money over at the table, with

100

Maisie. He was thrilled: he'd picked up some new bits for his Black & Decker and a whole pile of OS maps to add to his collection.

The sun was breaking through the clouds now and sweeping across the view like a searchlight, from the edges of the little town on one side to the lush country falling away on the other. It's a beautiful place, thought Heather. Full of great people. It had been one of the best mornings she'd had for ages. She loved it when everyone was in the same boat, pulling together, all going in the same direction. And she loved it most when she was actually in there with them. Too often in her life, she'd had that feeling that everyone was indeed in the same boat but she, Heather, was clinging on to the edge at the back somewhere, not quite able to scramble on board, getting cold and wet.

And actually, she hadn't just been in the boat this morning. She was its captain. And this whole success, it had all been down to Heather. All that worry, all that stress, all those lemons . . . Though everyone had done their bit on the day, this triumph she knew to be hers. Henceforth she was finally, indelibly, marked on the St Ambrose map.

Clover came stomping over the grass on her short legs, her two children lurking behind her. 'Oh, well,' she said, miserably. 'Never mind.'

'Never mind? Never mind what?'

'Well, it was a hell of a lot of work for you, wasn't it? Poor love. And for what, eh?' Clover looked about her, shook her head, dropped her voice to a mourner's whisper. 'For what?'

'Guy thinks we made over three thousand pounds! It might be more!'

'Ttttt. Oh dear. Is that all? After all that effort?

101

It's a shame.' Clover put her meaty little hand on Heather's and shook her head. 'Well. You must've learned one thing at least.'

'Must I? What? What have I learned?'

'Love-y. Come on. You've learned "never again", haven't you, hmmnn? Never again.'

*   *   *

Georgie watched Mr Orchard walking towards the exit, clutching his purchases: *The Secret History*, *The Accidental Tourist* and some old orange Penguin Graham Greenes. She gave a short sniff of approval. So he wasn't just a number cruncher, then. 'Well done, Mrs Stuart,' she heard him call as he passed the Passat. Bea was back in her THE BOSS apron now, she noticed. 'That was a triumph!'

'Oh, thank you so much,' Bea called back. 'It seemed to go off well enough, I think.'

'Terrific. You can go home now, and relax.'

'You are sweet.' She disentangled her headset with a show of relief, shook out her long buttery locks, half closed her eyes, stroked the head of her youngest who was clinging to her long, long legs. 'I must say,' she smiled a self-deprecating smile, 'I know it's awful but I just am *absolutely shattered.*'

*   *   *

Rachel didn't have much packing up to do. She seemed to have sold pretty much everything, including—she giggled to herself—her very late husband's personal effects. Oops. Soz. How did that happen? Never mind, she'd made him more than a fiver. Though, obviously, she did have to deduct her commission.

The newbie, five-star general, saviour of the Mason girls came back to her car.

'Thank you. So much.' Rachel went over to her. 'You brought us all in from emotional apocalypse there.'

'You're welcome. And I enjoyed myself. Well, not the emotional-apocalypse part, obviously. But Poppy's good company. We had fun. How've my boys been doing?'

'Made a fortune, I think, judging by the steady custom. What were you selling?' Rachel came round to her car for the first time, and saw the few remaining flowerpots, a couple with strong woody shrubs in, some holding no more than little green shoots.

'Wowser. They sold loads. It's just all the things we grow from cuttings. We raise them all in the greenhouse at home. Roses, lavender, fruit bushes, that sort of thing. Can I interest you in anything? . . . Sorry, I don't know your name.'

'Oh. Sorry. Rachel. Hi.'

'Hello, Rachel.' The two women shook hands. 'I'm Melissa.'

12 P.M. LUNCH BREAK

'So how's it going then, the self-sufficiency programme?' Rachel asked her mother cheerfully. It was, after all, Be Nice to Mother Day. 'How certain is your own personal survival in a post-nuclear world?'

'Ooh, it's all coming along very nicely, thank you. Here, put this on before we go in.' Her mum handed Rachel her spare beekeeper's outfit. 'So well that I am expanding the veg patch. I've got Pamela's Graham coming round next week to do the digging.'

As Rachel struggled to get into the charming beige gabardine onesie, an aroma drifted across the garden and hit her. It nearly knocked her over in fact—came at her like a playground bully. Roast lamb, if she was not mistaken. Roast lamb, rosemary, roast potatoes and—she sniffed again—a representative of the brassica family, broccoli possibly though she couldn't be sure. Someone close by was doing exactly what she had done nearly every Sunday of her life from Josh's birth up to the middle of July: they were about to sit down to a proper lunch. Mint sauce or redcurrant? she wondered. Personally she preferred the latter . . .

Not that she would be given the choice today. No, Rachel was instead enjoying—huh—the first of the alternative Sundays of the rest of her life. Which were, of course—look on the bright side—just a painful vaccine to prepare her for the worst that was yet to come. The every-other-Christmases—Christ. Her gut lurched. How was she supposed to survive them? And the weeks— and weeks and weeks—of separate holidays. When Chris and the kids and the bloody intern—she could picture her now, scrubbering away in her bloody intern's string bloody bikini, scrubber— were off re-enacting Kodak moments in the sun. And she, Rachel, rattled around on her own at home, luxuriating in a bit of—what did that silly cow Clover call it?—yes, that's right, me-time. Was that really what she was actually supposed to want? Me-time?

Well—hey!—it was great so far, the old me-time. Cracking. First day of me-time and it's like totally wild, guys. Here she was, stuck in her mum's back garden, waddling about in her dead dad's wellies, her face veiled, all her flesh covered, reduced to something small and squat and anonymous. She shuffled about on the patio, stabbing the toes of her Wellingtons into the edge of the lawn, waiting. She was starting to feel marginally less nice. God only knew what her mum was fiddling about at. Starting a fire in a watering can, it looked like. For reasons best known to her slightly batty self.

'It's a smoker,' she called over to Rachel as she worked. 'Bees hate smoke, it's the one thing they're scared of. So this is how we control them.'

'Really,' Rachel called back. 'Gosh. Who knew?' And Zzzzzzzz, she thought, returning to her boot and the stabbing. Who even cares?

'OK. I think that's it. We can go in now.' They walked down to the bottom of the garden, automatically falling into the positions established some time back in Rachel's own infancy and practised through shopping centres and along beachfronts in the decades since: her mother striding ahead while she shuffled along behind. In turn they went through the small gate. The noise was already loud, but as soon as the top of the hive was opened it became quite overwhelming. Rachel was used to seeing solitary bees, sticking their whatevers in a flower, doing their whatever bee thing. She was quite unprepared for this sight, the sheer impact of thousands of them concentrated together like this—quite a force to be reckoned with. They were almost unrecognisable from the common insects she thought she knew. The single bee, she felt, was a thing she had the hang of. You could either live with it or you could wave it away. But this multitude here was a different organism altogether. It was as if the process of combining was itself transformative. An alchemy. Instinctively she recoiled. Even in her lame protective clothing, Rachel felt really quite acutely vulnerable.

'Right then,' she said briskly. 'Jolly good. Everything seems to be in order.' She backed further away. 'Shall we be off then?'

'Don't be silly, Rachel. We've got to check everything first.' Her mum's voice was transformed too. Softened, sweet, intimate. 'Honestly, girls. Listen to her. Didn't I tell you?' she murmured as she slid out the top frame and studied it.

'What? What did you tell them?' Rachel's voice was not soft or sweet. A few bees flew out and around her. She stepped back further, flapped her hands in front of her face and started to hiss at them. 'Bugger off. Leave me alone. It's my me-time, damn it. Me-time.'

'Do be quiet, dear,' said her mum over her shoulder. And then into the hive: 'She does come out with some funny things. Even I don't know what she's on about half the time.'

'Um, hello? I am here, you know.' Were they actually ganging up on her? That was what it felt like. They were bloody ganging up.

'No one's interested in you, Rachel.' Now there was a phrase she'd heard before. 'They're only the guards of the hive. Just doing their job.'

Oh. No inverted commas there then. This, this buzzing around like a nuisance, was obviously what passed round here for a proper job.

Her mum put that frame back and slid out

another. 'Everyone's got their own jobs here.' She studied the frame and brushed away some debris clinging to the side of the honeycomb. 'It's all highly organised. Runs on a strict routine. And they all take everything in turns. A rota. Some of them stay behind to run the nursery or do the cleaning. Others go out and about, looking for new places to nest or checking for danger.'

'Yeah. Whatever.' She flapped at the bees around her a bit more. 'What did you mean by "Didn't I tell you?"? What did you "tell" them?'

'Oh, only that you wouldn't like it here.' She put that frame back and slid out one lower down in the hive. 'Because you don't like large groups of females. Never have. Not a girl's girl. Never were. Aha!' She tilted the honeycomb towards the autumnal sun. 'There's the queen. Look. All the worker bees are the same size, but she is much longer. More sleek somehow. Glossier. And looking lovely today, ma'am, if I may say so.'

'What? Honestly, Mother.' Rachel was outraged. 'How could you? Talk about me like that?' She could feel actual steam building up in her stupid hood.

'That's the other job, of course.' Her mother hummed on, ignoring her. 'Looking after the queen. There they all are, gathered around her. Cleaning her on one side, feeding her from the other. That's the life, isn't it, Your Majesty?'

What? Not a girl's girl? Really, what absolute rot. 'Is this still because I wasn't a Brownie? You know, it might be time to look for closure on that one.'

'It's a shame. Forty years old and still she's on about the Brownies,' her mum murmured, shaking

107

her head, as she put their hive back together again.

'It's you who's always banging on about them.' Rachel was keeping her distance. She was now pinned to the furthest fence. 'Anyway, I didn't like them because of their stupid uniform. I don't like this lot on account of their venomous sting. It's not even a valid—'

'Excuse me. I didn't bring up the Brownies. Or how you never made a team. Or how you had to come back early from that camp because you couldn't stick the dorm.' She clipped the lid back on the white box and the noise diminished.

'Mother. Stop it,' she whined. Sod the being nice if this was where it got her. 'Will you please stop presenting me as some weirdo no-mates?'

'Perfectly sociable, mind,' she added obligingly. But only to the ones still buzzing around outside.

'Well thank you.' Rachel repeated loud and clear: 'Yes. Perfectly sociable.' She just wanted to make sure the bees inside had heard it too.

'I don't know why you're shouting at them. They can't hear, you know. I only talk to them out of habit.' She patted the top of the hive affectionately, picked up her smoker and headed back to the house. Oh. Still, Rachel didn't really want to leave things there. She felt a pressing need to put all that in context; explain to the bees that this was a temporary blip, that she just so happened to be down one husband and one best friend, just at the moment, it could happen to anybody, and that— Christ, no!—her emotional landscape did not normally look quite so barren. But her mum was already off, which left Rachel no option but to fall in and stomp behind.

'So that was fun. Why did I even have to be here

anyway? You seem to be managing—'

'Well, it can be dangerous. One shouldn't ever go in there alone. You never know what can happen with bees. So thank you for your support.'

'You're welcome.' She might try the nice thing again. 'Nothing else much on anyway.' Even that sounded sarcastic, although for once it was actually true.

'Oh good. In that case you won't mind taking on my chickens.'

'Eh? Hang on a minute. What chickens?'

'The ones I've got coming. That nice new couple down the road have promised to knock up a hen house. I don't see why it should take them long. That will give you something to do.'

3.15 P.M. PICK-UP, MONDAY

Bubba waylaid Heather, who was in a tearing hurry.

'Heather, can I have a word?' Which sounded more like 'E'er, an I a a ur?' Her lips were horribly swollen, uncomfortable-looking. Almost deformed.

'Bubba! Are you OK? Have you been stung?' Heather had stopped in her tracks. She was always hyper-reactive to any medical situation. The thing was, in Heather's opinion, you just never knew . . .

'No, no, I'm fine. Well. I feel like I have been stung, actually. But there's nothing wrong with my lips.'

'Sorry? Oh. Well there is, you know.' Heather had started to speak a little louder, was doing her very best enunciation. 'I've got some Piriton in my travelling first-aid pack.' Guy had taught her never to leave home without it. She started rooting

109

around in her tote bag.

''O. Eally. It's perfectly normal on the first day. My problem isn't my lips, it's this ball. This Christmas Ball. I had counted on doing it with Bea, to be honest. Between us, we just do tick all the boxes—no getting away from it—and I thought it would be, well, *fun* for us.'

Heather noted the 'us'. She wished she was an 'us'. Bubba's only been here five minutes and look at her, ussing away.

'But now, she says, what with her new job, she really can't and I'm to form a committee! But I don't really know anyone! Well just a few . . . You were brilliant with the car boot sale. Would you be on my committee? *Pleeeeeeease?*'

Time was that Heather would have had to beg and connive to even get near a committee. Last year, Bea had thought it 'probably for the best' if she just served the refreshments. See how her position had changed since Sunday? Not only was Heather now in that boat. Sisters, she had an oar in her hands.

'Course I will. Love to. But right now I must get on. I've got Bea's children for tea.'

*   *   *

Rachel's hands were deep into the pockets of her aviator jacket. There was a bite in the air today, the afternoon darker even than just last week. Nice bowl of soup for tea, she thought. Just the ticket. Come on, Poppy. Hurry up before I'm nobbled.

'A'el!' It was that Bubba. No, it was a caricature of that Bubba—Gerald Scarfe? From the school of, definitely—bearing down upon her. Huge,

Jaggeresque lips airbrushed each cheek. She was trying to say something urgently, but Rachel couldn't quite make out any of it . . . until the word 'committee'. The word 'committee' Rachel heard loud and clear.

No. That's what she would have said. Before she had been so ruthlessly deconstructed in The Psychiatrist's Bee Hive. She might have said, 'I'd love to. But I'm already an artistic adviser. I don't think I could take on another thing.' But now she felt she had probably better join something, and sharpish, if for no other reason than to shut her mother up. It might be too late for her to link hands and skip round a toadstool, but she could, she supposed, with a heavy heart, help out with weird Bubba's stupid ball.

So she just said, 'I'd love to.'

'Great. The Copper Kettle. Friday. Straight after drop-off.'

'Lovely,' Rachel lied. And then in the new spirit of Mason glasnost, she went further still: 'How have your children settled in here, then?'

And Bubba was off. Everything was amazing. It was actually official: Milo and Martha were the world's happiest children. St Ambrose was the world's best school, their last snobby prep school was the world's worst. St Snobbo's said Milo had 'problems'. As it happened, he was probably gifted. If you have an exceptional child, you just can't beat a state primary. The teachers were wonderful, the other children were so special. The whole family just loved, loved, loved it. So many of her friends had said to her, state school? Was she actually *mad*? With everyone there so *rough* and *sweary*? She must need her *head* examined. But in fact it

111

turned out that the people here didn't actually seem to be too rough and sweary *at all.*

'Oh look,' said Rachel, sidling away. 'There's my daughter.'

*   *   *

Heather was still waiting at the door. Where were they all? She needed to get the tea on . . . Ah. Here came Maisie, and just behind her came Colette, holding all three of Bea's children firmly by the hand.

'Oh, thanks Colette,' said Heather, darting forward. 'They're all coming home with me tonight.'

'Oh no they are not.' Colette sidestepped Heather neatly. 'It's my night. Bea said it was my night.'

'But it's my night. I'm sure. She said . . .'

'It's my night,' spat Colette. And then she half ran, half frog-marched the Stuarts towards her car, her own boys scrambling along somewhere behind.

Scarlett looked over her shoulder. 'If only they'd made two of me!' she called out to Maisie, smiling sweetly.

'Maisie, love, I'm so sorry. I can't think what happened. There must have been a mix-up.' Heather could hardly bear it when Maisie was subject to emotional pain. They were like those identical twins separated at birth: when Maisie was hurt, Heather was in screaming agony. The pain was building within her now. Her breath was shortening. Her brain giddy with adrenalin . . .

'Mummy, I couldn't care less. Honest,' said Maisie, in a voice that she somehow controlled to make it sound completely normal. 'Is Mrs Green around?' Maisie spotted Bubba, and skipped over. 'Excuse me, but, well, I thought you ought to know: Milo's crying in the boys' changing room and he won't come out.'

THE DAY OF THE PLANNING MEETING
FOR THE BALL

9 A.M. ASSEMBLY

Bubba looked around the table and felt a flush of pleasure. Meetings were her favourite thing, always had been—they just were the perfect showcase for her own, specific skill set. Yet she hadn't been to one for absolute yonks. That was the thing about domesticity: no meetings. Unless you counted telling Kazia what to pick up in Waitrose. Anyway, now here she was, and it was just like old times: Bubba in the chair, surrounded by eager slaves just waiting to carry out her every wish—only kidding! OK, so the Copper Kettle was not exactly the sort of state-of-the-art committee room to which she was used. The waitresses were actually wearing pinnies and mob caps, which was a total hoot. And there were no piles of fresh fruit and bottles of water provided for them on the table. Instead, Jo was tucking in to an iced bun the size of her head. No waitress had approached the table since she'd arrived. She was in serious danger of death by thirst. But otherwise, yeah: business as usual.

It wasn't quite the top team. Heather was on the far side with Rachel, Georgie and Jo. Colette and Clover were opposite. Bea had promised to try and come, but she did have a 'mare of a morning', apparently. Bubba still hoped she would make it, though—just for that bit of input she could properly trust.

'So . . .'

She was planning to start with a small rallying speech. She had this gift, well known in the world of HR, for team-building.

'Shall I take the minutes?' interrupted Heather.

'Oh God, you're *gorgeous*,' said Bubba. 'But I think that so restricts the *spirit*? We want to be loose? Let it flow? Find those ideas. Kick them about and straight out of the . . . whatever.' Informality had always been one of her trademarks as a boss: it drew people together, in her experience.

'Oh. K then.' But for some reason Heather looked crushed. Utterly crushed.

'Right. Anyway. The thing is, this ball is quite some undertaking, and while I can manage a lot of it myself, what is so great and fabulous about St Ambrose is the sense of community and everyone helping everyone else which you just don't get in the private sector, or at least not the bit of the private sector we've just escaped from, which felt like the break-out from Alcatraz quite literally because everyone there was so stuck up—'

Rachel and Georgie suddenly got the giggles but Bubba pressed on. She might have to separate those two.

'—especially if your child is that tiniest little bit different which you would think they would want to celebrate but no.'

An ancient mob cap—possibly older than God—came to the table. Finally. 'Long skinny latte for me, please.'

The mob cap looked uncertain. 'Black or white?'

'Tell you what, Roz,' cut in Jo. 'Bring us a pot of coffee and a jug of milk and we'll do the rest.'

Bubba was gobsmacked. It was extraordinary: Jo

actually seemed to know this person. Which meant that there were just two degrees of separation between Bubba and a mob cap! Actually, it was rather wonderful the turns her life was taking at the moment. She really relished its new depth and its breadth and its texture—

'Shall we crack on?' asked Rachel.

'Where was I? Yes: the caterers. Now—'

'Hiya. Made it at last,' said Jasmine. 'Budge up.'

'Sorry we're late,' added Sharon. 'Bea says she's going to try and pop in but you know, now, with her job, it's'

'just juggle, juggle, juggle,' finished Jasmine, sighing.

'When I am Prime Minister,' pronounced Georgie, 'the use of the verb "to juggle" will be restricted to those with proven employment in the circus profession—'

'Shall we crack on?' Rachel said, a bit louder this time.

'Yes. The caterers. Bea has given me a steer on this, which is really, *really* kind of her. They're called "A Moveable Feast". I don't know if anyone here knows them?'

'Well, I've passed their snack van in the lay-by on the way up to the motorway,' offered Georgie.

'I *think* that must be a different one, though I really value your input. Bea seemed to think there was a school connection? Someone actually in the St Ambrose community?'

'I'll bet it's to do with that Pam, the dinner lady, you remember, who was sacked by the old head over something or other. All very hush-hush it was,' chipped in Clover. 'At your peril, if you want my opinion. At your peril.'

'I don't think so,' said Bubba. She was starting to feel quite cross. 'Bea is hardly going to recommend someone unreliable, is she? No one, *no one*, cares about this school and its kids like Bea.' Was it her imagination or was there negative energy building up here? She was hyper-sensitive to negative energy. If only Bea would arrive. 'Does anyone use any other caterers, then, for their own general entertaining? That they would like to recommend?'

'Enterwhatting?' said Jo.

'Lolz,' yelped Sharon.

'Rofl,' squeaked Jasmine.

'There we are then.' Time to get firm. 'A Moveable Feast it is. Now. Pressing forward. The music. Any suggestions?'

They all sat in silence for a bit, and then Jo of all people sprang to life. 'Do you know what?' She sprayed bun crumbs everywhere. 'I'd forget my own bum if it wasn't so enormous. Course I do. Wayne. Wayne's my mate,' she said to Georgie. 'Good bloke. Look after his mum over in the care home. Terrible old trout. He owes me one.' And then back to the table: 'Yeah, Wayne's all right. Sorted. He'll do it.'

'Fabulous contribution. Thanks, Jo.' Bubba would have loved a bit more information, but she did find Jo a bit intimidating. She was one of those people who could suddenly turn on one. 'So could I *possibly* task you with reaching out to, um, Wayne? See if he's free? Would you *mind*?'

'Listen here.' There we are. Bubba knew it: Jo had turned. 'Read my lips. I said Wayne'll do it. And Wayne'll do it. This is starting to get on my nerves.'

'Sorry. Great. Lovely. Wayne it is. Now then.

117

The theme.' This was the part where Bubba felt on the firmest ground, actually. She was brilliant at themes. Loved them. Any opportunity. Last time they had a curry, she wore a sari and turned the kitchen into Kerala. It had worked really, really well.

So it was odd that this was the point at which Bubba seemed to lose the meeting. Totally. Sort of mislaid the whole process somehow. She started her pitch about how she wanted a paradise beach theme, because that was what she had planned when it was a summer ball and she had a vision and a dream. And when she had a vision she had to stick with it, when she had a dream she could not give it up. And then Bea arrived. And then everything became a blur. There was a lot of argument about Christmas. And England. And the climate. And the snow upon the ground and the robin on the twig. As if any of those things had anything to do with people dressing up and having a glam night out and just tuning up that party vibe. And suddenly, before Bubba had any idea what was going on, Bea was saying, 'Right then. We're all agreed. Compromise time. The theme is the English Seaside in Winter.'

'Hang on a minute!' Bubba was yelping as if in pain. 'Hold that thought. If we can just walk this one back up the agenda a bit—'

But Rachel and Georgie were giggling, so loudly this time, so disruptively that Bea couldn't even hear her yelping and just pressed on to the next thing as if she was in charge, and not Bubba at all. 'Now,' she said to the table. The table which had been Bubba's table. Once. 'Another thing I want to suggest—I mean, just a suggestion, it's not *my* ball, so it's not *my* decision—is an Auction of Promises, which can raise such a lot of money. Of course, I couldn't possibly get one together, already got enough balls in the air as it is, but it will only take a nanosecond of somebody else's time—'

'I'll do that, Bea,' said Colette, sounding keener than she had sounded all morning.

'Thanks *ever so*, Col,' said Bea. 'You're awesome. You know the sort of stuff we usually go for. But I thought, this time, as we're lucky enough to have Bubba on board these days, she could get one of her smart London friends to offer something? Dinner with a celebrity, perhaps?'

'Huh? I don't know any ce—'

But everyone was suddenly oohing and aahing and looking at Bubba with a bit of respect for once and Bea said, 'There we are! You can't refuse now! Listen to the excitement. Time for you to share. Dinner with a Celebrity Friend of Bubba's.' Sharon did a drum-roll on the table. 'It's the Big Draw.'

And then Bea was off, and most of the others left after her. Colette had to sort out some cellulite. Sharon and Jasmine had their garden business to tend to. Georgie had to get Hamish from playgroup. Jo had to go and sleep off her night shift. And Heather was telling her to turn that frown upside-down. And Clover said she should keep it exactly where it was because this, in her view, had all the makings. And Bubba had a funny feeling. A feeling she wasn't used to, and couldn't quite identify. But one that, she decided, felt a bit like the feeling one might have after one had been run over by a very, *very* large vehicle.

10 A.M. MORNING BREAK

Rachel sat alone waiting for a coffee she didn't really want. She had wanted to scarper the minute that ludicrous meeting finished, but everyone else had had the same thought. And poor Bubba looked so pathetic and dejected that it seemed a bit mean to just dump her. Heather had taken her up to the counter to pick a large confection of trans fats and carbohydrate in which she might seek some sort of solace.

She looked about her. The café was hot and steamy. A real English-seaside-in-winter sort of rain was bucketing down on the people outside, and evaporating off them once they were in. It was packed in here—there was not a free seat at the tables around the counter or in the two rooms behind—and yet it wasn't noisy. And it wasn't noisy, Rachel realised, because it was packed with quiet, well-behaved women. Well, that wasn't quite true. At the table next to her there was one man with his wife, sunk in marital silence. His large hands held a delicate pastry fork with which he gave his cream puff the occasional doleful prod. Otherwise, it was as if she had stepped into the pages of a nineteenth-century novel; one in which the menfolk were all away at war, at work, or just had something better to do.

A few were younger than her, with babies in buggies and bottles that needed warming. But the rest, they were all late middle age. Elderly, some of them. The next stage on in life from the motley members of the English Seaside in Winter Ball

Committee. The seniors to their juniors; Lower Sixth to their Upper Third.

She listened to the women behind her. She couldn't see them, didn't know them, could only hear the age in their voices, but their topic of conversation—that was instantly familiar.

'And in the end it was just the coursework that let her down . . .'

Of course. The children. Or possibly—they were definitely that little bit older—the children's children? Or the children's godchildren or the children's children's in-laws or the children's children's next-door neighbours. The A-level results of children they would never know were being shared with people to whom they could have no meaning. And yet everyone was riveted. Nobody was standing up and saying, 'Enough. I do not know this girl. I am not interested in her offer from Leeds. Cease forthwith your tiresome prattle. Now, have you read the new McEwan?' Nope. They were rapt. They were genuinely worried about her retakes. Delighted with her A star. Crossing fingers that she chucked the dodgy boyfriend. They were actually prolonging the tiresome prattle with informed and interested questioning. It was just like Rachel's mum and her friend Mary and the wretched Queen of the Canadian Ice Rink, being played out again and again all over this coffee shop and—Rachel had a horrible feeling—all over the Home Counties.

She was desperate to get out of there and back to her desk. Subsumed with a desire to do something creative, substantial, that would pull her up and out of this . . . well, it was a dependence culture, wasn't it? Were they any better than the people government ministers were always banging on about on the *Today* programme who were dependent on benefits? It seemed not, just then, just there, to Rachel. They were parasites—living on the lives, the news, the emotions, the progress of others. If they were so bloody interested in A levels, why didn't they go off and bloody take some?

Was this how her own future was going to play out? Years dominated by her children's schools to segue into years talking about somebody else's schools? The rest of her life yawned before her like one long double period of French on a Friday afternoon. She reached behind her chair for her coat. She had to get out of there, get going, get on. She had just got her arm in her sleeve when Heather, Bubba, three coffees and a slab of chocolate brownie came back to the table. She took her arm out again, defeated.

'Oh great. Lovely. Thanks.' She picked up the teaspoon and stirred. 'Just a quick one.'

'You do realise,' began Heather, 'that this time next year we'll be getting ready for our SATS.'

A noise—a sort of death rattle—came out of Rachel's throat.

'You OK, Rach? Mmmm?' Heather's eyes were soft with concern.

Be nice, said Rachel to herself. Just be nice.

'Oh fine. Yeah. Just, you know . . . SATS. All that . . .'

'Well, you've got nothing to worry about.' Heather turned to Bubba. 'Her Poppy's on Top Table!'

'Anyway,' Rachel burst in. 'When's our next rung on the lunch ladder? It's been a couple of weeks. It's the only time I actually eat these days, you know. I might just starve to death, not that you'd care.' Rachel was doing her best cheerful smile, but Heather was not even meeting her eye.

'Um. Well. Bea's doing one the Friday after half-term.'

'Great . . .'

'She. Um. Was wanting to restrict numbers I think. So it's just invitation-only this one. You know, what with her job . . .'

So she really has dropped me, Rachel realised with a thump. I was just like all the others, all along. There had always been this kaleidoscopic pattern to Bea's social life: people hitherto unnoticed emerging from the shadows, brought into the light, spinning in the golden glow of being Bea's new friend. Until something or other happened and they spun off again, back to the shadows, slightly stunned, wondering where it had all gone wrong. Rachel had witnessed it for years, in an unconcerned, disconnected sort of way—a mortal who somehow believed in her own immortality, even though the evidence of death was all around. OK, so she'd lasted the longest, had a good innings, as they said. But now look at her—come a cropper and cast out like the rest of them. Well, well, well.

'Of course,' she said to Heather, with sympathy. 'Fine. The job. Understand. Totally.' She shrugged, spread her hands—a familiar Bea-like gesture. 'The Job. Of course . . .'

'She's having a lunch?' Bubba, Rachel was beginning to realise, did not do dissembling. She worked out her emotions like a well-trained Year 6 its maths: the workings-out all on display so that everyone knew exactly how she got the sum.

'*Bea?* Is having a *lunch*?

123

'Bea is having *a lunch* . . .

'. . . and she hasn't invited *me*?'

There were the workings-out: right there, all over her face.

'What a fucking *bitch*.'

Tick, thought Rachel. Correct. Got there quicker than I did. She jumped to her feet before anyone could stop her. 'And while we're on the subject, it doesn't have to be the English Seaside in Winter Ball, you know. If you want a Paradise Beach Ball, you have it, girl. You just do whatever you like.' She flung on her jacket—'Great coffee, great fun, see you at school'—and broke through the door. Out in the grey High Street, she gulped down the damp air and turned her face up to the rain.

3.15 P.M. PICK-UP

Georgie was propping herself up against the fence, her back to the school, her eyes on the car. The sight of Hamish snoozing in his car seat brought a lump to her throat. His long lashes flickered on his cheeks as he dreamed. Was there anything more beautiful on this earth than the rolling, folding, undulating, multitudinous chins of a well-fed, happy baby? A watery autumn light was making its way through the clouds and she willed it on. The garden could really do with a bit of sun. She sighed happily and pushed her hands deeper into her pockets. It was a while before she realised that Rachel was slumped beside her.

'Afternoon. What are you doing out here on the wrong side of the tracks?'

'Did you know Bea's having a lunch after

124

half-term?'

'Good-afternoon. I'm fine. Thank you for asking. Yes, a very nice day . . .'

'Sorry. Hello. How are you? Etc., etc. And did you know? About Bea's lunch? Her invitation-only sodding lunch?'

'Um, yeah.' She produced a packet of Marlboro Lights. With her thumb, she pushed one towards Rachel. 'Not going though. Want a fag?'

'No. Ta. So you were invited? Bloody hell. You know what? Maybe I will.' She took a cigarette and bent towards Georgie for a light. 'What did she invite you for?' She inhaled. 'No offence.'

'None taken. Been asking myself the same question. Committee this, lunch that—wretched woman won't leave me alone. Harassment, that's what it is. Pure and simple. As a matter of fact, I'm considering a restraining order.'

'So you're not going?'

'Why would I go, for God's sake? You should have seen it, the invitation. It was all the same old, same old. That's what's wrong with this school: they never learn.' Georgie shook her head in despair. 'Shocking punctuation, as usual—it was A Lunch for Mum apostrophe S.' Her fury was mounting. 'And the emoticons. Littered with the buggers. Smiley faces, party blowers, the works.' She flicked her ash on to the grass verge. 'One couldn't be seen dead after that, of course.'

'You know, she used to be my friend. My best friend.'

Georgie gave a splutter of irritation. The corruption of the verb to juggle was one of her hates, poor punctuation another. But this was a top-of-the-pops pet hate—grown women describing

125

other grown women as best friends. Mutton employing the semantics of lamb. It was like donning a ra-ra skirt and frilly panties. Or snogging in the street. Totally inappropriate behaviour. She was, quite frankly, disappointed in Rachel of all people.

'One of my best friends. And this term, this term of all terms, when everything else has been falling apart around my ears, she has been a complete and utter cow to me.'

Georgie presumed that Bea's sudden warmth towards her had something to do with this. It was a way of sending home the message that Rachel was properly, officially excluded. But she wasn't going to demean either of them by standing outside school and discussing such a thing.

'Some of the more perceptive of us might not see that as so wildly out of character.'

'Well, I suppose I've never been on the wrong side of her before.'

'Course. As you were saying. Best friends . . .'

'It's not been anything major, just one slight or little snub after another, so I wondered if I was just imagining it. But now . . . And it hurts, is the thing.' She coughed on the smoke. 'She has hurt my feelings.'

Georgie felt like asking for her fag back. It was an investment in the conversation, a cigarette, and she expected some sort of decent return. You never got this sort of drivel and nonsense from Jo, that was for sure, but she wasn't around again this afternoon. She was having to work more and more hours at the care home and harder and harder in the house while that pillock Steve lay around being 'depressed'. Georgie was missing her. You could always have a laugh with our Joanna.

'I would dearly love to get my own back on her somehow. Just bring her down a peg or two, you know what I mean?'

Aha. This, thought Georgie, is more like it. She flicked her ash over her shoulder and squinted into the middle distance. 'Hmmm. Well. You could just do us all a favour and thump her one, of course . . .'

Heather joined them, clearly distraught. 'Rachel, I'm so, so sorry. I didn't mean to upset you. I should never have blurted it out like that, about the, you know, the . . .'

'Bea's lunch. You can say it, Heather. I'm not going to top myself. It's fine. Really. I need to work anyway. Haven't got time for all this lunching about.'

Georgie was studying Heather intently, her head on one side.

'You are good. Thanks, Rach. To tell you the truth,' Heather leaned in towards them, dropped her voice, 'I'm quite worried about it all, personally.'

Georgie, still staring, walked around Heather, picking up a few strands of hair at the back. Heather bravely carried on.

'I'm worried that Bea's taking on too much at the moment. What with, you know . . .' Heather's eyes were following Georgie nervously.

'The lunch?' offered Rachel.

'Yes, the lunch and the . . .'

'The job?'

'The job. Yes. Georgie, what are you doing? Why are you staring at me like that?'

'Well, the most extraordinary thing has happened, Heth. It took me a while to recognise

127

you, to tell the truth. You've gone blonde. It's very rare, that. Sudden-onset blondeness. Did you catch it from hanging out with Bea so much, do you think? Are highlights contagious?'

'Stop it. You're being mean. Colette did it. And Bea just said it looked really nice, so there.' She turned back to Rachel. 'Anyway. Back to the, you know . . .'

'The Lunch,' Georgie intoned in her Archbishop of Canterbury voice.

'Yes. Thing is, Bea has asked Colette to bring a dessert! I mean, that's not like Bea, is it?'

Georgie gave a low whistle. 'What, you think it's, like, a cry for help?' She made the nee-naw sound of a siren. Hamish, still in his car seat, opened one bright eye. 'Should we stage an intervention?'

Rachel laughed. 'It's not like her, though. Heather's right. It's weird how she's being with this ball. Normally she would have organised the table decorations by now and had us all folding the napkins into the shape of exotic wildfowl of the less-developed nations—'

'Oh my God,' swooned Heather. 'Do you remember that time she did those birds of paradise?'

'Please,' said Georgie, irritably.

'—but she just seems, sort of, detached. She's never given up control of anything in her life before.'

'Mmmm. Ve-ry interesting.' Georgie became thoughtful. 'It's Descartes, innit?'

'Oh, is it?' Heather looked eagerly around, her Welcome-to-St-Ambrose smile already in place.

'Yeah. Well, no. Not driving into the car park right now, it's not. I meant, Bea's behaviour . . .

128

Oh, never mind. Hey. Look over there! There's someone really thin in yoga pants. Heather, don't waste your time with us. Off you go.'

And Heather went skipping off.

'My point was,' Georgie turned back to Rachel, 'that Bea is in control of everything. That is exactly who Bea is. It is her id. The essence of her Bea-ness. She is the Woman Who Controls Everything. Ergo, if she stops so doing, then is she still Bea? Eh?'

Georgie was enjoying herself—bit of amateur philosophising before the kids come out, what could be nicer? She noticed that Rachel was smiling, too.

'You know what?' Rachel seemed to perk up. 'I think you may just have given me a berrrilliant idea!'

THE DAY OF BEA'S LUNCH

8.40 A.M. DROP-OFF

'Hey, I only just noticed: you're in civvies.' Rachel took in what Heather was wearing: all new, if she wasn't mistaken. All new, and not quite right. She could see what was happening here: there had clearly been a half-term shopping trip and Heather had been taken in hand by either Bea or her gang. The new blonde hair, the lip gloss, the skinny jeans tucked into the boots should, Rachel understood, all add up to the Bea effect. And yet, of course, they didn't. They couldn't. Although her strenuous new fitness regime had slimmed her down a little, this new Heather was still, very recognisably, the old homely Heather. It was like Rubens trying to do a Degas ballerina. Rachel longed to tell her to stop, to save her from that coven, to save her from herself. Getting into a synchronised stride, she mumbled, 'Um. Er. Nice earrings.'

The girls were up ahead, balancing along the kerb as if it were a tightrope across Niagara Falls. Rachel was nervous of them falling into the school-run traffic and yet Heather—the woman who had once tried to get felt pens banned in school because of their obvious and terrifying fatal properties—seemed to be blithely unaware.

'Bea texted last night that there'd be no time for exercise today, and she was right, of course.' She gave a little shudder of excitement. 'The lunch.'

Rachel had one ear on the girls. There was something going on there.

'Whoever falls in first has to talk to her first.'

'Bagsy not me!'

She would quiz Poppy later. She was more interested in Heather this morning. For once.

'Big day.' Rachel nodded encouragingly. 'Big day. So did you follow through with my suggestion?'

'I did.' Heather's face was glowing. 'I'm doing the starter.'

'Excellent.'

'Step on a crack,' Rachel heard her daughter's little voice, 'and you break her back!'

'Stepped on it!' She heard Maisie shout in triumph and both girls giggling. This was not like these two at all . . . But back to more important matters.

'And what did you decide on?'

'Filet de canard avec sauce de raisin et des pines kernel thingies et tempura des endives et with, um, er, cauliflower dumplings.' Heather was beaming with pride.

'Golly.'

'I know! I think I first saw it on *Come Dine With Me*.'

'Hmmm. Did it win?'

'No, but they said it was "way overcomplicated" and "a collision of cuisines".'

They were at school now and Heather went running straight off. She'd spotted Bea, who was, Rachel noticed, in her pilates pants. But of course. Everyone else was doing her cooking for her. So she had plenty of time to exercise this morning.

Rachel kissed Poppy goodbye, turned to get on with her own day and smiled quietly to herself. It was like art, she thought. Those rare but magical minutes of pure creation that make up for the miserable hours, days and years of trying to be an artist. When you start painting one thing and by some chemical reaction beyond your own control something else quite wonderful is born. When a picture you hadn't thought of is just brought down somehow by the process of painting itself. When you find yourself making something you never even suspected was lurking in the blind spot of your own mind's eye.

OK, this was not as good. But it was quite good. She had just had the little idea that if everybody took something for Bea's lunch, then Bea herself would not be doing anything towards Bea's lunch and that would remove from Bea the oxygen of being at the centre of all operations. It was an amusing, harmless prank, and an exercise in crowd psychology. Nothing more. But here was dear old Heather, elevating it into something much more dramatic. She had rendered it extraordinary. And with a bit of luck, it sounded like she could poison the whole bloody lot of them.

'Christ! What's happened? Lemme guess. Chris's intern got genital warts? Bea's come home to find Tony dressed in ladies' underwear?'

'Hi, George. Wotcha, Hamish. No. Not as far as I know, anyway. Why?'

'There's an actual smile on your face for once. And you know, for those of us on Rachel Mason Misery Watch, it has been rather a long time since we logged one of those in our little book . . .' She patted her pockets. 'Lemme just find a pen . . .'

'Oh, it's just that it's The Bea Lunch today. And at last my Dick Dastardly plan is to be put into action.' Rachel laughed like Muttley, then her face fell again. 'Only trouble is, I won't be there to see it

132

happen.' She stopped. 'Here, Geo-orge?'

'Nope,' said Georgie firmly and carried on moving.

'But would you? Change your mind and go?'

'No,' she threw back over her shoulder.

'Pleee-ease?'

'No-ooo,' she sing-songed, dancing towards the car park.

'For me?'

'You see this thing here?' Georgie stopped and pointed to Hamish, who looked up at her with a genuine interest. 'This is what the government calls a "pre-schooler". It is called that because it does not go to school. It hangs around its parent or its designated carer nearly all day long. But do I complain? I do not. Because you know what I call it? I call it a get-out-of-jail-free card. For it is my excuse to do nothing with you lot in the daytime at all. Get it? And that is why, when it does go to school, I am going to have to produce yet another one. To keep you all off my back.' She growled— she did actually growl—picked up Hamish and started to walk off.

'Hamish?' Rachel ran after them and changed her mode of attack. 'Do you want to spend the day with Auntie Rachel, sweetheart? Shall we get out all Josh's old cars and make a garage? Would you like that, love?' Hamish swung with a casual grace from one set of arms to the other, like a baby monkey in a tree.

'Go on,' said Rachel to Georgie from over the baby's head. 'You know it'll be a laugh. In its own horrible, gothic sort of way.'

'You know what you are, don't you? You're a right saddo.'

'Yup.'

'And a loser.'

'Mebbe.'

'And a no-mates.'

'Ah, no.' Rachel held up a warning finger. 'That is the one thing I am not.' She put her spare arm around Georgie and walked her towards the car park. 'I am, in fact, perfectly sociable. I've got my mate Hammy here. And, Georgina Martin,' she gave her shoulder a squeeze, 'admit it: I've got you.'

11 A.M. MORNING BREAK

Heather drew up outside Bea's large, detached house and turned off the ignition. The purr of her hybrid engine gave way to the flat quiet of the cul-de-sac, but she didn't move at once. She was just going to sit there on her own for a little while, enjoy the moment. It seemed almost impossible that the girls had been in the same class for the past five years—Maisie had always adored Scarlett—and yet Heather had never actually been to Bea's house before this very day. Of course, she knew it from the outside—although this was the first time she had seen the new car port—because she had often driven past. Well, just once or twice. Even though it was in a cul-de-sac. And even though it was right at the very cul itself. It wasn't that she was a stalker or anything. But she did seem to spend quite a lot of her day thinking, wondering, about the Stuart family in general, and she merely wanted to get a bit of concrete detail on the exact sort of residence in which to picture them. That was all. No big deal.

The Building of the Car Port had been a

major issue in Bea's life a while back, Heather remembered. It was last spring term because it was when cycling proficiency was on, and she always managed to stand quite near to Bea during those lessons, if she got there early enough, and could hear a lot of the chat about the builders and so on. Bea had, if she had picked it up correctly, doubts about the cost of it all and what it did to the line of their house. It was nice for Heather to get a good look now, having been told—well, having overheard—so much on the subject. She bent slightly, to look under the driver's mirror for a better view. Hmm. She wasn't sure she was a car port fan in general or, indeed, a fan of this car port in particular. They'd had a nice little herbaceous bed there before; she remembered admiring the peonies and making a mental note to track down the variety so that she could—well, not copy exactly, but just get some too. It did though give the Stuarts' house the illusion of being the biggest in the street. Hey ho. Had Bea asked for her opinion at the time, Heather might have rustled one up. But Bea had not asked for her opinion. Because, back then—back in her own personal dark age—Bea had not even known Heather's name.

Well, that was then, this was now. And here she was, with a back seat covered with the components of the world's most fancy starter, about to go into Bea's kitchen and cook lunch for her and all her friends. Heather almost had to pinch herself. How far had she come?

One thing about taking on such a complicated recipe was that Heather had to get going pretty early. And she was, she noticed with satisfaction as she got out of the car, the first. So it would be just her and Bea for a bit then, she thought, as she bent in to gather up all the crates and boxes and cool-bags. Just her and Bea—she shut the car door with her foot. Just her and Bea in Bea's kitchen— she adjusted the weight of her heavy load, tossed her new hair and staggered down the path to the white front door. Mates together. Just hanging out and shooting the breeze.

12 P.M. LUNCH BREAK

This will earn me some Brownie points, thought Rachel as she pushed Hamish up the drive. She never 'popped in' on her mother. Ever. In fact, she never 'popped in' on anyone at all. Didn't believe in it. It was, without being too grand about it, an article of personal faith: if God had meant us to go 'popping in' on each other all the time, He would never have gone to the bother of creating the lockable front door, would He? Needless to say, her mother was a devout observer of the opposite persuasion—practically the patron saint of the popping in, and the 'Go on then,' and the 'Just a quick cup.' It was this sort of profound religious conflict, indeed, that had given relations between them that piquant Arab/Israeli-with-a-twist-of-Northern-Ireland flavour they had been so enjoying these past few months. 'Well this,' she murmured to the top of Hamish's head, 'is by way of a peace mission. Just look on and learn, my boy. Look. And. Learn.'

'We can just squeeze by,' she smiled at a man busy hammering the fence, and manoeuvred the push-chair down the side of the house and

136

through to the back garden. 'Mind the ladder! You don't want any more bad luck!' called Bea's dad cheerfully, from up near the guttering. 'Rachel!' Her mother looked up from the flowerbed, on which she was spreading old newspapers. 'What on earth are you doing here?' She seemed surprised but not, noticed Rachel, overtly pleased.

'Just thought I'd pop in.' Rachel forced out the last two words without gagging.

'Whatever for?' She was more than not pleased: she was quite cross.

And, put on the spot like that, Rachel couldn't quite recall. 'Um. Well. We were just out for a walk and—um—wondered if you wanted—er—help?' She looked around Old Ma Howard's Organic Homestead, a.k.a. the garden of 32 Webster Close, and saw it was already full of helpers—loads of them, everywhere, all quite ancient but busy hoeing and tilling and planting and building. It looked, this afternoon, almost picturesque—the very model of an early agrarian commune. Where was Breughel when you needed him?

'Doh. I don't need any help,' scoffed her mum, creaking up on her feet. 'Quite self-sufficient round here, thank you very much.'

Clearly. 'What about your bees? Shall we do them while I'm here?'

'Oh, honestly, Rachel, you're far too late for them. I shut them up weeks ago.' She picked up a trowel and a trug.

'Shut them up?' Rachel looked towards the end of the garden, where the hives were. 'Do they hibernate then?'

'Hmm? Noh.' Her mum's 'noh', like her 'doh', was riven with contempt. 'Course not. But the hive

137

has to be shut up properly for the winter, or it won't make it through. It's danger time for them.'

Rachel rocked Hamish's buggy rhythmically, deep in thought. All those bees, so full of life, so full of themselves just a few weeks ago. And now it was danger time for them. 'Why? What danger?'

'The winter. It's one big danger.' Her mum threw the words over her shoulder as she worked. 'Cold. Disease. Death. And the wet. The wet is the worst thing for bees. If the rain gets in, it's a killer. So now they're all clustering together in there, huddled around their queen, keeping her going. Keeping everything going. How're you doing,' she called over the garden, 'on the compost?'

Rachel's gaze was riveted on the hives. Extraordinary. Just three white boxes, that's all they looked like, three very ordinary white boxes. And yet inside a heroic Darwinian struggle to survive.

'But, Mum. If you don't open them up, how will you know whether or not they have made it through?'

'We won't. Not until the spring. And even then, we won't know at once if the queen has made it. You can't really tell if a queen has died until it all starts up again. But then it's pretty obvious.' She pulled up some carrots and shook off the earth. 'Because then it's chaos.'

'Is it?' asked Rachel doubtfully. 'Then why don't they just get a new queen?'

'A new queen?' Her mother stomped down the path in the veg patch. 'A new queen?' She tutted and raised her eyes to the sky. 'Like it's the easiest thing in the world?' She called over to Bea's dad: 'Did you hear that one, Graham? Get a new queen!'

138

'Can be done, though,' admitted Graham, lining up his hammer with a nail. 'You can even just send off for one, you know.'

'Huh!' Her mother was now thoroughly irritated. 'Course you can. Money can buy you anything. But your bees aren't going to accept her just like that, are they? They'll choose the queen they want and there's not much we can do about it.' She straightened up and took in her daughter properly for the first time. 'Oh, *Rachel*.' She pointed the carrots at Hamish and adopted her now-what-have-you-gone-and-done voice. 'That's not *your* baby.'

'WHAT?' Rachel twisted round and looked into the buggy with mock horror. 'Oh my God, Mum! You're right!' She slapped her hand over her mouth. 'What have I done? I have no recollection . . . One minute I was outside the supermarket . . . then . . . Christ . . . I must've blacked—'

Bea's dad laughed.

'A-ha. So that means Georgie's there, then.' The carrots were now pointing accusingly at Rachel. 'Even Georgie's at Bea's girls' lunch. But not you. Of course. You,' she wiggled the carrots emphatically, 'are left holding the baby.'

'I don't blame her,' called Graham cheerfully. 'That's cos she's not daft as all that. Are you, Rachel?'

Rachel gave a smile and a grateful wave in the direction of the guttering and turned to leave. 'I think I'll be off. Before you call the police.'

She reversed back down the side path, smiling. She liked Bea's dad. She had liked her own dad, of course. She'd visited more back then, she knew— when her dad was alive. When she could expect some sensible conversation and a bit of peace

139

and quiet. It had been much calmer then. Now the whole house and garden were in a state of perpetual motion, she just didn't fancy it so much. She shook her head as she set off. How her dad would have hated all this self-sufficiency rubbish. It was a blessing, probably, that he had been spared it.

Starter
Filet de canard avec sauce de raisin et de pine kernels et tempura des endives avec dumplings de cauliflower

Preparation time: well, days, really, what with all the thinking and planning and what-have-yous

Cooking time: not enough. Nowhere near enough

Heather passed the last few plates around the table and sat down among the silent lunchers.

'Gosh,' said Bea sweetly. 'What fun. What did you say this was again, Heather?'

Heather closed her eyes as she answered. Perhaps, when she said the words, they could magically become true. 'Filet de canard avec sauce de raisin et de pine whatsits and tempura des endives avec dumplings of cauliflower.' She opened them again. No change.

Georgie took her knife, lifted up her duck fillet and peered underneath it. Heather felt self-conscious enough without Georgie playing up.

'Except, um, the dumplings didn't quite work so I thought we could manage . . .'

Georgie lifted her plate up to eye level and tapped the bottom, listening for evidence of a secret compartment.

'And then, um, the tempura, well . . . Colette

140

took the whisk—'

'Don't you go blaming me,' Colette cut in. 'You had the kitchen to yourself for most of the m—'

Bea raised an eyebrow. Colette shut up.

Georgie tipped her plate gently, to establish the presence of moisture.

'Oh,' finished Heather mournfully. 'The sauce. I . . . must've . . . forgotten the sauce.'

'Let's just call it Duck and Nuts, shall we?' asked Bea of the table as she picked up her knife and fork. 'Two of my absolutely favourite things and practically *Atkins*. All protein, few carbs. Heather, you're totally awesome. How yummy. Tuck in.'

Heather was too miserable to pick up her fork. The morning had not gone according to plan. All that cosy hanging out and breeze-shooting had not come to pass. Instead Bea had answered the doorbell, exclaimed about Heather's new look—she had noticed everything, the boots, the cardi; Bea just sees more than Rachel, that's the thing—and then disappeared off to the shower. And no sooner had she dumped her stuff on the kitchen island and wandered over to the noticeboard to check out the invitations and appointments than the doorbell had rung again and then again and all the other volunteers had trooped in and spread around the kitchen like smashed eggs so that Heather had been practically falling out of the back door and into the painted box that said WELLINGTON BOOT'S. Even though most of their stuff seemed to come out of a carton labelled TESCO FINEST, and she was trying to do proper, actual cooking.

Heather dared to raise her eyes to the table, and saw, to her amazement, that they were all doing exactly what Bea had told them. They were tucking in. It was another miracle. And now Bea was raising a glass, about to propose a toast. Not to the Duck and Nuts, surely? Although, actually, it was a rather good, if simple, combination . . .

'I am *so* pleased to see you all here today. You see, this lunch,' Bea smiled around the table, 'is more than just another fund-raiser. It is a Thank You. A Thank You from a totally grateful me to the *totally* awesome all of you, for helping me get through the juggling act'

Georgie winced.

'of my first half-term as *a working woman.*'

'It was a pleasure.'

'We had such a good time with your kids.'

'I did not,' Georgie pointed her knife towards Bea, 'help you in any way.'

'I'm surprised,' said Clover, 'not to see Bubba here. Didn't she take them all to Thorpe Park for you?'

'Mmm.' Bea was nibbling on a pine kernel, making it last. 'She couldn't make it today, sadly.' She stopped and put down her knife and fork. 'I do hope they're settling in all right. Scarlett's a bit worried about poor little Milo, says he's terribly unhappy, suspects he's Special Needs. Has anyone else mentioned him at all?'

'My boys said he was annoying,' said Colette. 'They asked him to go in goal the other day and he went and lay down in it. He is a bit strange—'

'Do you think she gives him Fruit Shoots?' butted in Clover anxiously.

'—but I can't say they were worried exactly.'

'Oh, I'm sure it's nothing. I'll have a word with their teacher—I've got the staff all coming to supper next week. But you know what Scarlett's like—little mother to the whole school.'

'Lovely girl.'

'Defo the next head girl.'

'I don't know,' Bea sighed. She looked genuinely worried and uncertain. 'The whole Green family seems . . . Oh . . . What is it, do you think?'

'They don't fit in,' put in Colette firmly.

'What? You think they don't *belong*?' Poor Bea sounded so worried.

'Nor do we want them to, if all they do is knock back the Fruit Shoots,' added Clover.

Bea was astonished. '*Really?* Do we not? And is *that* what it is?' She shook her head sadly. 'Is *that* the general view? I always thought it was sort of lovely for our children to mix with *all* different sorts. But you all think it's better for the poor little *different* ones perhaps to be somewhere where they can really *thrive*?'

Heather wasn't at all sure that, somewhere in the back of her mind, she didn't have a few worries about what Bea had just said. Didn't Maisie rather like Milo? But before she had a chance to clear the mental space to think it through—it was a knotty one, this—Georgie just suddenly boiled up and over like milk in a pan.

'Well, fortunately it doesn't really matter what you think, Beatrice.' She was spitting nuts. It was actually revolting. 'The national education policy on inclusivity in mainstream education is one teeny weeny thing you can brush off your overburdened shoulders.' She stood up. 'Cos it's not bloody up to you. God, I need a fag.' And she just blew out the door.

Well, thought Heather. They were only chatting. There was certainly no need for all that. Heather

143

gazed across at Bea, sitting in the middle of the oval table with a faint furrow to her brow, looking fantastic. While Heather was trying to cook, Bea had washed and straightened her long blonde hair and she looked so gleaming, so elegant. From time to time, she twinkled her narrow cornflower eyes and folded her neat straight features into a pretty smile as the voices recovered, swirled and bubbled around her. Oh Bea, Heather thought dreamily as she looked upon this vision. Oh Bea . . .

*   *   *

The noise had been registered by her subconscious some time ago, but it was only now that her conscious mind tuned in and identified it. Humming. Rachel was actually humming. She was strolling up the hill, pushing Hamish in his buggy, and she was humming away like a . . . like a . . . like an actual happy person or something.

Rachel had forgotten all this—what a positive thing it was to have a little one around the place; how they imprinted their wholesome routine upon the days of everyone about them. It was only 1.30, and she had already run around down at the rec, had fruit, juice and a mid-morning story, got some work done while Hamish played around her on the floor, and partaken of a delicious luncheon of fish finger and green vegetable. She'd even popped in on her mum. It was so much more than she normally achieved that Rachel felt quite ashamed. Where did it come from, this idea that it was small children who killed your fun and tied you down? The freedom of having her own kids at school had resulted in hour upon hour of a freedom which she spent trapped, staring at her own four walls, subsisting on meagre rations and achieving, on an average day, sod-all.

She walked around the school fence and turned left, past the little Budgens. Hamish nodded off. Right at the sub-post office and there she was at the top of Mead Avenue. Didn't that lovely Melissa say she had just moved into Mead Avenue? It seemed incongruous, somehow, to think of that exotic creature settling here. Rachel turned in, to take a better look. It was a long, narrow road that fell down the hill and wrapped itself around the curve of the land, but that was its only decent distinguishing feature. All the houses were recently built and exactly the same—neat, square pods, designed for the raising of neat, square families. Not a sharp, pointy irregular triangle like her own. The humming, she noticed, stopped.

This was prime St Ambrose catchment, so Rachel knew quite a lot of the Mead Avenue set. They were indeed a set, with their Avenue Fireworks and their Avenue BBQ and their matching Avenue Christmas lights; they were always busy hatching something. All that community this, community that—it got right on Rachel's nerves. A weak wintry sun shone down upon the trimmed lawns, reflecting off the cleaned gutters. Presumably it always shone on Mead Avenue; it wouldn't have the nerve to do otherwise. Or was this merely the natural radiant glow of neighbourhood smugness? Just because estate agents called their address 'desirable', they seemed to think everybody wanted to live there. Well, not Rachel Mason, thanks very much.

She pushed on down the hill, holding tight

on to the buggy to resist the strong gravitational pull. The buzz of the hedge trimmer assaulted her even before she rounded the bend. Wretched things, she tutted. Surely not even Hamish could snooze through that racket. And then she turned and saw ahead a house that she had never before noticed. How had that happened? It was hardly new: possibly even Victorian, definitely pretty, significantly larger than its neighbours, substantial rather than grand. It was sitting behind a high Leylandii hedge, atop a large, upward-sloping front lawn, and quite clearly she had never noticed it before because she hadn't been able to see it. A huge old tree in front of the house was in the process of coming down. That place must have been hidden for decades behind all that foliage. The machine droned on. Another branch was for it. Rachel and the buggy passed the tall hedge, got to the drive, peered round into the garden. And there, with mufflers on her ears and the hedge trimmer in her hand, was Melissa.

Main Course
Sweet and sour duck salad

Preparation time: hard to say really, because Sharon went round to Jasmine's to get started, but what with a coffee and a catch-up the morning seemed to run away with them

Cooking time: a lot longer if you haven't got that Heather hogging the stove, thanks for asking.

'Oh, how lovely,' said Georgie as the mains was put in front of her. She'd only come back in because

146

she was still starving after Heather's lamentable effort and now look: 'Duck.' She picked up her cutlery with a weary air.

Across the table, she could see Heather as she had seen Heather so very often down the years: nervously sensing some sort of disaster, trying to gauge how much of it was all her own fault. Not really having much of a clue.

'Well, this is a disaster and a half, isn't it?' said Clover in helpful clarification. 'Thank God I bought those canapés . . .'

'Sorry,' Heather mumbled. 'We—I—should have had more coordination.'

'Not at all!' said Bea sweetly. 'We're so lucky that you've done all this and it is all so special and such a treat. Next time, Jasmine, you might perhaps use a bit more sesame oil? And I think, Sharon, just two minutes more on the duck? Otherwise, wow, delish.'

'Cooking,' said Georgie, in her *MasterChef* voice, 'doesn't get tougher than this.'

Bea broke the respondent silence. 'Now, is there any more in that bottle, Abby?'

The bottle was in front of Bea. Abigail got up, went round to her side of the table and filled Bea's glass. Georgie held out hers too—if she must be here, she may as well take the opportunity to knock it back a bit—but didn't get any. 'I hope you'll all still have me back next year when I've moved up to senior school.' Abby shuddered. 'God. I can't believe it's actually about to happen. Terrifying.'

'My friend's boy's just started this term,' said Clover. 'She says it's sheer hell.'

'We're all watching you, you know, to see which school you go for,' said Jasmine to Abby. 'You can try it out for us.'

Georgie yawned a spectacular yawn.

'So hard, so hard,' Abby continued. 'What is the right school? Ashley's mum, you know—'

'The fat one,' said Colette.

'Talk about Fruit Shoots.'

'Yeah. Well. She—'

'Oh dear,' whimpered Heather. 'Can't we change the subject?'

'No, really?' drawled Georgie, rolling her eyes. 'From schools?' She made a snoring noise. 'Must we?'

'All right, Georgie,' said Bea, smiling brightly. 'How about work? Why don't we talk about *work?*'

Here we go, thought Georgie: now I'm for it. 'Ah yes, Bea,' she replied, all enthusiasm. 'Work. You yourself have a very interesting new job, I gather? Please, fill me in. I long to hear all about it.'

'It is actually *fascinating*,' said Bea to the table, 'to be out in the world again. And *independent.*'

'I've always been out in the world,' protested Colette.

'We're so independent,' said Sharon and Jasmine.

'But don't you think someone as *clever* as Georgie would be happier back in the workplace? Remind us, Georgie'—Bea's eyes were feasting upon her. It was quite putting her off her duck—'what was it that you did that was so *terribly* clever?' Georgie scowled back. 'The law? Is that what it was?'

'She was so high-powered,' squeaked Heather.

Wasn't I just?

'Quite brilliant at it.'

Yep. Hard to argue . . .

148

'And it was so interesting . . .'

Ah, thought Georgie. I ought to stop you right there. And tell you that it was all right. OK. Pretty interesting. Sometimes. And other times—which seemed to take longer, though perhaps they didn't—it was boring as hell. She looked down at her plate, tore at a bit of duck.

'*Amazing*.' Bea gazed at Georgie while nibbling on a spear of endive. 'And yet look at you now. Just vegetating at home with the children.' She shook her head in sorrow.

Georgie leaned over and took seconds, looking only at the table, avoiding all eyes. And I could stop you right there, too. And point out that in fact it is the opposite.

That her life now was one of pure, fine, distilled creativity. That everything she made—meals, gardens, babies, a home, a family—brought with it a depth of satisfaction she had never before known. And that while she was creating them she read more books, listened to more music and enjoyed more freedom to simply think than she had ever been able to do as a professional. She could just think whatever she wanted to think, whenever she wanted to think it. It was an amazing privilege, really. And Georgie felt cleverer now than she had ever felt before in her life. So clever, indeed, that she knew to keep shtum and eat up.

'*I* believe,' Bea continued, 'that if you are qualified in something so *terribly high-powered* then you *should* carry on working? It's sort of *immoral* not to? If you've been *trained* to do something then you *ought* to just do it?'

Georgie took thirds. And thought of her time working as a trained lawyer. And the thousands of trained lawyers with years of experience up ahead of her. And the thousands of trained lawyers coming out of college crowding up behind. And that sensation, which had driven her quite close to bonkers at the time, of them all shuffling along in one long, highly qualified queue that seemed to stretch pointlessly from cradle to grave.

'Now for dessert,' announced Colette, leaping to her feet.

And then the moment, the revelatory moment of her life, when she had held Kate in her arms for the first time, and looked down at that scrunched little face, into those worried eyes trying to make some sort of sense of the first images ever to flash before them. The moment when Georgie had thought: Ah. Here it is. Finally. Here's the one thing only I can do.

She got up and waved the packet of Marlboro Lights. 'Just nipping outside to pollute your garden a bit more, if I may.'

*   *   *

'Now then.' Rachel parked Hamish in the hall and walked through to the kitchen. 'How can I help?'

There was a pause, a wing-beat, while her words hovered in the air before Melissa replied.

'That's kind.' She smiled as she slipped her gardening jacket on to the back of a chair. 'But I think I can *probably* rustle it up all on my very own. What sort do you like?' She opened the cupboard above the kettle. 'Earl Grey? Builder's?'

'Hmm?'

Rachel was so lost, so absorbed in her new surroundings that she wasn't quite listening. Wow, was what she was thinking at that very moment. Wow, and: What a kitchen. A disproportionate amount of Rachel's professional life was taken up drawing kitchens—imagining them, designing them, inking out little views of them which had to form together to make a coherent whole—because in her little corner cupboard of world literature, kitchens mattered. Kitchens were where the action was. They were to kids' books what the attic was to horror: the place to which, at some point, your hero—or your hero's wellies—had to go; the place where stuff could always be relied upon to happen.

'Have you got a lesbian?'

But even her fertile imagination and graceful pen had not come up with a kitchen quite as, well, as kitchenly as this one. It was painted a shade of ochre that shone with a warm, golden glow. The entire back wall was taken up with a dresser on which black-on-white crockery obediently lined up, like maids in a stately home ready for service. There were a couple of eye-level cupboards, and Rachel always went for open shelving where possible. But even they could be forgiven, as they had glass doors revealing tasteful contents—she could see pleasantly arranged home-made jam and chutneys, jars of local honey. It was all, to Rachel, a wonderful sight: not trendy, not frightful antique-y, but a perfectly timeless hymn to domestic virtue in which anybody—Mrs Bridges, Mrs Tiggywinkle, Nigella—would feel at home.

Rachel, sitting at the large oak table in a reverie, suddenly remembered herself . 'Sorry. Miles away. I meant a herb tea. If you have one, that is.'

Melissa turned around from the kettle and grinned as she passed a cup to Rachel. 'What did you think I thought it was? A sexual orientation or something?'

Rachel giggled, delighted. Hello, she thought. I knew I'd like her.

'Mmmm. Mint. Lovely.'

Rachel smacked her lips and reached for a biscuit. The warmth of the kitchen, Melissa's hospitality, the depth of Hamish's slumber all combined to make her feel unnaturally relaxed; drunk almost. She put her feet up on the next chair and leaned back.

'So what brought you to these parts then? You're new round here, I take it.'

Melissa blew across the top of her cup and nodded. 'Well, a good opportunity opened up for my work down here. Also my husband has to fly a lot for his new job, so we needed to be nearer the airport if we ever want to see him. Which, as it happens, we rather do.'

'That's nice,' said Rachel, taking another biscuit. 'My husband's flown off altogether.'

Melissa looked at her steadily over the lip of her cup. 'How did it go with your kids the other day? With their dad?'

'Oh, I dunno.' She rubbed at her neck. There was a muscle right at the back there that had been in almost permanent spasm since the day Chris moved out. 'They don't really say much when they get back. He's going the wrong way about it all, if you ask me. Always late, always rushed, always a different day of the week. And he just drags them round neutral territories—football stadiums, cinemas, Pizza Expresses—when all they really want to do is hang out at home and be normal. But there we go. If he screws it up with them, that's his

152

look-out, isn't it?'

'Absolutely!' said Melissa supportively. 'Let him get on with it.' Then she got up, went over to the sink and, with her back to the room, in the voice of one thinking aloud, said, 'Oh. Except—I suppose—they are your children too.'

'Yeah.' Rachel sipped her tea. 'True. That is the other side. No point me worrying away about how to keep them together if all he's going to do is blow them apart.'

'Must be so hard.' Melissa was bent into the dishwasher. 'No longer a couple, and yet co-parents for ever.'

Rachel swallowed. There seemed to be a lot to take in in Melissa's kitchen. And she'd had too many biscuits. It was hard to digest them all at once.

Dessert
Soufflés de chocolat et Grand Marnier

Preparation time: honestly, minutes. Everyone thinks soufflés are so hard, but, really, I knock them up just like that.

Cooking time: I don't even know. Pop them in and they will rise.

Note: I promise you, all men love this one.

'Well. Just look at this,' said Bea warmly. 'I think we have our winner! Colette, this looks *amazing.*'

Heather looked down at her perfect, puffy little individual soufflé and felt her gut twist as it tried to process all that duck. Winner? She didn't know there was going to be a winner.

'I think we all did our best,' said Sharon.

'Of course you did. You've all been fantastic. Such a help. Do you know?' She smiled around at them all. Her teeth were so even and white. 'I just don't think I could have managed all this without you.' And they smiled back at her.

'Not for us, thanks, Colette.' Sharon and Jasmine each held up a hand. 'I mustn't.'

Heather was just picking up her spoon, on the verge of digging in—she couldn't deny it looked delicious—when a chorus started to spring up around the table.

'No, nor me.'

'I really shouldn't.'

'I daren't.'

'Well I bloody will.' Georgie was back at the table, smelling of smoke. 'Pass one over here, Colette. In fact I can probably manage a couple more . . .'

One by one, ramekins were pushed in front of Georgie until they formed a little circle around her, cutting her off from the rest of the table. She set to, silently, methodically demolishing.

'I'd love one, but I am so bloody huge. I don't know what's happening to me,' said Jasmine, who Heather thought looked a bit like a twig.

'I'm worse, look!' Sharon had taken up her shirt and was holding a layer of epidermis up to the table.

'My arse,' Colette stood up and turned her back to the table, 'has never, ever been this size before.' She wiggled it to demonstrate. 'Is there a disease, do you think, when your arse just, like, takes on a life of its own? Like giantarseitis or something?'

'Don't! Bigbumorrhoea,' shrieked Jasmine, jumping to her feet.

Heather licked her chocolatey spoon and smiled. Suddenly the lunch had come alive. It helped that Georgie was now occupied with all her soufflés and had stopped scowling. But it wasn't just that. There was a new joyfulness in the room. Everyone was jumping up and down and shrieking and giggling. They were all united. They were as one. They were all in that boat that she liked so much, and pulling away, together. It was just adorable to watch.

Someone found a tape measure and they took turns standing up on the table to establish exactly how enormous their hips and waists actually were. Heather thought it was so funny. Each person was desperate to prove that she was the fattest and yet they were all tiny weeny little things. Georgie couldn't join in, because she was skinny as can be, and anyway, Georgie never joined in anything. She just wasn't a joiner-inner. And Clover was still sitting there too, which was interesting because Clover wasn't the slimmest. So that was weird. Perhaps she just wasn't a joiner-inner either. Well Heather jolly well was. Or longed to be, anyway. She leapt to her feet and on to the table.

'I'm fattest! Bet you! Bet I'm bigger than all of you put together.'

Colette looked over at Bea, who shrugged, then nodded. She stretched out the tape measure, wrapped it around Heather's hips and snapped it back.

'Er. Um. Well. Yes. You are.'

Heather smiled triumphantly around the table.

'See?' she trilled. 'Told you!'

And yet nobody congratulated her. Or said

anything. Or even looked at her. They weren't all together any more. No longer as one. They were all finding their chairs again, sitting back down in silence. The joy had flown out of the room. Heather was not quite sure what had happened. She knew it had something to do with actually being fat instead of not being fat. Even though she wasn't even fat. Was she? She was struggling to make any sense of any of it, but this much Heather knew: she was out of that boat, and—splash—back in the cold and wet and hanging on for dear life.

She clambered down from the table, slunk back to her seat and cast around the table in search of some emotional support. Georgie, she noticed, full of soufflé, was fast asleep like a digesting python.

'Now then,' said Bea. 'Who had volunteered for coffees? I can't remember the list . . . Oh heavens. Look. Is that the time? Girls, girls, girls! We're due back at school any minute. And help! Look at the state of this kitchen!' She laughed happily, sitting still.

'I'm not due to pick up till four-forty-five,' said Heather. 'Maisie has judo this afternoon. Can I help?'

'Oh, Heather. You are a *complete star.*' Bea stood, and put her hands on Heather's shoulders. '*God*, how I love this girl.' A new sense of well-being flowed through Heather. Any discomfort she had felt from the unfortunate tape-measure business just faded away. It was a bit like that moment in church, when you are at the communion rail and the vicar puts her hands upon you. Even if you're not totally convinced of the whole God thingummy, you somehow always do feel a bit better for it. Or Heather did, anyway. And that was how she felt right then: Bea had laid her hands upon her. And she was blessèd.

'If you've finished before I get back, just pull the front door to, would you?' Bea stopped, hand over mouth and gave a panicked little squeak. 'I nearly forgot! The money! Remember, ladies, there's no such thing as a free lunch. Can I trust you all to put your lovely cash in the pot on the way out?'

*　　　*　　　*

Melissa walked out into her front garden. Rachel followed behind, pushing the buggy.

'It's a bit larger than the Mead Avenue average, isn't it?' Rachel could now see that Melissa had at least an acre, which was unheard-of in that neighbourhood.

'All of Mead Avenue was this garden, until about twenty years ago. The previous owners sold the land for building. This used to be the countryside.'

They looked around them. It was early afternoon now, and the houses were starting to come back to life. People were returning home, cars were driving down, lights were going on. Rachel could picture the beauty of the place as it had been, before this estate had been thrown up, and shook her head.

'What a shame,' she said with sympathy. 'Imagine it. You could have had this beautiful house, practically in the middle of nowhere . . .'

Melissa laughed and strode down the garden, breaking off a wayward branch as she moved. 'I can't think of anything worse. Look at all these gardens—so beautifully cultivated. And I love being smack bang in the community like this. Why on earth would I want to be stuck out on the side of a

157

hill, up some long drive, with nobody else around?' She looked down at the buggy. 'Very nice of you to have someone else's baby for the day . . .'

'Do you know,' Rachel stroked the sleeping head, 'I've loved it. And the funny thing is I've achieved more with Hamish today than I have on my own for weeks.'

'Weird. And why was that, do you think?' Melissa was puzzled.

'Phhh. I dunno.' Rachel shrugged. 'Cos he's got a timetable, and such a good routine, I s'pose . . .'

'*Really?*' Melissa stopped short while she digested this astonishing revelation. 'And you think that made things better for *you*?'

'Yeah.' Rachel thought about it. 'I do actually. The imposition of order upon chaos—seemed to be just what I needed.'

Melissa was looking at her like she was, at the very minimum, the new St Francis of Assisi. 'So you believe in routine, in pattern, in order? That those things can make everything seem better, the hard things of life feel easier?'

Er, apparently so. Rachel had never given it a moment's thought and yet suddenly the idea was taking flight before her eyes—a fully fledged, long-held philosophy of life. 'Yes,' she said firmly. 'I do.'

'Fascinating.' They walked together, each matching the step of the other. 'Jeez Louise, does this baby *never* wake up?'

'Almost never.' Rachel leaned over the buggy and wiggled it a bit. 'Hamm-y. Come on. Let's go and find Mummy.'

Hamish opened one eye and gave a fleshy, gummy smile.

158

'It certainly seems to work for him,' agreed Melissa.

3.15 P.M. PICK-UP

Georgie was leaning against the fence. A lit cigarette was between the fingers of her left hand and her eyes were closed. At the sound of Rachel's approach—she recognised the light wheels of Hamish's buggy—she peeled back one eyelid and glimpsed her baby. Asleep, divine, delicious. And coming to the end of one whole precious day in his life that she could never now reclaim. She was some distance from being able to forgive anybody for the ordeal that she had been put through today.

'Do you know,' said Rachel, parking Hamish beside her, 'I've realised something. It's just occurred to me, walking here. It's Hamish who made me see it . . .'

'No, thank you for asking,' interrupted Georgie irritably. 'I did not have a nice day. Actually. I have just returned from a living bloody hell.'

'We need a routine. That's all.' Rachel was abstracted, in a world of her own. 'Me and Chris and the kids. We can't muddle on like this. We need a routine, an order, a pattern. We can't move on because our whole system, our organisation has fallen apart.'

'Hello? Remember me? The mug you sent round to Tight-wad Towers for an entire lunch? I'm wiped out. I've been on my best behaviour all day, I'll have you know. You cannot imagine the rot that I have been forced to listen to. God, it's exhausting always being so polite. How does a normal person cope?'

159

'From now on, we're going to have a timetable. None of this swirling chaos of Chris turning up when he feels like it and doing what he likes with them. We're going to draw up a system and stick to it.'

'That house. Christ,' Georgie continued, shuddering. 'Everywhere you look there's a rogue apostrophe or exclamation mark. I've got a very low pain threshold for that sort of thing, you know, and I don't think you take it seriously enough.'

'Sorry.' Rachel was back with her at last, and smiling. 'Tell me. Did they end up really hating the old bag?'

'Did they hell. They all cooked and cleaned and served her while she sat there on her big fat arse—'

'It's not, to be fair, a big fat arse.'

'OK, her hard little bony arse, and practically awarded them marks out of ten and then charged them at the end. Fifteen quid! You owe me fifteen quid.'

'Fair enough. But surely even they must be a bit pissed off with her?'

'Nope.' Georgie shook her head in despair. 'All as delighted at the end as they were at the beginning. I fear I have to declare your little experiment a right flop.'

She went through the rigmarole with her fag end and gathered up Hamish, who buried himself into her neck without waking.

'Trouble is,' she was rhythmically stroking the baby's back as she thought out loud, 'they do just worship her. They're like in some weird cult for weirdos.' She gave, in her view, an excellent rendition of the *X Files* sting. 'A weird cult for weirdos who, I can tell you, eat a weird amount of

160

duck.'

She looked across at Rachel, nervous that all this might upset her again, only to see that Rachel was smiling. Beaming. She was leaning forward, flickering her fingers in a flirty little wave, like a . . . like a . . . well, like a weird weirdo in a weird cult, as it happened. Her big brown eyes—all warm and deep and soupy—brought back to mind the eleventy million soufflés Georgie had eaten and her stomach gave a lurch. Ugh. She might actually puke.

'Hi. Hey. Thanks so much for today,' Rachel was saying, as someone Georgie had never met came gliding towards them. 'This is my friend Georgie, who I told you about.'

Georgie gave one of her speciality gruff nods, and was nearly dazzled by the returning smile.

'Georgie,' said Rachel with pride, 'this is Melissa.'

'Well, well, well.' The vision before her came into focus and Georgie started to smile. 'And he-llo'. This was odd. She'd been given bugger-all to drink and yet she was starting to feel a tiny bit squiffy. Someone must have spiked those soufflés.

'Melissa has just moved here for her—' Rachel stopped. 'Sorry, what is it you do, anyway? I forgot to ask.'

'Psychotherapist,' Melissa answered, smiling at Georgie. 'Just part-time. Over at the hospital.'

'Huh!' replied Rachel. 'See why you came our way. Plenty of nutters and loonies round here to keep you busy.'

'Interestingly,' Melissa intoned, 'since post-Victorian reforms, the terms "nutter" and "loony" have fallen from professional use . . .'

Gosh, thought Georgie, properly impressed. That Stephen Fry impersonation was quite close to brilliant.

THE DAY OF THE BALL

8.50 A.M. DROP-OFF

If Heather had been facing forward as Rachel walked up the hill towards her, then the shock might not have been so great. As it was, Heather was bent over Maisie, fussing and fiddling with the strap on her backpack—she was always fussing and fiddling over something or other—so it wasn't until she was at close range that Rachel first saw it: the new Heather. The new, specs-off, contacts-in Heather Carpenter, dressed top to toe in white and doing more than a passable impression of a newly shorn sheep—pale, blinking, vulnerable. Rachel gave a little jump of alarm.

'Morning.' Heather smiled. 'Feels funny, I must say. Funny but amazing. First time without glasses since infant school. I can't believe I've never done it before.'

'And what made you do it now?' The girls were already ahead and giggling. More of Mr Orchard's Funny Jokes, she presumed. That was all that Poppy ever talked about these days: Mr Orchard and his Funny Jokes.

'Colette. Colette has just taken me over.' She beamed.

'Aren't you the lucky one?'

'Hey, Rach.' Heather stopped and grabbed her arm. 'I bet I could get her to take you on, too. I mean, I could ask anyway.'

Rachel carried on walking. 'That is so sweet of you, but you know what? I think I'm fine as I am.

163

Just at the moment.'

Heather nodded with sympathy. 'I know. It's early days. But if or when you decide that the time has come for a makeover, you just let us know, OK?'

Let 'us' know?

'Colette did say she was dying to get you into her Serenity Spa and give you a good old seeing-to only the other day.'

'Really? Is that what she said?'

'Mm. She was saying that she thought you had real potential.'

'Gosh. Well. Hey.' Rachel's hands were balled tight into fists. 'That's really sweet of you to pass it on.'

'You're welcome,' Heather trilled. 'So. Looking forward to tonight?'

'Well. Ish. S'pose. Hey, I meant to ask you: do you want to go together? I don't mind driving. Won't drink much anyway. I could chauffeur you and Guy, how about that?' And Guy could lecture her on the niceties of the Highway Code and her miles per gallon.

'Aw, Rach.' Heather scrunched up her face. 'We're all going to Colette's to get changed together. It's going to be a total hoot, actually. Six of us! Nails. Hair. Dresses. C-razy. Then we're going to meet the boys'

The what?

'there and—hopefully,' she gave an atypical little wiggle, a wiggle that she had obviously borrowed from someone and in Rachel's view really ought to give back, 'stun them with our awesomeness.'

'Oh. Right. OK then. Doesn't matter.' Oh hell.

'Colette's so excited about her silent auction.

She's got the headmaster to put himself up!'
Heather laughed with glee.

'Himself?'

'Yes. Isn't it brilliant? He's a lot all on his own:
Dinner at the new French place in the High Street
with the headmaster. And Colette is going to win
him, whatever he goes for. She thinks tonight might
just be her night.'

'Poor sod.' How utterly humiliating. Rachel
could just imagine how he would feel unable to
refuse that. She felt genuinely sorry for him.

'It's going to be a great little earner, I think, the
auction. Bubba's got lunch in London with Andy
Farr.' Heather was still beaming.

'Oh,' said Rachel, flatly. 'Who the hell is Andy
Farr?'

Heather stopped walking, and—temporarily—
beaming. 'Do you know, that's what I thought,
but I was too embarrassed to say anything. I just
presumed he was really famous and I was being
thick. But he's a celebrity, apparently. So Bubba
says.'

'Can one be a celebrity, would you say, if no one
has actually heard of one?'

That was a bit semantic for Heather. She
brushed it away. 'Help, we're a bit late. Would
you mind scooting Maisie in for me? I've just seen
everyone's already waiting over by the car. Tennis
this morning. What a day. Mustn't be late.'

Rachel walked with the girls, down the corridor
to their neighbouring pegs. The cloakroom was
quietening down now; the bell would go any
minute. She grabbed a wrist of each and crouched
down to them.

'Hang on a minute, girls. Before you go. The

165

other morning, I heard some not very nice stuff coming from you two about someone or other and I would appreciate the low-down, if you don't mind. And right now, pronto.'

Maisie and Poppy chewed their lips and consulted each other with their eyes.

'I'm waiting. Are you or are you not in training for the Big Bully Olympics?'

Poppy went first: 'No. Scarlett is, Mummy.'

'Scarlett?'

'She's just being so mean to Milo,' added Maisie.

'Like really mean, and he cries every single breaktime.'

'And we feel really sorry for him.'

'And Miss Nairn couldn't care less.'

Then the bell did go.

'We'll talk about it later, OK? Now have a good day and don't get yourselves in the middle of anything.'

10 A.M. MORNING BREAK

Rachel opened the fridge door in search of something to help her celebrate. And there was the same old mould and stale stuff that everyone had turned down at breakfast. Fancy that. Yet again, a fridge elf had failed to nip down to Waitrose and fill it up for her. Who'd have predicted it?

She leaned against the cool door and sighed. It was a brutal truth of single parenthood—one that slapped her in the solar plexus a minimum of three times a day: nothing ever went into that fridge any more unless she put it there. She had once known a time when she could open it and the cheerful

166

little light would shine its sun upon some wonder never before dreamed of in her philosophy. Not a full family shop, admittedly—it would require swine flu or actual childbirth on her part for that to happen. But still, some small and beautiful domestic miracle—an M&S meal for two or half a cheesecake that Chris might have bought at the station or the remnants of a bottle of wine. Not any more. Its powers had shrunk. Her fridge was no longer capable of any existence independent of Rachel. Like the rest of the cottage, and the garden, and the wretched, useless car, it had become yet another dependent, colonial outpost of the sovereign state of her own mind. Which was a bore, because she really was starving.

And she did want to celebrate. Ellie's wellies had had their adventures, and were back in the cloakroom. The book was finished and, in her expert opinion, it wasn't half bad. It might not be an artistic masterpiece, she may just miss out on this year's Turner Prize—though the way she captured the light on those shiny toes was actually pretty brilliant—but it had a certain charm. And she was at last due a certain pay cheque. So she could now even afford to eat.

She picked up the milk and sniffed it—approaching the turn but not as yet in full pong—and was immediately shot back into her marriage. She smiled. While others may be transported to their memories by music or madeleines, there was nothing like a 'best before' to remind her of Chris.

It was in the last month before he left that she and the kids had come bowling back from the leisure centre and into the kitchen at eleven o'clock one sunny Saturday morning. And they had found

Chris sitting alone at the table, staring into space, tucking into a couple of dry pork chops without any evident pleasure.

'Hungry?' she had asked him.

'Not really.' He was chewing hard, in a busy, workmanlike, let's-get-it-over-with kind of a way. 'But they go off tomorrow, and we're going out.'

'Oh. I see. Would you at least like some apple sauce, to cheer them up?'

'Nah. I'm all right.' He swallowed in lumps, washing it down with the occasional slurp of cappuccino. 'Be a waste.'

And that was the moment, the tricky moment about which neither of them had ever spoken, when Rachel caught the look in Josh's eyes. And it really was only a moment, because as soon as Josh saw that his mother had seen it, he wiped his eyes clean, with a shake, like his head was an Etch A Sketch. And his look was then a blank one, which told nobody anything. But Rachel knew what she had seen: she'd seen a flash of disloyalty, and a hint of confusion and shame, and words that if spoken would have said something along the lines of 'Man, dood, why is Dad like this totally tragic freakin' dweeb?'

Looking back from where she stood, Rachel found she could only agree with him. It was interesting that Chris had shown such scant regard for his marriage vows, when he worshipped the sell-by date like something Moses might have carved on a tablet. She picked up some bacon. It didn't go off till next Tuesday, yet it was dried up, greenish, crusty. 'And guess what?' she said to herself. 'You can chuck it. Just like that. Throw it out. Your colony, your rules.' The phone rang and

168

she almost skipped over to it.

'Rachel. It's Bubba. Are you free?'

'Yes. Yes. That's exactly what I am. I'm free. I am a sovereign in control of my whole empire and I am free.'

'Oh, thank God.'

Rachel noticed there was a shake in her voice.

'Can you come over?'

In fact, she sounded very rocky.

'It's A Moveable Feast.'

Was that a stifled sob?

'I gave them a four-grand deposit. Bea *told* me to give them a *four-grand deposit*. And I did. And they've taken it. And I think, well, it seems, no, they have . . . they've just totally buggered off.'

12 P.M. LUNCH BREAK

Bubba sat at the kitchen table, which was covered with bits of paper. Every time she picked one up, her hand shook. And everywhere she looked there were numbers. Numbers numbers numbers. Numbers that never seemed to add up or do the decent thing and at least balance each other out. Numbers galore, every single one of them hell-bent on negativity. And Bubba had always disapproved of negativity.

She had never even liked numbers—much more an *ideas* person. And empathy, of course. That was her big thing, the Bubba trademark: *empathy*. Numbers had always bored her rigid. And it was funny, looking back on it, that numbers were there, a constant, at her introduction to motherhood. All that incessant counting which was supposed to help—according to every childbirth know-all and clever-clogs—with the pain. So like a good girl she'd sat there, fatly, on a bean bag, puffing and chanting and expecting that baby to just sort of pop out on the count of three or whatever and after a few days of that—or was it years?—she had finally been wheeled into theatre for a Caesarean.

And then those first few months at home, before she had hired the first nanny. (God, nannies: something else she didn't want to count.) All those ounces and millilitres—she'd never even *heard* of a millilitre before she had a baby. Why would she? So small it was quite *pathetic*—and hours in the night and doses in a Calpol bottle. Counting, counting, numbers, numbers, and all so boring and *unsympathetic* really that she had just gone running off back to work where there were huge *departments* full of people just there to do the counting for you. They completely *loved* it, sitting there with their little machines adding everything up so that she, Bubba, could concentrate on her *sympathy* and her *empathy* and all the other things for which she was valued.

And then ten years later, after all the nannies that couldn't be counted, she was back home and counting all over again. Sit-ups in the gym and sausages per person and standing in the petrol station which she seemed to do about ten times a week—it *guzzled* the stuff, that bloody car—just watching the numbers spin up and up and willing them to get to the top before every single one of her mental marbles was lost and gone for ever. So, just to keep her sanity really, she had come up with this huge project, this ball, which would be the perfect showcase for all of her creativity and originality and social—well, *genius* for want of a better word, and what happened? She was sitting at the kitchen table, looking at the numbers and knowing, just knowing, that they were never going to add up.

She wanted to cry, but she mustn't. She really mustn't. The others would be here soon, and she needed to hold it all together, but really, if she had just one regret in the whole history of her forty-whatever years—and Bubba did not like regrets, on the whole, didn't *approve* of them really, they were just more negatives—that one regret would be ever thinking up the St Ambrose Christmas Paradise Lakeside in Winter Seaside bloody Beach Ball.

*   *   *

Rachel and Heather swooped on to the gravel at the same time, ripped their keys from their ignitions, flung open their doors. Sharon and Jasmine were just getting out of their cars and running under outstretched coats through the pelting rain and into the house. Clover's large rear was disappearing through the front door. This is rather exciting, thought Rachel. Get us. We're practically *The Sweeney*.

Bubba was wringing her hands, both trying and failing to suppress her sobs. 'I gave Bea the cheque last week when she asked and they cashed it the bastards cashed it'—sob—'I just heard from the bank and it was my money I just thought I'd float it you know just till we'd sold all the tickets'—sob—'and then I thought this morning this is jolly odd isn't it jolly odd that they are supposed to be

171

doing dinner here for one hundred and fifty people in'—wail—'God in about eight hours and there's nobody here and no equipment they said they'd be bringing ovens and warmers and of course food there's no food here nothing at all not a fucking sausage not a loaf of bread and so I rang them and—'

'OK, I think we get the picture,' said Rachel.

'As I thought,' chipped in Clover. 'Pam the crooked dinner lady. Got her fingerprints all over it. Her MO completely. I did warn—'

'We need a Plan B,' Rachel said over her.

'—you but did anyone listen?'

'How much have we got to play with?' Rachel went to the kitchen table in the hope of finding some sort of budget.

'That'll teach you.' Clover shook her head, more in sorrow than in anger.

'Shut up, Clover.'

But there was no budget here, just thousands of numbers scrawled over hundreds of pieces of paper, as if Bubba was a mad physicist trying to crack a new theorem rather than a parent running a fund-raiser. How on earth, thought Rachel to herself, did this woman ever hold down a job?

'And where's the marquee? Have they done a bunk too?'

'No, no.' There was a pause for some sniffing and nose-blowing. 'You just can't see it from here. It's away from the house. Down by the lake.'

'Why?' Rachel felt a mounting panic. She spoke slowly and clearly, like a negotiator in a delicate hostage situation. 'Why. Is. The. Marquee. Away. From. The. House. And. Down. By. The. Lake?'

'Because it's going to be a lakeside ball.' A bit

172

more sobbing. 'Isn't it? Wasn't that the point?'

'Well, yes it was. When you were going to have it in the middle of summer, remember? But it is now December, Bubba. It's pissing down with rain. We won't be able to see the lake. We won't even know there is a lake unless someone happens to fall in and bloody drown in it. And we'll probably lose a few revellers to exposure even before we get to the sodding lake . . .'

'Oh my God,' put in Clover with satisfaction. 'This is a complete nightmare.'

'Well look, Mark is on his way. I called him at the office and he said he'd come straight back.' Bubba dabbed at her face. 'He'll know what to do. He always does.'

Rachel felt a twinge of envy. She could see him now, the Clooneyesque Mark Green, putting the phone down on his distraught but still beautiful wife, grabbing his Armani jacket, leaving the City as fast as he could—leaping into a helicopter? Piloting his own sea plane off the Thames?—and coming home to assert his masterful control. OK, so she, Rachel, was free. So she was a sovereign in control of her own empire. But she also thought that it might, occasionally, do to have a co-sovereign from time to time. A bum on the seat of the throne next to her. A consort who—

'Wowser, that is wet.' The back door opened. 'I was ringing the bell but I wasn't sure you could . . .' There was a gust of cool, clean, washed air.

'Hi!' Rachel flung herself upon the new arrival and kissed her on each cheek. 'Thanks so much for coming. Bit of a situation brewing here.'

She turned to the rest of the room.

'Everybody, I thought we could do with some

help so I called for some top-level reinforcements. For those of you who have not yet had the pleasure: this is Melissa.'

8 P.M. THE BALL

Drinks

'Oh, Bubba, you look fabulous.'

'So do *you*. Yummy! Is this new?'

''Tis actually.' Jasmine gave a little twirl. 'Splashed out rather. We all have. We had a girls' outing last week, up to London. Specially. Spent a fortune.' She looked around for her husband, who was over at the bar with Tony Stuart. 'Don't go on about it in front of Richard, though, will you? Put it on the plastic. Haven't quite broken the news yet.'

Bubba had been feeling more relaxed since Melissa had sorted the crisis, but something in what Jasmine just said had created another little bead of worry, which she could feel was rolling off to find all her other little beads of worry, and sooner or later they would connect and make a chain, a big long chain of worry that could throttle her. But she wasn't sure what it was. She couldn't quite focus. And anyway, what she should be doing right now was enjoying herself.

'Hi. Thank *you* for coming. *Amazing* shoes.'

The marquee was looking great, with the sand on the floor and the starfish and the netting, the cobalt-blue and white striped ceiling and the parasols above every table. It looked better even than she had imagined. Kazia—bless her—had been slaving for days. It wasn't even that cold in here. And you could, if you wanted to, pretend that the rain thumping down on the roof was a waterfall . . .

Everyone was here, that was the best thing. They were all here and *determined* to have a great time. The tent was filling and the conversational bubble was inflating and you could just feel the excitement in the air. It wasn't only the parents from school; there were friends of parents from school, and quite a few grandparents from school. The staff were here—even the grumpy secretary had put on her glad rags. And what glad rags they were. Poor thing. Tom Orchard was over there, chatting to Bea, looking rather adorable in his DJ. Lucky old Colette. And all the governors had turned out, she was glad to see. It was exactly as her instincts had told her: these were lovely people and they were just really grateful for the chance to get out and enjoy themselves. The plan was: drinks drinks drinks and chat chat chat for the next hour, so that Colette had a good chance to flog away at The Silent Auction, and then the wonderful Melissa had promised that dinner would appear at about nine. Yum yum. She for one could not wait.

Oh look, there were the Farrs. Another triumph! She really had pulled out all the stops tonight. *So* sweet of them to turn up at what was after all a pretty humble little gathering. She pressed her way through the crowd—

'Do you like it? Well, we wanted to do something a *little* bit different . . .'

—and hurried over to Andy's side. She needed to circulate him around before dinner, she thought. Sprinkle the stardust. Everyone would want to meet him. Mustn't disappoint.

'Andy! Jen! *Brilliant* of you to come all this way.'

*　　　*　　　*

Rachel had only been there for ten minutes but already had an overwhelming need for peace, quiet and a solitary fag. They were only two weeks into the new Mason family system of every other weekend and Wednesday nights with Chris, and Rachel still felt very wobbly on her feet—like a new foal learning to stand. The last thing she needed was this extravaganza. Her programme for the evening was to turn up, melt into the background and get home as early as possible, job done. She was just slinking, subtly, towards the exit when her path was blocked by some short fat bloke with a damp upper lip. 'You must be Rachel,' he puffed as he thrust a glass into her hands. 'Bubba said her new best friend was the hot redhead, and I spotted you soon as you walked in.' With a bit of panting and considerable effort, he lifted his short fat arm to pour her some champagne. 'I'm Mark Green. Cheers.' They chinked glasses. 'Well, what do you think? Early yet, but we seem to be getting away with it so far, eh?'

'Mmmm.' She gulped the booze back while she studied the man before her. Not quite the Mark Green she had envisaged. Even if this one did manage to squeeze himself behind the controls of a sea plane, the basic laws of physics would mean it could never take flight. Why must people persist in having such unlikely spouses? It was most disconcerting. 'It all looks fantastic. Very nice of you to do all this, you know. Everyone really appreciates it. I was just on my way to . . .' She gestured towards the flap that led to the Portaloos.

'You carry on. Catch up with you later.' He waddled off and Rachel ducked outside. It was raining hard now so she stood beneath the awnings, lit up and cursed Georgie for getting her smoking again. Still, she thought to herself, she was under a lot of stress here. Last time she'd gone on a night out as a single woman, it was back in another century . . . She puffed out and up to the moonless night as a large hand came from behind and gripped her left thigh. She heard herself shriek.

'You're looking particularly gorgeous tonight, Mrs Mason.' Tony Stuart peered over her shoulder, his alcoholic breath in her face. He put the other arm round her waist as he moved his hand towards her groin and she stepped smartly away.

'Bugger off, Tony. Are you turning into an old perv?'

He gave a good-natured chuckle. It was, Rachel remembered, one of his saving graces that you could say absolutely anything to Tony Stuart and he didn't care a damn, whereas his wife went through life with her umbrage on permanent red alert.

'Aw, come on. Only being friendly. Why don't we see you any more anyway? I miss you, Rachel.'

'Yes, well, I think that's how Bea wants it at the moment.'

'But we're old mates, you and me. She can't keep me away from my old matesh.' He really was plastered. It was not yet nine o'clock. 'We should get together. Just the two of us.'

'Oh yeah?' She was holding out her arm like a policeman directing traffic.

'Yeah. I'm always here for you, Rachel. If you just want a drink. Cup of tea. Hey, even if you only want a quick shag. I'm here for you. I'm your man. OK?'

'That's, er, good to know, Tone.' Rachel backed away, dodging the guy ropes.

He stumbled slightly. 'Do not,' he wagged his finger at her, put on his serious, professional businessman voice, 'outsource the shagging.'

'I'll bear it in mind . . .' She backed slowly towards the Portaloos.

'Just don't forget your old mate, is what I'm saying.'

Rachel turned and dashed up the flimsy steps of the Ladies and closed the main door. Sanctuary. The face that looked back at her in the mirror was a bit damp and highly coloured. Time for some essential repair work before she returned to the fray. The lavatory behind her flushed and out came Bea.

'Well, hello.' She took up position at the other sink, and they both stared into the mirror, side by side.

'Hi. You look fab tonight.'

'Well thank you, Bea.' Rachel had forgotten that feeling. When Bea with her lovely voice said a lovely thing it made you feel all warm and fuzzy and . . .

'You seem to have stopped making any effort at all lately. It's really good to see you still can.'

'Well. Thank you. Bea.'

Bea put down her make-up bag and turned to face Rachel in person. 'Sorry. That came out all wrong. I didn't mean it like that. I just meant, *you* have been looking pretty down and *I* have noticed.'

'Yes. Well. My marriage broke up. That is generally recognised to be a bit of a downer.'

'And I'm sorry we haven't seen you lately, but it's so difficult for us, Rachel.'

'Yeah. God. It must be awful for you. I haven't thought enough about that. How awful this is for you.'

'Rach, you and Chris were our best friends. We can't take sides.'

'Sides? Sides? What sides? On the one side, he is screwing an intern. On the other side . . . what? What is the second side, Beatrice?'

'There are always two sides to everything in marriage. And, love, you really mustn't let your anger get in the way.' Bea put her hand on Rachel's. 'Try and get through this with your dignity intact.' She smiled, gave Rachel's hand a final squeeze and returned to the mirror, her bag, her lipstick. Through puckered lips she added, 'Tony misses you too, you know.'

'Mmm.' Rachel made for the exit. 'He mentioned that, actually.' The top step made a clanking sound and shook as she stood on it. 'Just now. Out there. When the disgusting old perv was hitting on me.'

And she fell back outside into the wet night.

Dinner

It was a real moment of theatre when the fish-and-chip van drove over the lawn and parked outside the tent. The gales of laughter and gasps of delight would stay with Bubba for a long time. It was the most perfect solution to the terrible crisis of this morning: cheap, cheerful and—most importantly to Bubba—it fitted in with the theme. She did so wish Melissa was here to witness her

179

own success. Not fully integrated yet into the St Ambrose social whirl, the Spencers: staying in the shadows slightly . . . We must bring them in more. Because it was actually amazing what Melissa had pulled off today: not only had she had the brilliant idea in the first place, she even *knew* a fish-and-chip man—imagine! So Bubba was only two degrees of separation away from him too! *Hilarious!*—and finally somehow summoned him out of nowhere, just like that. Bubba would simply have to be her *slave*; her *slave*, practically for *life*.

She stood by the entrance, making sure that everyone got their lovely warm newspaper parcel.

'Well done, Blubber,' said Georgie cheerfully. She seemed to be a little unsteady on her feet. 'Pulled it off in the end. And how much we gonna make, eh?' She wobbled. 'Twenty quid? Twenty-five?'

Another little bead of worry formed and rolled off in the general direction of its mates. 'We stand to make a healthy profit, actually.' No numbers, please. Don't ask for any numbers. Not now, not yet. 'You look great tonight, by the way. Where's this from?' Bubba picked up an edge of Georgie's full round skirt and rubbed the hot-pink fabric between her fingers.

'Place used to be in the High Street. Closhed down, owph, fifteen years ago now. Shame. Nishe place. Never bought a dress since. No need, really. This,' she gave her skirt a little flutter, 'is my dresh.'

'Gosh.' Bubba did, personally, like to shop and indeed this Stella McCartney was new on this evening. Since children, she found that she did require a bit more tailoring, more designer *effort* than once she had.

180

When she looked around the party, Bubba was impressed by how good the women looked tonight, considering how many babies they'd had between them and how many years on the collective clock. Apart from Ashley's mum, of course. Bless her. But with her expert eye Bubba could look at every figure and see straight through to the exercise or dietary regime behind it. It was almost a *gift*, really. She didn't like to bang on about it, it wasn't a party trick or anything, but she could even spot a just-irrigated colon from at least twenty paces. Of course, all secrets safe etc. Anyway, suffice to say, of all the waists around, very few were here by virtue of their own natural elasticity. Rachel probably looked the most sensationally skinny, but in a way that wasn't fair: she was going through a nasty divorce, and that was always just the *best* for weight loss, a nasty divorce. It was technically cheating, really.

But here was Georgie, happy as a clam and who had—well, she had no idea how many children, she was not sure if Georgie herself knew how many children, they were practically the *von Trapps*, they had so many children—wearing some cheapo rubbish from a whole different era and looking sensational. And she'd brushed her hair.

'Don't panic, though.' Georgie took her fish and chips from Will. 'Thanks, babe. Scrummy. Everyone else has bought something just for tonight.' She gestured around the party. 'As far as I am aware, every single dress and pair of shoes has been purchased specially.'

Out comes another little worry bead, thought Bubba nervously.

'Oh, and every leg has been waxed and brow

181

threaded and every nail painted courtesy of our Colette at her delightful shed-slash-spa.'

They both looked over at the Silent-Auction table. Bea was relieving Colette, it seemed, so that she could go and get something to eat. Sweet of her, really, thought Bubba. Bea *could* be really sweet.

'Yup. They've all spent a fortune.' She picked up a chip and spoke through it. 'You can congratulate yourself, old Scrubberdubbadub. You might not have raised a penny for the poor old school, but you've sure given one hell of a boost to the local economy.'

Beads of worry, legions of them, plopping out, plop, plop, plop, rolling everywhere . . .

'Ha. Only joking.'

'Oh Bubba,' interrupted Heather. 'What a party. You are amazing.'

'*Heather!* Look at you. *Transformed.*'

'Thanks. It's new. Hi, Georgie.'

Georgie held out her hand politely. 'Hello. Shorry. Do forgive me. I don't believe we've met.'

*   *   *

Rachel sat alone, elbows on the table, licking the salt and vinegar from each fingertip with sombre deliberation. It had been a day of shocks, the biggest of which was that Jo's Wayne-with-the-disco who 'would turn up' did actually turn up. And yet Jo herself had not. She hadn't been that keen all along, Rachel knew that, but she had said that she would come. And she had bought a ticket. It probably had something to do with Grumpy Steve. Miserable old bugger.

Unlike our Wayne here. Boy, did he know how to get a party started. Freddie Mercury was requesting—at a very high volume—that nobody stopped him then because he was, apparently, havin' a good time . . . Bully for you, thought Rachel. I'm not.

Bea's parents were at the other end of the table, but the music was so loud that it was well within the boundaries of acceptable social behaviour to just wave, smile and stay silently where she was. With a bit of luck, she could just sit here for a bit and then slip away, back home. Even get an early night. The key thing was not to engage with anybody else, and not to draw attention to herself.

Colette came and sat down next to her. She tried her silent smile, cocking her head towards Wayne and his deck, shrugging at the booming noise around them, but Colette was there to talk.

'WON'T BE LONG,' she bellowed into Rachel's ear. 'ANY MINUTE. MY BRILLIANT PLOT IS ABOUT TO COME TO ITS DRAMATIC CONCLUSION.'

It was bad enough sitting on her own while all the tent was getting up to dance; it was even worse to be seen to be sitting on her own talking to Colette. Wayne introduced 'The One, the Only, the Completely Fabulous Gloria Gaynor, Who Will Sur-*vive*', and Rachel noticed that to add to her joy, her mother was tottering over towards them, rubbing her arthritic hip.

'At first I was afraid, I was petrified,'

'OH DO LISTEN, GIRLS,' Bea's mum shouted over to Rachel and Colette. 'WHAT A SCREAM.

HE'S PLAYING YOUR SONG.'

And whoomph: Rachel's mum went straight into battle. 'OH NO, PAMELA. YOU'VE GOT IT ALL WRONG,' she bellowed back over the table. 'IT'S ONLY A TRIAL SEPARATION. THEY'RE JUST WORKING THINGS OUT.'

'Mu-um. God'sake,' said Rachel, but through teeth so clenched her mother couldn't hear her.

'I should have made you leave your key,'

'THAT'S WHAT YOU SHOULD DO, RACHEL.' She pointed to Gloria Gaynor's imaginary door while jigging along in her seat. 'DON'T HAVE HIM BACK, WHATEVER YOU DO. I DON'T LIKE THE SOUND OF WHERE HE'S BEEN.'

Bea's dad intervened, clearly urging some sort of caution before proceeding down that particular route, but Pamela was not for turning.

'APPARENTLY SHE'S HAD A SPOT OF BOTHER, HIS BIT ON THE SIDE, WHOEVER SHE MAY BE.'

What? Rachel was racking her brains to think what on earth the mad old trout was on about.

'PAMELA, WHAT DO YOU MEAN?' Rachel's mother went straight in, head-first.

'A NASTY CASE OF SOMETHING VIRAL. MOST UNPLEASANT. THAT'S WHAT I HEARD, ANYWAY.'

Bea's dad got up and went.

'OH, *RACHEL*.' Her mum turned on her with dismay. 'HOW *COULD* YOU?'

'WHAT? DON'T BE RIDICULOUS, MOTHER. IT'S NOT MY FAULT.'

184

Her mother still sported a disappointed look.

'AND SHE HASN'T ANYWAY.'

Both old busybodies were turned on her now, eyebrows raised.

'IT'S NOT EVEN TRUE.'

Excellent. Here we go, thought Rachel. Now I'm the Great Defender of the Bloody Intern. Thank you, Mother.

'IT WAS JUST ONE OF GEORGIE'S STUPID JOKES. SHE HASN'T *REALLY* GOT'

The music stopped, the mike started to crackle, the tent fell silent. Rachel seemed to be having an out-of-body experience. She was somewhere up on the cobalt and white striped ceiling, with the fishing nets. She was looking down, she could see herself quite clearly. Yet somehow, she could do nothing to intervene.

'GENITAL WARTS.'

'Fascinating though that sounds,' announced Mark Green to the stunned crowd.

Some feedback in the sound system gave a little shriek.

'. . . it is now time to put you out of your collective misery. At last, we have '—Wayne put on a little drum-roll—'the Results of the Silent Auction. And here to give us the results is the One, the Only'—the drums rolled again—'ANDY FARR!'

And then there was another roll, of thunder this time, and an ear-splitting crack. It was almost overhead. And when it finished, yet more rain hurled itself towards the Greens' garden with a ferocity that Rachel had not heard for years.

The Silent Auction

Bubba looked on as Andy Farr took to the little stage. She could not help but notice there was a little rustle among the ball-goers. They were all so excited to have someone like Andy among them, which was really sweet. Bubba hadn't realised that so many people would be so aware of late-night history programmes on BBC4, but that was St Ambrose for you. Not just one big happy family: one big *brainy* happy family. *So* much *cleverer* than those in the private sector.

Bea was passing him the notes on the lots, and the winners. Bubba had thought that it had all been Colette's baby, the Silent Auction, but she was sitting down next to Rachel, with excitement all over her face. Ever so sweet.

Some of the things that had been put up were—whilst being really, really generous and though every little did of course help just so much—not actually that, well, glamorous. But still, Rachel's mum was obvs over the *moon* with Georgie's half a pig and the headmaster had nicely bought Rachel's mum's year's supply of honey. Heather's offer to cook a dinner party for six went to Heather's husband, which was sweet. He must really love her cooking. Adorable. The week in Bubba's Cornish cottage went to the Farrs, which was kind of them. Bubba had been slightly hoping for a sort of St Ambrose club-together on that one. It was very much a cottage—it was where they went for their absolute back-to-basics, *total* Bear Grylls—but it did sleep fourteen to sixteen. Although the pool was mi-*nute*. She hoped it was grand enough for the Farrs . . .

'Lot number six: one day of pampering in the Serenity Spa Sanctuary Beauty Therapy Suite, kindly donated by Colette. Thanks, Colette. It sounds fantastic, ladies, but only one lucky winner and that is'—Andy leaned in to the mike and looked out at the tent—'Rachel Mason.'

Bubba was pleased. Rachel did actually look fabulous tonight. That plain black halter-neck looked incredible with her red hair and slim, pale shoulders. But generally, Bubba felt, she did not make the best of herself. Perhaps this was the beginning of her own personal new dawn. Although at the moment she was frowning and looking baffled. And sort of screwing her nose up . . .

'And lot number seven: lunch in London with the TV celebrity Andy Farr'—Andy smiled—'kindly donated by . . . the TV celebrity Andy Farr.' Bubba led a smattering of applause. 'And the lucky winner is . . . Once again, Rachel Mason!' Everybody clapped. Rachel held both arms out, bent at the wrist, in a kind of er-hello-what's-going-on? sort of way.

'I'm looking forward to it too, Rachel. And now, the final lot of the evening, dinner with the headmaster at the new French place in the High Street, kindly donated by the headmaster.' Much more interest in the tent for this than the last lot, Bubba noticed. Which was odd. Colette was sitting up straight and grinning widely. 'And the winner is . . .' Wayne—good old Wayne, *such* a laugh— did another drum-roll, 'as if we couldn't guess, our local millionairess . . . RACHEL MASON!'

Bubba was so touched. She did like Rachel,

really felt a natural bond. It was lovely that she had shelled out so much on making tonight a success. Bubba tottered over to congratulate her on her purchases—*so* happy for her. She was surprised to encounter something of an atmosphere.

'Hello? Excuse me? What the fuck?' Rachel was hissing to Colette. 'What the actual fucking fuck just happened to me?'

'I might ask you the same thing.' Colette stood up. 'Thanks a bunch, sister. Thanks a bloody bunch. How could you?'

'I didn't—'

'You knew I'd set up that date for me and Tom. And you know how much I was prepared to pay to get it. I cannot believe you snatched it away from me like that. And where are you getting all this money from, that's what we want to know?'

'I didn't bid for anything, Colette. I haven't got any money. And I don't want your bloody date. My avowed intention is never to go on another date for the rest of my life. I didn't do it. This is a'

She was looking wildly around. Bea—Bubba just happened to notice—was standing in the corner watching them all. Wearing a secret, knowing sort of smile.

'set-up.'

Then Tony Stuart, on his way to the bar, leaned in to them and sort of slurped, 'Well aren't you just the moneybags, Rachel? I think my mate Chris had better get himself a better lawyer.'

And Mark was suddenly with them and stage-whispering, 'Rachel, listen, sorry about that. Just that nobody had put in a bid for lunch with Andy. He didn't seem to float the St Ambrose boat, and I'm not surprised. He's a right little prick.'

'*Mark!*'

'Sorry, love. But I bought it, didn't I? Someone bleedin' had to.' He patted Bubba on the back.

Then Heather slipped into position next to her. 'That's a present from us—the spa day!' She beamed into Rachel's really quite ashen face. 'Are you thrilled? We all clubbed together! You know how I was saying Colette was just desperate to get her hands on you?'

'Hey. I hear congratulations are in order.' Georgie swung towards them, toasting Rachel with an almost empty glass. 'To genital warts! Thought I was making 'em up but Destiny's mum says it's all true!'

Dancing

Georgie and Will had taken to the dance floor for 'Walking on Sunshine'. Rachel watched them dreamily, and she wasn't the only one. Their performance was attracting quite a bit of attention. It wasn't just that they were both such good dancers. It was that together they looked really, well, hot. In fact, they were practically shagging.

There were quite a lot of people dancing now. Even the grumpy secretary, with Wayne-with-the-disco gyrating behind her, doing a slightly unsavoury charade of grinding his pelvis into her bottom. They too were practically shagging, but Rachel's mind did not want to go there.

She returned her focus to the Martins. They were such an advert for the state of marriage, those two; they should be put on a billboard to promote it to a disenchanted nation. Even before her own ugly dramas—when Rachel had thought herself to be loved, in love, generally content—she had not always liked to look upon the spectacle of most other marriages in the raw: couples sitting in restaurants in a cloud of silence, or dragging around the shops with tetchy boredom. All those people might think themselves to be perfectly happy, yet their marriages never looked so great, it seemed to her, in the beholding eye.

'Dancing in the Moonlight' was on now, which Rachel knew to be a favourite over at Martin's Farm. Georgie was spinning around Will, and he was gazing at her with a mixture of adoration and open lust. How do they work, these relationships that go on and on for year upon year without any fatigue or dissatisfaction? Perhaps they never quite move on, or never notice that they have moved on. Looking at Will, looking at Georgie, Rachel could see that he was seeing the girl he had first fallen in love with. The eyes of someone who met her tonight for the first time would take in a great long list of marks and stains upon her appearance, from age and childbirth, hard bloody work and sheer neglect. They would look and see a woman bedding down into middle age. But his eyes weren't seeing that. His eyes were clearly seeing all the way back to how she was before.

It had been the same thing with Rachel's old family home, the one she had grown up in. They had all loved it for years—it was still her ideal house—and when all the children had left home and her parents had decided to sell it, they sort of presumed it would go for a fortune; that someone else would love it as they had done. So they were all shocked when the estate agent billed it as 'in need of modernisation' and listed all the cracks and droops and failings and general out-of-dateness of it. The decline had happened so gradually that none of them had even noticed. They had fallen in love with the place when they moved in and they had never had cause to revisit their original opinion. That's how Will and Georgie were with each other. And obviously, now, that would never happen to Rachel. It was too late. She was officially past it. Who would ever take her on these days, with her droops and failings and out-of-dateness?

'Good-evening. I thought I'd better come and say hello, as you were kind enough to spend so much on the privilege.'

'Ah. Mr Orchard. Thanks so much for coming over.' Rachel was about to make an arse of herself again, she could just feel it. 'A few things,' she coughed in a businesslike way, 'to clear up.'

'Tell you what, call me Tom. Seeing as how you went over the three-figure mark—'

Three figures?

'I think I might just throw in a first name.'

'Ah. Well, you see, I didn't. This is all frightfully embarrassing but I didn't want to, you know, buy you at all. And I didn't, in fact.'

'Is that right?' Tom thrust his hands into the trousers of his DJ in what was, Rachel thought, quite a dishy sort of way. 'Well I'll let you in on a little secret. You might not believe this, but . . .' he leaned towards her, turned sideways and whispered out of the corner of his mouth, 'I didn't actually want to be put up for sale.'

'Oh. God. Sorry. Course you didn't. I'm having this really rubbish time . . .'

He drew up a chair and sat beside her, right foot

191

on left knee. 'Bet you mine's a whole lot worse.'

'At the risk of offending you yet again, I really don't think it can be.' And out poured everything: Tony Stuart's pouncing, the Unfortunate Incident of the Mothers and the Warts, the horrors of the auction and the set-up by Bea. He laughed quite a bit along the way, but she thought she could forgive him. She even thought that she might laugh about it all herself. One day.

And then he reached for her hand and pulled her up. 'OK. You win. But come on. Everyone's staring. We've only got one course of action left at this particular juncture.

'I think we should dance.'

Carriages

Bubba was very tired and pretty tipsy so perhaps not all her reflexes were on top alert. She was watching Rachel and the headmaster, who were still dancing—and chatting and laughing—together even though the fast track had become a slow one . . . The first inkling that something was going horribly, catastrophically wrong went right over her light head.

'Bubba, you're even cleverer than I thought,' Jasmine shouted at her over the music. 'Lolz!'

'Awesome!' bellowed Sharon. 'You've got the tide coming in!'

Bubba smiled and lifted her glass in response. It was lolz. And she was awesome, actually, wasn't she? It had gone *so* well. It was actually *brilliant* to have a beach party in December. She gave a little wiggle of her hips. Everyone was in the mood for it. She shuffled around a bit, in an attempt at solo slow-dancing. Mark was perfect in every way, but for some odd reason she could never get him near a dance floor. So now I've got the tide coming in! That *is* clever, isn't it? Because, you see, it goes with the theme. Sensational! I *am*, as Jasmine says, *so* clever.

And then, suddenly, the dance floor started to empty, and more than a few people started shrieking about shoes and dresses and someone mentioned an inability to swim. And then the music stopped and Wayne was pulling out plugs as fast as he could and lifting up his equipment but when he put some large black box on top of one of the tables everything seemed to sink and then people were running—no, not running, they were *wading*, really fast *wading*—to the door and up to higher ground.

So it *isn't* a pond, she thought calmly to herself as the water level rose and the chairs down at one end started to lift up and sort of bob, bob, bob around. It *is* a lake—not quite the size of Windermere, it's true, but a serious body of water. Definitely a serious body of water. So serious, the hem of her Stella McCartney was now completely underwater. And then lots of little beads of worry—far too many to count—started to rush out and tie her up in knots and this was it, here they came, they were all going to come and throttle her. Or could it be that she was just drowning?

*   *   *

It had been a strenuous couple of hours. Everyone else had fled, in a state of some panic. Bubba, hysterical, had been bundled off by Mark and somehow it seemed to be left to Rachel and Tom Orchard to deal with the crisis. Tomasz and Kazia had stayed, of course; they had been brilliant. Tomasz was beside himself. He said that he had been wanting to fortify the banks of the lake since he'd started work for them, and that he knew it would flood with a rise in the water table, but 'Mrs Green she does not listen.' Eventually Tom had sent them tottering off to bed too.

So now it was just the two of them, alone. They had salvaged as much as they could and were now collapsed, worn out, on a pile of rolled-up carpeting at the back of the marquee. They lay there together, side by side like holidaymakers on an atoll, beneath the stretched-out fishing nets and the cobalt sky, relaxing while the gentle waters lapped around them.

'Should've brought a picnic, really,' said Tom, leaning back. 'Silly of me. Didn't think.'

'Well, you'll know next time. We at St Ambrose generally like to end our evenings like this.' Rachel slipped off her sandals—ruined—and looked down at her bare feet. She rather wished she had indeed gone for a mani-pedi over at the Serenity Shed. 'Whenever possible.'

'Do you know, I used to think you threw a fund-raiser for a tsunami—'

'But now you know it can also work the other way round.'

They giggled. She tucked her toes under the wet hem of her long dress.

'It's your first headship, isn't it? Experience is everything.'

'Tell you what: the learning curve is a little steeper than I had anticipated. All those training courses did nothing to prepare me.'

'So, um, where were you before this?' At last, her opportunity: the pop star, the footballer, the punch . . . ?

'Well, I started out as a teacher, then had a quick detour into the City for all the obvious reasons. Did that for a bit, and then really felt the urge to, you know, give something back.'

'So a bit like when you're on the motorway, and there isn't a petrol station and you have to come off the motorway to fill up, so that you can get back on it again and get on with your journey?'

'Exactly.' Tom picked up a bottle that came bobbing past on a wave. 'Except not quite.' He took a swig. 'Because my girlfriend decided she'd stay in the petrol station, as it were, rather than get back on the motorway—'

'Ah.' Pop star by any chance?

'—and that she would be keeping fifty per cent of the metaphorical petrol. For her own separate metaphorical tank.'

What, no triangle of lurve? That Destiny in Year 3—she's a right fibber. Still, this version was pretty riveting. But at that moment Mark Green came sloshing back in. They both pulled themselves up, perhaps a bit too quickly.

'Nah, nah, don't bother to get up. Give her one for me.'

'Oh! Gosh! No! We were just—'

'Bloody relief to see someone actually enjoying themselves, to be honest. Fuck a nun sideways.' Tom and Rachel each gave a startled, synchronised little jump. 'Got to hand it to my missus.' He looked about him. 'Full of surprises.'

'Oh dear.' Rachel sank back again. 'How is

Bubba?'

'She was pretty pissed anyway, so I threw some sleeping pills into the mix and now she's mercifully out of it. But she keeps muttering numbers in her sleep—three thousand divided by twenty and ten thousand minus twelve thousand and all sorts of crap and I thought'—he tapped the side of his head—'I know what's going on here. She's worried about the profit side of things.'

'That's sort of understandable,' said Rachel, looking around at the debris. 'There are going to be a few insurance issues, I shouldn't wonder.'

Mark brandished his chequebook. 'Yeah, well. I can't take any more of this. I've had it up to here. Having to buy that up-himself bugger Farr in the auction was the last bloody straw.' He leaned on the table and started to write. 'This should do it.'

He handed the cheque to Tom, who took one look and began to protest.

'Nope. Take it. Give it a good home. But I only give it to you on two conditions.'

Tom propped himself up on one elbow and nodded.

'One: I never hear any mention of this bloody ball ever again.'

'I think that might be a relief for all concerned.'

'And two: I take my kids out at the end of the summer term. I'll clear it with Bubba much later on. But I tell you, they're going back to yet another nice toffee-nosed fucking academy for the offspring of vulgar arseholes where you don't have to do a fucking thing but show up and flash your wad about and that's that. Christ, I can't afford any more of this state-school shit. One more year of it and we'll all be in the sodding workhouse.'

And with that he turned and sloshed back out again, away from the drooping tent, back presumably to the ravings of his unconscious wife.

Rachel and Tom sat on their carpet atoll in silence, listening to the whooshing sound of the departing wellies. When she was sure the coast was clear, Rachel said, 'Bubba was worried, when she chose St Ambrose, that we might be a little *"rough* and *sweary"* for the Green family, but she was willing to take a risk . . .'

'Glad they did, though,' said Tom, showing her the cheque. 'Look at that.'

Rachel gave a low whistle. 'You might get your library after all, then.'

'*Our* library.' Tom stood up and pulled Rachel to her feet. 'I mean, everybody's library. Yeah. And you get to do your timeline!'

Gulp. The sodding timeline. 'Ah. Yes. Jolly good.' Totally forgotten about that . . .

'I'm sure it will be fantastic. Have you started work at all?' He took off his jacket and wrapped it round her bare shoulders. 'You'll need this.'

Together they waded out of the marquee. 'Sort of, you know, early thoughts . . .' Not a bloody jotting. Hell. She flicked each leg at the knee to get her sandals back on, and then they walked back to the road. 'But now we know it's definitely happening . . .' the rain had stopped now, but the air was chilled, 'I can start properly getting down to it . . .'

Rachel got into her car and handed back the jacket. 'Anyway, um, thank you—'

'No, no.' Tom, smiling, leaned in as he held the door. 'Thank you'—he straightened up—'for what was a truly memorable evening.'

197

They laughed. She pulled the door in. He waved. She drove herself home. There you are, Mother, she thought with a smile. I have made a whole new friend.

MONDAY MORNING

8.50 A.M. DROP-OFF

Rachel walked up the hill, hearing Heather twittering on about something or other but not really listening. There was a minor malfunction with her concentration this morning. The world seemed to have slightly tipped on its axis. She was feeling a bit dizzy, had lost her bearings. When they got to the playground, the little gathering was already there under the tree, humming.

'Hi,' said—who? Jasmine? Sharon? Someone or other. 'We were just going over it all. Performing the autopsy. Wasn't it a complete disaster?'

'Mmm? What? What was a complete disaster?' Rachel couldn't think for a moment. 'Oh. The ball. Was it?' She pointed Poppy towards the door with a floaty gesture. 'You think so? I thought it was all rather . . . wonderful.'

'Glad to hear someone got something out of the evening,' Georgie said with meaning, and narrowed eyes. 'I wonder what it was? Going to share it with the rest of the class, are we?'

'Funnily enough,' chipped in Jasmine, 'my Richard said if only he'd known it was fish and chips and home for half-ten he would've looked forward to it more.'

'Ssssh. Act normal. Here she comes.'

They watched as Bubba's Range Rover drove into the car park at a snail's pace. She emerged with the children, and dragged behind them as they made their way into school. Her hair was

199

unwashed; it had not recently been brushed. She wore tracksuit bottoms and a droopy maroon cardigan. 'Pssst,' Heather whispered to the others. 'Look. Furry slippers.' Her sunglasses covered her eyes, but the rest of her face was unmade-up, and ashen.

'Poor thing . . .' said one.

'She seems . . .' trailed off another.

'She looks . . .' tried Heather.

There was only one person who could actually put a finger on it.

'She looks,' Georgie said briskly, 'just like one of us.'

Georgie's mobile rang and she passed the baby to Heather while she dug into her pocket to find it.

'Ye—

'Wha—?'

There was something terrible in the tone of her voice. They all turned away from Bubba and clustered around Georgie.

'I'm coming. OK, love? I'll be there.'

She lowered the phone and raised wide, blue, terrified eyes to the group. Her face was contorted with panic.

'That was Jo.

'It's Steve.'

Her voice broke. She was trying to say something but it wasn't coming out clearly. They only caught the last word.

'. . . suicide.'

9 A.M. ASSEMBLY

The school bell had rung a while ago, but nobody

200

had moved. The adrenalin-shot panic in the immediate wake of Jo's call had given way to a deep, dull collective misery. Rachel stood, a little apart from the others, pinned to the spot, incapable of speech. There goes another one, was all she kept thinking: another seemingly normal St Ambrose family picked off and blown to pieces by the violent, mindless hooligan that is fate.

She looked around. The morning was gloomy so the school was lit from within; the arched, church-like windows shining with a confident glow. Rachel stared at it, wondering at how it could still stand there, just going on, as if nothing had happened. St Ambrose was, after all, no more than the composite of its families; they were its DNA. It is only what it is, she thought, because of us. Because our little individual units have miraculously chosen to combine together. We are the cellular structure, the building blocks, of the school. And yet these cells are all so fragile. They keep splitting. Molecules keep dying. How much more of this can the place take before it, too, starts to change, or decay?

The group under the tree had grown and Rachel was now gathered in. Most, like her, were silent. Only the dimmest among them felt there was something to say.

'Poor kids.'

'But my boys are in the same Sunday team as their boys. They saw Steve every week.'

'And a week before Christmas . . .'

Rachel was grateful for her inability to comprehend the horror of a suicidal depression, but she could just about grasp that, if Steve had been locked in ferocious battle with his demons, it

201

would have been a struggle to hold them off just for the sake of a bit of turkey and a cracker. The black, bleak awfulness of it all was overwhelming, and she felt trapped, suffocated, by the group pressing in around her. She stood there, with the rest of the herd, shivering, like the rest of the herd, unable to escape. She listened as they exchanged little anecdotes—'*I've* known them since NCT'—their credentials that they might claim this tragedy as, in part, their own. All Rachel wanted to do was get home, slump down and sob, alone. If only she could move . . .

Georgie suddenly lifted her head, sharp and alert—a wild animal with the scent of danger. For a moment Rachel was worried she was going to pick a fight. She certainly wouldn't put it past her. But no. Her eyes were narrowed, her nostrils flaring. She was taut and focused on what was going on over by the prefab, at the entrance to the school.

'I do not believe this. Tell me this is not true. What. The. F—' And off she flew, with the group falling in behind her.

Bea was standing by the door, holding a clipboard and wearing black. Her eyes were dry, but her features were neatly arranged into the accustomed positions of grief. She spoke to another parent in a murmur—'Thank you, that's kind. It is very hard. A *lovely* family. A *terrible* shock'— and wrote down a name. Then she saw Georgie's approach.

'Oh Georgie, I'm *so* sorry to be the one to have to break it to you. I'm afraid I have some tragic, *tragic* news. Steve—that's, you know, Jo's husband?—has . . .'

'Thank you. So much.' Georgie's voice was

thickened by tears, but plenty loud enough. 'I do know who Jo's husband is. And I do know the tragic news . . .'

Bea put her hand to her chest. 'Well that's a relief for *me*, at least.' She shook her head and smoothed away her hair. 'This really is one of the hardest mornings I've ever had to—'

'But how do you, eh? How on *earth* do you do it, Bea? She only just found him. She hasn't even managed to get hold of his brother yet. So how come *you* know it all?'

Bea took a few paces back towards the prefab wall. Georgie advanced on her.

'You're like one of those tabloid creeps who's written up the story before it even happens.'

A proper crowd was gathering now.

'Have you got an ambulance crew on retainer? Have you got a mole in the police? Eh?'

She was right in Bea's face, and hissing into it.

'You don't like Jo and she does not like you. You never knew Steve. You know nothing, nothing about their lives. How dare you stand there with your clipboard, dressed like an undertaker, and act like this is anything, anything whatsoever, to do with you?'

Rachel was just about to burst into spontaneous and what would have been quite shockingly inappropriate applause when she was saved by Mrs Black, the school secretary, opening the front door.

'Ah.' She too had clearly been crying. 'I can see you've all heard already. The headmaster is very keen to deal with this as carefully as he can within the school. So he has asked me to come and see if Mrs . . .'

She paused as she put her glasses on to read

203

from the spiral-topped notebook. Her hand was shaking. The assembly on the tarmac held its breath. Georgie clenched her fists. Bea started to reach towards the school steps, as if she were in the final throes of drowning and Mrs Black a rope.

'. . . Spencer? Yes, Melissa Spencer might be willing to come in and offer her expert support to him at this horrible, difficult time.'

SPRING TERM

SPRING TERM

THE FIRST DAY OF TERM

8.45 A.M. DROP-OFF

'And a happy new year to you all.' The day was vague and sluggish; it was not yet quite light. Rachel's breath turned to cloud as it hit the chilly gloom.

'Thanks but, you know what?' Heather was chewing her lip, shaking her head as they fell into step. 'I've got a really bad feeling about this one myself.'

'Jolly good. That's the spirit. Have you ever thought of applying to be a ray of sunshine? You'd be a bloomin' natural.'

'Sorry. I'm sorry. Happy new year.'

'More like it. Personally, I feel I'm owed one, as last year was so spectacularly crap.'

Poppy and Maisie were holding hands and skipping up ahead. How lucky they were, to be able to just bond together like that.

'OK.' Rachel linked her arm through Heather's and softened her tone. 'Take me through what's bothering you and let's see how much we can get sorted by the time we get to school.'

'Rachel, you are brilliant. Aren't friends just the best? I missed you in the break. I feel better already.'

Of course, it went without thinking that Heather was wet. Sopping. Wringing. So Rachel was becoming increasingly alarmed by their mutual sympathies. But once again, she had found the school holidays almost purgatorial; at most a

207

half-life. Her first post-Chris Christmas—a rushed lunch, a sticky pick-up, then a joyless, toyless, endless afternoon with her mum on the sofa, the Queen on the telly and an increasingly hopeless struggle to tell them apart. Yes she had survived it, but only just. And those quiet dead days afterwards. Josh off on the school ski trip. Poppy with a horrid cold. It really was, honestly, good to be back.

'Right, here goes.' Heather took a deep breath. 'Number one: Bea sent a text last night saying "Exercise tomoz. Gentle start. Walk the dogs" and then an x and a puffed-out face.'

'O-K. Just for scale, is that the absolute worst of your problems, cos'—Rachel raised her arms to her face, a shield from the full horror, and started to tremble—'I'm not sure I can take any more . . .'

'BUT I HAVEN'T GOT A DOG!' Heather wailed. 'I've always wanted one, always, but Guy's allergic so we never got one and now look . . .'

'All right. Steady on. Well, what's our schedule here? Nine? So buying one is out. We could nick that half-dead smelly one from The Old Stables, on the way up. Or, last-ditch but worth a thought: why not just go on the walk, without a dog, and see if anyone even gives a shit?'

Heather's face cleared. 'And you think they won't mind?'

'Hey. Trust me. Next?'

'Oh dear.' Heather had that scrunched-up look again. 'Well, the thing is, I happen to know, it's Bea's fortieth the Friday after next'

That's right, thought Rachel. So it is. This time last year we went out for an Indian, just the four of us. Bea had said that was all she wanted.

'and of course we all ought to be doing

something. But no one's started organising it yet'

Or they have and they're not asking you. Or, obviously, me . . .

'so should I mention it to someone? Colette? Or even Tony? I've sort of met him. Ish. Or should I step in myself? Am I the person? Should I be The Organiser?'

Rachel doubted that very much, unless there had been a recent local nuclear wipe-out and she'd missed it. But she was determined not to expend a kilocalorie of precious energy on Bea Stuart's Happy Birthday.

'You must remember,' she said patiently, 'things are different for Bea now. What with—'

'Of course!' Heather slapped her gloved hand over her mouth. 'You're so right. The Job!'

'Indeed. The job. And what else, the . . .?' Rachel hoisted Poppy's games bag on to her shoulder and mimed the keeping of balls in the air, making the odd helpful *thwok* noise when pretend-catching one.

'The juggling!'

'Correct-a-mondo. The juggling. The likes of you and me, we just can't begin to know what it's like. So let's just wait and see . . .' Hours of fun to be had with this one. Would a HAPPY 40TH BEA banner at the roundabout be pushing it? Rachel smiled. It would be nice . . . 'Right. Next.'

They had now arrived at school. It had got as light as it was going to, and the sky was cold and flat, a uniform grey. Small children, big coats and huge bags were dragging towards the door, or being dragged there by pinched, exhausted parents. Milo Green was sobbing as Kazia coaxed him from the car. There was no trace of back-to-school

209

excitement in the playground this term.

'This one isn't so easy, I'm afraid.' Heather looked like she might cry. 'It's Jo.'

'Ah. Yeah. There's some helpful perspective for us . . .' Rachel could cry herself.

'I don't know what to do. I think about them all the time, all the time. Christmas Day, and Boxing Day and New Year's Eve and all the days in between I thought about her, and those kids and what they're going through, and my heart aches, just aches for them. But I haven't done anything. I tried to write a note but it was all wrong. So I've done a big shop to make a meal—you know, a family meal, something comforting, like we all did when Laura, the twins' mum, you know, passed. But should I do that? I mean, what's happening, do you think? What exactly are we all doing?'

Instinctively, reflexively, Rachel looked over to Bea. She was, of course, under the beech tree— looking neither pinched nor exhausted—swaddled in a cocoon of chocolate-coloured nylon and fake fur, surrounded by women in tracksuits with dogs. But she was not holding her clipboard. Indeed, Rachel realised with a start, she did not even seem to have a pen.

'Well,' Rachel began uncertainly. She too had done nothing, and it weighed heavily. She had meant to do something, wanted so much to do something, knew she should do something. And yet hadn't. She had just left Jo as another thing-to-do, in her emotional in-tray, for the whole of the holidays. 'I know Georgie is round with her today. They're finally able to organise the funeral, and Jo wanted some moral support when the vicar came round.'

'I think I will cook for them. Pop it over. I mean, we always do do something. It's what St Ambrose is famous for.' Heather, with her eyes on the women under the tree, and the pack of dogs, was chewing her lip again. 'After all, we are one big happy family.'

10 A.M. MORNING BREAK

Georgie sat on the hard, resistant sofa and looked around. The walls were bare. There were no pictures, no bookshelves, no printed matter to be seen—it was an entirely characterless space that took the war against pretentiousness to a whole new level. The only object adorning Jo's sitting room was the enormous blank television screen, standing proud against the far wall like an altar. Nothing was quite as Georgie had anticipated, and right then, she was feeling slightly uncomfortable. Jo was just as pale and exhausted and unkempt as anyone would expect, but she was also, unexpectedly, aggressively bullish. And although Georgie was quite prepared to offer moral support—she was desperate to do anything to help—she wasn't sure if it was Jo who needed it, or the poor vicar.

'Look, I'm sorry, no offence, Rev—'

'Please. Do call me Debbie.'

'—but we're not having it in church, that's that and stop wasting your breath. I'm not great at God at the best of times—and Steve could never stand the old sod—and right now I just don't want to have anything to do with Him. Know what I mean? Look at us. We're in a right bleeding mess now. Me, the boys, the money, the house . . .' She broke off, gulped, carried on. 'Are you getting my drift? I'm like, yeah, cheers, God. Thanks for everything, God. Thanks a bloody bunch.'

The vicar put her mug of extra-strength PG Tips down on the patterned carpet and her hands on her knees. This, thought Georgie, should be interesting. After all, they did have to declare their Christian faith to get into St Ambrose in the first place. School custom dictated that parents like Jo, whose homes clung to the margins of the catchment area, should observe a level of devotion that would have Thomas à Becket hanging up his hair shirt. The Reverend Debbie took all that very seriously indeed. In ordinary circumstances, no parent would ever dare to out their doubts in front of a school governor, of all people.

'It is always difficult to find the hand of God in the darkest moments of your grief . . .'

But these circumstances were, of course, extraordinary: when one parent comes home from a night shift to find the other parent hanging, cold, in the garage. Jo was currently struggling, thrashing, choking her way through something beyond our worst nightmares. Georgie bit her lip. She mustn't cry here, now, with Jo beside her. But how, she wondered, will any of us ever be normal around her again?

She looked over at the sideboard, where Steve's face was still grinning back from the happier times of his life, when he didn't know what was coming down the pike to hit him: Steve with Ollie as a baby; Steve with Freddie in matching football strips; Steve, sunburned and pissed with his blokey mates, sharing a Liverpool scarf. Nothing of Steve with Jo, but that was family life for you: one parent vanished, invisible, behind the lens.

'So if we do opt for just the crematorium—' The vicar was trying again.

'We've opted.'

'—we can still include a religious element in the service. Favourite family hymns and so forth? Some people like to revisit hymns and prayers from their wedding?'

Steve and Jo did get married, quite recently— when he was made redundant the time before this one, and a financial adviser had told them to get on with it. But it had just been the two of them, down at the Town Hall, while the boys were at swimming. On the Monday morning at school, Jo had said with some satisfaction that they'd been done, dusted and home in time for *Football Focus*. So there weren't even any old wedding photos, sadly. Georgie would love just a glimpse of them together, younger, happier, before family life snuck up on them like a mugger and robbed them of their individual identities.

'Or "Abide With Me", then? That can be a comfort.'

'Chrissakes, Debbie. It's not the bloomin' Cup Final.'

Georgie hadn't known Jo for that long—just five years, since Ollie and Kate started Reception. But in many ways, she thought she knew her more intimately than closer friends she'd had for decades. She knew her favourite sweets (Gummy Bears, inexplicably—and a matter of furious debate) and the state of her sex life (non-existent) and that of her pelvic floor (shot to pieces). They met every single day, generally twice, often more; plenty of time to pore over the fine print of each other's lives,

213

plus footnotes. And so much more than Georgie ever got to spend with even her dearest soulmates from college. That must be three times a year, if they were lucky, at meetings so rushed they had to shout the news from their lives in banner headlines: 'PREGNANT!' 'CHUCKED HIM!' 'PREGNANT AGAIN!'

And yet, sitting here on Jo's sofa this morning, she was struck by how much she did not, or had not, known. She had never been in this lounge before, for example. Georgie knew nothing about the rest of the house, had never penetrated beyond its kitchen door. She had only ever existed in her friend's everyday. Her normal. Her humdrum. She couldn't begin to imagine how Jo might cope with something as abnormal and monstrous as this. After all, though she had known that Steve was depressed, and that Jo was finding him difficult, Georgie had had no idea that things were so awful that they might even come to this. Because, most importantly, she realised, as she looked around his house, at his wife, at his things, she had not actually known Steve at all.

*　　　*　　　*

Heather stood in the kitchen, eyeing up two different lasagne dishes. One was too big, definitely—she didn't want to burden Jo with leftovers or extra wet-food recycling. But the smaller one was a bit of a useful old favourite—she would definitely like it back at some stage and didn't want to burden Jo with having the bother of returning that. How much did they eat, she wondered? There were two boys round there, sports-mad, and Jo did

214

like her food; that was a well-known fact. But would they even have an appetite right now at this terrible time? It was all very tricky, and she did so want to get it right.

She felt a little unguided, to be honest. Without a proper rota, she was just sort of swirling around. Nobody was blaming Bea for not doing one, of course, after Georgie practically beat her up in the playground that horrible morning that Steve . . . she couldn't even bear to think about it . . . But they did all feel the same. They'd talked it through on the walk earlier, and there had been general agreement: no blame, but lots of swirling.

On the other hand, Heather did have to admit that rotas did not always work to her own particular advantage. When nice Pat down the road got pancreatic cancer, she put herself down to do the drive in for the chemo, but that gang who lived in the turning circle had just gone and grabbed the first few weeks for themselves even though they didn't know the poor old soul from a piece of cheese. And then Pat had gone and died, very sadly, before they had even got to Heather on the list. Which she still thought was a real shame, because they had both always really enjoyed their little chats. And that reminded her of something else: Laura's twins and the Brownies drop-off. Heather still hadn't had her turn with them yet, thank you very much, and she had been on the waiting list for months. It was always the same people that got picked, in her experience, and while it was nice that everyone wanted to do their bit—and that was what was so really lovely about St Ambrose, after all—it was also nice for everybody who wanted one to get a go.

The smaller dish: that's what she would go for. If a job's worth doing . . . It was much nicer to look at, and there was plenty there for three hungry people. Ah—help!—not dishwasher-proof. Still, she'd stick a little Post-it on the foil on the top, with just the briefest of washing instructions, and saying that she'd come round and pick it up in a couple of days. That would be all right. She hoped it would be all right, anyway. She certainly didn't want to do anything that might add to Jo's grief . . .

*　　　*　　　*

I knew everything about him, Georgie was thinking, and yet I knew nothing at all: intimately familiar, and yet completely remote. Like a celeb, almost: she had the same relationship with Steve as she did with any member of the celebrity first division. She was kept constantly updated on where they were, what they were up to, their likes, their dislikes, in everything from the bedroom, via the wardrobe, to the kitchen. The private facts of their lives were all around her, in the ether, and she seemed to have to absorb them, breathe them in, whether she wanted to or not. But she did not actually know the people themselves. OK, she had seen a bit more of Jo's Steve than she had of Becks or Clooney—if you were going to nit-pick—but not enough to write home about.

It was the same with all the dads at school: they were present, of course, and turned up at the school gates all the time—so much more than her dad ever had, which wasn't hard as that was precisely never. But they didn't loiter or chat beyond the rudimentary. They were fantastic about their own

216

kids, but they did not seem to share our biological reflex to retain infinite amounts of extraneous information about the children of others. They didn't remember each other's birthdays or move in at times of emergency. Loads of them had seen Steve every Saturday at Lads and Dads footie. But apparently not one had noticed that he was even fed up, let alone suicidal.

Georgie continued to sit in silence while Jo and the Reverend Debbie wrestled over the funeral. There had been a rare moment of harmony over 'You'll Never Walk Alone', which politely ticked both boxes, the football and the—sort of, at any rate—spiritual. But for the rest of it, Jo seemed to be using the dog collar in the armchair opposite as a useful focus for all the dark energy of her dry-eyed, furious grief. Georgie thought that she probably didn't really, deep down want a reading from *My Liverpool Home* by Kenny Dalglish instead of the Lord's Prayer—she was just doing it to piss Debbie off—but hey, what did Georgie know?

For the umpteenth time that morning, she heard the back door go and the sound of footsteps shuffling around the kitchen. Georgie thought perhaps she might be more useful investigating what was going on out there and making some more tea for everybody. She got up, collected the mugs, slipped through the door, shut it quietly behind her, turned and beheld a kitchen in a chaos—visible even to her undiscriminating eye—that was certainly not there over an hour before and to which, on first sight, she could attribute no discernible meaning.

It seemed that some time after half-past nine there had been a sort of eruption. For every horizontal plane of Jo's kitchen—table, chair seats, worktop, doormat—was now buried beneath a geological crust of shallow, foil-covered baking trays, each with its own Post-it stuck firmly on its top. What, wondered Georgie, was the collective noun for one-dish pre-baked all-major-food-groups-combined family meals? A kindness? No, that was ravens. A nurture? That did nothing to convey the confusion that had been visited upon this place this morning. An interfering? Yes, that was more like it. A thoughtless, disorganised, misguided and mightily off-pissing interfering of cottage pies and tuna bakes.

Georgie moved over to the table and peeled up the nearest Post-it. LASAGNE WITH CURRIED LAMB. She tried to imagine the human misery or misfortune for which lasagne with curried lamb might be the balm, and failed. *Please return dish Friday as needed for weekend. Ta, Clover.* Of course. Clover. On Friday, Jo was going to be cremating the man she had chosen to share her life with. Perhaps the best thing would be if she could get the cortège to stop round Clover's on the way? How about that?

The back door opened again. This time it was Heather. Heather holding a foil-covered baking tray. She peered into the kitchen, her face puckered with worry.

'Oh dear,' she whispered. 'Is this, you know, coals to um, er, ah, wherever you get—got—coals from . . . um . . . you know . . . up north?'

'What the hell is going on?' Georgie hissed back. 'What are you all trying to do to poor Jo? Whose idea was all this? Who exactly instructed Clover to create this toxic filth and then issue a load of instructions about her sodding kitchenware?'

Heather took a few nervous steps across the threshold. 'Well, it was nobody in particular. I mean,' she put down her dish and gestured a washing-machine type motion with her hands, keen to give a proper explanation, 'we've all been swirling, you see, and—'

'Swirling? We're arranging the funeral and you lot are swirling? Well stop it. Stop swirling. Immediately. And what the hell is Bea doing, might I ask, while you lot swirl?'

'Well that's just it, you see. She hasn't done anything. That's our problem. You see, we've had no guidance.' She put her hands together, palms facing, neat parallel lines, stared at them. 'And so we've been swirling.' And then the washing-machine started up again.

'Then bloody well tell her to. Tell her to get on with it.'

'Well, the thing is . . . I mean . . . I think . . . um . . . well, Colette says that she's sort of gone on strike . . .' Heather dropped her eyes from Georgie's, and studied her own boots. 'We think— well, Colette thinks it might have something to do with you telling Bea to, um, effing eff off and mind your own effing business for an effing change. Oh dear.' She hadn't noticed the lounge door opening. 'The Reverend Debbie. Hello there.' She mumbled something that Georgie didn't quite catch, but sounded suspiciously like 'Thanks be to God.'

'Hello, Heather. Any chance of that tea, Georgie?'

'Sorry. My fault.' Heather picked her dish back up again and headed for the door. 'I'd better get on, anyway. The headmaster has called for a meeting of

COSTA this lunchtime.'

'Has he? Sorry, nobody told me . . .' Georgie, indifferent, turned towards the kettle, reached up for clean mugs.

'Well, Bea said not to. She said you don't have to come any more, apparently. She said you had quite enough on with Jo, and told us we should completely leave you out of everything from now on.'

Georgie snapped back around. 'Did she indeed?' That came out too loud. She dropped her voice back to a hiss. 'Well in that case, I am bloody coming. Jo's mum is taking over in a minute anyway, so—'

'What's happened?' They hadn't noticed Jo coming in behind the vicar. 'What have you done?' Her eyes were wide and pale in the dark circles of their sockets. 'What is all this crap?' She staggered like an invalid towards the table, read Clover's note, collapsed on to the edge of a chair. 'Why is it in my kitchen?' She looked from Georgie to Heather. 'Why would you do this? Why? Now? To me?'

And whatever it was, the magical adhesive that had been holding her together, enabling her to function, at that moment spectacularly gave way. And for the first time since Steve's death, and indeed for the first time ever, Georgie held her dear friend in her arms as her knees buckled, she slumped down and fell apart.

'Oh dear.' Heather looked from Georgie, kneeling on the floor, to Jo, falling out of her chair, and back to Georgie again, her eyes full of tears. 'I knew it. It's all my fault. I knew this would happen. I'm doing it, aren't I?' she mouthed the words, holding her hand to her neck. 'I'm adding to her grief.'

THE ST AMBROSE EXTRAORDINARY COMMITTEE FOR FUND-RAISING (COSTA)

Minutes of the Second Meeting
Held at: The Headmaster's office
In attendance: Mr Orchard (Headmaster), Beatrice Stuart (Chair), Colette, Clover, Jasmine, Sharon
Secretary: Heather

THE HEADMASTER informed HEATHER that before they began, he wanted to say that he had read THE MINUTES of the meetings so far, and that the detail and organisation of these was quite simply brilliant, possibly the best he had ever read in all his whole life.

HEATHER responded that they did represent the doing of her very best.

THE HEADMASTER wanted to add, however, that perhaps in future she might just write it how it is, just exactly what everyone says and not bother so much with trying to make it sound too sort of posh and official if she knew what he meant.

HEATHER replied that BEA had told her to.

THE HEADMASTER: Yes, well, perhaps this term, we might try and do things a little differently

BEA: Thank you everyone so so incredibly much for coming at such short notice and at what I know is a difficult time for a lot of us. Tom felt he would value the opportunity to catch up at the beginning of what I am sure will be another amazing term for COSTA.

THE HEADMASTER: I promise this won't take long. It can't, actually, as I'm teaching War Horse to the Year 6s straight after lunch.

CLOVER: Really? My Damian read that when he was five. To himself. Only five.

THE HEADMASTER: So. New term, take stock. We are now already over halfway to reaching our target, and for that we must thank everyone who has participated. Last term saw a sensational start, and I can announce today that work on our library begins this week. Indeed, if you look out of the window there, you can see the first delivery of the materials needed to turn those useless old sheds into our beautiful new space. There's Mr Baines the caretaker sorting it all out right now.

COLETTE: Ooh, I haven't seen him before. Is he new?

THE HEADMASTER: It's an exciting moment for our school, and for making this possible, I have to thank you all. But there is one person in particular whose efforts were quite simply astonishing:

BEA: First, I must say that I am only as good as the incredible team behind—

THE HEADMASTER: Mrs Green. Without the Christmas ball, we would not be in the excellent shape we are now in and she deserves our grateful thanks. Is she not coming?

BEA: what a shame. Perhaps she didn't get my message . . .

The Minutes record the arrival of RACHEL

COLETTE: Can we help?

222

BEA: Sorry. Do excuse us. We're just having a private little meeting of COSTA. If you'd like to come back later?

THE HEADMASTER: Ah, Rachel. Great. Thanks for coming. Rachel has agreed to help with the decoration of the new library so obviously her input is vital. I thought it made sense to have her with us now, in the committee stage.

RACHEL: Artistic adviser, I am, apparently.

COLETTE: Well, get her. Who is she then all of a sudden?

CLOVER: Nice for us all to be put in our place, I'm sure.

BEA: We're all equals here on COSTA so I do hope that's not too much of a struggle for you. Anyway. To get on. This term's programme of events—

The Minutes record the arrival of MELISSA SPENCER

CLOVER: Perhaps we should have put up a 'Do Not Disturb'?

THE HEADMASTER: Excellent. Welcome. This is Melissa, everyone, who saved the ball last year after the débâcle with the caterers—

BEA: What did happen there, btw?

THE HEADMASTER: and who I'm sure will be an excellent addition to our committee.

The Minutes record the arrival of GEORGIE

BEA: Ah. Gosh. What a turn-out.

CLOVER: A free-for-all, if you ask me. Call us PASTA and be done.

COLETTE: Hang on. I hope they're not all expecting wristbands.

RACHEL: How's Jo doing?

223

GEORGIE: Pretty awful, but her mum's with her now.

BEA: So. This term. I think—

THE HEADMASTER: If I might just say a few words? THE BALL was an excellent opportunity for me to mingle with the parents—

GEORGIE: Heh heh heh.

COLETTE: So we noticed . . .

THE HEADMASTER: and I was concerned to hear that there were grievances about how COSTA had been operating so far. Many people, new parents in particular, seem to feel that there is something a little—well, the word 'cliquey' was used more than once.

BEA: Oh, Tom. Tom! Please. Stop right there. I cannot believe you said that. With the deepest respect . . . ST AMBROSE? Cliquey? O. M. G. That is like so so so so wrong. Nobody has ever—

CLOVER: We're one big happy family.

THE HEADMASTER: Apparently—well, so I've heard anyway—these lunches have been putting various noses out of joint. They seem to have developed a reputation for . . . well, sort of, exclusivity.

BEA: Well I can't think why, but of course, it goes without saying, that the last thing COSTA wants is to be accused of being cliquey when what it is about really is a group of people who are working damned bloody hard giving up their evenings and their weekends for the good of the school and the benefit of—

THE HEADMASTER: Something to do with being invitation-only?

BEA: OK. So let's make the next lunch Open

House. How about that? Will that help to quell the revolt, do we think? We don't want to end up with our heads on sticks, do we? Just because some of us have to—

GEORGIE: Aargh. Please. No. Don't say it.

BEA: juggle—

GEORGIE: Damn.

BEA: families and jobs and fund-raising. Right. Let me see. Heather? Would you be willing to kick off the COSTA fight-back? Will you be the person to tear those barriers down? Let's call it THE PEOPLE'S LUNCH LADDER, shall we? Would that send the right message?

HEATHER: Um. Gosh. Well.

BEA: Heather, do you know the two things I have learned this academic year? One, that you are amazing, and two, that you are awesome. And I love that shirt, btw. Yes. Let Heather be Our Healer. The Friday after next suit everybody? Then the Friday after next it is: Lunch for Anybody and Everybody willing to give up their time and their money for Their School. At Heather's. Excellent. Now. Do you have any further complaints you want to fire at us, Headmaster? Any fresh disappointments for which we must do penance? Just that some of us do have jobs to get back to.

MELISSA: Is that actually OK with you, Heather?

HEATHER: Gosh. Well. I mean. I don't want to be difficult, and I'm really flattered, but my house isn't really quite big enough for the whole school . . .

MELISSA: Of course. And you're not being difficult at all. It is surely possible to control

225

the numbers of the lunches without seeming exclusive. Just mention it to people beyond the committee, perhaps? And may I suggest, if we still need to have an open-house event, I have a COFFEE MORNING at my place to which everybody would be welcome.

BEA: That is so completely sweet of you, um, sorry I've forgotten your name, but I think that is just too big an ask. You can't possibly have room for all—

RACHEL: Oh but she does. I've been round. It is huge.

JASMINE: How many bedrooms?

BEA: But those of us lucky enough to have the larger houses should not be expected to always be the ones who—

RACHEL: Don't worry, it's way, way bigger than yours.

MELISSA: I don't mind at all. Really.

SHARON: Has she done it up nice?

RACHEL: Gorgeous. They'll all love it. We'll make a small fortune.

HEATHER: We can all pitch in.

BEA: Well, there we are, headmaster. I don't think that it would be actually humanly possible to be less exclusive. THE PEOPLE'S COFFEE MORNING, round at, um, whoever's. Even someone as sensitive as yourself would find it hard to find fault with that. Now I, for one, really must get back to work—and preferably before the world caves in, if poss.

THE HEADMASTER: As must we all. Thank you for coming.

THE MEETING closed at 1.15 p.m.

Everybody collected their things and drifted towards the door.

'Oh, Rachel?' Tom, with his back to the room, was at the bookshelves, his hand at the M for Morpurgo. 'Could I just have a quick word? Artistic Adviser?'

Georgie winked at her, bundled Heather and Clover down the corridor and shut the office door. The sound of the school was muffled again. They were alone.

'Sorry about that. I don't know what came over me . . . I'm not normally quite such an idiot.'

'We're all a little altered in that particular environment, I find.'

'Well you weren't an idiot. You were dead brave taking that lot on. Gold medallist at the Dead Brave Olympics.'

'Excuse me?' His face was straight, but a smile was creasing round his eyes.

'Sorry. So sorry. Just something I say to Poppy sometimes.' Christ, she really must get out more. 'I mean, the Man Who Told Bea She Was Cliquey. Blimey.'

'Didn't quite come to anything though, did it? I fear I lost the meeting round about three minutes in. Yet again. I seem to have instituted something called the People's Lunch Ladder. How did that happen? You do have to hand it to her . . .'

'Come on. All that long experience in the world of high finance, all those masters of the universe— surely you can handle our little Mrs Stuart?'

'It turns out to have been no sort of preparation at all.' He grinned back at her. 'A few years up a mountain with the Taliban might have been a bit more useful. Well, a grounding, at least . . .'

227

Something somewhere deep inside her gave a little jump. As if it had been caught on something; hooked. Right at that moment, she could not quite speak.

'Anyway,' he went on. 'I just wanted to show you something.' He opened his desk drawer and produced an old album of dark brown card. 'For my prep on *War Horse* I thought I'd check out what impact the First World War had on St Ambrose, and I found this.'

Rachel stepped forward and they bent their heads over the pages. 'One of my predecessors, Mr Stanley.' There was a sepia photo of a tall, handsome young man in uniform. In the background was some sort of parade, and the hill that Rachel walked up every day.

'He was headmaster? He looks very young . . .'

'He's only twenty there.' Tom was visibly moved as he looked down on him. 'He was a heroic figure, apparently. Destined for amazing things: politics, the Bar.' He turned the pages on a few years. 'Until he came back like this.'

Rachel gasped at the next photo: still Mr Stanley, but with one eye patched, one arm missing, listing to one side, a dazed expression. 'Oh, the poor man . . .'

'Indeed. He wasn't going very far after they'd done that to him. But he was head here for over twenty years. So who knows what we all owe to him? Anyway.' He shut the album and handed it to her. 'I don't know if you've got to that point yet, but I thought it might be useful for your timeline?'

Her—? Oh shit, the bloody timeline. 'Yeah. Brilliant. Definitely still space to fit that in . . .'

'Great. And the one other thing was: we have a

dinner outstanding.'

'Oh. No. Really. You don't have to do that. At all. Honestly. It was . . .' she gibbered.

'A prank. Yes. No need to go over it again. We've cleared that up.' He was looking down at his desk, collecting bits and pieces—pencils, paper, a photo of a horse with a soldier on its back. 'But still, I do owe the lucky winner one dinner. And I do like to settle my debts.'

'Even though,' she found her voice, 'you were in the City?'

'One of the many reasons I felt I had to chuck it in. And anyway,' he looked up then, his eyes locked on to hers, 'I'd very much like to. If you don't mind. Do you have a free evening next week by any chance?'

Let's think—only about seven or so. 'Hmm, that should be OK.'

He slipped his jacket on and held open the door for her. The grumpy secretary looked up from her screen to give Rachel a filthy look. The racket of lunch was easing into the quiet of classtime with a slow diminuendo. 'Shall we aim for Thursday?'

3.15 P.M. PICK-UP

Heather stamped her feet while she waited. She had offered to drop Poppy back on the way home, so that Rachel could get on with her work. The girls were becoming inseparable now anyway—although Maisie still adored Scarlett—so they might as well share duties. Ah. Here they came. Oh dear. They did look worried. Heather's stomach clenched. She could hardly bear it. What had happened now?

229

'Are you all right, girls? Good day?'

They looked at one another and then Poppy nodded. 'I'll tell you when we're on the hill,' said Maisie, marching off to the gates with Poppy, so that Heather had to almost run along behind.

'What's up?' she hissed when they got out on to the pavement.

'It's Milo Green . . .' Maisie began.

'. . . and Scarlett,' finished Poppy.

'She's horrid to him every break'

'unless we look after him.'

'And we want to play our game'

'but we can't.'

'Because then she starts.'

'But Maisie, love, you adore Scarlett! She's your best friend!'

Maisie carried on as if Heather hadn't spoken. 'See, Milo says his favourite colour's orange, but he doesn't like eating oranges'

'and Scarlett says he can't have orange as his favourite colour if he won't eat an orange.'

'He has to have green.'

'But this is just silly, silly stuff,' said Heather crossly. 'Really, you two . . .'

'She started again today. Bringing in an orange and trying to force him to eat it.'

'She was doing it last term, and it makes him cry and we—'

'Look, girls, I think you should keep right out of this one.' It sounded a bit daft, to Heather, that someone should want to pick it as their favourite colour if they refused to eat the fruit. Sort of asking for trouble, really. Just drawing attention. 'Well, girls, it sounds to me like this is Milo's fight. He's been silly enough to pick it so he should jolly well get on with it.'

It would be a huge mistake, in Heather's view, for the likes of Maisie and Poppy to take on Scarlett. Or her mother, for that matter.

*　　　*　　　*

Thank God for the creation of tinted windows, thought Bubba as she hunkered down further into her car seat. She had arrived early this afternoon, with the sole ambition of bagsying the space next to the car-park gate. It was a coveted position, that space: the only spot on the school premises where you could see your children come out of school, stay in the car, and not speak to anyone. She had managed to nip into it just in front of grumpy Ashley's fat mum and had felt a small flush of triumph. Her first, she realised as she turned off the ignition, for some time. What on earth was she turning into? Once upon a time, Bubba Green was a woman of substance. She was used to making a difference, sometimes even, though she said so herself, changing actual lives. Now look at her: 'Good day, darling?' 'Yes, brilliant, thanks. I got to the car park *just in time* and nipped in front of grumpy Ashley's fat mum.' Christ. She had prepared herself for a quiet life with this career-break nonsense. She had no idea it would be actually, literally, The Night of the Living Dead.

As the parents started to drift in, one by one, pair up, form groups, she stayed firmly in her Range Rover, as assimilated as a traveller come ashore among the peoples of some obscure island in a distant sea—Margaret Mead or Michael Palin or someone. There she was, Bubba, used to running

231

the vast and teeming human resources division of a serious corporation, and yet somehow she had failed to make head nor tail of the human resources of St Ambrose. She had to be honest—and Bubba valued honesty; self-awareness was, in her view, a cardinal virtue—it was all going wrong. Again.

Of course, less than a month had passed since the ball, and time had not yet worked its healing powers upon the open wounds, the stigmata, of her savaged pride. She hadn't spoken to anybody here since the moment the flood waters had swept through her gorgeous, her bloody *fabulous*, tent, and the longer she left it the more remote it seemed that she might ever be accepted here again. But it wasn't just that. Even before the St Ambrose Tsunami, she was not—face the facts, Bubbs— fitting in. It was no surprise. She'd been here before. It wasn't that she was an unpopular sort of person, she was just—and she'd learned to live with it by now—almost *too* good-looking, *too* bright, *too* successful. Other women might want to *be* her but they did not, so much, want to *be with* her. And that was just the cross she had to bear. She had said it before, she would no doubt say it again: *Tall Poppy* would be the title of her autobiography.

She sighed, burrowed deeper, then started as she became aware of a face pressed up against the glass. 'Oh! Gosh! Scarlett!' She lowered the window. 'I literally jumped out of my skin!'

'I *love* your car, Mrs Green.' Scarlett was passing her open palms across the shiny bodywork like a prospective purchaser. 'Could I look inside?'

'Of course. Hop in out of the cold.'

Scarlett circled the Range Rover and pounced into the passenger seat in a flash. 'I *love* the cream interior, Mrs Green.'

'Well thank you, Scarlett. And please, call me Bubba.'

'Why are you called Bubba, Mrs Green?' Scarlett was twisted round, sizing up the room in the back. 'Is that your real name?'

'No, no. My name's Deborah really but my little brother couldn't say that so he called me Bubba and it sort of stuck.' Ah, there were Milo and Martha coming out together now.

'Gosh. You've got a little brother too! So have I.' Scarlett opened the glove compartment and peered inside. 'Aren't they funny? I *love* mine.'

Bubba leaned forward and shut it firmly. 'Not in there, if you don't mind. That's where I keep all my secrets.'

'I *love* secrets.'

'I'm sure you do.' But that little stash of emergency ciggies was top, *top* secret. 'Anyway. My little brother's thirty-six now.'

'Ahhhhh.' Scarlett's ah was a long, pretty, musical thing, full of meaning. For the first time, she was looking at Bubba rather than her car.

'So is he special-needs too, then? Your brother?'

'Special-needs? *Too?*' Despite the efficient seat-warming system, Bubba felt a sudden chill. 'Scarlett, what on earth are you talking about?' They both now faced the front, as the Green children approached. Smaller, younger, sturdier Martha was leading the way as Milo dragged behind, his face set down at an angle to the world. 'Nobody's special-needs. My brother is in property and making an absolute mint. And Milo . . .' Milo was shaking his left hand as he walked, like he did when he was stressed. She was trying to nudge him—gently, mind—out of it now that she was at home and they'd got rid of that psycho nanny, but he did still lapse. Though only very occasionally. 'Milo's more of the Talented and Able—'

'Gift-ed and Talent-ed. It's Gift-ed and Talent-ed,' corrected Scarlett.

What-*ever,* said Bubba. But only to herself.

'So is that why Milo writes backwards?'

'Mirror writing,' said Bubba firmly. How often had she said those words in the past two years? Mirror writing. Mirror writing. Some days it seemed to be all she ever talked about. 'It's called mirror writing. And it is most commonly associated with *extreme* intelligence.' Why she was always having to explain this, she simply did not know. Had nobody round here even heard of Leonardo da Vinci?

The children were now at the car.

'Ah. Yes.'

They opened the back doors as Scarlett let herself out of the front.

'How clever.'

Scarlett looked at Milo as if he was an exhibit in a museum and she was the expert who'd dug him up in some bog.

'I *love* mirror writing.'

And with that she flew off.

'Mummy?' Martha reached over for Milo's hand as together they watched Scarlett's skinny little shape melt away into the gloaming. 'What did she want?'

THE DAY OF HEATHER'S LUNCH

8.40 A.M. DROP-OFF

'So, really,' repeated Heather, 'if you look at it up
and down and backwards and forwards, all roads
lead to the one, um, thingy: Bea must've asked
me to do this lunch today, on her actual fortieth
birthday, because Bea must've wanted me to do her
actual fortieth-birthday lunch.'

'Mmmm,' murmured Rachel, again. She had lost
count of how many millions of times Heather had
been over this fascinating topic. To avoid being
driven completely bonkers, she had tuned out ages
ago, when they were still halfway up the hill.

Rachel had first developed this particular
mental skill back in her teens, when all she had
wanted to do was draw at the kitchen table and all
her mother had wanted to do was chatter on. But
now, during this past year of too much time spent
with Heather—who was actually, officially, an
über-chatterer—she had perfected it. It was easy,
really: all she did was envisage her brain as a suite
of rooms or chambers. Each had its own place, its
own purpose and its own infallible security system
so that unwanted personnel from one area of her
life could not intrude upon the thought processes
of another. Only the very special, like Georgie,
had access to almost all of it. Chris might have
had once, and Bea, but Rachel had recently had
to revoke their clearance, for obvious reasons.
Of course, the kids were allowed to burst in
wherever they liked—even into her work chamber,

235

unannounced. But nobody else could penetrate its reinforced, sound-proofed walls. And most people never even got beyond her foyer. Quite a crowded place, Rachel's mental foyer. That was where she liked to keep her mum, for example: she could always envisage her there quite clearly, standing in the entrance hall somewhere in a frontal lobe, calling her yoo-hoos, issuing forth instructions and opinions, wondering if any of them were getting through, if anybody was even at home.

And that was where Heather was right then, that morning: out in her foyer, wittering on about Bea's bloody birthday.

'It was code. It must've been. For "Please, please can you be the person to give me a birthday party?" So I've made a whopping cake. And ordered those balloons with a forty on them . . .'

'Mmmm.'

And meanwhile, Rachel could be alone. In her deepest, most private chamber of all. With a warm fire and a soft light. And the peace and quiet to think over—and over—the events of the night before.

Like most of the things in her life that turned out to be the best, the evening had got off to a rubbish start. Naturally, she'd been feeling sick all day— with nerves, with shame, with a morbid hatred of her tragic self. Not only was she the Oldest Woman in the History of Humankind to Go on a Date—no need to google it, it was perfectly obvious. Also, she was doing it—a nice touch, this; well done, Rach— with her daughter's headmaster. And it was only happening because her bestest frenemy wanted to make her look a pillock. How could she stack a few more odds against herself? Here's how: she could decide to walk down there—partly to quell the nausea, partly so that she could, if needs be, get completely rat-arsed—thus ensuring a turn in the weather. By the time she arrived at her 'date'—ugh, so embarrassing—rivulets were coursing down her pinkened nose. And not, she suspected, in a good way . . .

She opened the door and fought her way through an overgrowth of taffeta curtain. It had never occurred to her to go to the French place in Market Street before, and now she could see why. It was like entering a giant pair of old lady's knickers: flounces, frills, flock . . . This was not an actual smart restaurant, it was Colette's idea of a smart restaurant: two entirely different things. The headmaster sat alone, in the middle, sort of around where the old lady's gusset might be, looking totally out of place. Oh God, she thought. Oh God oh God oh God. How excruciating is this? We can't get through an entire evening in here. What are we going to talk about?

He had been studying his phone, but looked up at her approach. His eyes blinked into a smile. And, Gosh, thought Rachel, with a start, it's almost as if he's actually pleased to see me.

She sat down on the puffed-up chair and leaned across the table. 'What,' she whispered to him, 'are we doing here?' That was weird—straight from what-are-we-going-to-talk-about to this instant intimacy. What suddenly happened? Whatever it was, they were off.

'Ah.' He raised his eyebrows. 'Straight in there with the metaphysics.' He lifted the wine list, shielded his face from the waiter and whispered back. 'Or were you dealing more in specifics?'

'Specifics. Definitely. It's a bit, well, poncy, isn't it?'

'I thought we were contractually obligated. It's what you bid for, after all, Mrs Mason—dinner with the headmaster at the French place in . . .'

'I DIDN'T BID—'

A waiter turned round.

'All right, all right. You're the innocent pedestrian, I am the banana skin . . .'

'But this place was Colette's idea. This is the mood music by which Colette was planning to pounce on you.'

He blanched. 'Please . . .'

'Sorry. Only we don't have to be here, is the point I'm trying to make.'

'We? We? Mrs Mason, calm it . . .'

'Yes. See what you mean: ergo, why are we here?' He called the waiter over, ordered a nice-sounding bottle of white, and leaned back in again. 'You know what? You have actually made an extremely valid point.' He loosened the knot in his tie and undid his top button. Hmm, thought Rachel, that's better. 'You're completely right.'

'Oh good. Am I?'

'This evening just about sums it up. Why am I sitting here? Because some woman came into my office in not quite enough of a very tight top and told me to. I mean, I am the headmaster.'

'Indeed you are.'

'And do you know why I wanted to do this job? Because I thought here was an area which might offer both power and responsibility.'

Rachel snorted. 'Surely, in the City, you had a bit more power than you get at little St Ambrose. All that money. All those sea planes . . .'

238

'Not so many sea planes, actually. You'd be frankly scandalised by the paucity of sea planes . . .' The waiter poured the wine for him to taste. 'And it was all power and no sense of responsibility whatsoever.' He took a sip. 'Thanks. Yes. Very good.'

Rachel watched hungrily as her own glass was filled. Rat-arsed was still an option.

'But so far, St Ambrose has been all responsibility and precious little power over anything. The church, the governors, the parents, the children . . . It's been one long power struggle between me and the lot of them, and I don't even seem to have put up a fight. I tell you, I was never this biddable as a schoolboy.'

'Excusez-moi. Are you or are you not the Man Who Told Bea She Was Cliquey? I've only just come out of my swoon.'

'I'm also the man she squashed flat, if you remember, like a very, very small gnat.'

'Well, I guess you're still learning . . .' She raised her drink to him.

'Guess I am.' He clinked his against it. 'And yet you, apparently, know it all already—the holder of the key that unlocks the mystery of our existence. Who'd a thought it? You, Mrs Mason, are the philosopher's stone.'

'Why, headmaster, thank you.' She shimmied off her sopping blazer and draped it over the back of her chair. Apparently she was no longer planning to cut and run. 'I bet you say that to all the mums.'

11 A.M. MORNING BREAK

It was about the most manic morning Heather could ever remember. What with cooking lunch for goodness knows how many people and taking on the business of The Birthday. And running around the house from up to down to make it all presentable. Still, she was on top of it all now—'Make a list and tick everything off as you do it,' as Bea always said. She was actually ahead of herself by about fifteen minutes. Which was why she was having a quick shower in the first place. It was supposed to calm her down, because, although everything was organised, her head was still spinning. Indeed, it was still spinning to such an extent that initially she got her shower confused with her tidying up. And when she first felt it, she thought it was a marble. A marble that had got into the wrong place, and needed tidying up. Tsk, she thought to herself. A marble. How on earth did that get there? And only then did it hit her. It couldn't be a marble. Because it was in her left breast. And anyway, Maisie didn't even own any marbles. Heather would have bought her some if she'd wanted any, of course, but she'd just never shown the interest.

Immediately, she regretted having a shower at all. Why she had even thought it would calm her down she did not know. Showers were generally a disappointment, in her experience. In the films, people were always in these huge, clean spaces, with hot hot water beating down all over them, cocooned in luxury. The Carpenters' shower was nothing like that; partly because Guy had

240

installed it himself, and the door was so flimsy it sort of wobbled all the way through, but also the nozzle thingy was all built up with limescale so the not-very-hot water only came out in a limp trickle. Never very satisfactory, even at the best of times.

Her next thought was to blame Georgie. If Georgie hadn't simplified the menu for her in her normal bossy Georgie-Martin-knows-best way, then Heather would not have had the time to even think about a shower, let alone get in there and find the, you know—oh God, if only it was a marble. Heather's immediate instinct, when Bea had picked her for the People's Lunch Ladder-slash-fortieth, was dim sum. Home-made dim sum. Don't ask her why—it just popped up, a vision of a vast and varied Oriental spread that would have had them all gasping. And if she'd been making dim sum for up to twenty people right now, well, a shower would be right out of the question. But when she just mentioned it, in passing really, Georgie had grabbed her arm like she was about to jump off a railway bridge, really stuck her nails in—or what was left of them—and plain forbidden her. So now, as decreed by Madam, it was roast chickens with herbs, jacket potatoes, two salads—tomato and green—and a bowl of strawberries. Very simple. And very boring. And even after she'd put her signature twist on it, still simple and boring enough for her to think: I've got fifteen minutes. I'll just nip in the shower . . .

She was out now, wrapped in a towel, sitting on the edge of the bath and staring at herself in the mirror. Oddly enough, she looked exactly the same as she had ten minutes ago. Perhaps she was paler. Actually, now she was white as a sheet. And when

241

she let her hair out of its scrunchie, she noticed that her hand was trembling. Uncontrollably. But that was all. And right there, right then, she resolved two things. 1: She was not going to be bossed around by Georgie any more. She'd put up with it for thirty years. Enough was enough. It was time to take a stand. And 2: She was going to get through this lunch as if nothing at all was wrong. She had to. She would be brave. For the People's Lunch Ladder. And for Bea.

She reached for her mascara wand—she would jolly well paint on a happy face—and heard her phone beep. It was a text back from Bea, in response to the 'Happy Birthday' one she'd sent earlier: 'Thank U lovely! Feeling so spoilt :) !!!! Good luck with the lunch. Cld you pick up kidz for me 2day? Be with you by 6, 4 sure!! Love u loads!!'

12.30 P.M. LUNCH BREAK

Drinks

Georgie was just parking when she saw Rachel coming round the corner. 'Thank God for that,' she threw over her shoulder to Hamish in his car seat. 'We will at least have one human being to talk to. But I promise you, baby, it's in, scoff and out again as fast as we can manage it.' She turned off the ignition and jumped down on to the grass verge.

'Hi, Georgie. Hi, my scrumptious plumptious one.' Rachel was already at the rear car door, detaching Hamish and burying her face in his neck. 'Well this is a pleasant surprise. It's not like you to be arsed to turn out for this sort of thing is it?'

'Humph. How very dare you? When all one ever does, all day long, is One's Bit?' Georgie grabbed her bag and locked her car and together they walked down Heather's little drive. 'I thought I'd better just check that menus didn't get switched at the last minute. That we're not going to find ourselves at the mercy of Heather Blumenthal.' She mimed a quick vomit into the lavender border. 'Anyway, I had to come so that I could pin you down. Enough with the idle chit-chat. Now. How did it go last night?'

Then the front door opened, and there was Melissa.

'Hi!' said Rachel, far too loudly, as she threw Hamish back to his mother. 'How great that you're here.'

'Thank heavens you're here too.' Melissa stepped back to let them through.

'Why do you say it like that? Don't tell me it's just The Clique?'

Georgie went straight through while Rachel brushed her feet repeatedly on the doormat. Heather was practically OCD when it came to housework, known to hoover not just before and after social occasions but often while they were in full swing—or as full-swing as they ever got chez Carpenter. Georgie saw it as her moral encumbrance to always pig things up a bit round there whenever she got the chance. It felt that little bit healthier for all concerned.

'Quite the reverse.' Melissa dropped her voice as they headed back towards the kitchen. 'No clique at all. It really is the People's Lunch, or will be if we can only get a few more people . . .'

'Oh yeah, course,' Georgie stopped and said

over her shoulder. 'They've all gone on their stupid sodding spa day.'

'Is that where they are?' Melissa leaned forward and shut the kitchen door quickly before Georgie could get through it. 'And you *knew*?' Melissa sounded surprised.

'Oh yes. They only invited me along, that's all. Can you believe it? I mean how rude do I have to be to the bloody woman? Am I never to be left alone? Apparently not. It's all "Geor-gie"'—her Sharon-slash-Jasmine voice sounded exactly the same as her Katie Price voice, she realised, but so what? She was a busy woman, it would just have to do—'"we're going on a spa day for Bea's fortieth. Treatments in the morning and bubbly in the Jacuzzi. Wanna come?" I mean, I ask you . . . The sheer bloody cheek of it. Excuse me, but do I look like I'd want to go on a spa day?' She spat the phrase with contempt. 'I don't think I've ever been so insulted in my—'

She stopped. Rachel, her eyes wide, her hands on her face, had obviously got there before her.

'Oh . . . shit.'

'You didn't tell Heather they were going out for the day? Did you not know she was planning this big party?' Melissa didn't seem at all judgemental, just genuinely baffled at the turn of events. Still, Georgie thought it safer to head straight for the defensive.

'Well, now I think of it, there might have been a bit of prattling on . . .'

'Rachel?'

'Um, well, I think she might've mentioned it . . .'

'But look, Melissa, thing is, I've known her for donkey's years, and there's always been the

244

prattling on. You can't listen to all of it, else you'd go stark staring . . .'

'You do need a sort of filter . . .' explained Rachel.

'Yeah, a filter. Like on your computer. Against, you know, whatchamacallit . . .'

'Spam,' finished Rachel.

'That's it.' Georgie nodded. 'Exactly. Heather does talk a lot of spam . . .'

They were all three huddled together now, at the bottom of Heather's stairs. It had all the hallmarks of a medical briefing in a hospital corridor: the doctor, the loved ones, the horribly wounded patient behind the closed door.

'I got here a bit early,' Melissa whispered, the handle still firmly in her grip. 'We just had time to take down the banners and the balloons and hide the cake. I just don't see how the misunderstanding could have happened. How can someone throw a birthday party by mistake? Heather is trying to be brave, but she does seem to be—well—quite *unnaturally* upset about it all. Almost traumatised. Could there be something else bothering her, do you know?'

'Nah. This is just normal. Believe me, unnaturally upset is her default position. Get used to it. Heather is a teacup, life is a storm.'

'I see. A teacup,' repeated Melissa, 'which talks spam.'

'Precisely.' Georgie always appreciated it when people got her—not everyone did. That was a very nice little summing up indeed. She was starting to like the cut of this Melissa's jib.

'OK.' Melissa finally opened the door, cocked her head in the direction of the kitchen. 'You can

245

go through now.'

Main Course
Free-range corn-fed chicken roasted with garlic and thyme, jacket potatoes, green and red salads

Preparation time: almost nothing. Worst luck

'I was asked, of course . . .' Clover was clutching her plate to her large chest as they queued for the buffet in Heather's dining room, 'but Damian was seeing the ed psych this morning, and you know how long you have to wait to get a slot.'

Nope, thought Rachel.

'And anyway, the children just have to come first. That's my philosophy. So I said to Bea and the girls'—here Clover raised her voice significantly, spraying the sound around, pressure-hosing it into all ears—' "THAT'S SO SWEET OF YOU TO INCLUDE ME IN BEA'S BIRTHDAY SPA TREAT BUT VERY SADLY I AM GOING TO HAVE TO TURN DOWN YOUR KIND INVITATION." '

Rachel checked the room. Well done. It seems everyone heard that in here. And the kitchen. And probably the other end of the High Street.

'And then of course serves me right I had the most frustrating morning because Damian suddenly just like that went down with this head cold that's going around. I mean sod's law it had to be a head cold. Chop his leg off and he can do a page of level five maths blindfold, but with a head cold, well, just not himself. How's Poppy doing at maths?'

'Fine, I think. I mean, I haven't actually chopped her leg off yet.' Rachel slapped her own wrist, raised her eyes ceilingwards. 'Been that busy . . .'

Clover blustered on. Almost as if she wasn't even listening. Almost as if she didn't actually care about Poppy's maths, or her leg.

'And I did want it official, on a bit of paper, that he *is* exceptional because I think it just helps when you're dealing with schools . . .'

Rachel ducked out of the queue again. She'd rather starve to death than get stuck eating with that old baggage. She wandered past the lounge— like the dining room, too crowded to go into. Hamish and a few other toddlers were in the sun room on the back, curled up in front of a DVD. The whole house was suddenly heaving. Bizarre as it may seem, Heather, of all people, appeared to have pulled off a significant social success. Rachel poked her head into the kitchen, where the hostess-with-the-mostest was standing alone at the sink, vacant, ashen, like a zombie, and pulled it out again, irritated.

She caught sight of Georgie through the sliding doors, out on the patio, fag in hand: a forlorn sight, smoking on her own like that—a lone swan on a winter's day, pining for its mate. Its Benson & Hedges-smoking mate. She misses Jo, thought Rachel with a tug. We all do, in our various ways. Certainly nothing's the same without her. Rachel slid open the door and slipped out into the bleak air.

'Coming to join me?'

'Only if you can guarantee a Clover-free environment.'

'I can. She's an anti-smoking nutter.'

'Give us one, then, to ward off the evil.' She bent into the flame as Georgie lit it for her. 'How's Jo

247

doing? She does know we're thinking about her, doesn't she?'

'Yeah. She just can't face anyone at the moment. I'm still picking the boys up for her every morning, which means I can keep an eye. I think it's hell; how can it not be? But she's back at work—she had to—and they've given her day shifts now, which is something.'

'Is she getting any help?'

Georgie flicked her ash in the flowerbed. 'Your Melissa. She's going round three evenings a week, apparently. Counselling all of them, for nothing. Jo says she's just been completely amazing. And it's all been cooked up by your headmaster.'

Rachel felt a flush of pleasure. 'He's not my headmaster.'

'Really?' Georgie bent down while she stubbed her cigarette out on the side of a plastic urn. 'Isn't he?' She pulled herself up to her below-average height and pinned Rachel down with her clear blue eyes. 'Come on. Cough up. What happened last night?' She leaned in with a naughty, Year 7 sort of grin. 'Didja snog him?'

'Oh Georgie . . .'

'Hiiiiiii! Mind if I join you?'

'Oh. Hello, Bubba. Course not.'

'Sorry. Smokers only,' butted in Georgie.'You don't smoke.'

'I do, actually—on the sly. And you can't get near the food in there, so I need something to stave off the after-workout appetite. Funny. I wasn't even going to come. I don't know if you've noticed, but I'm just determined to lower the old profile this term, duck right down beneath *les parapets*. And to be honest I was starting to wonder if anyone

248

even *liked* me. I know, so silly, I don't mean my really lovely proper friends like you two—just, you know, the absolutely *teeming* masses, but then Melissa called and said she really needed me here cos nobody had turned up, and of course I dropped everything—well, I didn't really have anything *to* drop at that actual, precise moment but I would've anyway cos I just *adore* Melissa, I don't know if you know her at all but she *is* quite fabulous, I am totally *en-slaved*—and anyway I was just so *touched*. They *need* me, I thought, they *like* me. I've got nothing on until I take Milo to the ed psych and that's not till two-thirty. Anyway, so I get here and you can barely get in Heather's little *door*. *Sweet*, these houses, aren't they? So snug. I've never been in one before.'

Dessert
Strawberries doused in balsamic vinegar and tossed in passion-fruit purée; double cream with crème de menthe

Preparation time: a bit of fiddling about with the purée, thank goodness, so that stretched it out a bit and delayed the inevitable

The queue for dessert was snaking out of the dining room, down the hall and up to the front door. Sod that for a lark, thought Georgie. 'Sorry, excuse me, thanks, if I can just get through . . .' She travelled up it, sideways. This was her paramedic-in-a-crowd act: polite, professional, firm, it worked every time. They all pressed to one side to let her pass and within seconds she was at the table, piling fruit and cream into a bowl and heaping chocolates on to a plate. Why did anyone ever stand in line? It was a good question to which she had never found a satisfactory answer. She sighed. The human psyche was a wondrous thing, and not without its mysteries.

She darted up the stairs, kicked open the door to the spare room and slammed it behind her. Scoffing in front of everyone wasn't quite on, even she could see that. This would do nicely—might even have a nap straight after. She had just kicked off her shoes and curled up on the bed when the door burst open again.

'Oh. Thank God. It's only you. Not the pudding police.'

'No,' said Rachel, coming in. 'But I've half a mind to call them. Budge up.' She kicked off her shoes and sighed as she sank on to the bed. 'Can you remind me, in my second incarnation, to come back as an educational psychologist?'

'I'll make a note.' She still clutched her bowl in tight. 'You're not actually expecting me to share any, I hope?'

'Aw, go on.' Rachel laid her head on Georgie's shoulder. 'I'll tell you everything about last night . . .'

'Hang on, I said I was interested, not sharing-my-pudding interested . . .' She reluctantly held out the bowl. 'Come on then: snog or no snog?'

'Of course no snog. Really, George . . .'

Georgie wrenched it back again. 'No snog, no strawberry.' She took a mouthful and spat it out in horror. 'What the hell has she done to this? That woman's got cooking Tourette's.'

'Honestly. It's nothing. We just had to have this dinner, that's all. And now we're working on this pain-in-the-neck timeline that he's taking a bit too seriously. But he did walk me home. And it was raining, and we sort of huddled under his umbrella.'

'She just can't look at a nice simple ingredient and not bugger about with it. This isn't a recipe, it's an act of violence. Why does she always have to try and turn everything into something it isn't?'

'But nothing's going to happen with him. Nothing's going to happen with anybody. Ever. When I got home Josh was still up, and he was just looking out of his bedroom window, staring at us coming back. Arms folded. Didn't say anything, of course. Mind you, he hasn't said anything for months now. But can you imagine? Ever doing anything in front of your kids with someone who isn't their dad?'

'Colette seems to have got the hang of it. I said strawberries, cream, clear as day. Can she not follow the most simple instructions?'

'I mean, it was always "Er, yuck, get a room" if Chris so much as pecked me on the cheek. It amazes me how they cope with weekends with the bloody intern, but they do. I really think this timetable's helped so much. Normalised everything . . .'

'Christ. She's stuck some muck in this cream. Tastes like toothpaste.'

This marked a whole new low in St Ambrose cuisine, but Rachel wasn't bothered. She was picking out strawberries and popping them in her mouth with, it seemed, a total disregard for her inner self.

'He's nice, though, Tom. The amazing thing is that we've never met before. He grew up near me, you know, and was at college down the road from my art school. And we were on the same "Not in My Name" march and all that sort of stuff.'

She took another so-called strawberry and dipped it in the polluted cream. It was too awful to watch. Georgie had to avert her gaze. She focused instead on the dressing-table stool that Heather had made in her upholstery class.

'So that's funny. Cos, I mean, something could have happened. Once upon a time. If we had actually met. Life's like that, though, isn't it? You drive around, having no end of near-misses—and most of them you don't even know you've had. So, yeah, he's a lovely bloke. And we do get on very well. But there's no chance of it ever coming to anything.'

Of course, Georgie had noticed that the last six months had taken their heavy toll on Rachel. She had watched as her weight had dropped off and her natural ebullience dimmed. But it was only really then, that moment, as she witnessed her uncritical consumption of Heather's vile muck, that she saw fully on display the damage that had been wrought. This, here, was a woman with little or no self-respect.

'I mean, there he is, single as anything, swinging along with a rucksack on his back. Whistling a happy tune. Who on earth would want to join up with me and my excess baggage?'

Attitude to food was, in Georgie's world picture, the most reliable key to the spiritual well-being of any adult. She was surprised it was not subject to more government interest. Politicians were always banging on about 'national happiness', after all, and asking those sorts of nosy-parker questions about finances and health and sex that made people

252

complain about the nanny state. But surely, the most obvious questions of any nanny state worth its salt would be things like 'Did you sit down to a proper supper?' and 'What did you have for breakfast?'

'So we haven't arranged to do anything else. It was just that stupid auction thing. That's all. Nothing to get excited about.'

Oh yeah? Georgie sincerely hoped that this headmaster was planning on behaving himself, or he'd have her to deal with . . .

The door opened again. 'Here you are! I was wondering where you'd got to. Who are we hiding from?' Bubba barged in and sat down at the dressing table. 'There's no pudding left either. I *must* say I didn't get much for my fifteen quid. Still, I'm a good half a pound over at the moment. It's actually just exactly what I need right now: one proper, full day of nil-by-mouth.'

3.15 P.M. PICK-UP

Heather walked down the hill, with Maisie holding one hand and little Archie Stuart holding the other. Scarlett kept a few paces ahead of them, leading the way. It was a shame that Bea had asked her to look after the children today of all days. She had been looking forward to it being her go with them for months and so, of course, had Maisie. But now here they were, and it wasn't really the best of days for it. To be honest. What with one thing and another.

'Can't Poppy come to tea too?' whined Maisie. 'We've got this game going with the Sylvanian school.'

'Don't be silly, Maisie.' That was all Heather needed—a difficult child. 'You've got Scarlett today; she'll play Sylvanians, won't you, Scarlett?'

'Aww. I used to *love* Sylvanians,' said Scarlett, smiling fondly at the memory while she walked backwards. 'But I've grown out of them. Can we go on Facebook instead?'

'Golly, I don't think so. You're only ten! I'm sure Mummy doesn't let you. You can play in the garden . . .'

She didn't ask where Bea had been today—she wasn't a stalker, for heaven's sake, Bea had every right to do whatever she wanted. Heather had reviewed the whole Bea's-birthday-lunch confusion in her mind earlier, and had seen, quite clearly, that it had been an innocent misunderstanding and mostly, as usual, all her fault. There was no harm done. None at all. And those birthday bits and pieces would come in handy. At some point. Apart from the helium balloons. And the cake. The enormous cake.

Heather opened the front door and put all the book bags, shoes and coats in neat little piles. Frankly, she told herself, you might as well enjoy the next couple of hours while you can. Because outwardly, at least, life's normal. But soon Guy will come home. And Maisie will go to bed.

And then she would have to tell him about the . . . what she found. And that would be the turning point. Because that would be the moment when it—the thing—would stop being a secret hidden deep inside her body, known to her mind and her mind only, tucked away somewhere between the fear department and the imagination. It would be the moment when it turned into something much,

much worse: it would become a fact.

The children disappeared off, the girls to Maisie's bedroom and little Archie to the TV. Heather opened the fridge to see what could be rustled up for tea, and found nothing. Of course, that lunch had ended up so crowded that people had actually been in her fridge, grabbing what they could find like scavengers in the wake of a nuclear bomb. She moved on to the freezer. It really had been quite extraordinary—much the busiest of all the lunches there had been so far. And they had made an absolute fortune. Heather tried to remember it all, because Guy was bound to ask, the minute he got in. They could stretch that conversation out before they got on to the . . . you know. But the sad thing was, she hadn't really managed to enjoy it while it had been going on. Which was a shame, because, for two whole hours, her little house really had been the centre of the St Ambrose universe. And that was something she had always longed for, almost her dearest wish: to be at the centre of the St Ambrose universe. Instead of being a tiny little satellite, like a pinprick, buzzing around on its outer limits. Which was how she generally felt, the rest of the time.

Chicken nuggets or fish fingers? The girls could choose. She headed for the stairs, but stopped at the sound of scuffling in the dining room. Who was that? Oh. Scarlett, at the desk in the corner, on the computer.

'Hi!' Scarlett turned round and dazzled a surprised smile, as if the very last person she had expected to find in Heather's own dining room was, of all people, Heather. 'I *love* what you've done in here.'

255

'Really?' Heather looked around. 'It's only magnolia . . .'

'Well, it's *gorgeous*.' Scarlett turned back to the screen. 'I was just checking Facebook. Colette's already put up pictures of the spa day. I knew she would. I *love* Colette.'

Heather walked slowly towards the screen. At first she could only see bubbles, lots and lots of bubbles. Then some raised glasses came into focus. And teeth. Rows of exposed teeth, catching the flashlight. Then Bea's face took shape, and Colette's and Jasmine's and—whose was that?—Sharon's. There were a few more heads with their backs to the camera, but before Heather could identify them Scarlett had closed the page and somehow steered Heather out of the room and back to the stove.

'It looks really fun. I can't *wait* till I can go on spa days. I like fish fingers but Archie likes nuggets.' She opened a cupboard and spotted the enormous cake on the shelf. 'Oh wow! Look at that cake. Is that for Mummy? Mummy *loves* cake.'

'Does she? Well, we could have some when she gets here.' Heather was starting to feel quite dazed by the twists and turns of this day. She wasn't really used to anything very much happening. Ever. At all. Today, it really was quite a struggle to keep up.

'Oh, no. That's so funny!' Scarlett giggled. 'She *loves* it but she doesn't *eat* it. And anyway it's the huge main party tonight at our house. She won't want to eat before that, will she?'

*   *   *

The front doorbell rang and Heather staggered

256

towards it. Bea, gleaming, shining, wafted in on a cloud of lavender and ylang ylang.

'This is for you, though I cannot ever thank you enough.' She handed Heather a miniature scented candle. 'You are a *total* star. That vast lunch and then my unruly rabble for tea.' She slipped off her jacket and popped it over the banister. 'How did it all go? Bet it was awesome. I *so* wish I could have been here. Tell me *everything.*'

'Oh. Bea.' Her voice dropped to a whisper and tears sprang up into her eyes. She didn't know why, but somehow Heather couldn't hold any of it in for a second longer. 'Something awful has happened. I've got . . . I've found . . . a . . . lump.'

Bea sprang into life, as if this was a moment she had been training for. In the time it took for the tears to roll down Heather's face, before they even started to drip off the pointy bit of her chin, the children were all shut up in front of the TV, issued with a slice of cake, and Bea was back with her at the bottom of the stairs, with a box of tissues and kind eyes. She fired questions at Heather while simultaneously mopping at her. What was the shape of the lump? Was it Heather's first? Who was her GP? Did they have any insurance? Why on earth not?

'And who have you told so far?'

'Nobody.'

'Good. Let's keep it like that, OK?'

'Apart from Guy, obviously.' Heather blew her nose.

'I suppose so,' Bea conceded, pulling out another tissue. 'We've got a bit of a problem with it being Friday night, of course.' Bea pursed her lips and gave a little moue of crossness which Heather

257

presumed to be sort of jokey. 'Not perfect, finding it on a Friday, was it? We're going to have to wait all weekend, now, aren't we? And my Birthday Weekend, too.'

'Sorry,' mumbled Heather.

'Don't worry.' She squeezed Heather's hand again and Heather couldn't help but notice she was wearing a new wristband: BEAS' 40TH—GIRL'S SPA TOUR!!! 'I'll just have to put it out of my mind. We'll get going next week. First thing. The good thing about being at this age when it's *so* dangerous and can be *so* aggressive is that they do move quickly. Even without insurance.'

'Sorry,' mumbled Heather again.

'We'll just have to cope until then, won't we? But remember,' Bea put her arm around Heather— quite a soft arm, actually. Heather had expected something a bit firmer, more muscle . . . 'just keep it to ourselves for the time being, mmm? Good girl.'

THE DAY OF THE GOURMET GAMBLE

8.50 A.M. DROP-OFF

Every morning, Georgie hoped for a breakthrough. She was so lost, so all at sea, in this whole situation that she could not in any way predict what a breakthrough would look like when it came. But she did feel that she would know it if she saw it. It would be a change, that's what it would be. She would get to Jo's house and something would be different. Jo would look different, or say a different thing. And this terrible, miserable, hopeless stasis would come to an end. Something would shift.

She drove on to the main road that took her to Jo's part of town. The children were at top volume in the back this morning—they were teaching Hamish to rap, with consequences which were, to them, beyond hilarious—but she didn't mind that. Actually, she loved it—when they were all in one place like this, in the car, round the kitchen table, piled in the double bed on a Sunday morning. When she could see her family as one physical object, trace its edges, measure the length and breadth of it, calculate its mass, work out its—what was Kate learning about the other night? Newtons. That's right, newtons. How many newtons are there in that lot in the back? She looked in her mirror. Loads, she thought with satisfaction. Just check out all those newtons. Georgie didn't go in for life plans or any of that rot, but if she did have to come up with some explanation for her point or purpose it would probably be exactly this: to create the largest, noisiest, most solid family that she could. That was enough for her gravestone. That would do her.

It was the quiet that Georgie found so painful. Jo's reluctance to bang on about her private life had turned from refreshing to something really quite unhealthy. They saw each other every day, but communication between them had been gradually skimmed down until it was now reduced to practically nothing. As soon as the funeral was over and the boys were ready, Georgie had offered to take them in to school in the mornings. She could see that Jo wanted to hide away for a bit, but she had thought that was all it would be— for a bit. Now here they were, weeks down the line, and Jo was still hiding away. And it wasn't ideal for Georgie, adding that extra leg to every school run, and she was getting later and later as the term progressed. But neither of them seemed to be able to change the arrangement, because to change the arrangement they would have to have a conversation. And they hadn't had one of those for weeks.

She turned into Jo's road, drew up outside the house and leapt out of the car. Georgie knew that she was partly to blame—always late, always rushed, in a state of perpetual motion and only ever talking as she walked, like she was President of the United States storming around the West Wing instead of a Home Counties mother with time-management issues. It was pathetic. She needed to sort herself out.

'Morning, all.' She darted up the path to the back door, grabbed a couple of the boys' bags for them and moved back down the path again. 'How you doing, love? Much sleep?' Opened the boot, slung in the bags, shut it again.

'Not bad.'

'Is that your breakfast?' Georgie closed the car door on the boys, got into the driver's seat and lowered the passenger window to shout through it while she started the ignition.

'I'll get something else before I go to work,' Jo called back. 'Have a good day, boys.'

Georgie strapped herself in and reversed into the drive to turn round again. Jo was framed in her rear-view mirror, alone in her front yard—'garden' might have been the word for it once upon a time, but not any more—one hand holding a packet of Gummy Bears, the other waving. She looked shrunken, sunk in. Tiny. Utterly alone.

'How's your mum today?' She looked into her mirror as she asked the boys.

'She had that dream last night,' said one.

'About Dad,' filled in the other. 'She's never great when she's had that dream about Dad.'

Of course, one of the reasons neither of them wanted to change the system was because the boys obviously preferred it like this. While Jo had been busy cutting herself adrift, they had gone in the other direction—instinctively, it seemed to Georgie. They were always placing themselves in the middle of things—the school, the football team, the swim squad, the Martins' car. Hiding out in the crowd. Finding safety in numbers. How she wished she could somehow persuade Jo to do the same.

*   *   *

Rachel was walking up the hill; the two girls were up ahead on their scooters. Guy had dropped Maisie off at the Masons' cottage first thing this morning, without any explanation as to what Heather might be up to. Climbing the Ten Tors, Rachel presumed, or a spot of heli-skiing off K2. It wasn't easy, but she just had to accept that Heather was a full-time athlete now.

The quiet was useful, to be honest: there was so much to think about. Rachel had sat up late into the night with that photo album of the old headmaster from the 20s and 30s, and a memoir he'd written. She didn't need that sort of detail— you could knock off a sketch with a school building and a couple of war veterans without having to know any of it. But she'd been riveted, totally caught up in it. Something about what Mr Stanley had said when he retired: how glad he was to have come back from the war too mutilated to face the London future that had been ordained for him, what a privilege it had been to stay in the place of his birth and watch a generation of children go off towards a different future that—

The girls stopped, waited for Rachel and then took her side and matched her pace.

'Mu-um . . .'

'You know Scarlett'

'and Milo.'

'And how she's horrid . . .'

'Ah,' said Rachel, who had mentally parked all of that before Christmas, her own emotional traffic being rather busy at the time.

'We told Miss Nairn about the oranges—'

'It happens every day with the oranges.'

'—and she said that Scarlett was being nice and she couldn't tell a person off for giving a person oranges.'

'And we don't know what to do now.'

'Hang on.' Rachel stopped walking, to concentrate. 'Woah there. What oranges? You didn't tell me about any oranges.'

*   *   *

Georgie turned in to the school car park, shrieked to a halt, flung open the car doors and gave a quick sharp tug to the first child she could reach. They tended then to come out in clumps if you did that, she found, like clothes out of the washing machine—still basically separate objects, but temporarily engaged in a loose tangle which had the advantage of easier handling.

'OK, chop, chop, chop. Let's go.' She took up the rear position as they all headed for the playground.

Clover, standing by the gate, stood back to let them past. 'Tut, Georgie,' she said helpfully. 'You're really late.'

She got all the children into their respective classrooms just as the bell was ringing, and headed back to the car.

'You're always late, aren't you?' Clover was still at the gate, holding a book of raffle tickets. 'And you seem to be getting later. I couldn't bear it, always being as late as you. You need to sort yourself out.'

'Clover, do bugger off,' Georgie said politely. She went to pass her, but Clover blocked the way.

'Just saying. It would drive me mad. Being you. That's all. Anyway. Ticket for the Gourmet Gamble?'

'The what?'

'The Gourmet Gamble! You know, lots of us are

263

making lots of different dishes and then everybody else buys a ticket and then there you are, Bob's your uncle, that's your supper tonight. Honestly, Georgie. What is your head full of? How could you forget a thing like that?'

'What am I like, eh?'

'I know! So. Can I sell you a ticket?'

'No.' Georgie picked up Hamish and tried to squeeze by. 'You can't.' She gave a broad smile. 'You can bugger off.'

'I'm having to organise it all on my own. Of course. Heather and Bea were supposed to help. But they can't now'

Georgie got herself into the gate.

'obviously . . .'

And wriggled through.

'but I'm sure you've heard all about that.'

'Yep,' she called cheerfully over her shoulder. 'I'm sure I did.' She had no idea what Clover was on about and nor did she care. 'Buggeroff buggeroff buggeroff, off, off,' she sang quietly to herself to the tune of 'The Wheels on the Bus' as she turned back to the car.

*   *   *

Heather looked straight ahead as she steered out of the car park. The last thing she wanted to do was meet someone's eyes when she had done such a good job of keeping it all quiet so far. She did have very expressive eyes—her best feature, Colette said—and it would be typical of her—and her eyes—to give the game away now. It had been hard, this week, avoiding Rachel in the mornings and Georgie in the afternoons and not joining in

264

with any of the exercising. But she was sure Bea was right: it made everything one hell of a lot easier if all and sundry didn't know what she was going through.

She drove slowly past the St Ambrose world, going ahead with just another St Ambrose day. In her wing mirror she could see Georgie strapping Hamish into his car seat, and Rachel wandering over to talk to her. The sporties were gathering around Colette's Polo in running shorts this morning, all off to jog round the football club three times. She knew that because Bea had sent her the text anyway—as a sort of cover—even though they both knew that she wouldn't be joining in now. Ashley's mum and a few others were meeting by the gate. Of course, it's WeightWatchers this morning. They never seem to lose anything, bless them, but you can't blame them for trying . . . It was all so normal and yet to Heather—in her car when she was never usually in her car, alone with Bea when she had never been alone with her before—it all looked heartbreakingly remote. Like an old home movie of a past that was lost to her.

Heather pulled herself up. She mustn't think negative thoughts. She was so fortunate, really, that Bea had chosen to take control of the situation in the way she had: marched her down to the surgery first thing Monday morning, taken the day off work today to take her to the hospital appointment. 'I'll do this one,' she had said to Guy. 'You'll need plenty of time off later, don't you worry. Keep calm and carry on, that's the best thing you can do for us right now.' Even then, Guy had started arguing. And it wasn't like Guy to argue. Heather had had to give him one of her very meaningful looks—you

265

see, it was useful having expressive eyes—to make him shut up. But she didn't have to really because Bea was insistent and there was no changing Bea's mind once she'd set it to something, as Guy was just going to have to learn. Bea had held up her hand and said, 'I will drive her there myself.' And that was that.

Or it would have been, Heather was sure, but there was something a bit dodgy with Bea's car today, it was making a slightly funny noise—Guy thought it might be tappets—and she just didn't want to risk it. So Heather was in fact driving Bea to the hospital, which wasn't quite the idea. But it did mean that Bea could catch up with her texting and emailing on the way there—she was so busy and it was a nightmare for her giving up a whole morning in the middle of the week like this. And it was no bad thing really because at least it gave Heather something to do other than just worry.

11 A.M. MORNING BREAK

The wait seemed to be going on and on. Heather had read all the copies of *The Lady* and Bea seemed to be running out of things to do on her BlackBerry.

'Remind me again why you don't have insurance,' she said, with a lovely smile. And Heather obediently started a recap about how they had to choose, really, between the pension on the one hand and the health on the other and they perhaps could get both but now there was the worry about college for Maisie and how although she wasn't like Scarlett, wasn't going to set the world alight, poor love, she did like her books and she

266

could still pick up and they didn't want to not save for uni just because of how she might or might not do in her SATS . . .

Bea held up her hand to stop her. 'Thanks,' she said, 'but I didn't *actually* mean it.' She rooted around in her huge bag and took out an enormous book which Heather at first thought was, like, the Bible or Shakespeare or something, but turned out to be the Stuart family diary. 'I hope they don't give you Wednesdays, because they're no good for me at all, Wednesdays. We'd have to get a rota going from the beginning.' She turned a few pages. 'And then there's a whole week in May when Tony's parents are having the kids while we're off to play golf . . .'

Bea looked so worried there, twisting her mouth while she sucked on her pen, that Heather stretched her hand over to comfort her. 'You know, I probably shouldn't say this, I just feel it's not going to come to that. I told you, my GP was concerned and everything but he didn't look completely worried sick.'

Bea turned, her eyes alight with empathy. Nobody's eyes quite lit up with empathy like Bea's, and right now she had them on full beam.

'You do have to remember, they've seen it all before.' She squeezed Heather's arm. 'It's one in three, love. *One in three.* You mustn't forget that.'

'Yes, but . . .' Something felt a bit topsy-turvy to Heather about all this. She couldn't quite put her finger on it. But then nothing was really as it should be today. 'He did say it was "a good shape", didn't he?'

Bea flicked her eyes up to the ceiling and back again.

'And that all that fertility treatment I went through can do exactly this . . .'

'Listen.' Bea shuffled in her seat while she picked her words carefully. 'You have to realise that it's not yet a year since I lost poor Laura.' That was the first time Heather had heard that Bea was even close to Laura. She had no idea. She had never seen them together. But she could see that did make things much, much harder. 'And my motto for cancer is, and always has been, this: realism, not optimism. From the start. There's so much you're going to have to deal with, lovely. Why add disappointment to the list? That can be *so* painful in itself. Now.' Bea stroked Heather's hair, lifted a few strands, studied them with a frown. 'What do we think? Are we going to go for the Cold Cap? Or is it just not worth it?'

And Heather suddenly had a vision of herself, in a room, under a cold cap. With lots of realism. And not any optimism. And being given Wednesdays. And then Bea having to cancel her golfing . . . And her whole body seemed to sink, down, down into the hard plastic chair. She felt sort of homesick somehow. She wanted Georgie. She wanted Rachel. She really, really badly wanted Guy.

1 P.M. LUNCH BREAK

By the time Heather got back to the car, having dealt with the pay-on-foot parking ticket, Bea was already on the phone.

'I know. Lucky escape. Anyway, I thought you'd want to know as soon as poss.'

Heather turned the key in the ignition and

268

reversed out of the space.

'No, don't worry. I'll call her. I said I would.' Bea hung up.

'Who was that?' asked Heather as she pulled out on to the road.

'Only Colette.' Bea flicked through her phone numbers with her thumb. 'You feeling all right now, love?' But before Heather could reply, Bea was holding her phone to her ear and her finger to the air.

'Hi, Clover. You'll never believe it. *Benign!* I *know.* First time it's ever happened to *me.* I *know.* I *will.* Aw. You're lovely.'

Heather had not worried about her own death for years. It had simply not occurred to her, since she married Guy and had Maisie, to even consider it. Grief: that was her greatest fear. The loss of her daughter, or her husband—that was what kept her awake at night. And haunted her every waking second of her every conscious day. She couldn't help it, she was almost ghoulish about it all. She had a sort of mental scrapbook, and when she heard terrible stories, like that little lad who got leukaemia at nursery or that St Ambrose family whose daughter drowned in Majorca, she stuck them away in there. And then when she couldn't sleep sometimes, and she was feeling miserable anyway, she got them out and went over and over them and put herself in the middle of them and could work herself into such a state that the pillow was soaking and she was having to bite on the duvet cover to stop herself waking Guy, because she knew he'd only get cross with her for doing it to herself. But it wasn't as if she could help it.

It made a change, in a way, over the weekend,

having a whole new angle on the ghoulish fantasy. Her usual practice was to drive herself mad with images of Guy in a car crash—even though he was safety itself behind the wheel, it was always a car crash—and policemen coming to her door. Or Maisie in a hospital bed, and a life-support machine, and a switch. But instead, for a few days, she'd had Guy as a grief-stricken widower. And little motherless Maisie, living on roast chicken because that was all Guy could really do. And starting her periods and being too shy to say anything to anybody and nobody realising and . . . Still, the good thing was she could go back to normal now.

Bea was smiling over at Heather, wrinkling her nose, but still had her phone to her ear. 'Now then. On to the next thing. We Never Close! How are things looking for the Gourmet Gamble? Do you need anyone else to make any more dishes? Cos Heather's got the afternoon free now . . .' She raised her eyebrows at Heather and nodded, inviting consent. 'OK then. She'll knock something up for you. No problem. See you later. I *will*.'

She hung up again, and turned back to Heather. 'They all send their love. You *lucky* girl. Now then. Do you want me to call Guy for you, seeing as how you're doing the driving?'

3 P.M. THE GOURMET GAMBLE

Rachel dug her raffle ticket out of her pocket, got in line and shuffled along with everyone else into the hall. It didn't matter in the least what she got this afternoon; it was going to be her supper, even

270

if Clover cooked it. The kids were out tonight, so there would be no I-don't-like-this and I-don't-like-that. And she was genuinely excited at the evening ahead of her. She was going to start on the Second World War drawing for the library now that she had managed to pinpoint exactly where they'd had the bomb shelter—she couldn't wait to get down to that. And when was the last time Rachel had sat in her own house eating home-cooked food prepared for her by somebody else? It just was not part of the single experience. It simply could not happen in this post-Chris world. To be completely honest, it hadn't happened as often as it should have in a world with Chris. But it had happened sometimes. And when it had, it had been lovely.

It was only now that she was no longer married—well, still in the process of divorce, but it was not a reversible thing—that she saw all this in sharp relief. How all the things that she and Chris had done for one another—just making a pot of tea in the morning (him), or washing the socks (her)—that had seemed at the time to be nothing more than part of the diurnal routine were actually acts of love. Of course, they hadn't seemed like that at the time. Then, they'd just seemed like no big deal (the tea) or a total pain in the arse (the socks). But now, to her, they were romantic gestures that, in their sheer repetitiveness, reinforced the bond between them, renewed their vows in a practical way, over and over again. Until, for some reason, they didn't any more. And there was no bond. But it was only from here, from this bleak new world in which nobody did anything for her ever at any point on any day, that she could see it like that.

And even though the person who had made her

supper tonight could have had no idea that she would be eating it—may not know that Rachel even existed—she could still pretend. Tonight she would go home, pop it in the oven, smell it as it warmed and kid herself that someone had gone to the trouble of making this dish just for her.

All the dinner tables were out, and each was covered with plates with raffle tickets stuck on them. The children were still in class but the place was packed and almost buzzing with excitement. Rachel made her way through to the first one, and saw Heather standing behind it in what was obviously some tip-top majordomo official gourmet-gamble capacity.

'Sorry for staring. Only I used to know someone who looked just like you. Our kids were at school together.' She shook her head sadly. 'Ages ago now. *Tempus fugit*, eh?'

'Aw, Rach, I'm so sorry. I haven't been avoiding you, honest, it was just'—Heather's eyes darted around the dining hall in what looked to Rachel like an almost paranoid fashion—'look, I can explain later.' She reached across the table. 'But I'm so sorry. I've missed you, Rachel. I really, really have.'

'All right. Steady on.' She shook Heather's hand off. 'And don't explain it all to me right now, for heaven's sake. I need to concentrate. I have a rendezvous with a norovirus,' she said in her Ingrid Bergman voice. 'Just don't get in my way.'

Rachel moved on with her number 86. And there, on the next table, it was: fish pie. Her heart leapt in her breast. Yessss! Get in there! Only her favourite, that's all. She took a second to acknowledge that her jubilation was almost tragic, and then dismissed herself. This, this fish pie in a Nigella dish hailing from Bubba's own kitchen, clearly made by Kazia's fair hand—Jeez Louise, the potato on top was actually piped—was the best thing that had happened to her for some months. This, here, was a genuine piece of good fortune. She had taken a gamble and she had won. At last— hello, everybody—Rachel Mason's luck was on the turn.

She looked up from the yellow Post-it note and straight into the eyes of Tom Orchard.

'Oh. Hi. You OK?' There she went again— instant intimacy.

The headmaster carried the unmistakable demeanour of an innocent man recently condemned to death and yet to come to terms with it. 'Mm. Yeah. Fine, thanks.'

'What you got?' Rachel turned her head round to read upside-down. The label said BANOFFEE CHEESECAKE. 'Owph.' And the handwriting was Clover's. 'Oh dear.' She sucked her teeth in sympathy.

His face was a study in misery. 'I know. Looks delicious. Just what I fancied.' He looked down at his plate and shook his head again mournfully. 'Excellent. Anyway. How did you do?'

'Yeah. Good.' She mustn't sound too triumphalist—Christ, it was only luck after all and it could so easily have gone the other way. 'Just, er, um, fish pie. That's all.' She mumbled a bit, said it as casually as she could.

'Huh.' Tom bit his lip. 'Congrats.' He picked up his dish and turned to leave. She found the stoop of his shoulders too miserable to bear. She had to act, and she had to act fast. What else were friends for?

'Hang on! Don't go! Look!' Rachel rushed to his side and held her fish pie next to his banoffee cheesecake. She could feel that people were looking at them, but she didn't care. The grumpy secretary had her head down and was studying the next table. It was impossible to know if she was within earshot but somehow it didn't matter. At that moment, propriety meant nothing. And anyway, it couldn't be more innocent. They were just mates. 'Don't you see? Neither of these dishes is much on its own. But if we put them together, well, we've got a pretty decent meal here. Between us.'

His face cleared. 'Could we . . . ? I mean, sorry, forgive me, but are you saying . . . ?'

'Yes! We could! I am! There's masses and the kids aren't even in—pizza night with their dad.'

The grumpy secretary's back stiffened.

'And, actually it would be really brilliant. There's some stuff I wanted to talk to you about anyway . . .' It was time someone told him about Scarlett's reign of terror this year, and no one else was going to do it. 'Ooh! And I forgot! I've done lots of stuff since we last spoke. I'd love to show you my sketches!'

And at that, the grumpy face flicked back to administer a shocked and horrified stare.

'The sketches that I have done for the timeline in the library.' Rachel enunciated clearly so that everyone round there could be sure to have the right end of the stick for once.

'So bring it round. Seven-thirty. We can share.'

3.15 P.M. PICK-UP

Something hot, sharp and painful burned into the back of Rachel's denim jacket as she swung cheerfully out of the hall. She knew exactly what it was without turning back—the piercing sensation of the grumpy secretary's hostile gaze was nothing new. She shrugged it off as she made her way through to the entrance. Christ, can a single woman not even embark on some *pro bono* artwork for the school without reducing her reputation to tatters? They're actually sick in the head, this lot—they think everything's about sex, even when it could not actually be more innocent . . .

A mild drizzle had started to fall while she had been gambling her life away in there. She stopped to adjust the foil on the fish pie—couldn't take any risks with that piped mashed potato—and looked out on the playground. Georgie was in the middle of the tarmac, and the middle of her children. Kate was balancing Hamish on her hip with an experienced ease, Henry was on Sophie's back, George and Lucy were both looking into the depths of the same PE bag. They always stood out, the Martins; because they were so many, obviously. But also perhaps because they were always touching, connected: the only joined-up shape on a page of dot-to-dots.

She turned her gaze towards the gate, and felt the catch in her throat even before she realised what she was looking at: Chris and Poppy, heading for the car. She had never been there before when Chris met the children from school—why would

275

she? If he was meeting them then Rachel was, *de facto*, elsewhere—and it was curiously fascinating. Like watching a live scan of one's own internal organs—the very fabric of your being, going about its business, as you never normally saw it. For a moment, she was just riveted by the sequence of images: Poppy holding Chris's hand, Chris tucking Poppy's book bag under his arm, Poppy's ponytail swinging as she nattered on. And then she started to interpret what she was looking at: it wasn't just two people here; it was a whole relationship. And not just any relationship, either: it was a natural, vibrant, functioning, healthy one. The diagnosis was obvious, and most unexpected. It was against all the odds. A minor miracle. Despite all the trauma that had been inflicted here in recent months, everything seemed to be in reasonable working order.

She stayed in the doorway while Chris got in the car and drove away to pick up Josh. A subsection of a family—yes, of her family, as a matter of fact—was off for a subsectional family meal. She clutched the fish pie to her chest for safety, ducked into the rain and set off down the hill to home.

THE DAY OF MELISSA'S COFFEE MORNING

8.50 A.M. DROP-OFF

For the first time in months, the sun was shining down upon St Ambrose. Spring had chosen to arrive unnaturally early and in just a week all the leaves had suddenly appeared—as if nature had got out its best set of Caran d'Ache and coloured everything in.

Rachel kissed Poppy on the head and watched her skip through the gate. She, too, looked like she'd been coloured in. They had played tennis outside in the park for the first time yesterday, and freckles had erupted all over her face. And she was laughing a lot more now. A season had passed and what was once painfully abnormal seemed to have become something approaching ordinary. Rachel took a deep draught of fresh, green air. Perhaps everything might actually be all right after all.

'What are they up to now?' Georgie was beside her, holding Hamish and scowling.

The sporty group, carrying a large pole in each hand, wearing a heavy boot on each foot, were setting off at a brisk pace towards the hill. Colette and Jasmine were taking the lead; Heather was very much at the rear.

'OK. I'm no expert. I may have this completely wrong,' said Georgie in a loud voice. 'But are these people skiing?'

The group thrust onwards. 'Hurry up,' Colette panted over her shoulder. 'Bastard of a bikini wax at ten.' Heather, who seemed to be in a spot of bother with her pole, was lagging far behind.

'Is this normal? Skiing?' Georgie was almost shouting now. 'Car park? In spring?'

Colette neither paused nor turned her head, but Heather stopped quite near them, in a muddle with a strap and looking pink.

'We're Nordic pole walking, actually, Georgie.' Rachel had rarely seen Heather so cross. 'And it is said to be extremely good exercise. Clover? Will you wait? For me?'

'Ohhhh.' Georgie kept her voice up for all to hear. 'Nordic. I see. That's why they're all so blonde. Nordic. I say,' she bellowed to Rachel. 'Their English is terribly good, isn't it?'

'Oh God.' Heather's wrist strap was now completely undone and her eyes were filling with tears. 'They're going off without me.'

'Yuu vonnt catch upp vitt demm now,' said Georgie in a lilting Nordic sing-song. 'Day aahr hoff-vey down de piisst.'

Heather threw both poles down on the ground in a fury and crossed her arms in such a stroppy-kid fashion that Georgie and Rachel both had to laugh.

'It's not fair,' Heather added, for the full effect. 'It's all cos of my lump. Bea still hasn't spoken to me since and now they're all trying to get rid of me, I know they are. This is the second time they've left me behind this week.' She sniffed dramatically.

'Well, you can't blame Bea, can you, Rach?'

'Nah, you can't blame Bea. Blimey, it was her aerobics morning . . .'

'. . . And it was only benign.' Georgie droned the last word with contempt.

Rachel yawned. 'Be-oring, more like . . .'

278

'Be-no-lolz.'

Heather shuffled over to stand by them. 'I've been silly, spending all my time with Bea and that. You know, I'm starting to think'—she leaned in and dropped her voice to a whisper—'they're not always very nice people.'

Georgie staggered back in horror, clutching Hamish to her chest. 'No. You can't mean it.'

Heather shook her head. 'They're really not, you know. Georgie, will you forgive me? Can I hang out with you guys more? With your group?'

'For crying out loud, how many more times?' Georgie picked up Hamish and stormed back to her car, shouting over her shoulder as she did so: 'WE ARE NOT A BLOODY GROUP!'

Rachel smiled and called, 'See you all at eleven-ish.' She had to get out of that car park, back down that hill and home to get some decent work done before coffee. But her feet, she noticed, had turned around—quite of their own accord—and were taking her back, yet again, in the direction of the school office.

Since the happy day of the Gourmet Gamble, she seemed to have been popping in most days to have a quick word with Tom. They'd each had so many ideas about the timeline over the fish pie that the conversation was still going on. None of it was any big deal: she had wanted to know more about the Education Act when the school had been founded, and he had dug stuff out for her. She had found a description of the visit by the Prince of Wales and he was longing to see it. Each occasion was as minor, inconsequential and—honestly—completely innocent as the last. When her mum's neighbour produced the hat he'd worn to school back when

279

England won the World Cup, well, of course she had to go running in with that. He just loved it—they both did. But the funny thing about little chats was that they seemed to breed. One just led to another, and on and on it seemed to go.

Rachel could see it happening with Heather, too, just from walking to and from school together this year: Heather would embark on some daft, meaningless micro-conversation about something minor and inconsequential one day, Rachel would follow up on it the next, and before they knew where they were, there was this dialogue between them; Rachel could envision it now, as she trotted across the playground in the spring sunshine: a thread that got longer and stronger every day and that, she could see, had been woven into the fabric of their lives.

Of course, as soon as their daily routine changed that thread would snap. She was hardly going to be good friends with Heather for the rest of her life. Imagine. You needed a few macro-conversations if you wanted to go the distance with someone, and she couldn't go macro with Heather. Christ, that would do anybody's head in. Although, when she thought about it, the only macro-conversations she had recently enjoyed had centred around the shagging of interns, and they hadn't been that great . . . Still. Her friendship with Heather was a temporary thing. Like a holiday romance. Without the romance. Or the holiday.

The classrooms were just settling down to their mornings as she passed by them and strode on towards the office. Towards her other no-romance, nothing at all. She just wanted to find out how the meeting of the governors had gone last night, because she knew Tom had been concerned about it. He'd said so when she dropped off her copy of *Possession* for him yesterday. Which he said he hadn't read on Monday, when they were micro-chatting about the Victorian sketches for the library and poetry came up and . . .

She smiled cheerfully in the direction of Mrs Black—who didn't look up and didn't smile—and went straight through to the inner office.

'Good-morning.' Tom looked up, and he smiled.

'Hi. Just wondered how you got on last night.'

'Nice of you. I think it was all fine.' He put his pen down and pushed back his chair. Rachel was struck by how much more at home he looked now, nearly two terms in. 'They all seemed to be in general agreement with the Orchard budget so far. Your mother is certainly my strongest supporter. She was nodding and beaming at everything I said.'

Uh-oh. Rachel had an instant sense of unease. What's she up to?

'Though at the end the Chair asked if we could meet for a "private chat". She's coming in later today.'

'Pamela?' Uneasier still. What is *she* up to? 'You do know she's Bea's mum? And Scarlett's granny?' This was going to be about the bullying, she just knew it . . .

He laughed at her. 'Yes. And I think I can cope. Hey.' He tapped his own chest. 'Gold medallist at the Dead Brave Olympics, remember?'

He looked so confident, sitting there in the sunshine, linking his hands behind his head, feet up on the desk. But Rachel was worried. Properly worried. 'Look, I'll just pop in later, see if you're still in one piece.'

10 A.M. MORNING BREAK

Heather jostled her way through the crowd and got to the front of the cake table. Melissa was running it all on her own and besieged by customers this morning, yet she looked so calm, unflustered, elegant.

'Can I help you? Let me do something. Please.' Heather always preferred to be part of the team at these events—people had to talk to you then.

'I'm completely fine, thanks.' Melissa really smiled with her eyes. Heather loved that. 'It's just great that you came. What can I get you?'

Heather looked down at the scrumptious cakes on display, and there it was: the very Malteser cake that had literally saved her actual life back at the car boot sale. She popped a bit on to a paper plate. 'Did you make this?' She proffered her 50p. 'You're amazing.'

'Why, thank you.' She chinked the money into the pot. 'Ancient family recipe. Dating back—ooh—all the way to the discovery of the Malteser itself.'

'Wow.' Heather had never realised the Malteser was— Oh. She was joking. So witty, Melissa. Heather must be on her guard for that, if she was going to be her friend.

'Hi.' Colette was beside her, sticking her elbows in. 'Melissa. What can I do? How can I help?'

Heather pressed back through the customers and into the room. She stood alone for a moment, coffee in one hand, plate in the other, and looked about her. People were crowding in this morning, of course. It wasn't every day that most of them got their noses into a house like this. Even most of the residents of this very street had never been over this threshold before. Melissa's arrival here marked a whole new dawn.

None of the gang was here yet. Rachel was bringing Georgie, so they were bound to be late. Who should Heather talk to while she waited? She wandered over towards Ashley's mum—looking like she'd lost a few pounds, daw, so pleased for her—who was by the window with Abby. And then she caught the snippets: acceptance letters, induction days, uniforms, buses. And, Oh no, she thought. No, no, no, no thank you. Not The Next School. Let's not ruin this happy day by going over all that again.

She so dreaded the next stage, it made her quite dizzy. The patterns on Melissa's retro rug started to leap up at her and she had to blink and take a moment to pull herself together. Ever since Maisie was born, she'd been dreading the next stage. That first day, sitting up in the hospital bed, had been so joyous, she felt sad when it became the second. She adored having a baby, and worried about a toddler. And on it had gone. Why did no one tell you this about parenthood? That all it was, when you boiled it down, was a dull ache of regret for what was flying past, broken only by the sheer terror of what was coming at you. The actual present seemed very hard to grasp. She could hardly bear to look at parents walking around the shops on a Saturday with great big hulking miserable teenagers. It felt somehow intrusive to even witness their collective private grief. And as for adults with adult children—how did anyone even begin to cope?

283

She had trained her ears not to listen when the children sang that hymn at the end of every school year. That ghastly one, 'One More Step Along the World I Go'. The very words made her shudder. It shouldn't be allowed, in her view—too graphic, crude. Insensitive. She might have a word with Mr Orchard about it. Have another go at getting it banned.

Maisie still had one more year, thank God. So why torture herself by hanging round those tragic people who were already facing the end? It was like that day last summer when they were halfway through their holiday in Tunisia. She had come away from the pool for a minute to go into reception and check they had their places for the gala dinner, only to find it was changeover. And there were all these other holidaymakers—people she only knew in swimsuits and shorts and strappy dresses—standing in the air-conditioned gloom in jeans, socks, with their shirts tucked in, waiting to get on the coach, resigned. Heather forgot all about the gala tickets and rushed back outside. The very sight of those suitcases on trolleys in reception just made her want to splash wildly about in the sun while she still could.

She would do the same here—circulate in the sun on Melissa's flagstone floor. Study this amazing art on her walls. Look out of the French windows on to that pretty, sloping garden. Possibly sneak upstairs and just have a bit of a look . . . Ah, there were the others now.

'Hi, guys!' She was conscious of her voice being a touch too loud. 'Isn't this just totes awesome?'

'Heth.' Georgie closed in on one side of her, a hand on her arm.

'Please.' Rachel pinned herself to the other. They forced her into the corner.

'We're all very glad'

'you've come over from the Dark Side.'

'And a very warm welcome'

'back.'

'But now, you know . . .'

'it's time'

'to stop'

'talking'

'like a complete'

'and utter'

'arse.'

*   *   *

Georgie slunk away from the kitchen in search of somewhere to sit in the sun and snooze. She had precisely thirty-seven minutes before getting Hamish, and she planned to use them wisely. The throng around Melissa and her tasteful cake table and her welcoming coffee stand was large and loud. Those wretched keenos had taken over the place, tripping over one another and everyone else in their desire to help. She had to get out of there before she was crushed by the mob. There was a note of wholesome collective positivity to the occasion, and frankly it was starting to play on her nerves.

She wandered into the warmth and peace of the pale, pretty sitting room at the front and looked out of the window on to the quiet of Mead Avenue. Just one solitary car drifted up and down the hill, slowing when it came to Melissa's house, speeding up a little before it turned and came back. Perhaps they were under surveillance. Perhaps Melissa was a drugs baron or a terrorist or a Russian spy. That would be amusing—if it turned out that she was, after all, too good to be true. Instead of being just plain old, boring old perfect.

Georgie turned and toppled into the depths of the yellow checked sofa, raised the sluice that held back the fatigue and let it flood through her bones. Every time was more extreme than the time before. Of course, she would get used to it, get on with it, get through it. She always did. But this one, she had a feeling, was going to be just that little bit more of a struggle.

And then the door opened. 'Here's Georgie, in here.' Of course. Heather. Was she never to be left alone? Bloody cheek. Just carrying on with their stupid coffee morning, while some people were trying to have a snooze . . . She kept her eyes closed and her pose recumbent, remained on standby, left her screensaver firmly up.

'Conked out already?' She could hear concern in Rachel's voice. 'A bit early in the day, even for her.'

'Oh, look.' Heather was behind her now, playing with the curtains, looking out of the window, knocking into the sofa with a wilful disregard for those slumbering upon it. 'Isn't that Bea out there, just driving up and down? That's a bit weird, isn't it? There are plenty of spaces. Why isn't she parking and coming in, do you suppose?'

'Hiya! Is this where we're all hiding?' Et voilà, they had reached it: the actual giddy limit. Georgie groped for a needlepoint scatter cushion and plonked it over her own head.

'Hi, Bubba. How are you?'

'Well at least I'm conscious. Actually pretty revved up after my spinning class. Such an intense

286

cardio burn. I'm literally on fire. Here, do you think she's all right?'

'Georgie? Well. I'm not sure . . .'

Uh-oh. Rachel was sounding thoughtful, and shaking her awake. Please, let her keep it to herself and not blurt it out right here. 'Psst. Georgie?'

'Leave me alone.'

'George?' There, she had it. 'You're not . . . You can't be.' The penny had dropped. 'Oh my God. You bloody are.' Rachel slapped her own thighs. 'Aren't you?' She was falling about laughing. 'You are! You are bloody up the bloody duff! Yet a-bloody-gain!'

Georgie opened one eye. 'P'raps. Well, yeah.' She took the cushion off her head. 'Might be. S'pose. Whatever.'

'Oh *no*.' Bubba had her hands to her face in horror. Which Georgie felt frankly was a bit rich seeing as how this baby was actually all her fault, dating as it did from the night of that stupid ball. After which, for reasons inexplicable, they did not seem to have the requisite amount of time to get to the bathroom cabinet. In fact—Georgie smiled to herself—they hadn't even made it up the stairs . . .

'Bloo-dy hell.' Rachel was still laughing. 'You guys! Are you never going to stop? What's the plan? How big is the Martin family going to be, exactly? Ballpark. I mean, will we be able to see it from space, for example? Great Wall of China, that sort of scale . . . ?'

That cheered Georgie up. What a lovely image: the Great Wall of China. Like the Ming, she was leaving her mark upon the planet; like their wall, her family could stretch and flow and rise and fall and live as long as the earth beneath it. She sat up

287

and laughed back and looked around her happily.

And then she saw it, spelled out for her—the reason she had been keeping quiet was right there, all over Heather's face. The envy and the hunger and the misery—the same envy, hunger and misery that Heather had suffered so openly with every one of Georgie's babies—writ large upon it. And a whole new layer of weariness overcame her. A weariness at the thought of the months ahead of witnessing Heather's pain, tiptoeing around it, making all those fine judgements that needed to be made about how much she must share, how much she should contain. And before she had even acknowledged to herself that she could not face the emotional fight, that this time she just did not have it in her to cope with that one extra, tricky, niggling thing, she was on her feet.

'Anyway. Had enough of this.'

She rooted around in her jacket pocket.

'None of anyone's business.'

Time for a spectacular. She made for the door, turned and, with calculated precision, lobbed in a bombshell:

'I'm off for a fag.'

*   *   *

As Rachel moved through the room, everyone stopped and smiled at her. Aw, she thought, how lovely. She smiled and waved back. It must be the early-summer sun this morning—warming all womankind. The crowd around the cake stall parted to let her through. So charming. Sharon and Jasmine seemed to be manning things for Melissa, who was just hovering at the back, in a purely executive role. Rachel took a scone and a dollop of jam and waited her turn to pay.

'Oh, after you.' Clover moved to one side, beaming, friendly. Hang on—that was weird. 'And when you've got a mo, I'd love to hear Tom's views on the New Phonics.'

Huh?

'That'll be seventy-five p, Rachel,' cut in Sharon. 'How is Mr Orchard, btw? Did that stuff work on his nasty cold?'

How did she know . . . ? Rachel mumbled something into her neck and backed away. Yes, she had made a mercy dash to Boots for him, and yes the stuff had worked. But . . .

'Word of advice.' Who on earth was this? Rachel had never even clapped eyes on her before. 'If he really wants to change things round here, he should get rid of that awful old bag in the office.'

She looked around the room nervously. Surely, she said to herself, surely nobody thought that they . . .

'Destiny does love Mr Orchard's funny jokes. She was telling me that before he came to us he was a stand-up comedian . . .'

She was clearly the centre of attention. It was completely absurd. Utterly ridiculous. She wanted to shout at them: No. Stop. There is nothing, absolutely nothing, going on between us. We are just working on this library thing, that's all. Nothing, absolutely nothing else . . . But she could see that not only was it all anyone was talking about, it was all anyone wanted to talk about.

Only Colette, tucked away in the corner with the widower dad of the Year 3 twins and a hefty slab of Victoria sponge, seemed to have other things on her mind.

Bubba stood in the middle of the room with
Heather, and had a sneaking suspicion that together
they looked faintly ridiculous. She was so much
taller and—well, how to say it?—*narrower* than the
squat little figure beside her. There was a worrying
possibility that, silhouetted by the bright sunshine
pouring in through the garden window, they might
just be mistaken for some ghastly, unfunny comedy
duo out of the *Jurassic Park* era. Random names
came crowding into her mind: Laurel, Hardy,
Morecambe, Wise—she didn't seem able to shoo
them away—Cannon, Ball—she really needed to
attach herself elsewhere before, no, too late, there
it was—Schwarzenegger, DeVito. Damn. Bubba
had never liked comedy. She just didn't *get* most of
it.

She looked down on the head of—hang on,
would Heather be the clown or the straight guy?
She could never tell the difference, mostly because
she never got the jokes; anyway, the point was, she
looked down on Heather's head and could not help
but notice that her roots had grown out something
shocking. And then she saw that, although Heather
had—*sweet*—had a stab at splashing on some
mascara, her eyelashes needed tinting. And her
eyebrows needed shaping. And her upper lip was
a little . . . And: Aha, Bubba thought to herself.
Because not much got past Bubba. She was a
people person, after all. So she could see that all
the things that Colette had done to Heather had
now grown out, and they *had not been redone*. Poor

love, she thought as they smiled at each other: they dropped you weeks ago.

'Hey, you two, I'm so pleased to catch you.' Jasmine was before them, holding a plate and a mug. 'I just wanted to say, you know, sorry. About tonight.'

'That's OK,' said Bubba. She was just grateful for the presence of a person of average height, to be honest. It didn't really matter what she was actually banging on about.

'What about tonight?' said Heather.

'Well, you know, Izzy's party. In a way, I'm not happy that she invited the whole year and only left out Milo, Maisie and Poppy. But the thing is, Scarlett did warn them . . .'

'Warn them? Of what?' Heather had turned quite white.

'Well, you know, that if they told the headmaster about the oranges then no one would have anything to do with them.'

3.15 P.M. PICK-UP

Rachel rushed into the playground, head down, staring at the concrete as she crossed over to the main door. She had to see Tom before the children came out. While there weren't many parents hanging about with nothing to do but stand, stare and then add two plus two and make exactly a googolplex. She had simply no idea that they had been the subject of so much scrutiny. She must make things clear. No more discussions about the sketches. No more meetings on the subject. No more coming round to watch a DVD when the kids weren't about. Even though all of it was completely innocent as can be—Christ, they just liked the same movies, that was all—she would tell him: no more. And she could also find out what that busybody Pamela was up to at the same time.

She scuttled, furtively, Secret Squirrel, down the corridor, round the corner, braced to brave old Boot-face one more time. But even before getting to the office, she could sense something wrong. She stopped and wrinkled her nose. She could actually smell it: danger. Danger, with a hint of Floris. The first thing she registered was that the grumpy secretary was already looking up, ready for her. Waiting, it seemed, and smiling. She was actually smiling. 'Sorry,' she chirped in a merry sing-song. 'Very sorry, Mrs Mason. But I'm afraid Mr Orchard is busy.'

'Yes, Rachel.' And then she turned and saw Pamela, her broad form in front of Tom's closed door. Her plump fingers, viciously bisected by rings that had been given to her younger, more attractive self, had possession of his door handle. 'Mr Orchard is *very* busy. When he is on school premises. Very busy indeed. Did you need to see him? Urgently? With a matter relating *specifically to the educational well-being of your own particular child*? If so, do, *please*, feel free to make a formal appointment with Mrs Black here.'

Mrs Black waved a pen in one hand and a large diary in the other, exuding the radiant demeanour of a woman who was at last enjoying one day of happiness in an arid, joyless life. 'We'll see,' she sang, 'if we can fit you in.'

Rachel's head swam in torment. Filled with a vision of Tom, writhing at his desk, tied to his

292

swivel chair, chewing at the gag on his mouth. Able to hear her. Unable to get to her . . .

Chrissakes, woman, pull yourself together. 'Um. Don't worry.' She backed out of the door. 'Non-urgent, I think. Few worries.' She turned. 'But I'm sure they can wait.'

She fell back through the corridors, out into the sun, and picked a spot against the prefab wall where she could stand alone and think. The past half-term looked so different now, refracted as it was through the light of the knowledge that everyone had been spying on her every minute of every day. She revisited her actions, and saw how they would all have appeared to the St Ambrose Special Branch lined up watching her behind their two-way mirrors. The way she went tripping into the office every day, like she owned the place. The bonding—blimey, the exotic mating ritual it must have looked like—at the Gourmet Gamble. Last Sunday, after the fun run, when they walked off into town for a coffee; just them. And, she had to concede, Special Branch didn't even need to bother with the two-way mirrors. Rachel had, most helpfully, paraded herself around as if nobody was watching.

What a spectacle she must have made. Her cheeks were hot. Her mouth was dry. She needed to get Poppy, get home. Change her name. Grow a beard. Emigrate.

'Rachel. I need to talk to you.' Heather was shaking and clearly furious.

'Look, there is Nothing. Going—'

'I just think it's perfectly ridiculous that Georgie's even having another baby. So irresponsible. The planet . . .' She gave her head a

293

short shake of disgust. 'But the smoking. It's simply appalling. I can't get it out of my head. The thought of that poor foetus . . . It is technically actual child abuse, you know that. We have to do something. We must act. We should . . .'

Rachel felt something snap.

'Heather, stop it. Right now. That's enough. Keep it to yourself. For once. Try and think it, without saying it. I don't approve of it either, but I also think it is nothing to do with me. Georgie is a responsible adult who has managed to produce a wonderful family without any help from anybody up to now. So, please, can you and every other busybody round here just . . . Mind. Your. Own. Bloody. Business.'

'OK.' Heather jutted out her chin and looked her straight in the eye. 'I will. And this is my business: when were you going to tell me that my daughter—MY DAUGHTER—was not invited to a party tonight? A PARTY! AN ACTUAL PARTY! When,' her voice was thin and taut, her lips and hands were trembling, 'were you planning to break that?'

'Well, first can we just remind ourselves what we are talking about here: exactly that, a party. A children's party. Not a place at Oxford. Not a cure for cancer. Not the last seat on a lifeboat. A fucking children's fucking party. And I might have brought it up if they actually cared about it one way or another. But they do not actually happen to give a damn.'

And there were the girls. Looking like they were full of something. Oh, Christ, thought Rachel: please, girls, please don't come out suddenly giving a damn . . . And Maisie was saying, 'Go on . . .' And

294

Poppy was saying, 'Shall I . . . ?' And Maisie was nodding like her head could fall off. And Poppy took a deep breath and said to Rachel: 'Is it true you're marrying Mr Orchard?'

'What? Oh, darling. No. No. Look, let's talk about this at home. I'm so sorry . . .'

'Only Destiny says she wants to come cos Kylie's flying in specially for it.'

SUMMER TERM

THE FIRST DAY OF TERM

7.30 A.M. BREAKFAST

Rachel stood by the window of her front room, eating toast and watching the road. She wasn't quite sure what was going on here, but could sense that the Mason family routine and order was coming apart at the seams. The deal was, and always had been, that on the nights Chris had the kids, he had the kids all the way up to dropping them off in the morning. Rachel didn't like it—every single morning that she woke up in that empty house she presumed, from the silence, she had died in the night—but it worked. It worked using school as a buffer between the two parents, and the two houses. And it also kept the meetings between her and Chris to a healthy minimum.

In fairness to Chris, he obeyed the rules and regulations of their system as he would a sell-by date: religiously. But then last night, she got a text saying he was bringing them back early. Then she got one saying he wasn't. And at seven o'clock Josh had called to say they were on their way. Rachel longed to see them, but she couldn't help but notice there was some swirling chaos going on here. And, with her St Francis of Assisi hat on—or was he more of a hood kind of guy?—she knew that was not a good thing.

The car drew up, the children and their myriad possessions spilled out; but by the time Rachel was through the door and on the pavement, the car had sped off again. Josh pecked her on the cheek as he

299

headed for the house.

'Oh,' said Rachel, kissing Poppy. 'Daddy in a rush?'

Poppy stood watching the lingering exhaust fumes. 'Mmm. I think he might be late for the Grumpy Olympics.'

'Ah.' They went through the front door, where Josh was constructing a bag mountain.

'You're not kidding,' he said, as he balanced his boot bag on the top. 'And I know why as well.' He headed for the stairs, and turned. 'It's cos she's dumped him.' And he clattered up to his room.

Wowser, thought Rachel proudly, watching him go. That was by far the longest speech Joshua Mason had made in the entire academic year.

8.50 A.M. DROP-OFF

Heather turned out of Beechfield Close on to the hill and strode into the morning sun. This was always her favourite term: white ankle socks, gingham frocks, grass, rounders . . . She took a deep breath of gleeful anticipation. Ah. She just couldn't wait. Maisie had to run at her heels to keep up. 'What about Poppy? Mum? Don't we walk in with them any more?'

'I don't think so, love. Mummy's in a hurry this morning. And think of all your other lovely friends you're on your way to now. You're going to see Scarlett and Kate and—'

'But—' Here we go again. Maisie at her most difficult.

'No buts. You have seen Poppy every single day of the holidays and you will see her again in five whole minutes. And this term you're going to have lots of different friends, not just— Oh.' Rachel was at her side, but Heather didn't break her step. She carried on marching while the girls lagged behind. 'Hi,' she said, still facing forward. 'How are you?'

'Um, I'm not really sure, to be honest. I wasn't supposed to be dropping off this morning, which was good, you know, because I haven't actually spoken to Tom since—well, you know. But now here I am. And it's all cos of Chris. So now I might have to see Tom. And there is nothing, you know that, don't you? You do know that there is nothing whatsoever . . .'

Quite honestly, Heather couldn't follow half of it, and also thought it might be quite nice if Rachel didn't just mumble on about herself endlessly. Just for a change? 'Well, I'm good, thank you very much. Yes, jolly good. Trying to get to school a bit earlier this term.' Melissa always dropped off early. Heather would too, from now on. It was clearly so much better in every way. 'How were your holidays?' She kept her voice deliberately cool.

'Um. Let me think . . . Didn't see anyone. Didn't do anything. Sat at my desk drawing daft pictures no one's ever going to look at of the school through the ages while the kids disappeared off doing their own thing . . . Yeah. Pretty crap.'

Well, that's where shouting at everyone about minding their own business gets you, Rachel Mason: on your own, with no one to talk to. And walking in to school on a perfect summer's day under your very own black cloud.

'But this morning—'

'Well mine were great, thanks.' Heather just thought she would get that in. Not that anybody was polite enough to ask. 'Really fun.' She hadn't noticed before how slowly Rachel walked. Was she always such a zombie? 'How's Josh?'

'Josh?' Rachel dragged her heels some more. 'Um. Well. Sort of . . .'

'Oh dear . . .' Here we go again. That was the thing with people like this: they always dragged you down.

'Well. No. Not oh dear. I don't think. You see, he just—'

And the thing with Melissa was, she was always so up. About everything. And whenever you were around her you went up too. And that was where Heather was determined to be this term: up. Way up.

'Hey ho,' she said briskly as she bent to kiss Maisie. 'It will all get better soon, I'm sure. See you later.'

There was Melissa, standing over in the direction of the big beech tree. Heather swung away from Rachel and headed towards her fast. Very, very fast. Even though her legs were just longing to run.

'Morning!' Melissa was beaming. She looked like a summer's day herself: a summer's day in human form. 'You don't have time to grab a quick coffee, do you?'

'Wowser! Yes. Please. That'd be great.' Heather beamed back. 'I love your dress.' She was, she could feel it, standing on the threshold of a whole new world.

'Georgie!' Melissa sang across the tarmac. 'Fancy a quick coffee?'

'Nah. Can't. Sorry.' Georgie didn't even turn around, which was a relief. She and Heather hadn't spoken since, well, since . . . Heather did not want

302

her lurking about on her new threshold. With a horrid fag on.

'Are you sure?' Melissa persisted. 'Jo's coming . . .'

Georgie stopped. 'Jo? My Jo?' She walked over to where Heather stood. 'Jo whose boys I just brought in to school and who didn't mention it?'

'Yes, isn't it great? She's decided to try and get back into her old routine this term, which I think is a brilliant idea. But she wants everybody to be as normal as possible. No in-deepest-sympathy, no grief counselling at table, OK? Oh, and by the way, from tomorrow, she'll be bringing the boys in herself.'

Milo Green passed by, being pulled by Martha. 'Have a good day, darlings,' Bubba called after them. Her voice was cheerful, but her face was all screwed up with worry. Golly, she's aged since she came here, thought Heather. She looks about ninety.

'Come for a coffee, Bubba,' said Melissa kindly.

This was turning into a bit of a free-for-all, thought Heather crossly. It was getting a bit crowded here, on the threshold of her whole new world. She could do with a broom, give it a good old sweep. The only person not lurking about was Rachel Selfish-Knickers Mason, and thank heavens for small mercies.

Heather looked around. Where had Rachel got to anyway? Ah, on her own, over there, away from the beech tree—just standing, stock still, staring at Mr Orchard. And there was Mr Orchard, on the steps of the school, with his hands in his pockets, staring back. The funny thing was, neither of them seemed to be about to move, either to speak to each other or to stop the staring—which would have been polite, really, because it is, as everyone knows, very rude to stare.

And then Melissa called over: 'Rachel, we're off for a coffee.' And with that, the spell was broken and Rachel was suddenly at her elbow.

'Goody. Do you mind, I mean, would it be OK . . .' Heather thought how needy Rachel sounded now and how, quite frankly, it had started to get on her nerves '. . . if I joined you?'

9.15 A.M. ASSEMBLY

Georgie was last to arrive at the Copper Kettle, after dropping off Hamish at playgroup. He was up to two mornings a week this term and a plurality of child-free hours stretched before her for the first time in a decade. Thank God she had another baby on the way to put a stop to any more of that for a bit.

The bell gave its melancholy tinkle as she closed the door on the morning sunshine and turned into the gloom. There were the others, at a large oblong table over by the coffee shop's only window. Georgie weaved between the customers—some St Ambrose mothers hurriedly catching up after the holidays, other older women with a more relaxed, all-the-time-in-the-world sort of air—and made her way over to her friends. Jo—thin, pale, brave—was on Melissa's left; Heather—too close, almost hugging her—was on her right. Rachel sat alone facing the three of them from the other side, like a candidate at an interview. Bubba was on the end. Georgie leaned over to give Jo a quick kiss and a

304

squeeze—'You all right, love?'—then sat down. Rachel pushed a teapot towards her: 'Got you a lesbian.'

The conversation was sporadic, a little awkward. While she waited for the ice to break, Georgie poured herself a camomile and eavesdropped on the table next door. Four women—late fifties? Sprightly early sixties?—were catching up. Somebody's A levels were imminent, not a child of theirs, perhaps a neighbour or great-niece or a godchild's godchild, but even at that genetic and emotional distance they all cared desperately. Of course, she had hit the stage of pregnancy when she could weep at frankly anything from footage on the news to an advert for Clearasil—but still, Georgie wanted to weep.

She cherished the growing of things, always had: marking the children's heights on the kitchen wall, tucking the tomato vines up another wire in the greenhouse . . . There was always a profound personal satisfaction to be had from helping something, anything, get a little bit longer without breaking, or snapping off a shoot. That, for Georgie, was life-affirming. And friendships were no exception. The longer they got, the more she cherished them. Why else would she put up with a yawning eternity of Heather Brainiac Carpenter, for Christ's sake?

'Anyway.' Rachel made an attempt at conversation. 'Anyone read the new McEwan?'

'Nah.' Jo put on her bored, cross face. 'McEwan's an arse.'

And those women there had obviously known each other for an even longer eternity, but here they still were: just like Georgie, Rachel, Jo and

Heather, but fifteen or twenty years on. That's just what we'll be like, she thought. Still talking, and caring, about not just each other's children but a whole new generation as well. Because how, after going through these years together, could they ever stop? Maisie had been an extension of Georgie's family since infancy. Heather had held all of the Martin children from the minute they were born. Since Steve died, she had seen Jo's boys every single day. This year alone, they'd travelled together through one suicide and one divorce and who knew what else life was going to throw at them? She could never back out of this now. That would be like chucking in a brilliant book when you'd only read to Chapter Four.

'Do you ever wonder,' Rachel tried again, 'when you see all these old biddies like this, where all the men are? What they are off doing that's so much better?'

'Nope.' Melissa shrugged and smiled. The sun was coming through the window now, and her hair was lit from behind. 'I don't. I mean, I neither wonder where they are, nor do I presume that what they are off doing is somehow better.'

And Georgie suddenly saw it all in another dimension: that here she had something more than a collection of separate, long, individual friendships. Something else, other, had grown out of that. There was now a group—a tight, taut network of people who cared about her and her children and who would never stop. Who, she knew, would always be hungry for any news or developments, who would take them in, consider them, pass them on with care. And she also knew, very deeply, that the more people who cared about

306

your A-level results, or your anything really, the better they would be. That caring was the sticky stuff, the adhesive, that kept it all together. And between them, by this interlocking, this latticework of their friendships, they had built this: a strong support beneath their offspring that would keep them safe, a firm frame on which they could grow.

She wiped a tear from her eye, turned back to the table and collected herself.

'Funny, isn't it?' Heather mused, looking over into the corner. 'That table there was where Bea and her gang always used to sit. Every morning. Till she got her job . . .'

Georgie looked over. 'Hmm. The Algonquin without Dorothy Parker . . .'

'It isn't really, you know,' said Jo.

'Yeah. I do know. That was sort of by way of a joke . . .'

'No. I meant it isn't really a job.' Jo still sounded quite bored and cross. 'What Bea's doing. Not what I call a job, anyway. She met this chef bloke, just starting out, and sort of took him over. Announced she'd be his manager and do his PR and all that. He never asked her . . .'

'Hang on.' Georgie could hardly believe what she was hearing. There was a buzz in her head. A lump in her throat. 'Woah there. Not so fast. This is important. Facts. Please. Jo. Think. What are you actually alleging here?'

'Well, he's not paying her, for a start, not a penny, and I think—'

'What?' Georgie interrupted, electrified. 'No actual way. I knew it.' She grabbed Rachel. 'Rachel Mason, are you hearing what I'm hearing?'

'Well bugger me,' Rachel thumped the table, 'if

307

it isn't an MUJ.'

'An MUJ!' repeated Georgie. 'She's got an MUJ! Christ, I should have known.' She slumped into her chair, slapped her own forehead.

'How on earth,' Rachel was shrieking now, 'did we not spot this earlier?'

Georgie took Jo's hands across the table. 'God, I've missed you. A bloody MUJ. You have made my day.'

'*What*' asked Melissa, 'is an MUJ?'

'A made-up job,' they chanted in unison. 'It's a made-up job.'

'And this,' explained Georgie, 'is a textbook case. Look. There are women in this world—like Jo here, Rachel, and of course you, Melissa—earning money doing proper stuff that needs doing and people want done. There are women like me and Heather, who have made the choice to stay at home and raise our families and can't be arsed pretending otherwise . . .'

Heather nodded.

'And I'm in HR?' Bubba reminded the table. 'This is just a career break?'

'And then there's the made-up jobs. People who say they do stuff and make a huge song and dance about it and bossy-bottom about looking down on the rest of us but they're not doing anything that needs doing and they're not making any money either.'

Rachel joined in. 'You can always tell who they are, because they go to Norfolk or somewhere for six weeks every summer and nobody gives a toss.'

'Like that Abby,' said Georgie.

'Oh, but she's in advertising,' put in Heather, in a respectful tone.

'She gives her opinions on domestic products in a focus group once a month, actually. And that Liz who's in publishing—a bit of proof-reading every now and then.'

'Destiny's mum's my favourite.' Rachel smiled fondly. 'Oooh, she's soooo busy with her career in politics . . .'

'She went canvassing once for UKIP,' finished Georgie. 'Ah, bliss.' She raised her cup of camomile to the table. 'An MUJ. This really is a very special day for us all.'

'The thing is, though,' said Bubba, 'you do have to have some sympathy? I mean, you know, if your husband *does* earn pots and *pots* of money, so you don't *have* to work, but then you want to do *something*, just so you can *say* . . .' Bubba was warming to her theme, shifting in her seat like a panellist on *Question Time*. 'I mean, then, it's terribly hard. Do you see? It's what I like to call "The Wealth Trap"—'

Still, surprisingly, in benevolent mood, Georgie patted Bubba on her hand to shut her up. 'I'd keep that one to yourself, if I were you,' she advised, and turned back to Jo. 'Tell me, tell me. How did you crack it?'

'We've got her mother-in-law up the care home now,' said Jo. 'Bea and Tony've dumped her in there, sold her house, say she's gaga. But she's always pretty lucid on the subject of Beatrice, I can tell you.'

'Anyway,' Melissa said firmly. She was never very comfortable during a good old bitch. Georgie had noticed this before. It was a shame—she was great otherwise. 'Are you guys forming a team for the quiz?'

'Christ, no,' scoffed Georgie.

'We're not losers, you know,' added Jo.

'The quiz,' explained Rachel patiently, a kindly prefect to a first-year, 'is purely for no-mates.'

'Well I'm going,' said Melissa. 'With Colette, Sharon, Jasmine and their partners.'

Georgie snorted. 'Pah. Good luck with that lot . . .'

'Well, it's not the winning that matters, it's the tak—'

'But that's Bea's team!' Heather was shocked. 'They're always Bea's team! Since for ever!' She gripped the table like it was the only certain thing in an uncertain world.

'Not this year. Bea told them this year she was going to win, and she didn't want any dead wood,' said Melissa. 'They were rather put out . . .'

'Oh yeah.' Jo came to life again. 'That's another thing. Apparently Bea's all puffed up because she's definitely got the quiz in the bag. She's stolen three of the players from last year's winners and she's recruited a secret weapon.'

'Has she?' Georgie wasn't quite sure what was happening to her. Was it the hormones? Was it the revelations of the morning? It certainly wasn't the piss-thin lesbian tea. 'Has she indeed? Well, we'll have to see about that.' She looked around the table. 'Girls. There's only one thing for it. Sorry, but here come the words I never thought I'd hear myself say. We are left with no choice.' She gulped, spread her hands out to the table, drew herself up to the full range of her limited height, put on her football-manager voice. 'We are going to have to make a team.'

'What?' groaned Jo.

'Really?' added Rachel.

'Actually,' said Bubba, 'I'm pretty good at quizzes.'

Heather clapped her hands with delight. 'I've always wanted to do the quiz, always, but nobody's ever asked us. Oh Georgie, you are brilliant.' She reached her hand across the table, tears in her eyes. 'And I'm so sorry. Please. Will you forgive me?'

'S'pose so.' Georgie squinted at her. 'Wha' for?'

'For not speaking to you. I haven't been speaking to you for a whole month.'

MINUTES OF THE MEETING OF THE COMMITTEE (COSTA)

Held at: The Headmaster's office
In attendance: Mr Orchard (Headmaster), Beatrice Stuart (Chair), Clover, Colette, Sharon, Angie, Melissa
Secretary: Heather

THE HEADMASTER: Let me just begin by saying, Heather, the Minutes you did for the last meeting were quite fantastic, extraordinary detail.

HEATHER: So pleased you liked them. I wasn't sure. Sometimes I get a bit carried away . . .

THE HEADMASTER: But I think probably this time we don't need quite such a verbatim report. If you could just list the topics covered, say, just make notes of your general impressions of the progress of the discussion and give a quick list of what's decided in the conclusion? That would be plenty. We couldn't expect more than that.

1. PROGRESS OF THE FUNDRAISING
This is going really, really well and not just because of stuff organised by COSTA or that was what THE HEADMASTER said, though I got the general impression that BEA wasn't very pleased to hear that—she did that raising her eyebrow thing at him. Apparently, the FUN RUN raised a lot—at least as much as the LUNCH LADDER and the GOURMET GAMBLE and all that. And it was actually fun, too. We all agreed on that. Except BEA who didn't come to it, although she hasn't said why. Everyone else managed to get there. ~~I got the general impression she's not as fit as she used to be. She's actually put on quite a bit of weight, she's almost jowly, I mean, not really but defo a bit heavier around the jaw, I mean, for BEA, and I just wonder if she didn't come to the FUN RUN because she can't even run?~~

Also some of the dads are running the Marathon—which is so inspirational because that is really, really hard—and they've got huge sponsorship which will get the red to the top of the thermostat thingy as long as they make it to the end. So fingers crossed for them this Sunday. And that's also nothing to do with BEA. In fact, she didn't even know they were doing it. She raised her eyebrow at that, too.

2. THE QUIZ
Everything is set for next Thursday night, at 7.30 p.m. in the Coronation Hall. BEA assured THE MEETING that it would all be a tremendous

success. MRS WRIGHT, Head of the Juniors, has set the questions. The Quizmaster will be THE RENOWNED TV CHEF MARTYN PRYCE which BEA said was very exciting ~~although I got the general impression the meeting wasn't as excited as all that. Nobody seems that sure where on the TV you're supposed to find him or if you need a special, like, box or app or something. And nobody's heard of him at all. Colette muttered something like 'Come back, Andy Farr, all is forgiven.' Anyway.~~ So far nearly 100 tickets have been sold and the licensed bar's all sorted. The idea was that every table bring its own picnic and THE RENOWNED TV CHEF MARTYN PRYCE would then judge the best picnic and award a prize. I got the impression BEA is expecting to win that. Also there would be a RAFFLE and all told BEA assured the meeting the QUIZ would make more than all the other events put together.

THE MEETING then discussed what help was needed before the big night itself, and who could volunteer to help BEA. But unfortunately there were no volunteers because everyone was too busy apart from CLOVER. But then CLOVER assured everyone that she and BEA could get it all done between them as long as BEA could give up a whole day and go around to CLOVER'S house for all of it. I got the general impression BEA wasn't too happy about that either.

3. DECORATION OF THE LIBRARY OVER HALF-TERM
THE HEADMASTER said that the plan was to

313

get the LIBRARY decorated over half-term, so that it would be ready for an official OPENING CEREMONY towards the end of this term, perhaps on SPORTS DAY with A BLESSING FROM REV. DEBBIE and so on. In order to save funds for books and furniture, THE HEADMASTER has decided that he will give up his holiday that week to do all the painting of the interior. RACHEL MASON had already agreed to paint an illustrative timeline of the history of the school as a frieze around the top, above the bookshelves. THE HEADMASTER didn't know whether MRS MASON was free to do this at the same time, ~~and I got the general impression he was too nervous to ask her because of all the rumours and the nasty gossip there was before Easter which was really unfair on both of them and I get the general impression people should just try and mind their own business.~~

MELISSA said that RACHEL would definitely be around then because her kids were on holiday with their dad and she would certainly be able to do it. She personally guaranteed it. THE HEADMASTER looked really delighted by that. ~~In fact, I got the general impression that he was thrilled. His eyes went all soupy and glittering like a sort of glittery soup.~~ He then asked if there were any other kind volunteers who would also give up some time in the holidays to help but no one came forward. I got the general impression that they were going to—COLETTE, SHARON, JASMINE and ME too actually—but when we went to put our hands up MELISSA gave a long hard stare and shook her

314

head. So we didn't. We just sat there in silence instead. ~~And THE HEADMASTER looked even happier.~~ But BEA raised her eyebrow at that too.

CONCLUSION
1. If we include the Marathon and THE QUIZ, the funds have been raised and the target has been reached.
2. THE QUIZ will be organised by BEA and CLOVER.
3. The decoration of the library will be done in half-term by THE HEADMASTER and RACHEL MASON. On their own. With no one else around. While the rest of the school is all shut up and quiet.

THE MEETING closed at 1.15 p.m.

*　　　*　　　*

Heather was just collecting her files off the chair when Tom Orchard touched her arm. 'Oh, Mrs Carpenter.' Bea, Heather noticed, stopped to eavesdrop. 'If you wouldn't mind staying behind so I might have a word . . . ?'

'See you later,' Heather said very firmly to Bea, who did then actually leave the room. She could not quite believe her own awesome power. 'I do hope everything's OK with Maisie?'

'Oh yes. Maisie's perfect.'

'Hardly.'

'It's not that at all.' Mr Orchard sat down and put his feet up on the desk, one at a time. 'I just have a proposal I want to put to you. Now, this is confidential at the moment, I'm not talking to

315

anybody else about it and I'm afraid I am going to have to ask you to keep it completely to yourself for the time being . . .'

Crikey, had anything actually this exciting happened to Heather in her life before? She steadied herself with the back of a chair—it was important that she didn't faint or have a heart attack just at this moment and miss it all, that would just be typical.

'Mrs Black, the school secretary, will be leaving us at the end of term.'

'Oh,' said Heather. Well, that was only the best news ever. 'I'm sorry to hear that.'

'I don't know how we're going to manage without her,' said Mr Orchard, smiling as he tossed a pen in the air and caught it. 'But we're just going to have to move on and find someone new.'

'Hmm.' Heather was racking her brains to remember if anyone had asked her advice on anything ever before . . . It was just the sweetest feeling. For once, she let herself just live in, luxuriate in, the moment. Ahhh. Now then, what was he saying? She mustn't miss it, if she was to be an adviser and advise . . .

'You may not be at all interested, of course, and please don't worry if so, but: I would really love to appoint someone who knows us all already, and who could be a friend to the children, the parents and the school itself. I was talking to Melissa Spencer about it earlier, and she thought that you were that person, and I must say, the more I think about it, the more I agree with her. I really do think you are exactly what we need. Could—is there any way?—I possibly persuade you to apply, do you think?'

3.15 P.M. PICK-UP

Rachel got to the playground a few minutes earlier than usual. She simply hadn't been able to settle to anything all day. Dumped, she'd kept saying to herself. Dumped. Dumped. Well, well, well. The dumper: dumped.

But however much she said it to herself, it seemed to make no difference to her life. She kept sending it down, like a sonic depth charge, waiting for the explosion to reach the surface. But nothing came up. Back in the autumn, it would have meant something: he might come back, they might try again. But now, after all she'd been through, it apparently meant nothing at all. Their divorce was just being processed. Chris had not felt moved to speak to Rachel this morning. And she wasn't sure how much she had to say to him. Two dumpeds, it turned out, did not amount to very much at all.

Yes, she had been lonely in the Easter holidays, and yes, there was certainly a hole in her life. There were loads of holes: she'd been avoiding her mother. She'd had it up to wherever with Heather. She hadn't had one of her innocent little chats with Tom Orchard since Pamela came at her like the heavy mob, and she must admit she did miss them. Rather a lot. Even though there was nothing going on there at all . . .

And there had also been a big change in her children. Their activities had always, up to now, caused Rachel to connect with the rest of the human race several times a day—picking up, dropping off, going out, going round. But the past

317

two and a half weeks, Poppy had for the first time been in the driving seat of her own social destiny— off round the neighbourhood with Maisie, in the sunshine, doing their stuff. Rachel had been relegated to the sidelines, there for emergency use only, hanging about in the lay-by of life like a traffic cop on a road that should be busier than it was. A bit bored.

But however much she picked over it, the tatty, torn netting that passed as her life, she could not actually find in it a hole that was particularly Chris-shaped. And forget the dumping. The best thing about Rachel's day was that little taste of adult human company in the Copper Kettle this morning. She was now hungry—ravenous, actually—for more. She went to find Heather.

'Do you know,' she began, 'that after the hurricane of 1987, this beech tree was the only living thing left standing for miles around?'

Heather didn't quite bother to stifle a yawn. Rachel felt a new, sharper stab of loneliness. Tom Orchard would have loved that little gem. She looked over towards the school office. She could just make out the shape of him, bent over his desk. That was just the sort of thing she would have rushed in there with, and he would have fallen on with delight. And they could have talked about for hours . . .

She collected herself, and as she did so saw for the first time that Heather looked completely different. Altered. Radiant. Like she'd spent the afternoon in bed with a toy-boy or . . .

'So how was your day?'

'Me?' Heather looked around her. 'You're asking me?' She blinked, momentarily taken

318

aback, and then smiled broadly. 'It's been absolutely fantastic. We had the COSTA meeting at lunchtime—which was completely and utterly amazing—and then, this afternoon I've been round at your mum's.'

'Well aren't you the crazy funster— Hang on . . . You've been round to my *mother's*?'

That was kind of world-rocking, albeit in a very minor way. God, it was only Heather and her mum, after all. But still, she had no idea that they even saw each other. That had bypassed Rachel completely. Perhaps she wasn't even hanging around in the right one of life's lay-bys . . .

'Mmm. Well, Guy was round there anyway, putting up her fruit cage, and she wanted a bit of help with her bees.'

Rachel groaned. 'I haven't been round for weeks. Did she say anything?'

'She did mention it. Once or twice. She has got a lot to look after there, on her own.'

'Well, she shouldn't have taken it on, should she? Honestly. The dramas about those bees . . . All for a few jars of honey.'

'I get mine from Lidl.' Jo had joined them. 'Nothing wrong with it.'

'Exactly,' said Rachel firmly. 'Why does she have to do it, eh?'

'Well,' put in Melissa, just back from the hospital, 'it is important, you know, bee-keeping. It's not just for the honey. They do happen to be keeping the planet going while they're at it . . .'

'I know. She was telling me.' Heather's eyes were alight. 'I thought they were amazing.'

'"Without bees, mankind could only survive for another four years,"' quoted Georgie, walking in

319

holding Hamish. 'Einstein, innit?'

'Is it?' said Jo, bored, cross. 'Who does he play for?'

'Science United,' shot back Melissa. Rachel watched as they high-fived each other and laughed together. Yet another relationship that had crept up on Rachel's blind side. Jo was tamed. Utterly tamed.

'Oh yes, very funny I'm sure,' said Georgie impatiently. 'Gosh, aren't we the hilarious anti-intellectuals? Now listen here, you lot. This is not the attitude that is going to win us The Quiz. Enough already. None of you is going to let this team down. From now on, no more pretending to be dumb.'

'But Georgie,' protested Heather. 'I haven't been pretending to be dumb.'

And then the bell rang.

THE DAY OF THE QUIZ

8.50 A.M. DROP-OFF

Bubba parked her Range Rover next to Georgie's God-knows-what. Was it a utility vehicle of some kind? Certainly not top of the range, whatever its range might be. She held Martha's hand and waited as the Martin children poured out of every door and all over their wretched, utterly knackered-looking mother.

'Hi.' Georgie sounded quite cheerful, though it was hard to see quite what she had to be cheerful about. 'No Milo today?'

They walked together towards the school.

'He's with the ed psych at ten, so no point bringing him in really.'

'Golly. Didn't he go quite recently? Hamish— don't run off.'

'We literally *live* in consulting rooms of ed psychs. I can*not* tell you. This must be the fifth. It's a full-time job having a boy like mine.' Bubba smiled broadly, as if she was enjoying all this Parenting the Gifted Child, although the truth was that she was starting to find it a little *wearing* . . . 'That last one was a Tom Orchard recommendation. He has been terrific, actually. Very patient. He sorted out that silly bullying business so brilliantly—*God*, he was brave the way he just took on Scary Scarlett like that! We're all just *slaves* now in our family. He's still very keen to do the right thing and get the right stuff in place so that Milo can actually start to flourish here instead

321

of being frightened witless. But the woman he sent me to was a total. Waste. Of. Time.'

'Oh dear— Lucy, grab him. Why?'

Bubba laughed. You had to laugh really, otherwise it got to you. 'Very nice report. Looked all professional. Cost a fortune, thank you very much. And it said, basically, just summing up in layman's terms'—Bubba stopped to face Georgie, to fully emphasise the utter lunacy of the ed psycho's conclusion—'Milo is *neither special needs nor gifted.*'

But even as Bubba started the guffaw in which she expected—was just waiting for—Georgie to join her, she realised that all the Martins were disappearing through the main school door.

10 A.M. MORNING BREAK

'Thanks for coming, love.' Rachel and her mum pottered together, side by side, up the garden towards the hive.

'No problem,' said Rachel, holding open the gate. 'I really want to have a look, too, actually.'

'I just need to check what's going on in here.' Her mum checked the netting over her face before opening the top of the hive. Rachel, keeping close, peered in. Her mum took out a frame and bent over to inspect it.

'Yes. Look. There they are.'

'There what are?' Rachel studied the frame full of honeycomb. Nearly all the cells were full.

'This is the brood,' explained her mother. 'The queen has come in here and laid her eggs, and the workers are feeding them with honey. But see here.'

Her finger pointed to four cells on the outside—twice the size of the others, sealed off at the top, large and somehow important-looking. 'These are new queen cells they're bringing on here. As I thought, they're thinking of requeening.'

'Who are? The workers?'

'That's the thing, you see.' She put that frame back and slid out another. 'The workers decide. When they reckon the old queen's a bit past it, they choose a few cells, feed them royal jelly instead of honey, and make some new ones.'

'They make the queens themselves?'

'Told you they were fascinating. The only living example of a democratically elected monarchy.' She took out a metal tray, like a grille or a fence. 'This is the queen excluder. Keeps her one side only. She should be here somewhere. Aha!' She pointed into the throng at what even Rachel had to admit was a very superior insect indeed.

'But what's going to happen to her, when they've got the new ones?' Rachel felt a twinge of sympathy, looking at her there. Confident. Busy. Little knowing that she was about to be flung over for a new model. It can happen to any of us . . .

'Well, either she'll take a little gang of bees and go off to start a new hive somewhere else—that's when they swarm . . .'

Her mum fitted the last frame back in and clipped the roof back on the hive.

'Or what?' Rachel followed her back through the gate. 'What are the other options?'

They were back in the garden, plodding down to the house.

'Mmm?' Her mum peeled off her gloves and unzipped her hood. 'That's better,' she said,

323

shaking her head in the fresh air. 'Oh. Otherwise she just gets stung to death.'

Rachel gazed back at the hives with a sense of awe. She shook her head. 'Amazing.' And then peeled herself out of her overalls. 'Thank you. So much. Oh, by the way.' This was going to go down well. Exactly the sort of thing her mum loved to hear. She'd be pleased with this. 'Yeah. Anyway. Um. So.' But Rachel was surprised to find that she still had to choke up the words like a cat with a fur ball. 'I'm going to The Quiz tonight at school.'

Her mum stopped what she was doing and snapped her head round.

'*Such* a fun get-together.'

Okey-dokey, thought Rachel, time to be off.

'I'll be doing the marking—over at the marking table—with Pamela.'

Rachel slung the suit over the back of the garden chair and picked up her denim jacket.

'Be sure you listen to the questions prop . . .'

She slipped her feet into her ballerinas as she put the jacket over her shoulders.

'. . . take the time to check your paper over before you hand . . .'

Picked up her bag and pulled out her keys.

'. . . can't ask for more than . . .'

And headed out for the car.

'Bye then, Mum.'

'. . . that you just do your best.'

7 P.M. DOORS OPEN

Georgie parked, leapt out of the car and thrust towards the hall. Her heart was pumping, her brain

324

electric with pre-match tension, her whole body taut with expectation. She burst through the door, Henry V to the battlefield . . . to find a handful of people moving tables around.

'Georgina Martin,' brayed Clover. 'Of all people. What on earth are you doing here? You're half an hour early.'

Oh.

'Lolz,' laughed Colette. 'It's only the people doing the table set-up here now! Don't tell me that's you.'

Sharon and Jasmine were either end of a tablecloth and stretching it smooth. Bubba and Kazia were busy erecting what looked like the set of *Heidi*. Bea wafted about while Pamela was drawing out the scoreboard with a ruler.

'Got the time wrong,' she mumbled as she backed out of the door. 'Christ. Not helping you lot.' She turned, displaying her small bump in profile. 'Good. Time for a fag. Might have two.' And she fell back out into the car park.

She took out packet and lighter from her bag. What on earth was the matter with her tonight? She was getting quite carried away.

She leaned against the fence and watched the smoke curl gracefully from the end of her cigarette, up and off into the clear evening, and determined to stay out here until the rest of her table arrived. She flicked her ash back on to the tarmac, and became aware of someone emerging from the dusk.

It was Melissa, arms full of a large tray of lavender and herbs in little pots.

'Oh, Georgie.' Her smile was warm and winning. She didn't break her step. 'Look at you. Do your kids know you don't really smoke?'

325

'Eh?' Georgie didn't quite believe what she had heard. Melissa's voice was so casual, so everyday. As if she was saying 'Hi' and 'Nice evening.' And yet it had sounded like . . . She flicked her ash again, mostly so that she could look down and away.

'What? Dunno wot you're on about.' Oh dear. Was that her grumpy-teen impersonation? How did that get there?

'I've been watching.' Melissa was level with her now, but still walking, still sounding mildly disengaged, her mind on other things. 'You light them. You flick them. You throw them away. But you never actually smoke.'

'You're nuts, you are. Totally nuts.'

'So what's it about? Are you hiding behind the smoke?' She had now got to the door but her voice was still soft, like she was just thinking aloud.

'Typical shrink—'

'Psychotherapist.' She turned round to push it open with her neat bottom.

'—mad as a snake.'

'Or do you use it just to keep people away?' She was now into the hall, yet still clearly audible. How did she do that? The woman was spooky.

'Don't tell me,' Georgie shouted after her, 'you actually get paid for spouting this kind of nonsense?'

But the door had already closed.

7.30 P.M. DRINKS

Rachel had been to several functions in the Coronation Hall in her time, each one more

326

moribund than the one before. So she was taken aback to walk through the solid-oak door and find the place throbbing with life. How sweet, she thought. The losers and no-mates, all excited for their big night out—one mustn't begrudge them. She checked her watch. Let's hope it doesn't take too long. The best possible outcome to this evening would be ten-thirty, tucked up, *Newsnight*.

She stood close to the entrance and scanned the room. Her mum and Pamela were over by the scoreboard. Pamela was sporting the very headset that Bea had worn to the Car Boot Sale, if she was not mistaken. They were either side of—oh Christ, she hadn't seen him for weeks—Tom Orchard. Rachel had heard that he wasn't on anyone's table yet. He was just going to fill in wherever he was needed. And right then he was just standing there while the two old biddies carried out a tug-of-love battle over his person. Obviously, they each had very firm ideas of where he should be placed. Right, Rachel thought: whatever was going on over there was to be avoided.

She swivelled to the tables, and was startled by the sight before her. Rachel's definition of 'picnic' was 'cheese and tomato sandwiches and a packet of crisps'. She'd been quite looking forward to it—might have thrown in a Twix—until Bubba had told her not to bother, that she and Kazia had it all in hand. Now, it was revealed that there was a whole other meaning to the word.

Bea's table was laid with white linen, gleaming silver and a range of candelabra. Bea herself was in a fuchsia strappy number, with the added adornment of a tiara that Rachel knew belonged to Scarlett; Tony the Perv—even fatter and redder

327

than he had been at Christmas—was squeezed into his DJ; their guests were clustered around them, sipping champagne. The name of their team—THE REIGNING CHAMPS—wedged in a floral arrangement, was sticking up like a middle finger to the rest of the room.

Clover, wearing a sombrero, sat at a table decked out with cacti, surrounded by teachers. Oh dear, thought Rachel. Mexican food, cooked by Clover: all the staff will be off tomorrow, puking. Melissa's table looked the prettiest from here. A checked green tablecloth, with little pots of spring flowers and home-grown vegetables: The Constant Gardeners, they were called.

And then Bubba, in full Tyrolean costume, her hair in plaits, waved her over to an Alpine scene. 'What do you think?' she beamed. 'Fondue!' She gave a quick yodel. Georgie, already sitting down, rolled her eyes. 'Tell you what, it was a bugger getting hold of the edelweiss.' Jo sat slightly apart, with crossed arms and a cross face. Guy Carpenter looked pale and abject. 'Trouble is,' Heather muttered to Rachel, 'he's not supposed to have bread or cheese.' Mark Green poured Rachel a glass of glühwein. 'Don't worry, my love. It'll all be over before we know it.' He dropped his voice to a whisper. 'I've taken the precaution of booking a work crisis for nine.'

Rachel stole another look at Tom Orchard. The fight between the mothers over his person was still going on.

'So who's the secret weapon going to be then?' Georgie looked over to Bea's table. 'We should lay bets.'

'My money's on Wittgenstein,' said Rachel.

328

'Oh,' Heather began, 'is he loc—' She caught Georgie's look. 'Sorry. Doing it again, aren't I?'

'Heth, after thirty years of stasis I think I can finally say: you're coming on,' said Georgie. 'I'm going Melvyn Bragg.'

'What about that bloke off *Eggheads* with the dodgy shirts?' suggested Jo. 'Someone once saw him in our Waitrose . . .'

The door opened and in walked Chris. He stood at the threshold, looked around, spotted Rachel and gave her a friendly wave. What on earth, thought Rachel, is he doing here? She felt cold all over. Has something happened to the children? Josh has burned the house down. He's dead in a ditch . . . And then she saw Bea stand up and beckon him over. No, she said to herself. He cannot be her secret weapon. Not Chris. She wouldn't do that. Nor would he. They couldn't join up against her like this. They weren't that awful . . .

She watched as Bea kissed him warmly on both cheeks, Tony the Perv slapped him on the back and he shook hands with the rest of the Reigning Champs.

How dared they? This was Rachel's territory now, not his. He had, as she understood it, sought pastures new and he could bugger off back to them. Rage was building in her. She was almost on her feet when she felt a kind and steady gaze coming at her from the next table. She turned, looked in Melissa's eyes and, even as she did so, the completely other point of view swam up before her: Actually, isn't it a good thing that Chris is here? she asked herself. After all, he is a parent too. And she sat down again.

'This is fantastic!' Georgie cackled, giving Jo a

high-five.

'Could not be better.' Jo was, unusually, laughing.

'Well, of course, I can see it's definitely a good thing,' said Rachel, who felt sick, physically sick. 'Obviously. But I don't think it's funny.'

'Don't you really?' asked Georgie, wiping away the tears of laughter. 'No, you probably don't.' She coughed, collected herself, straightened her own face. 'Listen, love, at some time you should know the truth and now is as good a time as any. The thing is, Chris—' She stopped. She gulped. She tried again. 'You see, Chris . . . is . . . Well, Chris . . .'

'I've already told her,' said Jo, firmly. 'Chris is an arse.'

'Yes. Thank you, Jo. Needed to be said. Good to have that cleared up. It's high time you realised, Rachel, that you were the brains in that marriage.'

'And Chris,' reiterated Jo, 'was the arse.'

'Indeed. And of course, what that means is: if that is who we are up against, if that really is her deadly secret weapon, then we are in with a shout.'

'Well, you say that,' said Bubba. 'But we do still only have seven players, you know.'

'Yes,' said Heather, chewing her lip. 'And one of them's only me . . .'

Indeed, thought Rachel, whose corporeal being was now consumed with a desire to win, greater than any desire she had felt about anything for years. And another one is your dull husband. And then there's Mark I'm-a-Spiv-and-I'm-Proud Green.

'Where's Will?'

'At home. Couldn't get a babysitter.'

God help us . . .

'Well I'm pretty good,' said Bubba encouragingly. 'Very strong in the arts, in particular. And anything that requires, you know, *emotional* intelligence or *empathy* . . .'

'Good-oh,' said Georgie. 'Fingers crossed for an empathy round.'

The microphone whistled.

'Hello, good-evening and welcome,' began Martyn Pryce, 'to the St Ambrose Annual Quiz Night.'

They all turned round to face the front.

'He's lame,' said Jo, quite loudly.

'First things first, every team needs a name'

Georgie turned back to the table. 'Got that,' she said. 'We are the Outsiders.'

'and a captain.'

'Me!' Georgie stuck her hand up before anyone else could. 'Me, me, me. I'm captain.' She wiggled her fingers in the air. 'It's me.'

At that moment Rachel's mother came bustling across the room, towing a sheepish-looking Tom Orchard by the lapel.

'Ah,' she said. 'Here we are, Mr Orchard. At last. A table with a spare seat. Perhaps we can squeeze you in here?' She pulled out the empty chair next to Rachel's, without letting go of his jacket. 'I see you're one player down on this team. Here's an extra man for you.' She forced Tom down by his shoulders. 'There you are, Tom. This will do. As good a place as any.' She pushed his chair firmly back into the table. His thigh brushed Rachel's. 'Just to make up the numbers.' And she bustled off again.

Round One: General Knowledge

'You'd better be scribe, Mr Orchard,' said Georgie, pushing the answer sheet towards him.

'OK,' he replied. 'But please, call me Tom.'

'RIGHT,' bellowed Martyn Pryce. 'WE'RE OFF. HERE'S THE FIRST QUESTION OF THE ST AMBROSE QUIZ AND IT IS THIS:

OF WHAT IS AMBROSE THE PATRON SAINT?'

They all knew that one. That was the first picture in the timeline that Rachel had done: him with his beehive.

'Good start,' Tom said. 'Where are the pencils?'

'Bea put them out. Has she not given us any?' asked Georgie. 'I don't believe it. How low exactly is she planning to stoop? Who's got a pen?' Nobody said anything. 'Brilliant. Two bloody fondue sets and a bunch of edelweiss, yet no sodding pen.'

'I've got my crayons,' said Rachel, opening her bag. 'But they are my favourites. You have to be careful . . .'

Georgie snatched them from Rachel's clutches and gave them to Tom. 'Here you are, Mr Orchard. Tom. Now focus, you lot. Favourites, indeed. Will you bloody well focus.'

'WHO OR WHAT IS THE STARBUCKS LOGO?'

'Ooh!' Bubba gave a little jump and whispered the answer. 'I forgot about coffee. I'm *very* up on coffee.'

'HOW MANY TEETH DOES A TORTOISE HAVE?'

'OMG!' squeaked Heather. She whispered the answer to Tom. 'Only pet Guy's not allergic to.' She clapped her hands in triumph. 'That's how I know.'

'WHERE WAS THE FIRST ESCALATOR IN BRITAIN?'

Bubba knew again. 'And retail!' she mouthed to the table. 'I'm *fabulous* on retail.'

'WHICH IS THE HOTTEST PLANET?'

Everyone knew that.

'OVER WHICH WATERFALL DID SHERLOCK HOLMES FALL?'

Rachel and Tom huddled together and conferred.

'WHAT CONTRIBUTION TO TEXTILES AND ANGLO-AMERICAN CO-OPERATION WAS MADE BY DR WALLACE CAROTHERS?'

'Me! I know!' squeaked Bubba. 'Fabrics too! I'm *brilliant* at fabrics.'

Well, well, well, Georgie thought to herself. Look at us. A proper, functioning team. Whoever would have predicted it? She stole a look over at the enemy. Bea and Tony were fussing around with drinks. The three ringers were hunched geekily over their answer sheet and Chris was sitting there, smiling. Georgie knew that smile. It was the smile of someone who is way out of his depth, but pretending otherwise. The smile of an idiot who has perfected the art of posing as an intellectual; the smile, in her experience, of an arse. Not for the first time did she feel a frisson of fury that he should have had the damned cheek to leave her Rachel.

'WHICH PUBLICATION HAS A SECTION HEADED "THE HERDING OF ANIMALS AFTER SUNSET"?'

Guy leapt forward and gave the answer to Tom. 'Then it must be *The Highway Code*,' whispered Heather. 'Only thing he's read.'

'OF WHOM DID CHAUCER WRITE: "AND GLADLY WOULD HE LEARN AND GLADLY TEACH"?'

'You can leave that one to me,' said Tom.

'WHO CREATED MR CHIPS?'

'And that,' he smiled.

'AND WHERE IN BRITAIN ARE THE REMAINS OF ST EDMUND INTERRED?'

Blank faces all round. 'Damn,' said Georgie. 'We were doing all right up till then.' Then Rachel whispered something into Tom's ear, and pressed up against him as he whispered back. And then she held her hand over her mouth as she said something else and he said she was brilliant and she said he got there first and they both hunched, tightly, giggling, over the table as he wrote it down. And when he got up, they were pressed together still. And, Well, well, well, thought Georgie again, as she watched them.

Well, well, well.

Round Two: Words and Numbers

'IF THERE'S ONE THING ST AMBROSE CAN PRIDE ITSELF ON IT IS THIS: ALL CHILDREN LEAVE HERE WITH AN EXCELLENT GROUNDING IN LITERACY AND NUMERACY.' There were murmurs of approval. 'BUT WHAT ABOUT THEIR PARENTS? THAT'S WHAT WE WANT TO KNOW. SO THIS ROUND IS ABOUT YOU

AND YOUR WORDS AND YOUR NUMBERS. PENCILS AT THE READY.'

Rachel sat back in her seat. She didn't need to test her own numeracy, thanks anyway. No one was going to win anything with her number skills. Georgie, Tom and Mark seemed to have this covered. Especially Mark.

'HOW MANY DOZEN IN ONE THOUSAND ONE HUNDRED AND FORTY?'

Blimey. He was incredible. Tom shifted in his seat slightly, and his leg found Rachel's again.

'HOW MANY SQUARES ARE THERE ON HALF A QUARTER OF A CHESSBOARD?'

Mark whispered the answer even before Martyn Pryce finished the question.

'HOW MANY WHOLE NUMBERS DIVIDE EXACTLY INTO TWO THOUSAND FOUR HUNDRED AND THIRTY-ONE?'

He was like Rain Man.

'I'm stronger on the arts,' Bubba murmured to the table. 'The humanities. And so on. . . '

'AND THE NEXT QUESTIONS ARE ABOUT THE ENGLISH LANGUAGE.'

Tom was predictably reliable on his pronouns, she was glad to see. No help required there.

'IF YOU COMBINE A FORM OF THE VERB "TO BE" WITH THE PAST PARTICIPLE OF ANOTHER VERB, WHAT IS CREATED?'

But now Rachel leapt forward again, and her thigh was pressing into Tom's. The rest of the team fell away, happy to leave them to it. Not surprisingly. For who round here could know more than her about the passive voice? Hey, she'd been really working hard on that lately, seriously swotting up: she was left by Chris; she was dumped

335

by Bea; she was made fun of at that ghastly ball. Yes, she was flirted with, for a brief—rather happy, looking back on it—period. Then she was frightened off by those two dragons.

'SPELL THE FOLLOWING: MILLENNIUM.'

Tom spelled it.

Blimey, she could be a contender at the Passive Voice Olympics. She didn't quite know what Bea and Chris were up to over there with The Reigning Champs but she did know that she was being put in a difficult position. And she was now being made to realise that that was enough of that.

Well, from right now, she was starting to take control of things.

'MEDICINE.'

And Tom spelled that.

Henceforth, her personal pronoun would be at the forefront of every active verb she could think of.

'AND LASTLY, HERE'S ONE FOR THE GARDENERS OUT THERE: ESCHSCHOLZIA.'

And he even knew that one too.

'Oh Mr Orchard,' she said. The warmth from his touch was radiating out from her thigh, spreading all over her lower limbs. 'You are a lovely speller.'

Round Three: Sport

'ANY JOKERS FOR SPORT?' asked Martyn Pryce.

'Christ, no,' said Georgie to the table. 'Oh shit. I was hoping this wasn't going to come up. Anyone know anything whatsoever?'

'Yup. Me. Give it here.' Jo grabbed a crayon,

hunched over the answer sheet and took herself into a zone of her own.

'Now that,' said Georgie, approvingly, 'is what I call teamwork.'

'WHAT ROLE DOES THE CYCLOPS PLAY IN MODERN SPORT?'

The rest of them were left with nothing to do but chat quietly and nibble on slices of schnitzel.

'HOW MANY TIMES DID RED RUM WIN THE GRAND NATIONAL?'

'So how long have you all been friends, then?' asked Tom. 'You seem like you've known each other for ages.'

'Well, Heather and Georgie met when they were eleven,' Rachel began.

'Oh, earlier than that,' said Heather happily. 'We first met at Brownies.'

'Shush, Heather,' said Georgie. 'Jo is trying to concentrate.'

'HOW MANY TIMES WAS GARY LINEKER BOOKED IN HIS WHOLE CAREER?'

'No actual way,' squeaked Rachel. 'Georgina Martin, you were never a Brownie.'

Georgie shuffled uncomfortably and gave Heather a sharp kick under the table.

'Oh but she was,' said Heather proudly. 'She was a wonderful Brownie. So committed. Badges all down her arm.' She beamed around the table. 'George was my sixer, actually. I worshipped her.'

'Shut up, Heather,' Georgie hissed.

'FOR WHICH TEAM DID ROY OF THE ROVERS PLAY?'

'Ooh, yes, shut up, Heather,' cackled Rachel. 'What happens round a mushroom—'

'Toadstool,' Georgie snapped.

337

'—stays round a mushroom.'

'TOADSTOOL.' She couldn't seem to hold herself back. 'IT'S A FUCKING TOADSTOOL.'

'EMLYN HUGHES PLAYED FOR ENGLAND SIXTY-TWO TIMES. HOW MANY GOALS DID HE SCORE?'

Bea was staring at them with her eyebrow raised.

'There we are then,' interrupted Jo, pushing her answer sheet into the middle of the table. 'Think we've done all right there. Quietly confident. If anyone else wants to give it the once-over . . .'

'Jo, you're a star. I wouldn't have a clue about any of them. You have saved the day.'

'You have,' added Rachel. 'Go on, sixer, give her a badge.'

'Actually,' said Jo, 'we should all be thanking Steve. I wouldn't have known any of those without him.' She got up. 'Might just nip off for a fag.'

'OK. Papers please,' called Martyn Pryce.

'The sixer does not hand out the badges.' Georgie held their answer sheet over her shoulder for collection. 'They are in the gift of Brown Owl.' And then she hissed, very quietly, the lowest, the dirtiest insult she knew: 'Boggart.'

Round Four: Popular Entertainment

'Good. Come on, team.' Georgie shook a fist across the table. 'We're strong on this. I can feel it. Best shot here. We need our best shot.' Rachel was not quite sure what had happened to the Georgie she knew and loved, but she certainly didn't recognise this one.

'WHOSE WAS THE FIRST ROYAL

338

WEDDING TO BE BROADCAST IN COLOUR ON TELEVISION?'

Georgie whispered the answer and gave a louder 'Yesss!' for the rest of the hall to hear. And there was that fist again.

'WHO SHOT JR?'

Heather got that. Georgie's excitement was growing.

'NAME ALL THE TELETUBBIES, GIVING THE COLOUR OF EACH.'

How could Rachel not know that one? Or Chris? Josh had been obsessed with them as a toddler. An entire era had revolved around Teletubbyland. They had effectively lived on Home Hill. They knew every uttering of every episode. Dipsy, Lala and their strange, fat friends were the principal icons of Mason family history. She stole a look over at The Reigning Champs, preparing herself for Chris's eyes meeting hers, guarding herself against a flash of recognition, a moment of intimacy . . . He was still chatting away to Tony the Perv. The question, it seemed, held no live significance to him. The Teletubbies were but ancient history. And Chris had never seen the point of ancient history.

'HOW DID LADY BELLAMY DIE?'

She and Tom both knew that one.

'OF WHICH REAL US CITY IS CARCHETTI THE FICTIONAL MAYOR?'

And that. The first time he had come round was the night of the Gourmet Gamble. Tom had studied her shelf of box sets while Rachel had knocked up a salad to go with the fish pie. It had become apparent then that their taste in TV was not just compatible, it was identical.

'WHO WHEN WE FIRST MET HIM WAS

SEVEN HUNDRED AND TWENTY YEARS OLD, HAD TWO HEARTS AND CAME FROM THE PLANET GALLIFREY?

Rachel looked over at Chris again. Another child, another passion . . . He was checking his BlackBerry.

'FROM WHICH FILMS DO THE FOLLOWING LINES COME:

'"TOMORROW IS ANOTHER DAY"?'

This round really was falling very nicely for them. Georgie was half out of her seat with excitement.

'AND FOR YOUR LAST QUESTION: "WHEN YOU REALISE YOU WANT TO SPEND THE REST OF YOUR LIFE WITH SOMEONE, YOU WANT THE REST OF YOUR LIFE TO START AS SOON AS POSSIBLE."'

Rachel whispered to Tom. Tom smiled as he wrote it down.

And that was it for Georgie. She could no longer contain herself. She was on her feet. 'Oh ye-ah, oh ye-ah'. She was wriggling, gyrating around the table. 'Outsi-ders. Outsi-ders.' Doing a strange stirring motion with her hands. 'Oh ye-ah. Oh ye-ah. OUTSIDERS. *Yeah.*'

9.15 P.M. SUPPER BREAK

'I'd better just go and say hi to a few people before supper,' said Tom as he rose. 'Excuse me.'

'Seems very nice,' said Georgie, watching him go. 'Solid player.'

'Yeah,' agreed Jo. 'Not an actual laugh a minute though, is he? I dunno. The boys go on like he's some comic genius, but I can't say he cracks me up.'

340

'Same,' agreed Heather. 'Sometimes Maisie just sits there giggling about some remembered Headmaster's Funny Joke. And we can't make head nor tail . . .'

'Anyway,' said Georgie. 'Back to important matters: I am a proud woman here tonight. Proud of our performance. Proud of the way we have conducted ourselves. The first half has seen some good solid play, with the occasional flash of brilliance—'

'Oh, it was just luck, really, with the retail coming up *and* the coffee,' put in Bubba, while she fiddled with the meths.

Georgie carried on. 'Looking at the scoreboard, that's a strong position we're in there. And we haven't played our joker yet. So . . .'

'What is she banging on about?' said Jo. 'Shut up, George. I'm starving.'

Time for the big moment: get this lovely cheese bubbling away. Bubba got out her matches, was just about to strike one when out of nowhere Bea's *ghastly* mother bore down upon them—like a huge giant monobosom out of, like, a monobosom horror film—and snatched it from her hands.

'No, no, no, you don't,' boomed Pamela. 'Health and safety! Health and safety! What more do I have to say than HEALTH AND SAFETY? Are you COMPLETELY MAD? There will be NO MATCHES IN THIS BUILDING.'

The whole hall was now watching them. 'But . . . We're having a fondue? It's our theme?' And it wasn't even fair: Bea had lit her candles. Where was Mark? She looked around wildly. He'd know what to do. Why was he on his way out of the door? 'Darling? Come back . . .'

341

'Sorry, babe,' he called across, waving his mobile. 'Can't stop. Work. Crisis. Gotta go.'

The monobosom thundered on. It did not care about Bubba's theme. It did care about burning the house down. It was confiscating the matches. And then off it thrust, this confiscating, thundering monobosom, to ruin some more fun elsewhere.

*   *   *

Rachel was outside in the car park, taking in several much-needed draughts of fresh night air. She had been unable to settle once Tom had left the table, she didn't know why. She was hot, yet her legs felt suddenly chill. And jumpy. Nervous. She needed to calm down.

'Hello.' Suddenly Chris was beside her. 'How's your team doing then?'

'Evening.' This felt weird. Although she had seen Chris twice a week for the past six months, they were never actually alone together any more. 'We're holding our own so far. You?'

'Good, I think. It's pretty easy, isn't it?' Was that a scoff? It was. He was scoffing. 'We've got a few geeks who seem to be taking it seriously, so I'm letting them do most of it. Just chip in when they're stuck. Don't want to steal anyone's glory.'

Rachel did not trust herself to reply.

'I know it's not one of "my days", but I thought I might pop round afterwards. As I'm in the 'hood. Kiss the kids. Perhaps we could have a nightcap.'

'Sure,' shrugged Rachel. Good idea. We're co-parents, so, obviously, it would be good to . . . But even while her head was saying all that to itself, her heart just carried on sinking anyway, entirely under its own steam.

'Great.' He patted her on the bottom. She flinched. He didn't notice. 'And may the best team win, eh?'

*   *   *

The Outsiders stared down mournfully at the Tyrolean tablecloth. Georgie picked up a bread cube and sucked on it sadly. 'That's that, then,' said Jo, with her head in her hands.

'Oh dear. Poor you.' Melissa was suddenly among them. 'Can I offer an emergency food package? We're a garden of plenty over there.' As she pointed, Sharon and Jasmine rose to their feet, lifted a couple of plates and brought them over.

'That's a goat's cheese tart with thyme, garden mint and early-summer vegetables,' smiled Melissa as she found a space on the table. 'All grown by our fair hands, and pretty delicious. And the first strawberries—best taste of the year, don't you think? Full of the promise of a future.'

Jasmine handed over two salads—one garden, one potato. 'And if you want any more,' said Melissa 'just shout.'

Bubba watched them all fall, like extras in *Les Mis*, upon Melissa's cast-offs. Which were pretty ho-hum-looking in her view and anyway nothing whatsoever to do with the theme. 'Nice bread cubes here,' she offered, 'to have on the side?'

She kept her eyes down. She couldn't see Bea's table. But they were laughing at her over there, she just knew.

*   *   *

343

Colette walked past on her way to the bar, beaming and pushing a man ahead of her like a supermarket trolley. She gave them all a wink.

'Hey,' said Rachel. 'That's not the same one, is it? Isn't that a different one? Psst, Colette! That's not the same bloke who came on the fun run, is it?'

Colette giggled and leaned in to the table. 'New one, as a matter of fact. They're like number nineteen buses at the moment. Turning up all at once.' She gave a cheerful shrug and wiggled onwards.

Georgie turned to Heather. 'I thought she was seeing the twins' dad.'

'Moved on to internet dating now.' She looked fondly at Colette's retreating derrière. 'Bless. She's so much happier. Every weeknight, she goes shopping for men on the web, and then when the kids are with their dad at the weekend she gets them delivered. It's ever so sweet.'

'Ugh, for God's sake,' spat Georgie in fury. 'That's disgusting. They're not turning up like number nineteen buses at all. That is a totally misleading analogy. The thing about the number nineteen bus, Mr Orchard Tom,' she leaned in to the headmaster, 'is that it turns up of its own accord. See?'

Tom took another slice of tart and nodded.

'Now, internet dating, that's a different thing altogether. That is like getting on to the bus depot and saying to the manager, "I would like to charter a series of nineteen buses and I want them to stop at my house and at my own convenience."'

'And then giving them one when they get there,' added Jo with a leer.

344

'Typical Georgie,' Rachel explained to Tom, as she forked in some nasturtium salad. She felt better with some food inside her. And sitting back here. With him. 'Couldn't give a monkey's what anyone gets up to in private, but wanton abuse of a metaphor? In public?' She gave a low whistle. 'Terrible . . .'

'I must say,' said Tom, laughing, 'it's good fun on your team. Even if we're not going to win.'

'Well we like having you, Mr Orchard Tom.' Georgie bowed her head in welcome. 'And we bloody are'—she thumped the table—'GOING TO BLOODY WIN.'

Round Five: Soaps and Celebrities

'Argh,' said Georgie, banging her head on the table. 'If I could have my time again, I wouldn't spend it doing a victory dance when we were only halfway through.'

'Regrettable,' agreed Jo.

'This,' explained Rachel to Tom, 'is our Achilles' heel. How are you on slebs?'

'Utterly useless,' he replied. 'I'm proud to say.'

'Hey, I'm pretty good,' said Bubba impetuously. 'Hand it over.' She took the answer sheet. 'Leave it to me.'

If Bubba was to be totally honest, she was feeling a bit down. The fondue thing was a blow, a heavy blow. Because really, without the fondue, then why the edelweiss? Or the Tyrolean folk dress? In which she was starting to feel a bit of a chump. She could do with a personal triumph, to perk her up. She'd been rather jealous of Jo, with the sport.

345

This should be good. After all, she has listened to *The Archers* religiously for, golly, months now. And *Downton Abbey*, of course. Absolutely *glued* . . .

'WHAT WAS THE NAME OF MINNIE CALDWELL'S CAT?'

Hmmm. Not the best of starts. Who or what was a Minnie Caldwell? She had simply no idea, but then who could? Just bung something down. Any old pet's name. Might strike lucky . . . Tiddles? Or something a bit more exotic? It would help to know if it was pedigree . . . Oh dear. She seemed to have just missed another question.

'IN WHICH LONDON BOROUGH IS ALBERT SQUARE?'

Very strange. Isn't that geography? Never a strength of Bubba's, geography . . . The Memorial is definitely Kensington & Chelsea, so presumably the Square . . . Gosh. Did another question just fly by?

The next one *has* to be *The Archers*. Come on. Come on . . .

'WHICH SOAP WAS WITNESS TO THE FIRST LESBIAN KISS?'

Um. Well. There's Shula? And Peggy? Surely they never. . . Anyway wouldn't that be incest, too? Or was she getting muddled with Jill . . . ?

'How's it going, Bubba?' interrupted Georgie. Who was taking this *way* too seriously. 'Are you getting them all?'

'Oh yes,' trilled Bubba. Why? Why did she trill that? Why was she even trilling? Damn, she just missed another question. He goes terribly fast, this chef chap. Steady on. You're not in the kitchen now, you know. 'All in hand. Over here.'

'OK. NOW ON TO CELEBRITIES.'

This would be better. Audrey Hepburn, Lady

346

Di—she'd known a cousin of hers, in actual fact—
Angelina Jolie, yadda, yadda. Bring it on . . .

'GIVE THE FIRST NAMES OF ANY TWO
KARDASHIANS.'

Huh? Sorry? What the . . . Who's a. . ..WHAT
THE FUCKING FUCK is a KARDASHIAN?

'Oh dear,' said Bubba, suddenly standing up. 'Do
excuse me. I believe I've been taken terribly *terribly*
ill.'

And she flung down her crayon and flew out of
the room.

Round Six: History and Politics

'Oh no! Politics!' bellowed Georgie into the four
corners of the hall. 'We don't stand a chance on
politics. Not against Destiny's mum.'

'Might as well upset a few people,' she said
quietly to the table. 'We're stuffed now anyway.'
She ran her hands through her hair. 'Christ. Why
did we trust her? She's a total nut-job. No points!
A whole round with not one point! That's it. We
are never going to recover. And Chris does actually
know about politics. The evening, my friends, is
lost.' She slumped down with her head on her arms,
inconsolable.

'AT WHOM DID PEEPING TOM PEEP?'

'Stop it, Georgie,' said Tom firmly as he dashed
off the answer without any consultation. 'We are a
strong team and this is a strong round for us. It is
not over till it's over and you will not give up now.'

'WHO ON THE FOURTEENTH OF
JANUARY 1963 SAID "NON"?'

Georgie pulled herself up out of her hands

347

as Tom knocked off another answer on his own. Rachel looked at the paper and smiled—shy, adoring.

'COMPLETE THE FOLLOWING: LINCOLN, GARFIELD, MCKINLEY . . .'

'Anyone?' asked Tom of the table. But before Georgie could reply, he'd written it down.

'NAME THE FIRST BRITISH PRIME MINISTER TO BE THE PRODUCT OF A STATE SCHOOL.'

'Interesting . . .' he said.

'Well,' said Rachel, whispering in his ear.

'Of course,' he agreed as he wrote.

'FIELD MARSHAL MONTGOMERY'S HABIT OF HAVING A GOOD BREAKFAST BEFORE A MILITARY CAMPAIGN GAVE RISE TO WHICH POPULAR EXPRESSION?'

Georgie knew this one, but there was something about Tom and Rachel and the atmosphere around them that made it seem improper to intrude.

'WHAT DOES THE S STAND FOR IN HARRY S. TRUMAN?'

Barging in now with the answer would be like barging through a bedroom door. Better off leaving them to it. If she just gave them space, they would get there in the end; they just needed to feel their way in, gently, explore a little, probe. And then . . . yes. Lovely. They've found it.

'WHICH TWENTIETH-CENTURY AMERICAN PRESIDENT NEVER WON AN ELECTION EITHER FOR PRESIDENT OR VICE-PRESIDENT?'

This was, quite blatantly, quizplay as foreplay . . .

'WHICH RIVER DID JULIUS CAESAR CAUSE A WAR BY CROSSING?'

348

Georgie fanned herself with the spare paper. She couldn't quite tell from here, but she really hoped that Chris was watching.

Round Seven: Geography, Science and Nature

'There you are,' said Georgie. 'Told you we were doomed.'

'WHERE IS BROWN WILLY THE HIGH POINT?'

'Hang on a minute,' said Heather proudly as Guy mouthed the answer across. 'You're forgetting one important person.'

'WHERE IS BITTER AND WHERE IS DISAPPOINTMENT?'

'This is Guy's specialist area, you know,' Jo chortled, but Heather ignored her. It was her big moment, and it was not going to be ruined by Jo or anyone else.

'WHICH SEA AREA AND WEATHER REGION LIES TO THE WEST OF MALIN?'

'He's brilliant at weather regions, aren't you, love?'

'WHICH TOWN IS HOME TO THE MET OFFICE?'

'So we went on a tour of that once? For his birthday? Fascinating, all the instruments . . .'

'YOU HAVE BEFORE YOU FIVE ORDNANCE SURVEY SIGNS.' The table groaned. 'PLEASE IDENTIFY THEM.'

'Oh Guy,' swooned Heather. 'It couldn't be better! His absolute favourite.' He looked like a different man, sitting there, setting to work on his symbols. Broader, stronger, healthier. So manly. So

349

confident. 'Look at him go,' said Jo, as astonished as the rest of them. 'He's incredible. Half man, half machine. It's like watching Messi on the pitch.'

'WHAT IS THE NAME GIVEN TO A LINE JOINING PLACES OF EQUAL RAINFALL?'

Guy was now in charge of the paper and the crayon. He tossed off the answer without speaking—casual, assertive, arrogant.

'FOSSILS FROM WHICH GEOLOGICAL PERIOD ARE LIKELY TO SHOW EVIDENCE OF THE LAND BEING COLONISED BY PLANTS AND INSECTS?'

'He's always had a thing for fossils,' smiled Heather wistfully. 'Haven't you, love?'

'WHAT NAME IS GIVEN TO THE TWELVE FINGERS OF THE SMALL INTESTINE?'

'As he knows to his cost,' she said around the table, her face screwed up with meaning. At which Guy looked up from his writing and declared: 'From now on, I would prefer it if you refrained from telling the whole world the secrets of my digestive system.'

Round Eight: Literature

Georgie waved their joker in the air. 'Right, you lot. This is it. All down to the last round. We're level pegging with The Reigning Champs, and only two points ahead of The Constant Gardeners. We cannot afford any mistakes.'

'And we're not going to make any,' Tom assured her. 'Trust us. This is our night.'

'WHO, IN 1941, WAS BRITISH CIVILIAN PRISONER SEVEN-NINE-SIX IN TOST,

350

UPPER SILESIA?'

'How are the Champs on lit then? Anyone know?'

'Well, Chris—' began Rachel.

'Chris is crap,' cut in Georgie. 'He's bluff, bluff, blow and show. Take it from me.'

'WHICH FIRST-CENTURY-BC ROMAN WAS WILFRED OWEN QUOTING WHEN HE WROTE THE WORDS "THAT OLD LIE, *DULCE ET DECORUM EST PRO PATRIA MORI*"?'

Rachel whispered to Tom. Georgie kept her eyes on the enemy. 'They don't have a clue,' she threw back over her shoulder.

'WHERE DOES MR SAUCEPAN LIVE?'

Rachel gave a jump, and then a giggle when she saw that Tom had got there even before her. He shrugged, and smiled a shy lopsided smile. 'Bit easy? As it's the greatest book ever written . . .' She smiled back. Tried hard not to cry. For that might just have been the most romantic, moving, beautiful thing she had ever heard. She pinched herself. It was important to ascertain what exactly was going on, right here, right now, in this hall, tonight. Was she actually sitting next to—were her bare thighs pressed against the soft worn jeans of—the world's most perfect man then? Was that what was happening?

'WHICH POEM, CELEBRATING THE BEAUTY OF ENGLAND, WAS WRITTEN IN AND ABOUT STOKE POGES?'

She watched him write its title, in his long, loose script, with her best Cherry Red. Until her hair fell across her face and she could no longer see the page. She needed to raise her hand, hook it back around her ear, but she knew that if she did that her closeness to him would be lost, that physical connection would be broken. And she wasn't sure that she could bear it. And then, very carefully, he laid down the crayon. And he turned towards her. His fingers were tender as they felt for the wayward strand, brushed it over her shoulder and smoothed it down her back.

'Geeks seemed to have got that one,' Georgie reported from her look-out.

'IN WHICH FICTIONAL TOWN DOES INSPECTOR WEXFORD FIGHT CRIME?'

Rachel moved even closer as she softly told Tom that which he already knew. His foot brushed hers, moved on; and she wanted to call to it: Stop. Come back. But then she felt it. Coming back again anyway. Of its own free will. Travelling slowly, tantalisingly, around the back of her shoe, and settling just there, between her legs. She stifled a gasp. She was blushing, she knew she was blushing. Had anybody noticed? Did she care?

'WHAT WAS THE CHRISTIAN NAME OF THE BRONTË BROTHER?'

Of course. Some things were simply beyond words.

'WHICH SHOP HAD ITS PREMISES IN PORTSMOUTH STREET, KINGSWAY?'

They were now at that rare, exquisite point— in a literature round, in a quiz, in an evening, in a lifetime—when the mundane becomes the sublime. When a relationship suddenly takes flight, transcending all ordinary expression, and hands over the controls to just the skin, the nerve endings, the meeting of minds. When communication needs to be nothing more than a look . . .

'Get in,' said Georgie.

'WHAT WAS INSCRIBED ON THE BROOCH WORN BY CHAUCER'S PRIORESS?'

. . . a touch . . .

'Oh yes,' said Georgie.

'IN *THE END OF THE AFFAIR*, AT WHICH RESTAURANT DO THE LOVERS SHARE FRIED ONIONS?'

. . . or a smile.

'Yessss.'

'WHAT, IN FULL, IS THE LAST LINE OF THE NOVEL *JANE EYRE*?'

Until they reached that moment, at the end, when neither could hold back any longer. And in that urgent, irresistible desire to give the final correct answer to the final question of the final round of the night, they both, in a single moment, fell upon the paper. Together. Triumphant. Fulfilled.

'YES!' Georgie hit the table. 'YES!' She leapt to her feet. 'YES. YES. YESSSSSS!'

'AND THAT,' announced Martyn Pryce, 'IS THE END. CAN YOU PLEASE CHECK YOUR ANSWERS AND HAND IN YOUR SHEETS FOR THE LAST TIME.'

Rachel flung herself back into her own seat, Tom into his. She exhaled deeply. Had she even been breathing at all for the last ten minutes? She couldn't say. Tom wrestled with his tie, undid the top button on his shirt and threw the crayon on the table. 'Well.' He thrust his hands into his pockets as he stretched out his legs. 'There we are. We've given it our best shot.'

'It felt pretty good to me,' said Rachel, blowing

353

her hair from her face.

'Yup,' agreed Mr Orchard Tom. 'In fact, it felt amazing.'

10.15 P.M. GOING-HOME TIME

Georgie and Jo still had their hands held high in a victory clasp. Guy and Heather were still locked in the remains of a passionate victory clinch. In the heat of the moment, Mr Orchard had put his arm around Rachel's shoulders in a polite victory half-hug. And Georgie noticed that, although the moment was over now, his arm was still in place.

The Outsiders' table was swamped with well-wishers, and they would not be going home in a hurry. Mrs Wright was delighted, Rachel's mum was wiping away tears. Melissa, Sharon and Jasmine—thrilled themselves to have won Best Picnic—were generous in defeat. Chris, who seemed to have swapped allegiance altogether, was sitting down in Bubba's vacant chair, gracefully receiving congratulations on behalf of the whole team. Georgie wanted to smack him.

Only Bea was separate and alone. Her geeks had scuttled off back under the stone where she had found them. Tony was drinking at another table with Colette's latest man. Pamela was clearing the scoreboard; her back was to the room; its very set screamed her displeasure.

'I'm thinking,' announced Georgie, loud enough for Bea to hear, 'victory wristbands? Something including the words "Outsiders" and "champions". What do you say, team?'

Bea was blowing out her candles, but her

eyebrow was raised.

'Brilliant evening,' said Chris, rising to his feet. 'But I'd love to get home and see if Josh is still up. Rachel? Shall we go?'

The well-wishers melted away. Georgie, Jo and Heather watched open-mouthed. There was a minute's silence before Rachel said, 'Of course.' She stood up and out of Tom Orchard's embrace. 'You must,' she said, 'see the children.' Her voice was robotic, her stride slow and deliberate as she walked away from the table and out through the door.

'Excuse me?' asked Georgie. 'What just happened there?'

'I don't know,' said Jo, 'but I don't like it.'

'It's sweet, isn't it?' said Heather happily. 'Such a great dad. So brilliant with the children now everything's settled down. Anyway,' she was hugging herself with delight, 'are we really getting wristbands, Georgie?'

'Course we're—'

'—bloody not,' finished Jo.

'Don't—' Georgie tried again.

'—be such an arse.'

*   *   *

Rachel stood at the open fridge, searching vainly for something white and sweet lurking in there that might just pass as a 'nightcap', when Chris came back down into the kitchen.

'All fast asleep,' he said.

'Yes, well, it is a school night.' She shut the fridge door again, as Chris would be going now. 'Never mind. You'll see them at the weekend.'

Chris opened it again. 'What you got in here? Not much by the look of it. I thought,' he said, not to Rachel but straight into the dairy compartment, 'perhaps I might stay the night? See them in the morning? They'd like that.'

'Sorry. Excuse me. But aren't you that bloke I got divorced from the other day . . .'

'Well, you know.' He turned now, looking, and heading, straight at her. She had to hand it to him: there was no hint of sheepishness or shame. 'There's still something there, you know. Even now.'

'Seems a shame to waste it, you mean?'

'Ex-actly.'

'What?' She stepped forward and shut the fridge in what she hoped was a final gesture. 'Like I'm a sodding pork chop?'

'Rach, Rach.' He put his hands on her hips. 'You're always too hard on yourself—' The doorbell rang. 'Who's that at this hour?'

'Another number nineteen bus, I presume.' She struggled out of his grasp and swung to the door. 'Golly.' Through the peephole she could see the back of a navy linen jacket. 'It is too.' She opened the door a crack. Tom Orchard turned around and looked her straight, deep in the eye. The one, small detached and sane part of her brain registered that if she flexed her knees back, hard, it did help to stop them buckling altogether, but also noticed that it did require a considerable effort.

'Hi.' He stepped forward, leaned against the door jamb. She didn't pull back. His face was close. Right up close. With his forefinger, he tipped her chin up towards him. She parted her lips. And Chris came into the hall.

'What sort of establishment are you running here, Rach?' He was quite jovial. 'Perhaps I should think about moving back in if—' His expression changed. 'Oi!'

He stuck his head over her shoulder so that the three of them were crammed against each other, like three teens in a photo-booth wanting to capture the moment.

'Hang on. Hold your horses.' Chris's face was now right in Tom's. 'Here. You. You're the headmaster.'

'I think he already knows that, Chris.' Rachel pushed him away. 'Thanks anyway.'

But Chris moved back in again. 'Oh no you don't, Mr Chips. You don't go around doing that kind of stuff. Not if you're the headmaster.' He was shaking his head, jabbing the other man in the chest. Rachel ducked behind him, grabbed her bag, pulled her key off the radiator shelf. 'That, matey, is way above your pay grade. That kind of behaviour is off the Chips Scale.' He was shouting now. 'The great British taxpayer, the decent hard-working families that live in this decent honest town, are not paying you far too much so that you can turn up on the doorstep of married women . . .'

Rachel reached behind Chris and lifted her jacket off a peg. 'OK, you can spare us the cheap politics.' Her heart was banging against her ribs. 'And actually, Chris, I'm no longer married. Remember?'

She guided Tom off her doorstep, followed him out and turned back. 'Oh. And you're right. About staying the night. You should. The kids will really appreciate it.'

She pulled the door in. Smiling, she stuck her

head sideways through the crack.

'So we'll just leave you to it. I'll be back first thing, OK?'

And shut it in Chris's face.

Out in the warm night, Rachel and Tom stood on the front path and looked at one another.

'So. Er. Hi.' Her giggle sounded small and awkward.

'Um. Hi.' Tom held up his right hand. 'I just popped by to give you these.' He was holding her crayons. Her favourite crayons. 'You left them on the table.'

Oh no, she thought. No no no. This is not happening.

'You said they were special. Otherwise, of course,' he shrugged, 'I wouldn't have bothered . . .'

She had just walked out on the kids for some bloke who was dropping off her crayons. He wasn't a number 19 bus. He wasn't even in service. And she'd just gone and jumped on him anyway. Jeez Louise, she made Colette look like a nun.

'I thought you might need them in the morning.'

She felt faint. Actually, she was willing herself to faint; then she wouldn't have to speak. Although the best course of action was, at that moment, suicide. She looked around the sparse front garden for something handy—hemlock, say, or a convenient asp.

'I hope my popping by didn't create any—you know—issues in there.'

'Uh . . .'

'I mean, I'd hate to . . .'

She looked up at him. He was grinning.

'Hang on. Is that it? Is that the celebrated Headmaster's Sense of Humour in action? Was

358

that an actual, genuine Headmaster's Funny Joke?'

He stepped forward and took her into his arms. 'Glad you liked it. Was one of my better ones, I agree.'

'It was RUBBISH.' She had not been held for nearly a year. The shock of the closeness of it made her flesh feel like liquid. 'You bastard.' But still, she managed to lean back a little, and hit him.

He kissed her. She had a taste of thyme. Garden mint. First strawberries. The promise of a future.

'You horrible, horrible, unfunny bastard.' She struggled in his arms, but could not have found the strength to extract herself had she wanted to. He kissed her again, for longer. She wondered if Chris was watching out of the window. She hoped he was. And that he could hear her say: 'Come on. Let's go.'

Rachel wrapped both her arms around his waist and held her own hands tightly. 'But you're still an unfunny bastard,' she grumbled into the cloth of his jacket.

'I don't know how you can say that'—Tom's left arm hugged her shoulders; his right hand stretched across—'after my recent triumph'—he cradled Rachel's head towards his, kissed the top of her hair—'at the Bloody Funny Olympics.'

And with matching step, they set off down the hill towards the headmaster's house. Joined up. Together. One solid shape against the pale summer night sky.

SPORTS DAY

6.30 A.M. LONG BEFORE DROP-OFF

There was already warmth in the sun that poured
through the gap in the ill-fitting curtains and spilled
over Rachel's face as she slept. She remonstrated
with it, turned over on to her other side, stretched
out her hand and realised, with a jolt, that there was
no one beside her.

'Where . . . ?' She propped herself up on one
elbow, sheet over her chest, as Tom strode into the
room.

'Morning, gorgeous.' He sat down on her side of
the bed, kissed her on the mouth and put a mug on
the bedside table.

'Blimey.' Rachel sank back on to the pillow,
squinted at him through her hair. 'The hour is
unearthly and yet you appear to be dressed.' She
took a sip of lemon-and-ginger and scowled.
'You're such a weirdo.'

'Just *carp*ing the old *diem*.' He looped his tie
round his neck. 'A big *diem* for me, as it happens.
The climax of my first year.'

'Humph.' She pouted.

He smiled as he kissed her again. 'The
professional climax of my first year.' He stood up.
'I've got a speech to write so I'm going in early. Else
you will get in my way.'

'Ooh. A speech. Get you. Full of the finest
Headmaster's Funny Jokes, I hope. What you going
to say? Go on, give me a heads-up. I must be due
some perks . . .'

He moved over to the chest of drawers and filled his pockets. 'Well, quite a lot. About the library. And the amazing timeline. Then I've got some announcements to make,' he mock-swaggered. 'Actually.'

'Announcements?' She purred and crossed her legs beneath the sheets. 'God, how sexy. Grrr. I love announcements.'

'Yes. About the new head boy and the new head girl.'

'Poppy, obviously.' She took another sip of tea. 'I mean, what do you think I've been doing here? Not wasting my time, I trust.'

'Wow. Was that your idea of a Parent's Funny Joke?' He whistled as he pulled a comb through his hair. 'Cos you are one sick, nasty—'

'Yeah. True. Everyone knows it's going to be Scarlett.'

'Does everyone? And does everyone know who the new school secretary is too?'

'OMG. Not a new school secretary! It's more than a body can bear. Tell me. Tell me. Before I simply burst,' she begged in her Southern-belle voice. 'Headmaster. Please. Who is the new school secretary?'

'Nope.' He blew her a kiss. 'You'll just have to wait and see.'

She listened to him clatter down the stairs, slam the front door and beat a retreat along the pavement. Then she smiled, stretched and soaked up the happy silence. Funny, she thought to herself as she finished her tea, that she used to dread Wednesday nights and every other weekend. Because she really rather loved them now.

9 A.M. JUST AFTER DROP-OFF

Rachel turned the corner into Mead Avenue with a steady, thumping tread. It was all downhill from here to home. There was time for a shower and a bit more work before going in to school for the big *diem*. She smiled at the thought of Tom—it was hard not to smile whenever she thought of Tom—as she breathed sharply in and puffed out-out-out. Almost immediately, she heard the hedge trimmer's whine. Were they never silent, the trimmers of Mead Avenue? They ripped at the air around them like guns at the Somme. Did they never rest? Was there never a moment when the poor shrubs of the Avenue were not being trumm? Breathe in and out-out-out . . .

Melissa's place was just coming up on the left. And it sounded like it might be her trimmer, at it again . . . Rachel rounded the bend, and even as she did so the last stretch of Leylandii in the front of that garden fell down and away. The noise stopped. The pretty stone house was revealed, and in front of it, waving the wretched saw, wearing the ear mufflers, were Sharon and Jasmine.

'Hi, Rachel,' called one.

'The Gardening Biz in action!' trilled another.

'Out training for the mothers' race?'

'Christ, no!' puffed Rachel, jogging on the spot. 'Just out for a run!' Although, now she thought about it, she didn't usually go out for a run. 'Perfectly ordinary run!' Hadn't for years. 'Course I'm not in training!'

Melissa came walking down the lawn. 'Wowser!

362

That is *so* much better,' she cried, delighted. 'Thank you, girls. Finally! Now I feel that I'm actually part of the neighbourhood at last.'

'You're so welcome,' said one.

'A pleasure,' sang the other.

They both put down their gardening clobber and took off their gloves.

'Now, what'

'can we get you?'

'That's very kind.' Melissa pushed her hands into her pockets and smiled. 'I'd love a coffee.'

10 A.M. ASSEMBLY

Georgie stood in her spot, on the other side of the green fence, rhythmically rocking Hamish in his buggy. She could see the playground clearly enough, and the sheds that were now the library. So she would just stay and watch proceedings from here. The children were all being led out now by their teachers, already in their red shorts, white polo shirts, trainers and sunhats. They were so excited for Sports Day, she couldn't see how they were going to contain themselves through an outdoor assembly with all their mums and dads, the governors, the vicar, the mayor . . . But she rather hoped, at least for nice Tom Orchard's sake, that they did.

'So not actually smoking, but still stuck out here in your smoking spot . . .' said a voice at her elbow.

'Huh? Oh. You again.' Georgie had been so deep in thought that she hadn't noticed Melissa landing behind her. 'Yeah. I'm here. And it's deeply significant. Something to do with my mum?

And the potty? In that sort of area, certainly.' Why was she being like this? She was in therapy for most of her twenties. 'But mostly because Hamish here needs a nap.'

The ceremony was about to start. Mr Orchard was taking to the microphone. Georgie waited for Melissa to glide off and join in. But she didn't.

'Hmm. I know Hamish and his powers of sleep. He won't be waking up in a hurry.'

The speeches were beginning. But Melissa still didn't budge.

'Such a friendly school,' she murmured, looking on. 'One big happy family.'

Georgie scoffed.

Melissa carried on. 'Such nice people.'

'Yeah. OK,' Georgie conceded. 'Individually they're all right. Most of them. Few notable exceptions.'

'Not collectively?' That was Melissa's vague, thinking-aloud voice.

'Yeah, small groups. Little cells. Split up. Subdivisions. Perfect.'

'But not all together?' she murmured. 'The whole community?'

'All together?' Georgie cracked. 'All together? Looking at them from the outside like this? That huge teeming mass of them? Christ, no. They're bloody terrifying!'

'Then perhaps you should change your angle? Why not try looking out from the inside instead?' And before she knew what was happening, Melissa's right hand was cupped around her elbow, her left taking the handle of the buggy. 'Come on.' And she was speaking so softly, it was almost a hum. 'Come on.' Together they moved across the

364

tarmac. 'Let's go in.' And found places in the centre of the crowd.

*　　　*　　　*

Quite how Mr Orchard had come up with such a generous speech about the grumpy secretary, Heather did not know. Nor was she sure how he had raised enough money to get that lovely bench the children were presenting to her. He was such a nice guy he probably ended up buying it himself.

And here it comes, she thought. My big moment. Oh dear. It's bound to go wrong.

'. . . and next year, there will be a new friendly face to greet you in the office.'

Heather had been to the Serenity Whatsit Spa this morning and was looking all groomed—threaded, tinted, waxed. But she was still so nervous. What if no one wanted her? Or something stole her thunder?

'After reviewing a great number of applicants . . .'

That was always happening—people stealing her thunder.

'. . . and giving it enormous consideration . . .'

Heather had never enjoyed a moment's thunder in her life before someone or other came along and nicked it. Guy, beside her, sought out her hand and squeezed it.

'I am delighted to announce that Heather Carpenter has agreed to come and join us.'

And then, suddenly, everybody was clapping. And Rachel was cheering. Jo was wolf-whistling. Georgie was laughing, looking amazed. Heather didn't think she had ever amazed Georgie before ever—at least, not in a good way. And she could see Maisie, in the Year 5 row, getting patted on the back and beaming and proud. And then she saw that the whole school was smiling at her. At last. This was it. Right here, right now, in the school, in the sunshine: her thunder. And it was going on and on and on.

'Very good news indeed,' resumed Mr Orchard, back at the microphone. 'And one last matter to attend to. This morning the staff had a meeting, before you even turned up to school. Lazy lot.' The children giggled. 'Don't worry, we know where you were: down on Bikini Bottom with SpongeBob SquarePants.' They laughed, hysterically. 'And we talked about who we think should be our head boy and head girl next year.'

Heather switched off for a bit. Guy still had her hand in his, he hadn't let go. She felt so safe, with him holding on to her like that, surrounded by her friends. Gosh, she thought, for the first time in years or possibly the first time ever: I'm so lucky.

'. . . we would like to ask Felix Spencer to be our head boy . . .'

Oh, that's Melissa's Felix. Heather approved of that. Lovely lad. A good balance to Scarlett, who might well be trouble . . .

'. . . and Maisie Carpenter to be our head girl.'

Maisie Carpenter? Was there another Maisie Carpenter? Which Maisie Carpenter? *OUR MAISIE CARPENTER?* And now everyone was cheering Maisie, and all the parents were looking at Heather again. And Guy. At Guy and Heather and Maisie. The three of them: they suddenly seemed to be in the very middle of the whole school.

'. . . before the vicar opens the new library building, let us all sing together number one-four-

366

eight-three in your *Songs of Fellowship*: "One More Step Along the World I Go".'

Oh, thought Heather, panicking. Typical. Then the music started up on the portable electric piano, and the children stood up and shared their hymnbooks. And Maisie looked straight at her, grinning, before she started to sing. And Heather realised that, actually, she was OK.

> 'From the old things to the new,
> Keep me travelling along with you.'

She looked around her, at the families she would be dealing with day in, day out, in the next school year. And the staff she would be working for. The letters she would be typing, the reports she would be sending . . . Ooh. Her heart gave a bounce of joy. Reports! Would she get a sneaky look at them all first? And she thought, too, of the little ones who weren't with them yet. Who were probably pottering about in a paddling pool somewhere, or snuggled down to an afternoon nap, but who in September would be putting on their scratchy uniforms and their stiff new shoes and coming to join them. They would all need Heather too, at some point, for some thing or other—little or big.

> 'All the new things that I see,
> You'll be looking at along with me.'

And, Yes, she thought, as they launched once more into the chorus. Carry on. Sing up. I can take it. It doesn't bother me so much any more.

> 'Give me courage when the world is rough,

367

Keep me loving though the world is tough.'

So Mr Orchard's announcements were quite something, after all. You could say that on the small scale, in the limited scope, of this primary school they amounted to a revolution. Grr, Rachel thought to herself. I do love announcements.

'Leap and sing in all I do,
Keep me travelling along with you.'

She scanned the people around her as they sang. There was Heather, looking neither tragic nor mousey, but perfectly radiant. It was nothing short of a metamorphosis, what had happened to her this afternoon. Then her eyes found Georgie, uncharacteristically in the middle of things. And Jo, sticking close by, looking so much better. Not recovered, obviously—could one recover?—but she was better, definitely. And she looked comfortable here, safe in these numbers.

'And it's from the old I travel to the new,
Keep me travelling along with you.'

The crowd was large now: more parents had arrived. And dense—everyone had to squash in together. It's funny, thought Rachel: we're all such quiet people, really. The adults and the children: well-mannered, nicely behaved, ordinary people leading quiet, polite, orderly lives. And yet we sound so strong out here this afternoon. Singing the same words, side by side. In the playground opened a century ago by the last Prince of Wales, standing on the very spot where Mr Stanley spoke

368

to the whole school, right where the old bomb shelters used to be. She turned her face towards the seasonally warm sun and watched an aeroplane draw a perfect curve upon the summer sky. They must be able to see us from up there, she thought: we're such a solid mass of individuals, all doing the same thing and on the same side. Bound together by the same roots. They could hardly miss us. We're quite a force to be reckoned with.

*   *   *

'There are two things I love about our new library. The first is: it's got books in it.'

The children roared in uncontrollable mirth.

'And the second: every single person here contributed in some small way to making it happen. This really is our library. And that makes it one very special place. Now, there is a plaque in there, with a quote on it in Latin, which Freddie will translate for you'—he clicked his fingers—'in an instant.'

They all, Freddie included, roared again, even louder. Bubba was struggling to keep up. One could really do with subtitles when Mr Orchard got going with the children.

'And our chair of governors—a very important lady—is going to unveil that for us now. Unfortunately, our library is a very small place as well as a special one, so we can't all get in there at once. Just for the unveiling, I wonder if the governors and the committee would come through first.'

Bubba wished she hadn't worn such a big hat for two reasons: the first was that nobody else was wearing one, and the second was that it was slightly too big to get through the library door. She ducked her way in, just behind Bea, in front of Colette, and was still busy cursing her sartorial decisions—so rarely did it happen, that Bubba did hate getting things wrong—when she stopped, looked up and registered what was around her.

The new St Ambrose library was simply one of the loveliest spaces that Bubba had ever been in. And Bubba knew a thing or two about lovely spaces. The old sheds and outhouses thrown up by those earnest old Victorians seemed to have the most incredible feng shui. Who knew they did feng shui back then? Knocking down all the internal walls had created a hexagonal space with books on every wall, and benches arranged like the petals of a flower. It was all painted in a deep warm yellow and Rachel's timeline, which she'd been fantastically boring about, quite frankly— old people, poor people, wounded people, dead people; the thing was Bubba was always much more of a *here* and *now* sort of person—anyway, here was the thing: it turned out it was absolutely, completely charming.

As Bubba looked at it in a bit more detail, she even got the feeling that she was actually learning something. Or certainly thinking about things almost for the first time. Fancy that, the boys and girls used to have to troop in through separate entrances . . . Not a bad idea. Milo would probably have been *much* happier then—separated from the brutal Scarlett. Something that was actually quite sweet, moving really, was to see the beech tree all the way through: almost a sapling hung with bunting for Victoria's Diamond Jubilee, and then building and growing—gosh! Look at Concorde

370

flying over in that one, so clever—until it became the majestic, towering thing it was now. And Bubba couldn't help but notice, when she came to the end, that Rachel had left a space to fill with the future. She approved of that—Bubba was very much a *future* sort of person, too. And then she couldn't help but have a little fantasy of an image of Milo in that space, one day—collecting his Oscar, walking through the door of 10 Downing Street . . . She did long to know: where would his special gifts, his *genius* if you will, lead him?

Her reverie was interrupted by Pamela the Monobosom, who marched up to the little piece of cloth that was hiding the plaque, preparing to reveal all. Bubba felt quite emotional. Because, really, how extraordinary that out of all those dreadful lunches, and nasty little sales, and that hellish fun run when she was pretty sure she did something ghastly to her metatarsal (Jo said she may never play professional football again) and the—well, she'd rather gloss over the whole Paradise Ball nonsense . . . Anyway. Here was what they were really doing all that time: they were building this library. And they were building it for everybody. Tom Orchard was standing by the wall, smiling with pride. It really was his big day. Bless. Bubba, Bea, Colette and Clover took up position in the front row. She wasn't sure who else was in the room, or if they could even see . . .

And then Pamela the Monobosom reached up, yanked at the cloth, and revealed the plaque that may well have had upon it a quote in Latin, which Freddie might well be able to translate. But all Bubba or anyone else in the front row could immediately see was a bright flash of orange paint.

And the legend:

FUCK OFF

1.30 P.M. THE SPORTS

'Who's winning?' asked Rachel, sitting down on the bench. She had missed most of the races: she and her mum had somehow ended up being the ones to have to clean up the plaque, before any of the children got near it and clocked what it said. Really, Milo ought to have been made to do it himself, but Mark Green swept him off the premises before anybody could collar him. And that was probably for the best: there was no saying what exotic form of corporal punishment Pamela might inflict on him, given half the chance. She was still rampaging around the corridors, bellowing, 'Special needs? *Special needs?* I'll give him special needs . . .'

'Ashley's coming first in everything,' replied Heather. 'She's amazing. Unbeatable.'

'God knows how.' Clover was cross. Of course, Clover was often cross, but nothing made her crosser than the subject of grumpy Ashley's fat mum having produced a sporting legend. 'Look at her,' she spat. 'Hasn't stopped eating all afternoon. Every time Ashley wins she cracks open another packet of crisps.' Neither nature nor nurture seemed to have made any discernible contribution, and yet grumpy Ashley just sped on, regardless. It was in direct violation of all Clover's strongly held child-rearing beliefs.

'Come on, Ashley,' hollered Rachel.

'There. She's done it.' Heather bent over her programme and added the result to a lengthy list.

'Heth . . .' began Rachel.

'Mmmm?' She had, Rachel saw, separate columns for *1st*, *2nd* and *3rd*. And a sub-section for *School Records*.

'What. You. Doing?'

'Just marking them all down. Else I can never keep track.'

'Of what exactly?'

Heather looked up. She was still glowing, still pink. 'Why, of which house is ahead!' She smiled. 'Silly . . .'

'Ooh!' Colette jumped up. 'Mothers' race now! Come on, girls. We'll let you off this year, Georgie.'

'Good of you,' scowled Georgie, who had never taken part anyway. 'Er, Rachel? You may not be aware of this but you appear to be standing up? By mistake?'

'Um,' said Rachel, chewing her lip. 'Er.' She slipped off her shoes. 'I was sort of thinking, I might just, I could kind of, you know . . . um . . . possibly . . . join in?' And she turned and jogged gently over to the start.

'Rachel!' called her mum happily.

'Joining in, Mum!' she sang as she passed. 'Just joining in!'

'ARE WE READY?' asked Tom, holding his whistle. Rachel liked him with a whistle. Whistles, she realised, were sexy too. Like announcements.

373

And jokes about SpongeBob SquarePants. It turned out there was all sorts of sexy stuff around. Once you knew what you were looking for.

'Where's Bea?' someone was asking.

'Well we can't start without her,' added another.

'ARE WE STEADY?'

There was a lot of jostling for position on the line. There were those still in their normal clothes who had bare feet, like Rachel. They found themselves giving way to those in their normal clothes but who just so happened to have brought their trainers. Colette, Sharon and Jasmine were all, of course, shod for action. And so was Melissa.

'HANG ON, MR ORCHARD. WE'RE NOT ALL HERE YET.'

Rachel felt a sharp elbow in her side and Bubba squeezing in next to her. She was astonished. Bubba had obviously hung around to support Martha, which was sort of fair enough. But still, Rachel would have thought that, after her child had pulled off quite such a spectacular public disaster, an ordinary person would have chosen to keep a lower profile. Yet here was Bubba, out in the throng, parading herself around for all to see. And she had changed into full running gear.

'Are you OK?' Rachel murmured into her ear, sympathetically, as she stretched. Surely, deep down, Bubba must be going through hell.

'Hmm. Got a *bit* of an issue with my metatarsal, but I'm going to give it a go . . .'

OK. It's official, thought Rachel. The woman is deranged.

'NOW. ARE WE READY?'

'Oh look. Here she is.'

Bea came jogging in: running shorts, ponytail,

sweatband, Reeboks. 'Sorry to keep you all. Thanks for waiting. I'll come back here.' She signalled to the next line-up. 'Give my traditional head-start.' And ran backwards behind them.

'Are you sure you want to do that?' Melissa called, with a genuine, warm concern.

'ARE WE STEADY?'

'Yes, thank you.' Bea's voice sounded quite sharp in comparison. 'I always do. It's only fair. Everyone else knows that.'

'GO!'

Rachel neither flew ahead with the front runners nor disgraced herself at the back, but remained firmly at the centre of the cluster in the middle of the field for the length of the race. Where she found, to her surprise, that she was enjoying herself. The afternoon was lovely. The sports field looked pretty much like paradise. The wind was in her hair, the grass beneath her toes. Her head was clear. Her mind was sharp. And she was perfectly placed to notice three very important things, one after another.

The first was: someone, at the halfway point, stuck out their foot and cropped Bubba. She fell, spectacularly, gracelessly, and lay sprawled across the track in front of the whole school.

The second: Melissa won by miles, and was already swigging water out of a bottle before the rest of them got anywhere near the finish.

And the third was: Hang on. Bloody hell. Bea's puffing and sweating away on her own back there. She's been left behind by us all.

* * *

There was quite a crowd already congratulating Melissa. Rachel was waiting her turn when her mum rushed by in a panic: 'Well done, darling. Got to zoom off. The bees! Swarming!'

'Eek. Do you want some help with that?'

'Don't worry,' she called over her shoulder on the way to the car park. 'Tom's coming over when he's finished here.'

Is he now? Rachel smiled to herself as she wiped the sweat from her face and took some water.

Then Bubba was there. 'I'm going. I'm finished. It's over.' She was gabbling, distraught, limping. 'Please. Bring Martha back for me. I simply can't take any more.' And without waiting for a reply, she too hobbled off to the car park.

The crowd around Melissa was thinning, and Rachel went over to join her. 'So we have a new champion.' Melissa gave an aw-shucks flick of the hand. 'We'll have to ask Heather if you've set a new school record.'

At that moment there was a crash, a screech, a horrible scrape of metal and a terrible scream.

'What was that?'

'Oh, Christ.'

They ran towards the noise. Bubba's Range Rover was out at an angle. The back of Rachel's mum's Fiat was smashed in. They must have reversed at the same time, smack, right into each other. And—oh—it looked like they might have hit someone . . .

Yes. There was Bea, lying on the gravel. Her hair was in the dirt, her huge bunch of keys had been thrown to one side. Her polo shirt had ridden up, and her midriff was exposed. Only Clover knelt by her side. Everyone else was holding back.

376

"Oh my *God*,' Rachel heard one person whisper. 'I *know*! She's *fat*,' hissed another in reply.

For a moment, they just stood there together. Frozen. Immobile. Not sure quite what they should do. Then the crowd came apart. Melissa stepped forward. And quietly and calmly, she took charge.

AUTUMN TERM

MEETING OF THE ST AMBROSE EXTRAORDINARY FUND-RAISING COMMITTEE

Held at: The Headmaster's house

In attendance: Mr Orchard (Headmaster), Melissa, Colette, Sharon, Jasmine, Georgie, Jo

Secretary: Heather

APOLOGIES: BUBBA has sent a letter of resignation, with deep regret, but is confident that THE COMMITTEE will understand, as her children are now at boarding school and she has returned to her professional commitments. She sent her deepest love to all, and a message that, in her view, boarding was quite the very best type of education for children from the age of seven or eight and that hers were thriving literally like triffids and that—

THE HEADMASTER felt that THE MEETING had got the general picture.

CLOVER and BEA entered the meeting, with apologies for lateness.

CLOVER requested that DISABLED ACCESS should be put on the agenda, as getting BEA in here with Zimmer or crutches was quite a struggle.

The first matter arising was a new Chair. After a show of hands, MELISSA was duly elected.

THE HEADMASTER proposed that the special project for this year should be the creation of an eco-garden within the school, to provide eggs and seasonal vegetables for the kitchens. This was duly passed.

MELISSA suggested that all fund-raising this year include the children and that meetings be held in school to hear their ideas for how money could be raised. This was agreed.

THE MEETING closed at 8.15 p.m.

'Is that it?' asked Clover. 'All that fuss and bother to get her here and that's it? I tell you,' she hoisted Bea up out of her chair and on to her frame, 'I would not wish the life of a carer on anyone. It is sheer, living hell.' She steered Bea through the doors, still talking. 'That was a shocker, wasn't it, you being voted out just like that?' And was clearly audible as they plodded down the hall. 'They all voted for you last year, I seem to remember.' They heard the latch being opened. 'And yet, this year, they all voted against . . . Every single one. What did you do to them, do you think?' The door closed.

'I do love what you've done in here, Tom,' said Sharon, looking around.

'We were right, weren't we?' added Jasmine. 'With the knocking through . . .'

'After all, it turned out you did need the space.'

And then the headmaster's wife put her head round the door. 'Meeting finished already?' She smiled. 'Well, don't rush off all at once. Let me get you something. Hands up who wants a tea? Coffee? Lesbian?'

So they all said, 'Go on, then.' And stayed, chatting happily, for hours.

ACKNOWLEDGEMENTS

First and foremost, I must thank Rosalind Wiseman for her insights into female social behaviour and its parallels with the beehive. Her book *Queen Bees and Wannabes* is an essential handbook for parents worried about their daughters. The later work *Queen Bee Mums and Kingpin Dads*, by Rosalind Wiseman with Elizabeth Rapoport, is just as useful for any parents worried about themselves.

John Corne and Elise Payne of the Newbury and District Beekeepers' Association opened up their hives to me and were extremely generous with their time, their knowledge and their honey. Any misrepresentations of the apian world are entirely my own.

I am enormously grateful to my wonderful agent, Caroline Wood, for her sharp eye and passionate support—this book would not exist without her. And to the teams at Little, Brown on both sides of the Atlantic. Antonia Hodgson and Reagan Arthur have been enthusiastic, kind and clever editors.

So many friends have helped in so many different ways and I thank them all, but particularly Catherine Bennett, Belinda Giles, Jo Love and Amanda Posey.

And finally to Margaret Hornby and Holly, Charlie, Matilda, Sam and Robert Harris: thank you, for everything.

CHIVERS LARGE PRINT
–direct–

If you have enjoyed this Large Print book and would like to build up your own collection of Large Print books, please contact

Chivers Large Print Direct

Chivers Large Print Direct offers you a full service:

• Prompt mail order service

• Easy-to-read type

• The very best authors

• Special low prices

For further details either call Customer Services on (01225) 336552 or write to us at Chivers Large Print Direct, **FREEPOST**, Bath BA1 3ZZ

Telephone Orders: **FREEPHONE** 08081 72 74 75